ALSO BY MARGARET BROWNLEY

A Match Made in Texas
Left at the Altar
A Match Made in Texas

The Haywire Brides
Cowboy Charm School
The Cowboy Meets His Match

Christmas in a Cowboy's Arms anthology
Longing for a Cowboy Christmas anthology

The Outlaw's Daughter

MARGARET BROWNLEY

sourcebooks
casablanca

For George, always

Published by Sourcebooks Casablanca, an imprint of Sourcebooks
P.O. Box 4410, Naperville, Illinois 60567-4410
(630) 961-3900
sourcebooks.com

Printed and bound in Canada.
MBP 10 9 8 7 6 5 4 3 2 1

"What gets us into trouble is not what we don't know. It's what we know for sure that just ain't so."

Haywire, Texas
1887

"HOLD IT RIGHT THERE, MISTER!"

Matt Taggert froze in place. The woman's voice sounded serious, as did the metallic click announcing she was armed.

Not wanting to alarm her, he held his hands out where they could be seen and turned to face her, taking it nice and easylike.

The owner of the voice stood at the entrance of the barn, the sun behind her back. The woman was small in stature but nonetheless looked like she meant business. Least her shotgun sure enough did.

Loosely braided hair the color of silken corn fell from beneath a floppy felt hat. Keen blue eyes looked him up and down, stopping momentarily to study the Colt hanging from his side and the badge on his leather vest. Apparently, nothing she saw relieved her mind as her weapon remained pointed at his chest.

"You can put your shotgun down, ma'am," he said. "I mean you no harm."

Matt's assurances won him no favor, and the

shotgun didn't budge. "What are you doing, snooping 'round my property?" she demanded.

"Name's Taggert. Matt Taggert, Texas Ranger," he said. When even his name and profession didn't convince her to lower her weapon, he added, "I'm looking for Neal Blackwell. I knocked on the door of the house, but there was no answer. Thought maybe I'd find him here in the barn."

"Well, you thought wrong, mister."

He studied the woman with narrowed eyes. "If you don't mind my asking, ma'am, who am I speaking to?"

"I'm Mrs. Blackwell."

"Mrs.—" That was a surprise. If her husband did indeed rob a stage, he sure in blazes hadn't spent any of the stolen loot on his wife. Her sinewy body looked like it had been shaped by hard work and even harder times. If that wasn't bad enough, her dress had enough patches to shingle a roof. The scuffed leather boots showing beneath the frayed hem of her skirt fared no better.

Nor did the animals in the barn, which included one skinny milk cow and a swaybacked mare.

Nevertheless, the woman earned his begrudging respect. Despite her shabby attire, she held herself with a quiet dignity that seemed at odds with her circumstances. He sensed that her squared shoulders stemmed from hard-earned inner strength.

"I need to talk to your husband," he said.

Some emotion he couldn't decipher flickered across her face. "Well, you won't find him here."

"If you'll kindly tell me where I can find him, I'll be on my way."

Suspicion clouded her eyes, and he could almost

see the cogwheels turning in her head. "What business does a Texas Ranger have with Neal?"

Before he could answer, a boy no older than five or six appeared by her side and tugged on her apron. "Mama?"

Dressed in knee pants and a checkered red shirt, the child peered at Matt from beneath a black slouch hat. A handsome lad, he had his mother's blond hair and big blue eyes. He also matched his mother's determined demeanor.

Matt grimaced. He hadn't counted on Blackwell being a family man. Nothing worse than having to arrest a man in front of his children. It was bad enough cuffing one in the presence of his wife. But if Blackwell couldn't answer Matt's questions, arresting him was a real possibility.

The woman's stance didn't waver, but her voice softened as she addressed her son. "Go back to the house, Lionel. Mama's busy right now."

Before leaving, the boy looked Matt up and down, curiosity written on his little round face. "Is he a bad man, Mama?"

"Let's hope for his sake he's not," his mama replied. "Now, go."

Lionel's face grew more solemn as his probing eyes met Matt's. Matt winked in hopes of relieving the boy's mind, but the stoic look remained. Never had Matt seen a child so young look so serious.

"Go," his mother repeated, and this time Lionel left without further ado.

Mrs. Blackwell gave her shotgun a shake as if to remind Matt she meant business. "You still haven't told me what you want with Neal."

Matt couldn't think of a tactful way to explain his business, so he came right out with it. "I need to talk to him about a stage robbery that took place last year."

Her gaze sharpened. "Why?"

Partly because of the shotgun and partly because something about the woman brought out his protective instincts, Matt chose his next words with care. "I have reason to believe your husband has... certain information that would be helpful in my investigation."

She discounted his explanation with a toss of her head. "Why would you think such a thing?"

"I'm not at liberty to say, ma'am. Least not till I talk to your husband."

Her blue eyes narrowed. "If you think Neal had anything to do with that robbery, then you're barking up the wrong tree."

"That may be true," he said slowly. "But I still need to talk to him. It's the only way I can wrap up my business and—"

"You'll wrap up your business a whole lot quicker if you just leave now."

Matt drew in his breath. If she were a man, things would be easier. For one thing, a man would have been disarmed by now. He would have seen to that. After letting his outlaw brother escape, Matt couldn't afford another blunder. Not if he wanted to keep his job. Still, he wasn't about to use physical force on a woman. Not unless he had to.

"I'm sorry, ma'am." He ever so slowly lowered his hands to his side. "I can't leave. Not till I talk to your husband."

"That's gonna be a little hard to do," she said with a wag of her shotgun.

He arched an eyebrow. "Why is that?"

"Well, mister, it's like this. My husband, Neal, is dead."

Ellie-May Blackwell watched the man ride away on his fine black horse. He'd said he was a Texas Ranger, and she had no reason to doubt his word. A man who rode that tall in the saddle probably had nothing to hide.

Still, she kept her shotgun ready. A woman alone couldn't afford to take chances. He wasn't the first man she'd had to chase off her land in recent months, but she sure did hope he would be the last.

If the Ranger thought Neal knew something about that stage holdup, then somebody was spreading false rumors about her husband, and she didn't like it. She didn't like it one bit.

"Mama…"

"What is it, Lionel?" she asked, keeping her gaze focused on the now-deserted road leading away from her farm.

"I'm hungry."

She turned to gaze at her son. "Hungry, eh?" No surprise there. The boy ate like he had a wolf in his belly. Affording him a loving smile, she tweaked the brim of his hat. "Then I guess we best rustle you up some grub."

Slinging her shotgun over her shoulder, she walked him the short distance from the barn to the house.

"Careful," she said when they reached the warped porch. Her farmhand hadn't yet fixed the loose wooden step. Since Neal's death, the house had fallen into disrepair. A window shutter hung from a single rusty hinge, but that was the least of it. The roof had lost some vital shingles, and several floorboards had come loose.

There just didn't seem to be enough time to do everything that needed to be done on that farm. Nor was there enough money.

What was the old saying? Too poor to paint and too proud to whitewash? Although in her case, pride had nothing to do with it. Even the cost of whitewash was more than her budget allowed.

"Was that a bad man, Mama?" Lionel asked, following her into the house and through the small but tidy parlor to the kitchen.

She glanced at her six-year-old son, and her heart ached. He was too young to know that bad men existed. She had tried her best to protect him—protect both her children—from such worldly matters. But now that they both attended school, her job had gotten a lot harder.

"No, he was just looking for someone," she said.

"Why-cha point a gun at him?"

"I didn't know who he was till he told me."

Lionel studied her. "I wish Papa was here," he said, repeating the refrain he'd heard her say many times over.

Sighing, she reached into the bread box and pulled out the loaf of bread baked fresh that morning. "So do I, Lioney," she said, calling him by his pet name. "So do I." Retrieving a knife from a drawer, she set to work slicing the bread.

Neal had been dead for a year, and keeping his memory alive in her children's young heads was no easy task. Lionel had only been five when his father died and Alicia six.

Still, she refused to let her children forget who their father was and what he stood for. Not only was it important to instill a sense of pride in them, but she never wanted Lionel or Alicia to go through what she had gone through as a child.

She'd only been eight when she'd watched her pa swing from the gallows. All through her growing-up years, no one had let her forget that she was an outlaw's daughter. Some had even gone as far as to say she had tainted blood. As such, she had been viewed with suspicion and distrust wherever she went.

At the age of ten, she had been accused of stealing a nickel from another pupil's desk. Though she was innocent, she was deemed guilty and expelled. Never again had she been allowed to attend school, and her lack of formal education still rankled.

Calling her a bad influence, parents had kept their children away from her, which only added to her loneliness and isolation. And it didn't stop there.

Throughout her teens, clerks had followed her around from the moment she entered a shop until she left. At church, all eyes had turned in her direction whenever the minister mentioned the word *sin*.

She couldn't believe it when Neal had taken a fancy to her. He'd said he didn't believe all that nonsense about tainted blood, and neither should she. She had only been seventeen when they'd gotten married. Out of respect for Neal, people then began looking at her with more tolerance. Still, there were those who refused to let her forget the past, and she remained an outcast in the town's social circles.

The women's auxiliary was off-limits to her. Same was true of the music club and quilting bee. She pretended that she didn't care. Told Neal as much. Said she had no interest in quilting bees or charity groups, even though secretly she longed for female companionship.

She'd heard it said that people had short memories. If such folks existed, they sure in blazes didn't live in Haywire.

Resigned to a lifetime of living in her father's shadow, she'd never expected to be fully accepted by the citizens of Haywire. Then the unthinkable happened; her husband had died a heroic death saving children from a school fire.

With his death, she had finally gained the acceptance she had longed for nearly all her life. As Neal Blackwell's widow, she was now treated with more respect than she'd ever known or even thought possible. Even the mayor had consulted her before deciding on the placement of her husband's memorial.

She considered it ironic that it took one man's death to ruin her reputation and another man's death to restore it.

Neal had died a hero, and she aimed to make sure he stayed a hero for her children's sakes. Never did she want them to experience the scorn and shame that she'd gone through.

Lord knows, she could barely eke out the bare necessities for them and sometimes not even that. But she had it within her power to preserve the memory of their father in a way that would earn her children the admiration and respect denied her throughout her childhood. That was what she had done this past year since Neal's death and she intended to keep doing it.

The Texas Ranger be danged.

2

MATT TAGGERT ELBOWED HIS WAY THROUGH THE
swinging doors of the Wandering Dog Saloon and
bellied up to the bar. The scent of freshly strewn straw
rose from the floor and mingled with the stale smell of
tobacco and alcohol that clung to the air.

It was still early in the afternoon, and the place
was empty except for the man hunched over a corner
table, snoring like a freight train. Even the poker and
faro tables stood deserted.

The bartender sauntered over to Matt. A tall, thin
man with droopy eyes and an even droopier mustache,
he gave the bar a quick swipe of his wet rag before
asking, "What can I do you for?"

"I'm looking for information."

Droopy made a face. "If it doesn't come in liquid
form, I can't help you."

Matt tossed a gold coin on the bar. "What can you
tell me about Neal Blackwell?"

Shrugging, Droopy pocketed the coin, proving that,
despite his disclaimer, he held no prejudice against solids,
long as they were gold. "Whatcha want to know?"

"For starters, how and when did Blackwell die?"

Setting his rag aside, the bartender glanced at Matt's badge. "You haven't been in town long, have you?"

"Arrived yesterday. How'd you know?"

"Only a stranger could ask a question like that. Anyone taller than a grasshopper knows how Neal Blackwell died. I'm surprised they haven't made him a saint. For now, he just has to settle for being the town hero."

Matt's gaze sharpened. "Hero? In what way?"

"The school caught fire, and it would have turned into a disaster had it not been for Neal Blackwell. He ran into the blazin' buildin' and got everyone out unharmed." Pausing for effect, Droopy gave the bar another quick swipe. "Unfortunately, the smoke got him in the end. The doc said his lungs couldn't take it."

"How long ago was that?" Matt asked.

Droopy rubbed his whiskered chin with his one free hand. "Guess it's been about a year now."

Matt did a quick calculation. The bartender might have answered one of the questions that had puzzled him—why none of the stolen banknotes had shown up. If Blackwell was indeed responsible for the holdup, he might have died before he had a chance to spend the stolen loot. Timewise, it made sense.

"The whole town turned out for his funeral," the bartender continued with a shake of his head. "Never saw anything like it."

"Guess folks 'round here are grateful to the man," Matt said.

"You can say that again." The bartender pursed his

lips before continuing. "Just to show how grateful, they're about to name the new school after him."

Matt furrowed his brow. "They're goin' that far, eh?" If he was right about Blackwell's involvement in the stage holdup, the town might want to rethink the wisdom of naming a school after him.

"Yeah, and that's not all." The bartender picked up a tin can and rattled it. "We've been collecting money to pay for the bronze statue of him."

Matt's eyebrows shot up. "There's a statue of Blackwell?" From what he'd heard and observed, the town was still dealing with the economic problems caused by the drought. A statue seemed like a waste.

"Why didn't they just give the money to his widow?" Matt asked. "Seems to me that would have been a better way to honor the man." God knows, the woman looked like she could use some financial help.

The bartender shrugged and set the can down. "Well, it's like this. Haywire is the only town that don't have whatcha call braggin' rights. Dallas has its Armadillo Days and San Antonio has the Alamo. Now we got our very own hero."

Matt scratched his temple. "Where is this statue?"

"In the town square. They're gonna…whatcha-call-it on Saturday?" Droopy's forehead creased as he searched for the right word. "*Dedicate* it. That's it! If you wanna be a hero, you best know how to die." He laughed at his own joke.

Matt didn't know what to think. When he set out to track down Blackwell, he'd been so certain of the man's guilt. He hadn't expected to find the man dead. Nor did he think to meet up with the likes of his widow. And he sure in blazes didn't expect Blackwell to be a hero, let alone the town idol.

His job had just gotten a whole lot tougher, that was for certain and sure. Thanking the bartender, Matt left the saloon and rode his horse slowly from one end of town to the other. That was no easy task, as the town had more twists and turns than a scared rattler.

Still it was just as the bartender had said. If naming the school after the man wasn't enough, large printed signs posted on lampposts proposed changing the name of the town from Haywire to Blackwell. There were almost as many signs for Blackwell as there were left over from the town's recent election for mayor.

Matt followed a series of winding dirt roads until he found the town square. Sure enough, a bronze statue of a man carrying a child rose from a pedestal at the center of the square. Dismounting, he walked up to the statue for a closer look. The larger-than-life image was surrounded by flowers and candles. Indeed, even as he stood in the square, a matronly woman laid a bouquet of wildflowers at the base of the statue.

"Excuse me, ma'am," Matt said, doffing his hat. "Did you know him?"

The woman lifted a tortoiseshell lorgnette to her rheumy eyes. A straw bonnet framed a well-lined face, and her gray hair was pulled back into a severe bun.

"Know him? I'd say!" she said in a voice that crackled with age. "He saved my grandson from that awful fire. He was a wonderful, wonderful man," she exclaimed with great reverence, and her stacked chins wobbled in agreement. She lowered the lorgnette and gazed at the statue as if witnessing a miracle. "Too bad he married that woman."

Matt frowned. "You have something against Mrs. Blackwell?"

A look of alarm crossed the woman's face. "Oh, don't get me wrong. That dear man just deserved… better."

The way she'd said it made Matt wonder if she would have deemed any woman good enough for the town hero.

She lowered her voice. "I'm not one to gossip, mind you. But it's the truth." Making it clear she intended to say no more about Blackwell's widow, she reiterated her high opinion of the statue's subject and then walked away as quickly as her old bones allowed.

The woman wasn't alone in her assessment of Neal Blackwell. Everywhere Matt went, it was the same story. *Saint* Blackwell did no wrong, and God help the man who said he did.

Ellie-May stood in the tall grass scanning the arid land that made up her farm. It was a small farm by local standards and barely produced enough to feed and clothe herself and two children.

It wasn't much, but it was hers. All hers. The good Lord willing, the drought would soon be over, and the land would once again flourish. The clear-blue sky and hot, blazing sun suggested it wouldn't be anytime soon. But for now, the ongoing drought was the least of her worries.

She had other things on her mind. Other things meaning a certain Texas Ranger. Why his visit upset her so, she couldn't say. The Ranger was mistaken. Neal had known nothing about a stage robbery. She'd stake her life on it.

Placing her hands at her waist, she scanned the distance with narrowed eyes. Where was Anvil? Maybe he'd heard something in town that would explain the Ranger's visit.

She hadn't seen her farmhand since early morning, and she couldn't help but worry about him. Lately, it seemed that he'd aged overnight. His step was slower and his back bent as he walked.

It had been a cold winter, and that seemed to have taken a toll on him. The barn loft couldn't have been that warm, though he never complained and had steadfastly refused to sleep in the house. Said it wouldn't be proper for a man to share the same roof with a widow-woman.

His concern for her and her children never failed to warm her heart. What a fine pickle she'd be in without him! Anvil was a slow worker, but he got the job done. Eventually.

But what he lacked in speed, he made up for in other ways. For one, he was willing to work for bread and bunk and enough money to support his Saturday-night whiskey habit. Not many men were willing to work for so little.

Sighing, she tramped through the tall grass until she spotted him propped up against the trunk of a sycamore tree, his felt hat covering his face.

While she debated whether to wake him or let him

sleep, he pulled his hat away from his face and pried his eyes open as if he'd sensed her presence. He stared at her for a moment before struggling to his feet.

"I was just resting my ole bones for a minute, Miss Ellie-May."

Though she had asked him to just use her Christian name, he'd insisted upon addressing her as Miss. He said that a fine lady like her should be spoken to properly, and that had made her laugh. No one had ever before called her a lady, fine or otherwise.

Anvil bent to pick his felt hat off the ground, one hand on the small of his back. After brushing off the dirt, he slapped the hat on his head. "I was gittin' ready to fix the fence."

Now, as always, he looked so eager to please that she didn't have the heart to make mention of the fact that he'd been doing a lot of that lately—resting. Sleeping.

He was more than her ranch hand. He'd been a good friend to her since her husband passed and was kind to her children. If it hadn't been for him, last Christmas would have been a bleak one indeed. But he had taken it upon himself to make Lionel a wooden wagon and her daughter, Alicia, a doll cradle. For that alone, Ellie-May owed him her undying gratitude and loyalty.

"I just wanted to ask if you'd seen anyone snooping around," she said.

Anvil thought for a moment. "Nope. Not since I caught that fella trying to sneak off with your chickens last month." The creases in his forehead deepened. "Why?"

"This morning, I caught a Texas Ranger in the barn. He asked about Neal."

Anvil's bushy eyebrows shot up. "A Texas Ranger, eh?"

She nodded. "Said something about needing information on that stage robbery they had a while back."

She remembered the robbery well. It was all anyone had talked about at the time. Senator Henry Miles had been one of the passengers, and him being robbed during his visit to Haywire had posed an embarrassment to the town.

"Pshaw." Anvil scratched a whiskered cheek. "What makes him think Mr. Neal would know anythin' 'bout that robbery?"

She drew in her breath. That very question had been all she could think about ever since her encounter with the Ranger. "I have no idea. Have you heard any gossip that might explain it?"

He shook his head. "Not a word. All I heard say is what a good man your husband was, and I know for a fact that's the God-honest truth. He was the kindest man I ever had the pleasure of meetin'. If it weren't for him, I'd still be sleepin' by the railroad tracks."

She watched Anvil open his toolbox and pull out a hammer. What he'd said was no exaggeration. She'd never forget the day Neal had brought Anvil home. What a sorrowful bag of bones he had been! His smell alone had been enough to topple a cow. She'd objected to letting the man in the house, but Neal had insisted that Anvil had seen hard times and deserved a chance to get on his feet again.

Anvil's actual name was Willie Williams, but Neal

had renamed him Anvil. He'd said that any man who'd survived living by the railroad tracks had to be strong as steel, and the name Willie didn't do him justice.

Ellie-May had been used to Neal bringing home strays in the early days of their marriage, but by the time Anvil had come along, things had changed. They had a young child to think about. Like a mother bear fighting to save her cub, she'd threatened to take the baby and leave if Neal insisted upon letting the man stay.

Neal being Neal expressed disappointment that she judged Anvil as harshly as the town had judged her. It was an underhanded way to win an argument, but she'd nonetheless given in, and she was glad that she had.

"No sirree," Anvil said after hammering a rail onto a post. He spit out a yellow stream of tobacco, and it plopped on the ground. "They don't make 'em like Mr. Neal anymore."

"They sure don't," she said and after a moment added, "When you have a chance, the step on the front porch needs fixing."

He nodded. "I'll get to it soon as I can. And don't you worry none, Miss Ellie-May. That Texas Ranger comes snoopin' around again, he'll have to deal with me."

She smiled. Anvil meant well, but he would be no match for the tall, strapping Ranger. "Thank you." Leaving Anvil to finish his task, she walked back to the house, mulling over their conversation.

How foolish of her to get all worked up over one lawman, but she couldn't seem to help herself. As much as she hated to admit it, Neal had had a quiet, dark side he'd always done his best to keep hidden from view.

She couldn't recall the number of times during the early days of their marriage that she'd woken in the middle of the night to find his side of the bed empty. Invariably, she'd find him pacing the floor or out on the porch staring at the dark of night.

At other times, she'd catch him gazing into space as if he were a hundred miles away.

But then he'd turn around and do something nice for her. Something nice for the children. For the town.

After one such episode, he whitewashed the church all the way to the steeple. Another time, he worked twenty-four hours straight to clean up his neighbors' yards after a tornado had ripped through town.

One night, he'd finally told her what haunted him; he'd accidentally shot and killed his best friend. He'd only been ten at the time and his friend eleven, but the pain and grief had never left him.

Helping others had been part of Neal's atonement. As much as Ellie-May hated to think it, she often wondered if marrying an outlaw's daughter had been his penance as well.

Dying to save all those children had been his final payment to society, though she doubted Neal would agree. He didn't have it in him to forgive himself.

He had even apologized to her for not being a better provider and promised that things would get better in the future. Had he lived, she had no doubt he would have found a way to fulfill that promise. That was the kind of man he was.

Shaking away her thoughts, she picked up her skirt and quickened her pace. There was no denying that Neal was a good man. A good husband. A good father. A hero. And that was what she needed to remember. That was what everyone needed to remember.

For the sake of her children.

3

SHERIFF KEELER LEANED BACK IN HIS CHAIR, HANDS clasped behind his head, and stared over his propped feet at Matt. "Let me get this straight," he drawled, and his mustache twitched. "You think Blackwell is responsible for that holdup?"

Matt lifted his gaze to the ceiling. It was hard to hear over the noise coming from upstairs. Prisoners confined to the second-floor cells were pounding the floor, and the hanging gaslight over his head swung back and forth like the pendulum of a clock.

"That's yet to be determined," Matt said, raising his voice to be heard over the racket. "It's possible."

"Quiet!" the sheriff yelled, and the stomping stopped. He made a face. "Wasn't that long ago that prisoners took their punishment without complaint. Now there's no pleasing them. Would you believe they're demanding steak instead of bread and water?"

Ignoring the question, Matt leaned forward. "About Blackwell…"

Sheriff Keeler dropped his feet to the floor and leaned forward. Hands clasped together, he propped his elbows on the desk. "What proof do you have that makes you think Blackwell was involved?"

That was the problem. Matt didn't have any real proof. At least none that would stand up in court. He nonetheless reached into his vest pocket and pulled out the stub of a train ticket, found in a Pinkerton file. The agency had never officially been on the case, but one of the detectives in town at the time had checked out the crime scene.

"This was found where the robbery took place," Matt said, holding up the ticket. "It was purchased here in Haywire."

The sheriff's eyebrows rose. "That's it? That's all you have?"

"According to the records, only two tickets were purchased that day at the Haywire station. And the station master distinctly remembers selling one of those tickets to a man named Harvey Wells."

The sheriff's gaze sharpened. "Wells?"

Matt nodded. "He's a local farmer and inventor."

"I know who he is." The sheriff pondered this latest information for a moment. "So why isn't *he* under suspicion?"

"Wells got off the train in Austin to visit his ailing grandfather and didn't return to Haywire until a week after the holdup. His story checks out."

The sheriff scoffed. "How would Hawkins remember who he'd sold tickets to? It was more than a year ago."

"Actually, he only remembered the one," Matt said. "That's because it was Hawkins's first day on the job, and he distinctly remembers Wells trying to sell him a mechanical ticket dispenser he'd invented. It was Wells who told me Blackwell boarded the train with him and planned to return to Haywire that same day. That puts him back in town at the time of the robbery."

The sheriff pondered that information for a moment. "Okay, Blackwell was back in town. So what? That don't make him a thief. He could have dropped that ticket or tossed it away. It could have blown to the robbery location for all we know."

Matt stuck the stub back in his pocket. As far-fetched as the sheriff's arguments seemed, they were precisely the same arguments a defense attorney would use in a court of law, and that was the problem.

"The ticket could also have been dropped by the thief at the time of the robbery," Matt said. "Don't you think it strange that there's been no other local robberies since Blackwell passed? How do you explain that?"

The sheriff sat back and folded his hands across his chest. "I don't know how to explain it. All I can tell you is that I knew Neal personally, and he wouldn't hurt a fly. He sure in blazes wouldn't rob anyone, let alone a stage."

As if to agree, the pounding of feet began again. It was so loud this time that even the windows rattled.

"Quiet!" Keeler yelled, and when that failed to gain results, he left his seat and grabbed a broom from the corner. Cursing beneath his breath, he banged the ceiling with the broom handle until peace had once again been restored.

Returning the broom to the corner, he sat. This

time, he regarded Matt with a look of disdain. It was no secret that the sheriff resented having to deal with the Texas Rangers, and he wasn't alone in that regard. Though one of the main responsibilities of the Rangers was to render assistance to local lawmen, their help was often regarded as criticism or interference. For that reason, the Rangers were seldom appreciated or even wanted.

"It's been a year since that robbery," the sheriff said. "Why all the interest now?"

"The senator's been pushing it. He still has hopes of recovering his heirloom ring stolen during the holdup."

The sheriff shook his head. "Not much chance of that. The thief probably sold it."

"Maybe, but the senator happens to be a friend of my captain and asked the Rangers to step in." Matt regarded his current assignment as a demotion for failing to arrest his outlaw brother when he'd had the chance. No one had called it a demotion, of course, but he'd been with the Rangers long enough to know that messing up was not an option. By letting his brother get away, Matt had messed up big time.

The pounding started up again, forcing the sheriff to raise his voice to be heard. "If you think Blackwell was involved, you're dead wrong."

"I take it you knew him well," Matt said, lifting his voice.

"Yes, and you'd be hard-bent to find a better man." The sheriff's next words were drowned out by the prisoners' noise.

Matt cupped his ear. "What?"

"His widow. Have you met her?"

"Yeah," Matt said, dropping his hand to his side. "I met her." No sooner were the words out of Matt's mouth than a vision of a blue-eyed woman holding a shotgun sprang to mind. A dainty thing she was, size-wise, standing little more than five feet tall. Despite her small size, she hadn't seemed at all intimidated by his six-foot frame or even his status.

That alone had been surprising. He'd seen burly men fold when confronted by a Texas Ranger, but not Blackwell's widow. Instead, she'd looked ready to fight him tooth and nail to protect her husband's honor.

The sheriff left his chair again and reached for the broom. After restoring order for a third time, he stood holding the broom, ready to wield it again if necessary. "If you met Ellie-May Blackwell, then you know she's as poor as a church mouse. If Neal robbed that stage, then what in blazes did he do with the loot?"

That was a good question and one for which Matt had no answer. Least not yet. "That's what I'm here to find out."

Keeler made a face. "Well, good luck with that."

Matt stood and donned his hat. Right now, it looked like he needed all the luck he could get. "I won't take up any more of your time," he said.

Sheriff Keeler leaned the broom against the wall. "You're wrong about Blackwell. You know that, right?"

Since Blackwell was regarded as a local hero, it sure did look that way. But Matt wasn't ready to exonerate the man. At least not yet.

"I hope you're right," he said and meant it. Not only for the town's sake but also for the sake of Blackwell's pretty widow and young son.

∞

"Lord almighty, will the man ever fix that step?" Mrs. Buttonwood's strident voice arrived at Ellie-May's door before the knock.

Ellie-May set her feather duster down on the mantel and crossed the room to let her neighbor in.

Mrs. Buttonwood strode inside, shaking her head and tutting. Dressed like a man in trousers, plaid shirt, and felt hat, she moved like one too, with long strides and broad movements. "Anvil better fix that step afore someone breaks his neck," she said and tutted.

The woman's reproving voice didn't fool Ellie-May one bit. Her husband, Ted, had died a year ago for no good reason that anyone could figure out. The doctor said it might have been the heart or maybe the liver. Others suspected Mrs. Buttonwood had finally succeeded in nagging him to death. Whatever the truth, she was now a widow on the prowl, and Anvil was clearly her target.

"Here's the fabric for Alicia's dress," Mrs. Buttonwood said. "I used it to make curtains, but there's enough left over for a dress." She was a large-boned woman who could ride and shoot as well or better than any man. But neither did she lack in feminine skills.

Ellie-May took the length of calico from her and ran her hand over the soft blue fabric. "It's beautiful," she said. It would make her daughter a fine frock indeed. "Are you sure I can't pay you? I have some egg money."

Mrs. Buttonwood turned down the offer with a wave of her hand. "Consider it payment for your husband's kindness."

The Buttonwood ranch had been hard hit by the tornado that roared through town two years earlier. The barn had been toppled and the roof ripped off the house. Neal had worked night and day to help the Buttonwoods restore order.

"Thank you. You're very kind." Ellie-May folded the fabric and put it on top of her sewing basket. Not only was Mrs. Buttonwood generous, but she was also one of the few people in town who knew what it was like to be alienated. The manly way she dressed had made her almost as much of a social outcast as Ellie-May. "Won't you at least stay for tea?"

"Thank you, but no. I have to get back to the ranch." Mrs. Buttonwood started for the door and stopped. "Will you have time to finish Alicia's dress before Saturday?"

"I'll make time," Ellie-May said. Her children would look their best for their father's memorial service if it killed her. "Eh…" She hesitated. If anyone knew the latest scuttlebutt, it was Mrs. Buttonwood. Surely, she'd heard that a Texas Ranger was in town inquiring about Neal.

Not wanting to raise her neighbor's suspicions, Ellie-May carefully phrased her question. "Do you think there'll be a good turnout Saturday?" Usually, it didn't take much encouragement to get Mrs. Buttonwood to share the latest gossip.

"From what I've heard, everyone and his brother will be there," Mrs. Buttonwood said and patted Ellie-May on the arm. "Don't you go worrying none, you hear? It'll be a day that'll do you and your little ones proud."

Disappointed that Mrs. Buttonwood hadn't taken the bait, Ellie-May forced a smile. "Do you think there'll be any out-of-town guests?"

"Who knows? We'll just have to wait and see, won't we?" After a beat, Mrs. Buttonwood asked, "Do you want me to remind Anvil to fix the porch step?"

Anvil had no interest in the overbearing woman and had begged Ellie-May to keep her away from him. "No, that's all right," she said quickly. "I've already spoken to him. He'll get to it as soon as he can."

The corners of Mrs. Buttonwood mouth drooped in disappointment. "Well, do tell him I said hello." With a toss of her head, she left without further comment.

∞

It was hot that Saturday, and the town square was already packed when Ellie-May arrived with Anvil and her two children.

Dressed in her Sunday-go-to-meeting calico dress and straw bonnet, she made her way through the crowd. Most women in her position would have worn black, the proper attire for a grieving widow. But dressing in widow's weeds following her husband's death would have meant having to purchase new fabric, and her budget hadn't allowed for such folly.

She did, however, take the time to polish her boots with soot and beeswax until she could practically see her face in the worn leather. Though she doubted anyone would look pass her faded floral print dress to notice.

Her lack of mourning clothes never failed to bring disapproving stares from some of the older women, and today was no different. The same women had criticized her attire in church. One had even told Ellie-May to her face that the absence of appropriate garb showed a lack of respect for her late husband.

Determined not to let anything spoil the day, she threw back her shoulders and lifted her chin. Let them gawk. See if she cared.

"Come along, children," she said and led the way through the crowd with Anvil following close behind.

The town gunsmith tipped his hat as she passed by, provoking the ire of his wife. "Your husband was a fine man," he said, ignoring his wife's elbow to his side.

Ellie-May rewarded him with a bright smile and a nod of gratitude.

"Saved my son, he did," called the newspaper publisher from beneath a stovepipe hat. The publisher had printed a glowing editorial on Neal's heroic deed and had urged the town to do something in Neal's honor. "You should be proud."

Ellie-May *was* proud and ever so thankful. Her children would never have to go through what she had gone through growing up. She'd lost a husband and her children had lost a father, but they had gained the town's respect. It had been a high price to pay, but she'd had no choice in the matter.

As she caught her first glimpse of the ten-foot-tall bronze statue in the middle of the square, her jaw dropped. Her husband's larger-than-life form standing on a pedestal nearly took her breath away.

"Oh my!" she gasped.

When the mayor first approached her with the idea of a memorial in Neal's memory, Ellie-May thought he'd meant something small like a plaque. Never had she imagined anything as impressive as a statue.

Statues were for important people. For presidents and generals and kings. It was hard to believe that the image of her simple farmer husband was now enshrined for all eternity.

Knowing Neal, he would be horrified! No doubt he would think the statue put him further in debt to society.

Next to her, Lionel and Alicia gazed wide-eyed at the mass of people, and Ellie-May sympathized. Her poor babies looked as overwhelmed as she felt. She gave their hands a reassuring squeeze.

"There's your pa," she said, directing their attention upward away from the crowd. "What do you think?"

Lionel stared up at the statue with solemn eyes. He was a serious child, and for that reason, she worried about him.

He looked less impressed with the statue than he had with the large gathering. "Why are all these people here?" he asked, his voice hushed.

"They're here to pay their respects to your papa," Ellie-May said. "He was an important man."

Never had she imagined that so many would show up to honor her husband. As pleased and touched as she was by the turnout, the crowd reminded her of something she'd rather forget. The last time she remembered seeing so many people at the town square was at her father's hanging. Thank God that Neal had convinced the town to ban public hangings. Never did she want her children to witness such a travesty, and Neal had seen to it that they wouldn't.

Pushing her thoughts aside, she watched the mayor thread his way slowly through the crowd to the make-shift podium next to the statue. A robust man as round as he was tall, he stopped to shake hands and chat with some of the spectators.

Always eager to take credit for everything good that happened in the town, he was no doubt prepared to give a long and painful speech, praising himself as much as Neal.

Shoe-Fly Jones, owner of the town's boot and leather shop, led a motley group of musicians in a rousing rendition of "Oh, Better Far to Live and Die." In the introduction, Shoe-Fly told spectators that the song was from *The Pirates of Penzance.*

Another man walked through the crowd, hawking the virtue of Bonnore's Electro Magnetic Bathing Fluid.

Ellie-May hadn't known what to expect at Neal's memorial, but she certainly hadn't imagined such a circus-like atmosphere.

She glanced down at her daughter. "What do you think about Papa's statue, Alicia?" Unlike Lionel, who mostly kept his thoughts to himself, Alicia wore her heart on her sleeve and had taken Neal's death the hardest. She still had nightmares, although they were now fewer than before.

"It's so big," Alicia murmured, her eyes rounded in awe.

Ellie-May smiled. To a child, the statue had to look enormous. "Do you like it?" she asked.

Alicia nodded. "Uh-huh. Is that Lionel in his arms?"

"It can't be me," Lionel said with a frown. "Statues are for dead people."

"That's not true," Ellie-May said gently. "Actually, I believe it's supposed to represent one of the children your pa saved from that awful fire."

She brushed a blond strand of hair away from her daughter's face. She had worked until the wee hours of the morning putting the finishing touches on Alicia's dress and was pleased with the results.

Alicia was a pretty child, and the blue calico enhanced the color of her fair skin and brought out the golden highlights of her hair.

Ellie-May had ripped apart one of Neal's shirts to make a new one for her son. Lionel had been all spit and polished when they'd started out that morning, but the look hadn't lasted long. Already, his shoes were scuffed and his knee pants dusty. To make matters worse, he had a smudge on his face, and his cowlick stood up like a flagpole. Sighing, she rubbed the dirt off his face with a handkerchief and worked a moist finger through his hair.

So much about Lionel reminded her of Neal. Certainly, he had Neal's good looks. Still, it worried her that, like his father, Lionel had a tendency to withdraw at times.

Anvil, who had stopped to talk to someone he

knew, joined them, and her troubled thoughts vanished. He pulled off his hat. His head falling back like the lid of a coffeepot, he gazed openmouthed at the statue. "That's a mighty impressive image," he said.

Ellie-May smiled. "Yes, isn't it?"

"It sure does look like Mr. Neal," Anvil added.

Lionel tugged on Anvil's sleeve. "You can be a statue even if you aren't dead," he said.

Anvil's gaze shifted downward. "Is that so?"

Alicia nodded in agreement. "Do you think they'll make a statue of you?"

"Stranger things have happened," Anvil said and winked at Ellie-May. He then lowered his voice in a conspiratorial tone to address the children. "Guess what I saw? A juggler. Whatya say we go and have a look?" He spotted Mrs. Buttonwood, and his eyes suddenly took on a frenzied look. "Oh no! Come along. There's no time to waste."

Before Ellie-May could object, Anvil had steered Lionel and Alicia away. "Hurry back," she called as they disappeared in the crowd. When the ceremony started, she wanted her children by her side. Their presence would be the only thing keeping her from falling apart.

Forcing herself to breathe, she glanced around. Then she saw him—the Texas Ranger—and he was looking straight at her. Shooting him a visual dagger, she quickly turned away.

Much to her annoyance, the Ranger failed to take the hint. Instead, he suddenly appeared by her side and tipped his wide-brimmed gray hat politely. "Mrs. Blackwell."

She glared at him. "If you don't mind, Mr...."

"Taggert," he said. "Matt Taggert."

"Mr. Taggert, the ceremony is about to start."

"Oh, I don't mind," he said. "Feel free to ignore me."

That she would have gladly done, had it been possible. But he wasn't an easy man to ignore. Standing as tall and straight as a maypole, his height alone made him stand out in the crowd, not to mention his broad shoulders and long, sturdy legs.

It was also hard not to notice what a handsome man he was. Piercing brown eyes stared out from a rugged, square face. The set of his jaw boasted a stubborn streak; the square of his shoulders touted strength and determination.

Everything about him suggested power and grit. He looked like a man accustomed to asking questions and demanding answers. A force to be reckoned with. Trouble with a capital *T*.

Regarding him with more than a little apprehension, Ellie-May's mouth ran dry. "I thought you would have left town by now," she said. If indeed he'd come to town to talk to Neal, there was no reason for him to stay. "Being that your business here is done." The last was a question as much as a statement.

Some emotion she couldn't decipher flickered in the golden-brown depths of his eyes. "Sorry to disappoint you, ma'am. But it looks like I'll be around a while longer," he said.

"Because of the stagecoach robbery?" she asked.

He hesitated a moment before answering. "It appears that someone from Haywire committed that crime, and my job is to find out who."

Ellie-May drew in her breath. Neal wasn't mentioned by name, but she got the distinct impression that the Ranger still considered her husband a suspect. Why else would he take the time to attend Neal's memorial service?

"So why are you wasting your time here?" she asked.

"Just paying my respects, ma'am. Just paying my respects." He tossed a nod at the motley band. "Interesting choice of music," he added after a short pause.

She stiffened. Until he'd mentioned it, she'd not paid much attention to the music. Had she known that the band would choose selections from an opera about pirates, she would have objected. "I had nothing to do with the choice."

The Ranger arched an eyebrow. "If you had, what would you have chosen to mark the occasion?"

"'For He's a Jolly Good Fellow,'" she said with meaning.

Affording her a crooked smile that made her heart flutter, the Ranger glanced at the mayor, who had now taken his place behind the podium. "Looks like they're about to get started," Taggert said with a tip of his hat. "I'll let you enjoy the ceremony in peace."

She locked her gaze with his. "I hope you catch… your man," she said.

"Oh, I will, Mrs. Blackwell. You can count on it."

4

MATT WAITED FOR THE 3:05 TRAIN TO PULL INTO THE
Haywire station. It was hot and humid, and the open-
air station offered no shade.

He had sent his captain a telegram requesting a
meeting. Captain McDonald had granted Matt five
minutes, the amount of time between train stops. A
firm believer that anything of importance could be
said in three minutes or less, the captain was being
uncharacteristically generous with his time.

Matt had accepted his new orders under protest. He
felt like his time would be better spent tracking down
his outlaw brother before Charley hurt someone or
got hurt himself.

So far, Charley was wanted only for bank robberies, but things could quickly escalate. Most victims of
holdups were shot by accident, and Matt feared it was
only a matter of time before Charley or one of his
victims suffered the consequences.

It was bad enough that Charley was a thief. A bank
robber, for crying out loud. Pa would turn over in his
grave if he knew how Charley had turned out.

Matt blamed himself. He was the oldest, and it had been his responsibility to watch out for his younger siblings, especially after his pa died and his ma had taken to a sickbed. Had he been too lenient with Charley? Too strict? What signs had he missed that Charley was heading for a life of crime?

Matt had been so close—so very close to catching his brother. Fool that he was, he'd expected his brother to surrender nice and peaceful-like. Never had he imagined that the boy who had once idolized him, the boy who Matt had nursed through illness and childhood injuries, would one day pull a gun on him. It hurt just thinking about it.

To make matters worse, Matt's failure to capture his brother hadn't just hurt him personally but also professionally. As a result, his captain had yanked Matt off the case. Said he was too close to the situation to be effective.

Matt disagreed. Okay, so he'd underestimated Charley that one time, but that was a mistake he wouldn't make again. Family apparently meant nothing to Charley. That much was clear. Never again would Matt let his personal feelings get in the way of his job.

But orders were orders, and the sooner he cleared up this matter in Haywire, the sooner he could persuade the captain that he was the best man to end his brother's crime spree.

Matt's thoughts fled as the train chugged into the station, right on time. Several passengers disembarked, including James McDonald, captain of Texas Rangers Company F.

Stepping onto the platform, the captain glanced around. He acknowledged Matt with a nod before heading his way. He matched Matt in height, physical power, and resolve, but that was where the similarities ended.

Never a man to waste words, the captain skipped the usual polite greetings and cut right to the chase. "Got your telegram. You said something had come up."

Matt glanced at the people milling around the station. It was hardly the place for such an urgent conversation, but there was no time to look for somewhere more private.

"Neal Blackwell is dead."

The captain didn't even blink. "Did you find the loot?"

"I'm working on it."

"So what's the problem?"

"The man is a hero around here, and no one is willing to say a bad word about him. There's even a statue of him in the town square, and they plan to name the school after him."

"So what are you saying?"

Matt sighed. For someone who held such a high position, the captain sure could be thickheaded at times. "Now that he's dead, I don't know that finding the stolen money is even possible. It's been a year."

The captain frowned. Not only had the Rangers failed to capture Matt's brother, but they'd taken a lot of heat of late for failing to put a stop to the fence-cutting wars. McDonald didn't look happy at the prospect of another failure on his record, especially since a senator was involved.

Not that Matt could blame him. The Rangers couldn't afford to lose more public support and were in desperate need of a positive outcome.

The captain's clipped voice cut through Matt's thoughts. "Have you been to Blackwell's farm?"

"I've been there," Matt said. He decided it was best not to mention being held at gunpoint by the suspect's widow.

"Do you think that's where Blackwell hid the money?"

"Possibly." Blackwell had died the day after the robbery. It hardly seemed possible that he'd had time to spend it.

"And?"

Spotting a man loitering nearby, Matt lowered his voice. "Blackwell left a widow and two children."

"I don't care if Blackwell left a whole orphanage of children." Seemingly oblivious to those around him, the captain made no effort to lower his voice. "Dig up the whole Blackwell farm if you have to. I want that stolen money found."

Matt's jaw hardened. "My time would be better spent tracking down my brother," he said through clenched teeth.

"I've got men working on it."

"But no one knows him like I know him," Matt argued. Or at least he'd thought he knew his younger sibling. But that was before Charley had pulled a gun on him. Before he knew how little family meant to Charley.

A flash of impatience crossed the captain's face. "Like I said, I've got men working on it. Your job is to find the stolen loot. That money from the stage has gotta be somewhere, and I want it found."

Matt spoke through wooden lips. "I'll find it," he said with more conviction than he felt. "But it'll take time."

"Take all the time you need. Just make it quick." Without another word, the captain spun around and headed for the train with minutes to spare.

∽

Ellie-May woke with a start. Something had pulled her from a sound sleep, but she didn't know what.

Rising, she donned her robe and quietly checked the children's room before plodding barefooted down the hall to the parlor. She paused for a moment to listen. Light from a full moon angled in the window and spread a luminous glow over the sparsely furnished room.

It was more of a feeling than a sound that drew her to the parlor window.

The moonlight spilled over her property like melted butter, and she immediately spotted movement. Pressing her face close to the windowpane, she narrowed her eyes. It was a man, and he appeared to be digging up her vegetable garden. What the—?

What possible reasons would anyone have for doing such a thing? Grabbing her shotgun from a corner, she ripped the door open with such force, it was a wonder that it hadn't come off its hinges.

She dashed outside to the edge of the porch and raised her shotgun. She could see only the dark form of the man, but it was enough to tell her the intruder was short and stocky.

"Who are you and what do you want?" she yelled. Without giving the trespasser a chance to answer, she aimed her gun high and fired. A screech owl left the safety of a sycamore tree and took to the sky in protest.

The man's arms shot up over his head. "Don't shoot, don't shoot!"

Ellie-May kept her weapon pointed. "Who are you?" she called again. "And what are you doing on my property?"

"Name's Wagner, and I heard there was stolen money buried here."

Anvil came running from the barn. Dressed in a white nightshirt and sleeping cap, he looked like a ghost. "What happened?" he called. "You all right?"

Her shotgun aimed at Wagner, Ellie-May said, "I'm fine. But that man claims he's looking for stolen money."

"Money?" Anvil said, sounding as confused as she was. "What money?"

Wagner kept his hands held over his head. "From last year's stage robbery," he replied.

Ellie-May frowned. "Why would you think the stolen money is here?"

Wagner lowered his hands to shoulder high. "Heard the Texas Ranger say it with my own ears."

Ellie-May gritted her teeth. Taggert again! "Well, you heard wrong. Now get your sorry ass out of here before I fill you with lead." To show she meant business, she aimed over his head and fired again.

The blast echoed through the night.

Seeming to need no further proof of Ellie-May's intentions, Wagner ran to his mount and practically flew into the saddle. His horse then took off in a flash, its hooves hammering the ground like war drums.

"You can go back to bed, Miss Ellie-May," Anvil called. "I'll keep watch."

"It's all right, Anvil. I don't think he'll come back. Least not tonight. Get some sleep."

"Mama?"

Ellie-May turned to her find both her son and daughter standing in the doorway. Alicia's and Lionel's pale faces seemed to hang in midair. The moonlight reflected fear in their rounded eyes.

"Don't be scared," Ellie-May said gently. "Mama thought she heard something, but...I was mistaken." No sense worrying them.

She glanced at Anvil before joining her children and herding them back into the house.

The Feedbag Café was empty when Matt took a corner seat early that morning and perused the bill of fare.

Breakfast was served at the hotel where he was staying, but the out-of-town guests had no personal knowledge of Neal Blackwell. Matt counted on the café to serve up a generous heap of local gossip along with his cackleberries and bacon.

What he hadn't counted on was coming face-to-face with Blackwell's widow. No sooner had his eggs and bacon arrived than he spotted her storming into the restaurant. She paused for the briefest of moments at the doorway. Even from a distance, he could see the fire in her eyes. Whoever had earned her ire this time deserved his sympathy, that was for sure. At least she wasn't packing iron.

Picking up his fork, he was just about to dive into his breakfast when her gaze zeroed in on him. As a Ranger, he'd been the target of angry men and blazing guns, but he'd never been as tempted to hide as he was at that moment.

Unfortunately, there was no time to follow through with his cowardly wish. For before he could move, she dashed toward him like a runaway train and stood next to his table, glaring. A bull tossed by a cowcatcher couldn't have looked more incensed.

"How dare you?" she thundered, turning the heads of the other diners.

He reared back in his chair. "I'm sorry?"

As if suddenly aware she was making a scene, she leaned forward and lowered her voice for his ears only. "You have no right spreading falsehoods about my husband!"

Now he really was confused. "Falsehoods?" He'd been accused of many things, but never had he been accused of lying. "I don't know where you got such a notion but—"

Blue sparks shot from her eyes, and she straightened. "A man named Wagner told me what you said about stolen money being buried on my property!"

Not having the foggiest idea who Wagner was, Matt was at a loss for words. "And you believed this man?"

She regarded him with narrowed eyes before dropping her gaze to his still-untouched plate. For an instant, a look of deprivation dulled her eyes. It was the same hungry look his father had shown all those years ago upon returning from that awful war.

As if to stop herself from staring at his plate, she lifted her gaze to his. "What reason would he have for lying?"

The café's proprietor, Mrs. Buffalo, stopped at their table. An apron was tied around her thick middle, and only a few strands of white hair showed beneath her ruffled cap. "Is there a problem, Ellie-May?"

Motioning to his plate with his fork, Matt answered for her. "No problem," he said. Right now, there seemed to be a more pressing issue at stake. "At least none that a plate for the lady wouldn't solve."

With a curious glance at the still-seething widow, Mrs. Buffalo nodded. "I'll see to it right away."

Not giving Mrs. Blackwell a chance to object, he pointed to the empty chair. "Have a seat," he said. "You look like you could use some vittles. My treat."

She lifted her chin. "I'm not hungry," she said, the deprived look in her eyes belying her words.

Ignoring her protests, he reached for the saltshaker. "So where did you meet this…man, Wagner?"

"On my property," she said, and her eyes blazed anew with accusatory lights. "Digging for the money you said was buried there!"

Matt furrowed his brow. Wagner. The name didn't ring a bell, but then he'd talked to a number of people around town. Still, the only time he recalled mentioning buried money was during his conversation with the captain at the train station. Had someone overheard? Perhaps the man he'd seen lurking nearby?

He sprinkled a generous amount of salt on his eggs. "If something I said gave the wrong impression, I apologize," he said, hoping to smooth her feathers.

His apology didn't take the wind out of the lady's sails, but she looked less inclined to throttle him. She did, however, draw herself up to her full five-foot height to subject him to a long, level look.

"Neal was no thief," she said.

She spoke with such conviction and heartfelt emotion that Matt found himself hoping she was right. "It's my job to consider all possibilities," he said.

She narrowed her eyes. "Why Neal?" she asked. "He's been gone for a year. Why are you suddenly interested in him?"

He took a moment to consider his answer. "We have reason to believe that the man who robbed that stage purchased a train ticket in Haywire." He purposely failed to mention that only two men had bought tickets on the day in question and one had already been cleared of any wrongdoing. "Anyone at the train station that day is of interest."

She studied him for a moment as if to measure his sincerity. "My husband was a good man."

"So I've heard."

"An honest man."

He drew in his breath. "Your husband has a lot of admirers," he said. Her expression softened at his words, and he was once again reminded what a pretty woman she was. Especially when she wasn't spitting fire.

He picked up his knife and fork and sliced off a piece of crisp bacon.

"He has a lot of admirers for good reason," she said. "And you have no right dragging his name through the mud."

His hands froze. "If that's what you think I'm doing, I apologize."

Mrs. Buffalo delivered a second plate to the table and left. Matt stabbed the air with his fork. "Eat your breakfast before it gets cold."

"I told you—"

"I know, I know. You're not hungry. But it would be a shame to let good food go to waste." He doubted she would let that happen. A hardworking woman like her. It was what he counted on.

Still she hesitated. She was no doubt torn between eating with the enemy and walking away from the best meal she'd probably had in a month of Sundays.

In the end, practicality won, and she yanked out the chair and sat. "Just because I'm eating with you don't mean I agree with what you're doing."

"Understood."

Eyeing him like a cat might eye a mouse, she picked up a fork. "My Neal didn't rob no stage."

Without waiting for him to agree or disagree, she dived into the food on her plate as if there were no tomorrow.

5

ELLIE-MAY DROVE HORSE AND WAGON AWAY FROM the Feedbag Café feeling more than a little guilt. The curious and, in some instances, shocked stares of other restaurant patrons had followed her out the door.

No doubt they were thinking she was a hussy, if not worse. Her poor husband had been dead for only a year, and already she had been seen dining with a man.

Ellie-May inhaled sharply. Holding the reins with one hand, she drew her handkerchief out of her pocket and mopped her damp forehead.

She could hardly blame anyone for judging her. Not only had she failed to comply with the rules of widowhood through dress and demeanor, but proper ladies didn't let casual acquaintances pay for their meals. She might not have much in the way of school learning, but she knew that much.

Still, it wouldn't have been right to let all that good food go to waste. The amount of food on her plate alone added up to nearly three days of rations.

If only she hadn't enjoyed the meal so much! But

she hadn't been able to help herself. The bacon was crisp, the eggs fluffy, and the flapjacks light as air.

The coffee alone had been worth the critical stares. It had been months since she'd allowed herself the luxury of a cup of coffee. What precious beans she had were saved for Anvil. He needed them more than she did.

Not only had she enjoyed the coffee and food, but never had she known the luxury of dining in a restaurant and being waited on. As a child, she'd thought that only rich people could afford the extravagance. Certainly, Neal hadn't been able to spare such expense.

"One day," he'd told her. "One day."

The view hadn't been all that bad, either, much as she hated to think it. It wasn't every day that a gal got to sit across from a good-looking man, and the Texas Ranger was that in spades.

The female diners might have glared at her in disapproval, but she didn't doubt for a moment that they envied her.

She sighed. It wasn't just that she'd allowed a man—a near stranger—to pay for her meal that had filled her with guilt; Matt Taggert obviously thought her husband was involved in some way with the stage robbery. True, he'd fallen short of calling Neal an actual suspect, but why else show so much interest in him?

Accepting anything from Taggert, let alone a meal, showed the utmost disrespect for her husband and his memory.

Such were her thoughts as she drove horse and wagon home, and her misery only increased as the day wore on.

By late afternoon, she was still mulling over her morning encounter with Taggert as she sat in her parlor ripping seams out of one of Neal's shirts.

The broadcloth was in good condition and would make a fine shirt for Lionel. The boy was growing like a weed and had outgrown the shirt she'd made him for Christmas. Here it was only five months later, and already the shirt was too short to tuck into his knee pants.

It wasn't that long ago that she could make Lionel two shirts from a single one of Neal's. Now it took careful planning and cutting just to make a single shirt.

A knock sounded at the door, drawing her away from her thoughts. Dropping the scissors and shirt into her sewing basket, she stood and hurried across the room to open the door.

The visitor pulled off his hat and held it to his chest with both hands. He appeared to be in his late thirties. "Sorry to bother you, ma'am. The name's Roberts. Dave Roberts."

Her gaze traveled past him to the brown horse tied to the hitching post in front. The absence of a wagon told her he probably wasn't a salesman.

Ellie-May shifted her gaze back to the man. The lack of a Bible and frock coat ruled out the possibility of him being a traveling preacher. Instead, he was dressed in canvas trousers and a plaid shirt. He looked like one of the cowhands who worked on the nearby cattle ranches.

"What can I do for you, Mr. Roberts?"

"Actually, I'm here to do something for you," he said with a magnanimous air that caused the upturned ends of his mustache to twitch. "I just got back from

Alaska, and I only just heard about your husband passing through the Pearly Gates."

She drew her eyebrows together. "Did you know my husband?"

"Know him? Why, we grew up together and were practically blood brothers."

"Oh? You grew up in Texas, too?" she asked, testing him.

He blinked. "Missouri, ma'am. Born and raised in Hannibal, Missouri. Just like your husband."

The man had the right answers, but Ellie-May still wasn't sure if she could trust him. "If that's true, how come Neal never mentioned you?"

"It's like this," Roberts explained in a conspiratorial tone. "Neal and I had what you might call an altercation. He didn't like me mentioning his past and what had happened."

She stared at him. "You...you knew about that?"

"Yes, ma'am, I did." He shook his head until his jowls wobbled. "Shooting his little friend took a terrible toll on him. Just terrible."

She moistened her lips and tried to think. It stood to reason that anyone residing in Hannibal at the time would know what Neal had done. Certainly, anyone growing up with Neal would know.

Still, coming face-to-face with her husband's past was unsettling. She'd thought Neal's secret was safe with her. Now that Roberts was in town, she felt threatened on yet another front. It was bad enough that she was an outlaw's daughter, but if it were known that Neal had killed someone—even accidentally—his reputation could suffer.

Roberts continued. "I didn't know he'd kicked the buck...eh...passed...till I saw the piece about his statue in the paper. Seeing that, I said to myself, *Dave Roberts. You've got to find the missus and pay your respects.*"

"That's very thoughtful of you," she said cautiously. She was still not sure that she could trust him. There was something too smooth, too slick, too polished about him.

"Yes, well..." He cleared his throat. "I hope you don't mind me saying so, but it looks like you have need for a handyman. I noticed your broken step and shutters. And your roof..." He shook his head and tutted. "If I may offer my services..."

"I'm sorry, I can't afford to hire anyone right now."

"Oh, but I wouldn't think of taking your money!" The man looked positively appalled. "Oh, no, no, no. I offer my services in memory of your dear departed husband who, like I said, was like a brother to me."

Ellie-May didn't know what to say. "That's...very kind of you, but I couldn't possibly accept."

"Oh, but I insist." He twisted his hat in his hands. "You won't even know I'm here. More than that, you'll be doing me a favor. I can't tell you how bad I feel for not making amends with your husband before he passed. Helping you is the only way I can think to appease my guilt."

"Well..." Ellie-May hesitated. The man seemed sincere, and God knew she needed the extra help. "I can't offer you room and board," she said. She could barely provide for the children, Anvil, and herself.

"There's no need. I work at one of the local ranches

and can only work on your place during my off-hours."
He glanced down at the warped boards beneath his
feet. "Shouldn't take me more than a couple of weeks
to do what has to be done around here."

Ellie-May shoved her hands in her apron pocket
and weighed the pros and cons of accepting the
stranger's offer. She desperately needed the help but
still wasn't sure if she could trust him.

"Mr. Roberts, as I'm sure you must know, Neal
didn't like to talk about what happened in Hannibal."

Roberts raised his right hand as if taking an oath.
"I swear I won't say a word to anyone, if that's what
you're worried about." He looked and sounded as
serious as a preacher delivering a sermon to a bunch
of confessed sinners. "Like I said, all I want to do is
make up for not making amends when he was alive."

Feeling bad for thinking ill of the man, Ellie-May
felt herself cave. "In that case, I'd be much obliged for
whatever help you can give me."

❧

Matt left the barbershop with a smooth chin but nothing in the way of information. No investigation was
complete without at least one visit to the town barber.
In years past, he'd gotten some of his most useful local
news from sitting in a barber's chair and listening to
the other patrons talk.

Lather a man's face with shaving soap, and opinions
tended to spout out of his mouth as easily as the
whiskers left his chin. At least that had been Matt's
experience in the past.

Today, he'd heard opinions aplenty, but none of any help. Though the Dawes Act had passed in February, the federal law turning Indians into farmers and land-owners was still being loudly debated. Any attempt on Matt's part to turn the conversation away from politics to local happenings was met with resistance.

Mr. Haines, the owner of the barbershop, said anything that had to be said about Neal Blackwell had already been said. Matt felt the same way about the Dawes Act.

That left him with nowhere else to go. No further clues to track. Nothing left to do but return to his company and hope his next assignment bore more fruit. If Neal Blackwell had indeed been responsible for the holdup, he sure in blazes hadn't left a trail. A man didn't steal that much money and not have something to show for it.

Just as Matt reached his horse, he was stopped by a lad in a slouch hat. "Mister, are you the Texas Ranger?"

Matt gazed over his saddle at the boy. Keen hazel eyes stared back from an angular face dotted with freckles. The studied expression contrasted sharply with the boy's careless attire. His wrinkled shirt and frayed trousers hung from his thin body like moss from a tree. Uncombed ginger hair fell from beneath his cap to his shoulders in long, stringy strands.

"Who wants to know?" Matt asked.

"Name's Jesse. Jesse James."

Matt quirked an eyebrow. Was the boy aware that he shared his name with an outlaw?

"Yeah, I'm a Texas Ranger," Matt said slowly. "You got a problem?"

"I want you to hire me," Jesse said. "I'm a hard worker, and you won't be sorry."

Matt furrowed his brow. "You want to be a Ranger? Is that what you're saying?"

"Yes, sir."

"How old are you, son?"

"I'll be fourteen in December. But I act older than my age, and I can shoot as good as a twenty-year-old."

"A twenty-year-old, eh?"

"Yeah." Jesse ran a hand down Justice's neck. "That's a mighty fine horse you got there, Mister. I've been saving up to buy my own horse. I've already got $1.47 saved."

Matt stared at the boy. That was hardly enough to cover the cost of horseshoes. But since the boy looked and sounded so serious, Matt tried to think of a way to let him down gently.

"I'm afraid you've come to the wrong man. I'm not the one who does the hiring."

Jesse scrunched up his nose. "But you could put in a good word for me."

Matt shook his head. "'Fraid that won't do you much good. You're not old enough to be a Ranger. Wait a few years."

Jesse frowned. "Boys younger than me fought in the war."

"Yeah, and most of them didn't live long enough to tell about it." The corners of Jesse's mouth turned downward, but he looked no less determined. Feeling sorry for him, Matt asked, "How come you want to be a Ranger?"

Jesse glanced around before answering. "I know things," he said, his voice hushed.

"Do you, now?"

The boy's eyes narrowed. "You don't believe me, do you?"

"Any reason I should?" Matt asked.

"I don't lie. Only cowards lie, and I ain't no coward."

Matt regarded the boy with keen interest. Something about the boy reminded him of himself at that age. "Okay. So what kind of things do you know?"

Jesse lowered the volume of his voice, but the same intense look remained on his face. "I know that the bank manager, Mr. Coffman, sneaks away during the day to play poker."

"That's not a crime," Matt said.

Unfazed, the boy continued. "I also know that Jeff Watkins stole money from Mr. Gordon's till when he wasn't looking."

"Okay, that is a crime. But it's a job for the sheriff's department, not the Texas Rangers."

"I also know who robbed that stagecoach a while back," Jesse said, saving the most startling information for last.

Matt pushed back his hat and stared at the boy. If Jesse James wanted to get his attention, he sure enough had succeeded. "Is that so?"

Jesse's dark eyes gleamed in triumph. "It was Mr. Blackwell," he said in all seriousness. "He's the one who done the robbing."

"You better not let anyone hear you say that," Matt said. "The man you're accusing of a serious crime happens to be the town hero. He also happens to be deceased."

"That don't change nothing. He still robbed that stage."

Matt studied the boy. Either the youth had a wild imagination, or he really did know something. Matt glanced around to make sure no eavesdroppers lurked nearby. The last thing he needed was for Blackwell's widow to get wind of this conversation.

"What makes you think Blackwell was responsible for that crime?"

"Heard him talking."

"You *heard* him?" Matt's sharp voice caused his horse to shake his head and a passerby to stare. Grimacing, he motioned the boy to follow him to the alley that ran along the side of the barbershop.

Satisfied that they were out of earshot, he turned to face the boy. "You said you heard Blackwell talking. Where was this?"

"On his farm. He'd hurt his back and hired me to help out. That's when I heard him talking to another man. I heard him say that he would keep the stolen money for twenty-four hours."

"Why twenty-four hours?" Matt asked.

Jesse James shrugged his shoulder. "Don't know, but that's what he said."

Matt weighed this new information against what he already knew, and something didn't add up. If what the boy said was true, that meant that the stagecoach robber hadn't acted alone. He had a partner. But neither the driver nor any of the three passengers had mentioned a second man.

Matt narrowed his eyes. "You're not making this up, are you?"

Jesse looked affronted. "Why would I do such a thing?"

"I don't know. To impress me?"

"I'm telling you the God-honest truth."

Matt studied the boy at length. He certainly looked and sounded sincere. If he wasn't speaking the truth, he sure in blazes was a good liar. "How come you didn't tell anyone what you'd heard? The sheriff?"

"I did, sir. The sheriff said he'd look into it. But before he had a chance, Mr. Blackwell died in that fire."

Matt ran his hand over his newly shaved chin. "The man you heard Blackwell talking to… Do you know his name?"

Jesse shook his head. "Nope. Saw him once in my pa's saloon. Haven't seen him since."

"Would you recognize him if you saw him again?"

"Yes, sir," Jesse said without hesitation. "A Texas Ranger never forgets a face."

Matt wasn't sure that was true, but he let the comment pass. "Anything else you can tell me about Blackwell and what you heard?"

"No, sir. That's all I heard him say. He would keep the loot."

Matt's thoughts whirled in his head like autumn leaves on a windy day. If what the boy said was accurate, then the money could well be hidden somewhere on the Blackwell farm. Unless, of course, the man seen talking to Blackwell had absconded with it. But since none of the banknotes had been put back in circulation, that seemed unlikely. The only explanation that made sense was that Blackwell had died before spending the money, and his partner—if indeed there had been a partner—had no knowledge of its whereabouts.

"If you think of anything else," Matt said, "I'm staying at the hotel. Room 10."

Jesse's face brightened. "Does that mean I'm now a Ranger?"

"No, it means if you recall anything else about the man, you're to tell me. No one else. Understood?"

The boy gave a reluctant nod. "Yes, sir."

Satisfied that he had Jesse's cooperation, Matt spun on his heel and left the alley. He still didn't know whether to believe the boy. He wanted to, but there were too many unanswered questions.

Jesse followed him to his horse. "What can I do?"

Matt untethered his horse and mounted. "Do?"

Squinting against the sun, Jesse looked as serious as an old cat. "You know. Till I'm old enough to join the Rangers?"

Matt thought for a moment before answering. "You might think about changing your name, son." With that, he tugged on the reins and rode away.

6

Ellie-May walked into Gordon's General Store
with Alicia and Lionel in tow. The pleasant scent of
cinnamon and freshly ground coffee beans filled the
air, along with a hint of tobacco.

The smell of coffee reminded her of the breakfast
she'd had with the Texas Ranger. Just thinking about
her crass behavior made her cheeks flare. It wasn't like
her to be so confrontational or outspoken, but she
couldn't let the Texas Ranger say things about her
husband that simply weren't true.

Standing behind the counter, Mr. Gordon looked
up at the sound of jingling bells, his spectacles resting
on the tip of his nose. "Mornin', Mrs. Blackwell," he
drawled.

"Morning, Mr. Gordon." Since Neal died, the shop
proprietor had been especially tolerant of her running
account, but she tried not to take advantage. Today, as
usual, she intended to pay him part of what she already
owed him from her egg money.

Adjusting her empty shopping basket over her
arm, she started down the aisle. Lionel had already

rushed ahead to check out the tin soldiers in the toy section.

There was no room in her budget for toys or any other luxuries. For that reason, she quickly walked past the tempting display of feathers and lace. No sense lingering on things that only made her feel bad.

She did, however, stop to check out a handsome straw hat that she would never be able to afford.

Alicia called to her. "Oh, look, Mama. Look!" Her young daughter pointed to a small cylinder box that played music. The lacquered black box was engraved with green leaves outlined in gold.

Eyes sparkling like sun-lit gems, Alicia carefully turned the little gold key at the back of the box, and a tinny tune began to play. Closing her eyes, she swayed back and forth, a look of pure joy on her face.

Ellie-May took a quick glance at the price tag, and her jaw dropped. The music box cost as much as it did to run her household for several weeks.

"All the way from Switzerland," Mr. Gordon called from behind the counter as if to justify the cost.

The music box fell silent, and Alicia immediately rewound it. Humming along with the tune, she lifted her head as if to catch every note.

"Come along, children," Ellie-May said. "We have shopping to do." Anxious to complete her errands and return to the farm, she quickly moved along the aisle. She needed rice, flour, and candle wax. If she used fewer coffee beans for Anvil's morning cup, she could make the current supply last for another month.

Alicia followed without argument, but each time the music box stopped playing, she would run back to rewind it. Fearing Alicia would drop the box or otherwise break it, Ellie-May scolded her. Mr. Gordon had a strict policy that required customers to pay for any breakage.

"Come on along, Alicia. You mustn't dawdle." She handed her daughter a block of candle wax. "Take that to the counter."

Mr. Gordon greeted Alicia with a look of sympathy. "You can come to the store anytime you want to listen to the music box," he said, drawing out his words.

Alicia responded with a happy squeal. "Oh, thank you, thank you!" She spun around, a wide smile on her face. "Mama, did you hear what Mr. Gordon said?"

"Yes, yes, I did," Ellie-May said. "Just be careful not to break it." Gratified that her children were shown more kindness than she'd ever been shown as a child, Ellie-May thanked the store owner and scooped rice into a paper sack.

After filling her basket, Ellie-May deposited a handful of coins on the counter to pay part of her prior bill. It cost every penny of that week's egg profit.

After adding her current purchases to the tab, Mr. Gordon adjusted his spectacles up his angular nose and handed each child a penny candy. Alicia ran back to rewind the music box one last time, and the tinny tune followed them out of the shop.

∞

After leaving Jesse James, Matt went to his hotel room and read and reread the sheriff's report on the Haywire robbery. Every word written on the one-page report had been committed to memory. Still, it didn't hurt to go over it again. There was always the chance that some small detail had been missed or that something that had originally seemed unimportant would take on new meaning in light of Jesse's information.

Three passengers had been on the stage, including Senator Miles. The other male passenger was a salesman who'd had nothing of value on him and had escaped being robbed. The third passenger, Mrs. Whittaker, had been relieved of her jewelry, but the contents of her purse had been left untouched.

Matt suspected that the robbery of the senator was more of an embarrassment to the sheriff than the stealing of the strongbox. The politician had been robbed of his watch and heirloom diamond ring. Miles never failed to mention the holdup in his speeches and had promised to help Captain McDonald carve out a future political career upon return of his cherished jewelry.

The passengers, driver, and guard all described a single bandit wearing a flour sack. Like Blackwell, he was of average height and build. The guard was positive that he'd shot the man as he was getting away, but none of the other victims could confirm it. Nor had there been any mention of a second bandit.

I heard him say that the stolen money would stay with him for twenty-four hours.

Now, as before, Matt puzzled over the time period. Why only twenty-four hours?

Still, if what Jesse said was true, then the road agent hadn't acted alone. If Blackwell did indeed have a partner, why had there been no other robberies after Neal's death? What had his partner been doing all this time?

Matt slid the report back into his portfolio. Something about this case didn't sit right. Correction. Nothing about this case sat right.

Having more questions than answers, he left the hotel and rode straight to the sheriff's office. Today as usual, Sheriff Keeler looked none too pleased to see him.

Keeler jabbed his pen into the penholder and sat back in his chair, the ends of his curling mustache twitching. "Thought you'd left town."

Matt seated himself upon the ladder-back chair in front of the sheriff's desk and balanced his hat on his knee. "That was the plan. But something came up."

Today, no sound could be heard from the second-floor jail cells. Either the prisoners had been released, or they had succeeded in their demands for steak. Either way, Matt was grateful for not having to raise his voice.

"Oh?"

"I bumped into a boy named Jesse James. You know him?"

The sheriff rolled his eyes. "Yeah, I know him. His mother died last year, and his old man lets him pretty much run wild."

"Jesse said he told you about a conversation he'd overheard between Blackwell and some stranger."

"He talked to me, all right." Keeler folded his hands across his protruding middle. "Just like he's talked to me about half the citizens in Haywire. If I arrested everyone he suspected of a crime, we'd have to shut down the town."

For some reason, Matt felt the need to defend the boy. "He wants to be a Texas Ranger."

"Good. Then he'll be someone's else's problem."

Matt frowned. "So, you don't think there's any truth to Jesse's story? About Blackwell, I mean."

Sheriff Keeler shook his head. "You're wasting your time. The kid's as wild as they come, and he's got an imagination to match."

"So what you're saying is that he made the whole thing up."

"That's exactly what I'm saying." The sheriff paused for a moment. "Who knows? Maybe he's just lonely and this is how he gets attention. He sure don't get it from his pa."

Matt leaned forward. "I don't understand. If his pa owns a saloon, why does Jesse look so needy?" It had been his experience that even during dire economic times, saloons were the last to feel the pinch.

The sheriff scoffed. "His pa don't own no saloon."

Matt sat back. He distinctly recalled the boy mentioning his pa's saloon. If what the sheriff said was true, the boy had lied about his father, and his credibility had just taken another nosedive.

Still, even in the face of all the evidence to the contrary, Matt was reluctant to discount the boy altogether. Without him, Matt had nothing to go on but Blackwell's train ticket and a number of improbable theories on how it had ended up at the crime scene.

"So you don't think there's anything to what the boy said?"

The sheriff made a face. "All I knows is this—Blackwell had nothing to do with the stage robbery. I'll stake my life on it."

7

ELLIE-MAY HAD JUST FINISHED HANGING HER WASH ON
the clothesline when she caught sight of Anvil heading
her way.

One look at his serious face told her something was
wrong. She sighed. *Please don't let it be another expense.*
She'd recently had to sell their best horse to pay for
new parts for the windmill. Last winter, they'd had to
sell a cow to fix the barn roof. She was now down to
one sorry mare, one skinny milk cow, and a bunch of
chickens.

She reached for her empty laundry basket before
addressing him. "Something wrong?"

"Yes, there's somethin' wrong," he said, his face
pinched. "It's that Roberts fella. What's he doing
here?"

"He was a friend of Neal's," she said. "He offered
to help 'round here in Neal's memory. Thought you'd
appreciate the help."

Anvil scowled. "Far as I can see, he ain't much
help. I told him to muck out the horse stall, and I
found him diggin' 'round the windmill instead. Said

he was weedin'." Anvil spit out a stream of tobacco. "When did weeds take precedence over muck?"

Ellie-May furrowed her brow. She hadn't counted on Anvil objecting to the man's presence. "I'm sure he means well. He refuses to take payment for what he does here."

"That might be the problem," Anvil said with a shake of his head. "Been my 'sperience, you get what you pay for. I'm tellin' you, the man's slicker than a boiled onion. He even works slower than I do."

"No one can take your place, Anvil," she said, hoping to soothe his feathers. "Like I said, he was Neal's friend. And I doubt he'll stay around for long. I'd consider it a big favor if you'd try to be pleasant to him." Since the same stubborn look remained on Anvil's face, she added, "It's what Neal would have wanted you to do."

Anvil shrugged in resignation. "I'll do what I can, Miss Ellie-May. But don't 'spect me to like it." Turning, he walked away, muttering beneath his breath.

Tucking the empty laundry basket beneath her arm, Ellie-May headed back to the house. Upon reaching the porch, she noticed Lionel's discarded shoes.

She stooped to pick them up and dropped them into the basket. She'd told Lionel time and time again not to run around barefooted. There were rattlers out there. Scorpions and the Lord knew what else. That boy would be the death of her yet.

Holding the basket with one hand, she shielded her eyes from the sun with the other and scanned the area. It wasn't a school day, and the children had left earlier to go fishing. It sure would be nice if they caught a bass or two for dinner, but Alicia's restless nature usually scared the fish away.

Shaking her head, Ellie-May started up to the porch, forgetting about the broken step. The rotted wood caved beneath her foot, and she was barely able to regain her balance and keep from falling all the way through.

Muttering beneath her breath, she tossed the laundry basket onto the porch. She then carefully removed her foot and stood staring down at the splintered step, hands at her waist.

Tired of waiting for Anvil or even Mr. Roberts to get around to fixing it, she decided enough was enough! She would fix it herself.

Crossing quickly to the toolshed behind the barn, she grabbed the toolbox in one hand and a length of wood in the other. The board was too long, so at least six inches would have to be sawed off. Maybe more.

Moments later, she dropped to her knees in front of the porch steps and pulled the loose tread away from the frame with a crowbar. The wood was so decayed and moldy that it splintered. Reaching into the toolbox, she pulled out the metal measuring tape.

As she drew the tape from one end of the step to the other, something caught her eye on the newly exposed ground beneath the porch. Something that made her lean over for a closer look.

It sure did look like a gunnysack. Curious, she reached down and grabbed hold of the burlap sack with both hands. It took some tugging on her part to pull the bag through the small step opening. Not only was the sack heavy, it was bulky. What in the world?

Plopping the sack down on an unbroken step, she brushed away the dirt. It smelled musty, like it had been there for a while.

She untied the narrow strip of rawhide. Peering inside the bag, she got the biggest shock of her life. Gasping, she blinked, not sure she could believe her eyes.

Thinking—hoping—she was seeing things, she reached inside the sack for one of the brick-shaped objects and pulled it out for a closer look, but there was no mistake. The object was made up of a stack of banknotes held together with a paper band. It was but one of many such bundles that filled the bulging bag.

Dropping the wad of banknotes into the sack as if it would bite, she leaned back on her heels. Hand on her mouth, she tried to think. Never had she seen so much money. She couldn't begin to guess how much was in the sack. Thousands!

But how…? Where? The answer came in a rush, shaking her to the very core.

Oh, no! No, no, no! Please don't let this be stolen money. Please, God, no! Brushing the dirt off the bag, she stared in a daze at the bank's name stamped on the side.

Shocked, she remained frozen in place, unable to move. There had to be a logical reason for how a sack of money had ended up under her porch. There just had to be. But the only explanation she could think of—the only one that made sense—was that Neal had put it there. And if that were true, it could mean only one thing. Her husband had robbed that stage.

A wave of nausea washed over her, and she clamped down on the thought. Hunching over, she grabbed her stomach and rocked back and forth. *No, no, no. It can't be!*

Shaken, she tried to still her hammering heart and forced herself to think. She couldn't keep the money, but neither could she turn it in. It would only tarnish Neal's reputation, and that had to be avoided at all costs. She would do anything—anything at all—to keep Lionel and Alicia from being exposed as the children of an outlaw.

She had no idea how long she'd sat there in a state of shock before the sound of horse's hooves yanked her out of her inertia. A quick look to check the road confirmed her worst fear. Someone was heading her way. Worse, the tall rider upon the fine, black horse could be none other than Matt Taggert!

Feeling herself begin to panic, she quickly pushed the gunnysack through the opening and shoved it back under the porch as far as she could reach.

Grabbing the wooden plank with trembling hands, she quickly covered the gaping hole left by the missing tread. The wood hung over the side by a good ten or twelve inches, but it masked the area beneath the risers, and that was all that mattered.

Forcing herself to breathe and willing her heart to stop pounding, she stood ready to greet her visitor. She hid her shaking hands in the folds of her skirt, but nothing could be done about her trembling knees.

"Afternoon, Mrs. Blackwell," Taggert said, touching a finger to the wide brim of his hat.

He dismounted and, after wrapping his horse's reins around the hitching post, sauntered up to the porch, his piercing eyes seeming to see right through her. He glanced at the tools scattered around her feet before locking her in his gaze a second time. Once again, she was reminded how tall he was, how straight he stood, and what a commanding figure he made.

Thankful that her knocking knees were hidden beneath her skirt, she forced a smile. "Mr. Taggert. What a surprise," she said, hoping he wouldn't notice her strained voice or trembling hands.

Tilting his head, he arched an eyebrow. "A not-too-unpleasant one, I hope."

She regarded him with narrowed eyes. "That depends on why you're here."

"I just have a question that I hope you can answer." He pulled a canceled ticket stub from his pocket and held it up. "Your husband purchased this train ticket," he said. "It was found in the vicinity of the crime scene. Do you have any idea how it might have gotten there?"

"H-how do you know that's my husband's ticket?" she asked, hedging.

"Only two tickets were sold on that particular day, and the other passenger had purchased only a one-way ticket. This is a two-way ticket, which means it had to have been purchased by your husband."

Feeling trapped, she chewed on a nail. Just thinking about Neal's train trip brought back all kinds of memories—none of them good. That ticket had cost them more than they could afford. That was one of the reasons she hadn't wanted Neal to take that trip, but he'd insisted. They needed a bank loan to pay for a new windmill, he'd said. They needed to replace the shingles on the roof, fix the back fence, and purchase livestock.

After being turned down by the Haywire Bank, he'd decided to apply elsewhere for a loan. But he'd had no better luck in the larger towns than he'd had locally and had come home feeling tired and depressed.

The Ranger hadn't said it in so many words, but his meaning was clear—things looked bad for Neal. As if she didn't already know it.

"The robbery occurred on a main road that my husband traveled many times," she said, her mind scrambling. "Neal had a habit of stuffing things in his pockets. He could have dropped it at any time." After a beat, she asked, "Does that answer your question?"

"Not exactly." Taggert returned the stub to his pocket.

She studied him with narrowed eyes. "Oh?"

"A Pinkerton detective happened to be in town the day the stage was robbed. He found the train ticket at the crime scene." Taggert paused as if to carefully choose his words. "That means your husband traveled that road between the time he returned to Haywire and the time of the robbery, eighteen hours later. Do you know what he was doing there?"

Ellie-May thought for a moment. "That's the road to the Petersons' farm," she said slowly, cautiously. "I'm almost certain that was the day of their barn raising." She leveled her gaze at the Ranger. "Neal never missed an opportunity to help a friend or neighbor."

As she spoke, he pulled paper and a small pencil from his vest pocket and made a note. "Peterson, did you say?"

She nodded. His note-taking told her he intended to check out her story. That was fine with her. If he found that Neal really was at the barn raising as she supposed, would that take him off the hook? She could only hope and pray that it did.

"Sorry to bother you," Taggert said, returning both to his pocket. "I hope there're no hard feelings. I'm only doing my job."

Surprised by his apology, she flashed a quick smile. "No hard feelings, Mr. Taggert."

"In that case, please call me Matt."

"Matt," she said, but only to oblige him. The bag of money weighed on her conscience like a massive rock, and she was in no mood for friendly chatter. She wanted him gone. "So when will you be leaving Haywire?"

"That's what I came to tell you," he said. "I'm leaving on the afternoon train."

"Oh," she said, relief washing over her.

He tilted his head. "You look happy to see me go." She started to protest, but he held up his hands. "Don't feel bad. I'm like the tax man. People hate seeing me come and love seeing me leave. I've learned not to take offense." He tossed a nod at the plank covering the broken step. "Let me help you with that."

"No, it's all right," she gasped. He looked at her all funny-like, and she hastened to explain. "I'm sure you must have more important things to do now that you're leaving town."

"The train doesn't leave till three, so I have plenty of time," he said.

"Not if you intend to check out my story with the Petersons," she said.

"Don't worry." He dropped down on one knee and lifted the board away from the missing step, exposing the ground underneath. "This won't take long to fix."

She knotted her hands by her sides. "You really don't have to do this."

He glanced up at her. "Fixing your step is the least I can do for the trouble I've caused you."

"You didn't cause me any trouble," she said. Just a few nights' sleep was all. And maybe a few years off her life.

He reached for the tape measure, and she cast a worried glance at the opening. The bag was hidden, but the end of the rawhide tie was clearly visible.

Dear God...

Gulping, she pressed her knotted hands to her chest.

Matt measured the open area first and then the board. Reaching into his vest pocket, he pulled out a pencil stub and marked the wood.

"I met a friend of yours in town," he said as he worked.

Ellie-May's heart was beating so fast she could hardly breathe, let alone talk. "Oh?" she managed, hoping he didn't detect her strangled voice.

He reached for the saw. Balancing one end of the board on the upper step, he began sawing away. "His name is Jesse James."

Anxiously eyeing the still-uncovered step, she cleared her throat. "How is Jesse? Haven't seen him for a while."

Faster and more efficiently that she could have managed on her own, Matt finished sawing, and the discarded length of wood fell to the ground. "Seemed okay."

He picked up the plank and blew away the sawdust before placing it across the opening.

He wiggled it in place, and it fit perfectly. Relief washing over her, Ellie-May quickly dug in the toolbox for the little box of nails and handed him one.

Their fingers touched as he took it from her, and something like a spark passed between them. His gaze flew up to meet hers, telling her he'd felt it, too. Cheeks flaring, she looked away and quickly reached for another nail.

Matt was the first to break the awkward silence that followed. "Jesse said that your husband hired him to work here."

"He did, but only for a short while." Careful to hold the next nail in such a way as to prevent physical contact, she handed it to him and reached for another.

Matt took the nails from her one by one and hammered each one in place. "Was there a problem?" he asked.

"A problem?" she echoed.

Matt paused for a moment to check his work before reaching for another nail. "You said he only worked here for a short time."

"No, no problem," she said. "Jesse is a hard worker. Neal was thrown from a horse and hurt his back. He hired Jesse to help out while he recovered."

It had been an added expense, but the ground needed to be tilled. Neal couldn't do it with his injury, and Anvil had his hands full taking care of the other chores.

After pounding in the last nail, Matt tossed the hammer into the toolbox and stood. "That should do it," he said, brushing his hands together.

Now that the bag of money was safely hidden by the newly repaired step, Ellie-May took a deep breath and felt the tension leave her body. Matt would never know how grateful she was to him. Not just for fixing the step but for also failing to notice what was hidden beneath.

"Thank you," she said. This time, she had no trouble smiling her biggest and brightest smile. If Neal did indeed steal that money, his secret was now safe. No one need ever know what lay under her porch, and her children would be spared the awful truth. "Perhaps you should take up carpentry as a profession."

He arched a dark brow. "You mean instead of pursuing law and order?"

She shrugged. "The work is less dangerous, and run-down houses don't generally fight back."

He afforded her a crooked smile that brought a rush of heat to her face and struck a worrisome chord inside her. She hated herself for thinking it, but he really was one handsome man. Especially when he flashed his pearly whites.

"Never thought about it that way," he said, his eyes warm with amusement.

Hoping he hadn't noticed her flaring cheeks, she offered him another smile. "And I'm sure there would be less chance for...error," she said.

"I'll keep that in mind." They stared at each other for a moment before he slanted his head toward his horse. "I best be going," he said.

"Do you have time for refreshment? Some lemonade?" It was hot, and now that her secret was safe, she could afford to be hospitable.

He looked about to say yes but then changed his mind. "I better not. I need to wrap things up with the Petersons so I can write my report."

Sighing with relief, she moistened her lips. If Neal had been building a barn, he wouldn't have had time to rob a stage. It didn't explain the money under the porch, but his reputation would remain intact, and she was willing to settle for that.

The thought lifted her spirits, and she smiled more freely this time. "Thank you, again, for fixing the step," she said. "It was a big help."

The Ranger flashed a crooked grin that sent her pulse racing. "Glad to be of service."

Surprised and more than a little dismayed by the way his smile affected her, she drew in her breath. "If you see Jesse before you go, tell him I said hello."

Matt mounted his horse before answering. "Will do," he said.

With a wave of his hat, he rode off. Watching him, Ellie-May tried telling herself that everything would now be okay. Matt Taggert was leaving town, and the Petersons were bound to back her story. That would take Neal off the hook as far as the Rangers were concerned.

But a niggling inner voice told her there would be no peace now that she knew what lay beneath her porch. She didn't want to believe that Neal robbed a stage, but no other explanation made sense. If Neal didn't put the money there, then who in blazes did?

Claudia Peterson opened the door to Ellie-May's knock. Looking pleased to see her, she motioned Ellie-May inside. "What a nice surprise. Come in, come in."

Ellie-May crossed the threshold and was careful not to trip over the children's blocks scattered on the floor.

As usual, Claudia looked harried. Her black hair had been pulled back into a messy bun, and her wrinkled skirt, shirtwaist, and apron would have benefited from a good pressing with a sadiron.

"To what do I owe this pleasure?" Claudia asked.

"I just stopped by to say hello and bring you this." Ellie-May handed her a jar of strawberry preserves she'd made herself.

"That was very thoughtful of you." Claudia studied the jar a moment before setting it on a low table next to a celluloid baby rattle. "How are you doing?"

"Better," Ellie-May said, "but it's been a rough year."

"I can't believe that it's been that long since your dear husband…" Claudia checked on the baby lying inside a cage made from two chairs wrapped in mesh. Seemingly satisfied, she turned her attention back to Ellie-May. "I owe you an apology," she said. "I've been remiss in my neighborly duties. I'm afraid time has gotten away from me. Why, it seems like only yesterday that your Neal…"

"I know," Ellie-May said. However, since finding that money under her porch, time had seemed to stand still. "There's no need to apologize. I have only two children and have no time to socialize. Whereas you have eleven." By the looks of it, a twelfth child was on the way.

As if to guess her thoughts, Claudia lovingly pressed her hands on her rounded middle. "We're expecting a December baby," she said and laughed. "That's the only month in which I haven't yet given birth."

Ellie-May laughed, too. "I guess now that you've run out of months, you're done."

"Lordy sakes, I hope so," Claudia said and then grew serious. "I still feel bad for not reaching out to you. After everything your husband did for us, it's the least I could have done."

It was the opening Ellie-May had hoped for. Prayed for. "Speaking of Neal, I was wondering…" She paused for a moment to gather her thoughts. "Do you remember when you last saw him?" It seemed like a dumb question, even to her own ears, but it was the best she could do. Since recalling that the barn raising had been on the same day as the holdup, she'd not been able to think of anything else.

Wrinkling her forehead, Claudia tapped a finger to her chin. "No, I'm sorry."

"Was it at your barn raising?" Ellie-May pressed.

Claudia stared at her. "Funny you should ask about that. A Texas Ranger came to the door yesterday and asked the same thing. I'll tell you the same as I told him. Neal never showed up at the barn raising. I guess he got busy or something."

Ellie-May gulped and tried not to let her dismay show. Busy like robbing-a-stagecoach busy? "Are you s-sure?" she stammered. "It was more than a year ago."

"Quite sure," Claudia said. "I remember my husband saying what a pity it was that we didn't get a chance to see Neal before…" She cleared her throat. "Why all this sudden interest in our barn raising?"

"It's just…" Ellie-May's mind scrambled for an explanation. "I know Neal wanted to come, and I thought—"

"Don't feel bad," Claudia said kindly. "Knowing Neal, he would have been here if he could have been." She frowned. "But why did that Texas Ranger—"

"I'm sorry," Ellie-May interrupted. Anxious to leave, she turned to the door. "I can't stay."

Claudia followed her out to the porch. "It was really nice seeing you again," she called, her voice reflecting confusion.

"Thank you. You, too." With a wave of her hand, Ellie-May hurried to her horse and wagon, her head pounding. Neal wasn't at the barn raising. He'd said he was going there. So why hadn't he? What had stopped him? In her mind's eye, she could see the gunnysack of money, and she felt ill.

Blinded by tears, she grasped the reins of her horse and frantically drove home.

8

Three weeks later

MATT WOKE THAT MORNING IN A TANGLE OF BEDDING.
Sunlight had already settled on the canvas roof over his
head, and it promised to be another hot day. Ranger
Madison's cot was empty, and the smell of coffee
drifted through the tent opening, a clue that Matt had
overslept.

Again.

Since leaving Haywire, he'd not slept well. Either
he'd fall in bed at the end of the day exhausted or wind
up twisting and turning until the wee hours of morn.
Last night was one of those nights. He tried telling
himself that his bouts of insomnia had nothing to do
with his failure to track down his brother. Nor did he
want to think it had anything to do with the other
Rangers singing "For He's a Jolly Good Fella" to him
on his birthday, which had reminded him of a certain
blue-eyed lady.

Sitting up, Matt planted his feet firmly on the
ground and rubbed his bristly chin. His company was

getting ready to move again. Standing, he donned his trousers and reached for his shirt.

It had been three weeks since he'd left Haywire. It hadn't been by choice, but there was nothing more to be done there. Mrs. Peterson had told him that Neal never showed up for their barn raising, but even that didn't prove Blackwell guilty. The most Matt had was circumstantial evidence, and that wasn't enough to convict anyone, let alone a town hero.

The captain hadn't been happy with the end result, nor had the senator. But unless something extraordinary happened, the stagecoach robbery that had taken place in Haywire more than a year ago would probably forever remain unsolved.

Matt had tried putting the matter out of his mind, though questions remained. Even after all this time, the unsolved robbery continued to be a thorn in his side. Not only had he failed to arrest his brother, but he'd also failed on another job. That sure didn't look good on his record.

He told himself that his obsession with the Haywire robbery and missing money had to do with job performance and had nothing to do with the pretty widow.

Ellie-May Blackwell had secrets, no doubt, and may or may not have lied about the Petersons, but for some reason, her combination of strength and vulnerability had left a memorable impression, crazy as it seemed.

The whole thing was crazy. Had a state senator not been involved, the holdup would probably have gone down in the annals as an unsolved crime, and the Texas Rangers would never have been asked to step in.

Even more frustrating, Matt had hoped to be back on his brother's trail by now. But Charley had apparently decided to lie low for a while, and the captain seemed in no hurry to reassign Matt to the case. There was nothing to do but wait until Charley made his next move. All Matt could do was hope and pray that a trigger-happy bounty hunter or lawman didn't get to him first.

Captain McDonald stuck his head through the tent opening. "Hey, Taggert," he said, breaking into Matt's thoughts. "Someone here to see you."

Puzzled, Matt finished buttoning his shirt. Who would possibly want to see him? The Ranger tent quarters were located ten miles away from the nearest town. It was still relatively early, and his company was getting ready to hit the trail, their job there done.

The captain stepped aside, and who should take his place but the boy Jesse James.

Matt couldn't believe his eyes. Jesse was the last person he'd expected to see. "How'd you find me?"

Stepping through the canvas opening, Jesse pulled off his slouch hat and shook his shaggy hair out of his eyes. "I stopped at Ranger headquarters, and they told me you were here."

"You traveled to Austin?"

Jesse shrugged as if it were no big deal. "Didn't know how else to find you."

Matt stared at him. It had only been three weeks since he'd last seen the boy, but he appeared even thinner than before. His bedraggled clothes hung from his bony frame like an empty potato sack. He also looked pale and smelled ripe as old meat. But first things first.

"Does your pa know you're here?"

"No, sir. All he knows is I'm not there."

Matt blew out his breath. *Oh boy.* "How'd you get here?"

Jesse hesitated before replying. "Stole a ride on the train."

Matt frowned. "No train comes out this far." A dispute between landowners and train moguls had delayed the laying of tracks, and Matt's company had been assigned to make peace. After much haggling, the two sides had finally agreed on a new train route a few miles west.

"I walked from the station."

Matt's eyebrows shot up. "You walked?" He glanced down at the boy's thin-soled shoes. "That's at least ten miles away!"

"I know, sir."

Matt studied the boy's gaunt face. "When's the last time you ate?"

Jesse thought for a moment. "Not since the day before yesterday."

Matt grimaced. He was willing to bet the kid hadn't slept since then, either. "I told you, you're too young to be a Ranger."

"That's not why I'm here," Jesse said and lowered his voice to a hushed whisper. "I saw him."

Something in the boy's expression made Matt sharpen his gaze. "Saw who? Who did you see?"

"The man I saw talking to Mr. Blackwell about that stolen money. I saw him at my pa's saloon."

"Your pa doesn't own a saloon."

"Never said he owned it. It's just where he spends all his time."

Matt rubbed his bristly chin. "Are you sure it's the same man?"

Jesse nodded. "I wouldn't have come all this way 'less I was sure."

Matt had all but discounted Jesse's prior claims, but this time, it was hard to ignore such sincerity. Nor could he believe the boy would go to all that trouble of tracking him down had he not been telling the truth. Still, it was a shock to realize that his reluctance to believe the boy had more to do with Neal Blackwell's widow than anything else.

He hoped to God for her sake that Jesse was mistaken or making things up.

Still, Matt had to be sure. If what the boy said was true...

He placed a hand on Jesse's shoulder and turned him toward the tent opening. "Okay, let's get you some chow." Soap and water wouldn't be a bad idea, either. "Then we'll talk some more."

∞

Ellie-May stifled a yawn and stared at the door marked MAYOR. Though she had done her best to hide the shadows under her eyes with powder, her sleepless nights had taken a toll. It had been three weeks since she'd found the money under the steps. She'd hardly been able to sleep since, let alone think of anything else.

If Neal did steal that money—and it certainly looked like he had—it meant that everything she believed in, everything she'd thought true, was a lie. Her whole life was a lie, and there was no getting away from it. Still, it was hard to believe that her husband and the father of her children was a criminal. But there didn't seem to be any other explanation. At least none that made sense.

She didn't want to believe Neal was guilty, but each time she stepped on the porch, she thought about the money hidden beneath. Thought about how close Matt Taggert had been to finding it. Thought about what would have happened had he done so.

She sensed the Ranger was a man of integrity, and it pained her to think how she had pulled him into her web of deceit. That she, herself, was forced to live a lie.

But it wasn't just the secrets or lies that seemed too big to bear. The mere act of riding into town had become a nightmare. Everywhere she looked, there had been signs of Neal. It was hard enough to separate the revered hero from the man she'd loved. But trying to connect a loving father with a man who'd robbed a stage was harder still. Neal had been so determined to set a good example for his children.

Never had she known Neal to miss Sunday worship. Nor had he let a day go by that he hadn't practiced the Golden Rule. She hated thinking of Neal as a hypocrite, but there was no other way to explain his duplicity.

In two weeks, the new school would be dedicated in Neal's name, and that only added to her nightmare. She hated the thought of little minds attending a school named after a man who appeared to be an outlaw. It was the school that had brought her to the mayor's office.

Dressed in her Sunday-go-to-meeting best, she smoothed the front of her blue floral skirt and reached for the doorknob with a gloved hand. As she stepped into the small reception room, a thin, dark-haired man looked up from the desk and peered at her over the spectacles balanced on the tip of his nose.

"May I help you?"

She closed the door behind her and stepped forward. "I'm here to see Mayor Wrightwood," she said.

"Do you have an appointment?" he asked.

She stared at him and wondered when the mayor's office had become so formal. "No, but it's most urgent that I see him. My name is Mrs. Blackwell."

That brought the man to his feet, looking apologetic. "Mrs. Blackwell, of course. I'll tell the mayor you're here." With that, he vanished through a side door.

Minutes passed before the clerk reappeared and directed her into an adjacent office. As soon as she entered, Mayor Wrightwood's hefty form rose in greeting from behind an oversized desk. With a wave of his hand, he motioned her to the ladder-back chair facing him.

He waited for her to sit before lowering his stout body onto his squeaking chair. "What an unexpected pleasure," he said, cigar clamped between his thick lips.

Ellie-May pulled off her gloves and clutched her purse on her lap. After years of living under the shadow of a criminal father, it had been hard to adapt to her newfound status as a hero's widow, but never more so than now. She doubted the mayor would have been so eager to see her if he knew what lay beneath her porch.

"Congratulations for winning the election," she said. It had been a tough race, and many had been surprised that the mayor had managed to land a second term.

Wrightwood removed the cigar from his mouth and smiled. "Thank you," he said, balancing his stogie on the edge of a copper ashtray. "I'm glad you came to see me, Mrs. Blackwell. Saves me a trip out to your farm."

"Oh?"

"Just wanted to know if you'd like to say something."

She sat back. "I'm sorry... Say something?"

"When we dedicate the new school. Thought you might like to speak on behalf of your late husband."

"Oh no, I..." She cleared her throat and stammered, "I-I'm not very good at public speaking." Even if she was, she wouldn't know what to say. Finding that money had changed everything, including her feelings toward Neal and their marriage.

"If you change your mind, let me know."

She would never take him up on his offer, but still she nodded. "Thank you."

He studied her. "So what brings you here today?"

Anxious to state her business and leave, Ellie-May took a bracing breath. "About the school..."

"You mean the *Neal Blackwell Grammar School*?" the mayor said with a flourish of his hand.

It was clear by the note of pride in his voice that he considered the building and naming of the school one of his greatest achievements as mayor. That made Ellie-May's job that much harder.

"I've been thinking about the school name," she said.

His eyebrows shot upward. "Oh?"

She fell back on her carefully rehearsed speech. "My husband was a...humble man. Oh, don't get me wrong," she hastened to add. "He would appreciate everything the town has done for him, but I'm afraid he'd be a little...overwhelmed. Maybe even... embarrassed." She had the mayor's full attention as she continued. "For that reason, I think he wouldn't want his name on the school."

The mayor sat back. "Not want his name on the school?" he asked as if he couldn't imagine such a thing.

"Like I said, Neal was a very humble man. And the town has already done so much. That statue..." She still couldn't get over the size of it.

The mayor sat forward and planted his pudgy hands on the desk. "I appreciate your concern, Mrs. Blackwell. And I'm sure you're right about your husband's modesty."

"Oh, I am," she said. Sensing that her argument had failed to persuade him, she quickly changed tactics. "Perhaps the city would consider naming the school after someone else," she said and, hoping to appeal to the high opinion he had of himself, added, "Perhaps someone like yourself."

"Well now," he said, looking both pleased and flustered. "That's very kind of you to say."

Feeling hopeful, Ellie-May leaned forward. "I'm sure that many others would agree with me."

"Yes, yes, I'm sure that's true." The mayor's mouth

drooped at the corners. "But I'm afraid it's out of the question."

"Oh?" Ellie-May frowned. "I'm not sure I understand."

"The sign is already in place for the dedication. To have a new one made at this late date would involve needless time and expense."

She dug her fingers into the purse on her lap and silently chided herself for not raising an objection earlier. "I see," she said.

"I'm sure the town will see fit to…uh…" He cleared his throat. "Honor me at a later date."

She swallowed hard. "Yes, of course."

"As for your husband…I'm sure he would have understood. Neal Blackwell was a fine man." The mayor's jowls wobbled as he spoke. "And I know he would want to do what's best for Haywire. It's not often that a town can claim its very own hero." He pulled his watch out of his vest pocket. Thumbing the case open, he rose from his seat. "Now if you'll excuse me, I have a meeting to attend."

Trying not to let her disappointment show, she gathered up her purse and stood. In her haste to leave, she dropped a glove and stooped to pick it up. "I appreciate you seeing me."

"My pleasure," he said. "Feel free to stop by at any time."

"Thank you." Ellie-May left the office feeling worse than when she'd arrived.

9

THE SUN HOVERED LOW IN THE SKY BY THE TIME THE train chugged into the Haywire station. Jesse had slept during the entire trip, his head bobbing against Matt's shoulder with each *clickety-clack* of the tracks. Now Matt shook him awake.

He'd made sure the boy had been well fed before starting on the journey, but there hadn't been time to do anything about his clothes, and he looked like a ragamuffin. The quick sprinkle of cold water back at Ranger camp hadn't done much, either, to improve his appearance. What Jesse needed was a good scrubbing from head to toe.

"You're home," Matt said.

Jesse blinked the sleep out of his eyes and stood. Yawning, he followed Matt off the train without saying a word.

Outside, they waited for Matt's horse to be unloaded from the animal railcar. "Will you be all right?" Matt asked. "Do you want me to talk to your pa?"

Jesse shook his head. "Pa don't care where I am."

Matt clamped down on his jaw. How could a man be so uncaring of his own son?

"What's our plan?" Jesse asked, and it was evident from his voice that he had regained his usual enthusiasm. It was amazing what a ton of food could do for the boy. That and some shut-eye.

Matt glanced around to check for eavesdroppers. He didn't want anyone knowing why he was back in town. Even his captain had expressed surprise that Matt had wanted to return and check out the boy's story.

"*We* don't have a plan," he said sternly. "I work alone." Had he hoped to discourage Jesse, he would have been sorely disappointed.

Instead, Jesse looked as determined as ever. "What's *your* plan?"

Matt sighed. "That's for me to know. No one else." Jesse's description of the man seen talking to Blackwell had left much to be desired. According to Jesse, the man was of average height, weight, and appearance. He sported a mustache and a crooked nose, but so did most of the male population in town. No other outstanding features or scars were mentioned.

Matt placed a hand on Jesse's bony shoulder. Finding such an average-looking man without involving Jesse would be a challenge. But even if he didn't need Jesse's help, he was concerned about the boy's welfare.

"You done good, son. Now go home and get some rest."

"Can't. If I don't show up for work, I don't get paid."

Matt blinked. "Work?"

"Yeah. I work at the Pittman Coffin Shop."

Matt frowned. "You work at a coffin shop?" That hardly seemed like the place for a boy Jesse's age to spend his time.

"Only on Wednesdays," Jesse said and swiped a strand of hair out of his eyes. "On Saturdays, I work at the general store, and on Mondays, I work at the telegram office."

"You have three jobs?" Matt regarded the boy's unkempt appearance with a frown. "What do you do with all your money?"

"I give it to Pa."

"'Course you do," Matt muttered under his breath. Jesse no doubt thought he was helping his pa and probably didn't have a clue that he was making it possible for his father to continue along his destructive path.

"What?" Jesse asked.

"Nothing."

Jesse wrinkled his nose in thought. "If I see the man again, where do I find you?"

"For now, I plan on staying at the hotel." Matt drew his hand away from the boy's shoulder. "Listen to me. I don't want you snooping around. You hear? If this man is guilty of a crime, there's no telling what he might do. You could get hurt. Understood?"

When Jesse failed to answer, Matt pressed him harder. "Understood?"

This time, the boy nodded, but it was clear he was reluctant to do so, and that had Matt worried.

Ellie-May sat on the edge of her daughter's bed as she did every night to listen to her prayers.

Alicia knelt on the floor, hands steepled, eyes squeezed shut. Her long, blond hair—braided to keep from tangling in her sleep—fell down her back in two long ropes.

"God bless Mama and Lionel and Anvil," she murmured. "And bless Papa in heaven. And please, God, make the chickens lay lots and lots of eggs. Amen."

Alicia jumped to her feet and quickly climbed into bed. Ellie-May drew the bedcovers up to her daughter's chin. Though the days had turned warm, the nights were still chilly.

"Lots of eggs?" Ellie-May asked, curious. Since when did chickens make it into nighttime prayers?

Head on the pillow, Alicia gazed up at her with a funny little smile. "It's almost my birthday," she said, her eyes shining with excitement.

Ellie-May groaned. "Oh no. Not the music box again." It seemed like that had been all Alicia could think about since seeing it in Gordon's General Store.

At mention of the music box, Alicia's smile practically reached her ears, and Ellie-May felt a tightness in her chest. Leaning over, she tapped her daughter's small upturned nose. "I've already explained that we can't afford it."

"But Papa would want me to have it," Alicia said. "I know he would."

"Shh. You'll wake Lionel." Ellie-May glanced across the room at her son's bed.

Despite her warning, she doubted a fired cannonball could wake him. The boy slept as hard as he played.

Turning back to her daughter, she took Alicia's hand in her own and spoke softly. "Now how do you know what Papa would want?"

"Because the music box played the song Papa used to sing to me," Alicia said. "'All the Pretty Little Horses.'"

Ellie-May stared at her. She vaguely remembered the music box playing that tune but had forgotten that Neal used to sing it to the children before bedtime. No wonder the music box had left such a lasting impression on Alicia.

In many ways, it seemed that Neal had become an even larger presence in death than he'd been in life. The town had turned him into someone Ellie-May hardly recognized. Were her children having the same problem relating the town hero to the pa they once knew and loved? Was that why Alicia had become so obsessed with the music box? Because it brought back memories of the pa with whom she could better identify? The father who had tucked her in bed each night? The father who had told her stories and sung to her?

Ellie-May laid Alicia's hand on the counterpane and reached up to brush a strand of hair away from her face. "It's late," she said. "And you have school tomorrow."

Grateful that her daughter had dropped the subject, at least for now, she tucked her in, then crossed to Lionel's bed. He'd practically fallen asleep the moment his head touched the pillow. The long eyelashes feathering his rosy, round cheeks made him look almost angelic, and Ellie-May felt a tender stirring in her heart.

While both children took after her side of the family appearance-wise, Lionel was sensitive, like his father, and that was a worry. If the truth came out about Neal, there was no telling what it would do to Lionel. Alicia would take it hard, but she would express her feelings openly. Her brother, on the other hand, would keep everything inside.

Dropping a kiss on her son's smooth forehead, Ellie-May turned off the lamp. She remained in the darkened room for a long while, comforted by her children's even breathing.

When she'd first held each of her babies in her arms, she'd vowed to give them the kind of life that had been denied her. A life that would allow them to hold their heads high and not feel ashamed. A life filled with goodness and beauty. A life filled with promise and hope.

And here, she couldn't even give her a daughter a coveted birthday present. Now that Ellie-May knew why Alicia wanted it, it near broke her heart to have to tell her no.

But Papa would want me to have it. I know he would.

Her daughter's words ringing in her head, Ellie-May tiptoed from the room and quietly closed the door. Leaning her forehead against the smooth, cool wood, she tried to think. She should have known that the music box had something to do with Neal. It wasn't like Alicia to be so obsessive and not take *no* for an answer.

Ellie-May drew away from the children's room, her mind in a whirl. She had to do something, but what?

She thought for a moment before hurrying to the

kitchen. Reaching on the high shelf over the counter, she grabbed hold of the porcelain cookie jar and dumped the contents on the table. The pitiful pile of coins represented her hard-earned savings for the past three months. Even so, they added up to little more than $1.50. She couldn't believe it. It wasn't even enough to buy her son a much-needed pair of new shoes.

She counted the coins twice to make sure she'd not made a mistake and returned them to the cookie jar.

Leaving the kitchen, she headed for her bedroom and rummaged one by one through the dresser drawers. She'd cut up most of Neal's clothes to make shirts for Lionel, so many of the drawers stood empty.

Finding nothing of value, she checked her jewelry box. She'd tried twice to sell her mother's mourning brooch, but because it had belonged to an outlaw's widow, no one had wanted to touch it. She reached for the man's gold pocket watch. After holding it for a moment, she returned it to the jewelry box. It was the only thing left of Neal's of any value, and she was saving it for Lionel.

She kept searching. There had to be something she could sell that would fetch enough money to buy the music box. There just had to be.

10

THE FOLLOWING MORNING, ELLIE-MAY DROPPED THE children off at the Masonic Lodge. Since the school had burned down, the lodge had provided temporary classrooms.

Dreading what she was about to do, she then headed straight for the heart of town, a single mission on her mind. Fearing the loss of courage, she urged her mare, Jingles, to go faster.

The wagon bounced along the narrow dirt road leading to the town center, dust churning beneath its wheels. Eyes squinted against the glaring sun, Ellie-May kept her mouth clamped tightly shut to keep out the dust and flies.

She kept her focus straight ahead. She didn't even glance at the soon-to-be dedicated new school. Nothing must be allowed to distract from the task she'd set for herself.

Reaching her destination, she guided her horse to the side of the road next to the water trough and set the wagon brake. It took several quick breaths before she could bring herself to walk into Gordon's General

Store, but nothing could be done for her pounding heart.

"Morning, Mrs. Blackwell," Mr. Gordon called from behind the counter.

Not trusting herself to speak, she returned his greeting with a nod and started down the aisle. Her back to the counter, she opened her purse and fingered the single banknote inside.

Last night, she had pried a tread off the porch steps and reached for the bag hidden beneath the porch. She'd been tempted, oh so tempted—God forgive her—to take out more than just a single note. Oh, what she could do with all that money!

Lionel needed new shoes, and Anvil could use a warmer place to stay before next winter. The roof was in desperate need of repairs, and the chicken coop would soon have to be replaced. The list went on and on. It had taken every bit of willpower she'd possessed to help herself to just the one bill and put the rest back.

The single bill was enough to pay for the music box and settle the rest of her account. Gordon might wonder where the money came from, but she doubted he would ask. If he did, she would make up some story about a deceased uncle on Neal's side.

The thought made her feel sick to her stomach. More lies. Would there ever be an end to them? Or an end to the shame she felt for taking even that small amount of money?

It felt wrong, all wrong. She snatched her hand from inside her purse and snapped it shut. Never before had she taken anything that didn't belong to her.

If only her heart would stop pounding and her

knees would stop shaking. If only she didn't feel so guilty. It was only one banknote. One out of what had looked like hundreds stuffed in that old gunnysack.

Standing in the aisle, she closed her eyes. *Was it stealing if you took something that had already been stolen?*

"What can I do you fer, Mrs. Blackwell?" Mr. Gordon called.

She opened her eyes. "N-nothing," she stammered. "I'm just looking." She then pretended to study a bolt of calico.

She envisioned her daughter's face when she opened her gift on the morning of her birthday. Ellie-May now knew that it wasn't just a music box Alicia had wanted; it was the memory of her father that she craved. Not the town hero, not the statue, but the pa who only she and Lionel had known and loved. The pa who'd sung "All the Pretty Little Horses" to her every night as he'd tucked her in her bed.

Never did her daughter need to know that the father she adored was a thief. Nor must she ever know that her mother was now one, too.

The squeezing pain in her chest almost made Ellie-May double over. She suddenly felt ill. Hot. She reached into the sleeve of her dress for her handkerchief and dabbed her damp forehead. Her children need never know the truth, but that still didn't make it right.

She'd spent nearly a lifetime trying to prove that being an outlaw's daughter didn't make her one, too. But it had all been for naught. All the accusations she had endured through the years had been proven true. Ellie-May Blackwell was now officially a thief.

It was this last thought that sent her fleeing from Gordon's shop.

Outside, she stopped to gasp a mouthful of air and gather her wits about her, but that was easier said than done. Such was her distress that it took a moment before she became aware of the commotion across the street.

Frowning, she watched Sheriff Keeler drag a protesting youth by the ear. Just as she started for her wagon, she thought she recognized the boy's voice. She whirled about for a closer look. The boy's hat had fallen off, revealing a mop of ginger hair.

Dash it all, it was Jesse James. Just as she'd thought!

Fueled by a maternal instinct to protect the motherless boy, she picked up her skirts and rushed after them, stopping only long enough to swoop the boy's slouch hat from the middle of the road.

Mindless of the stolen money in her purse, she darted around a horse and buggy, raced up the boardwalk steps, and followed Keeler and the boy into the sheriff's office.

"What do you think you're doing?" she demanded.

Sheriff Keeler released the boy and tossed a pair of handcuffs on his desk. Looking pale and shaken, Jesse pressed his back against a wall and rubbed his left ear.

The sheriff looked none too pleased to see her. "I'm teaching this boy a lesson, that's what!"

"By dragging him through the streets like a common criminal?" Her body shook with rage. "He's only thirteen!"

"I don't give a fiddle how old he is. He has no right accusin' people of doing things they ain't done! Now if you want to pay his fine, he's all yours. If not, git out of here and let me do my job."

She glanced at the boy, and her heart ached at how thin he looked. How pale. Tossing his hat to him, she asked, "How much?"

The sheriff sneered. "More than you can afford," he said.

She clutched her bag in her hands. "How much?" she asked again.

Behind her, the door burst open, and someone entered the office. Keeler glanced past her to the newcomer before answering her question.

"Five dollars or five days in jail."

She winced. She hated the thought of Jesse spending time in jail—absolutely hated it. But to pay his fine with stolen money was plain asking for trouble.

She was still debating what to do when Matt Taggart stepped to her side. Surprised to see him back in town, she gaped up at him, not knowing what to think. He looked taller than she remembered—looked even more commanding. He seemed to take up all the air in the room, and she suddenly had a hard time breathing.

Greeting her with a nod, Matt touched a finger to his hat brim before turning his attention to the sheriff. "What'd he do?" he asked.

The sheriff scoffed. "Accused the mayor of stuffing the ballot box to win the last election, that's what."

Matt turned his gaze on the boy. "Those are fighting words, son."

"It's true!" Jesse said with a defiant look at the sheriff. "I saw him with my own eyes."

Keeler looked about to argue, but Matt stopped him by slapping a banknote on his desk. The sheriff regarded the bill with raised eyebrows before turning to Jesse. "You're free to go."

Matt gave the boy a stern look. "Go home. We'll talk later."

Jesse darted past the three adults like a mouse pursued by a hungry cat. Leaving the office, he slammed the door shut with such force, the windows rattled.

Cursing beneath his breath, the sheriff pulled the chair away from his desk and sat. "That boy's trouble, and this ain't the end of it."

Having nothing more to say to the sheriff, Ellie-May met Matt's gaze and was once again reminded of his commanding presence. "T-thank you," she stammered. Matt's generosity had kept Jesse out of jail and saved her from doing what would have surely been a mistake. The banknote in her purse weighing heavily on her conscience, she turned to leave.

Much to her dismay, Matt rushed to open the door for her. Even more disturbing, he followed her outside.

11

ELLIE-MAY TOOK OFF LIKE A MUSTANG WITH ITS TAIL afire, and Matt practically had to run to catch up to her.

She glanced at him as he fell in step by her side. The look of gratitude she had shown him moments earlier when he'd paid Jesse's fine had now been replaced with something that looked like suspicion. Maybe even fear.

"I didn't expect to see you back in town," she said.

"I didn't expect to come back." He regarded her from beneath arched eyebrows. "But it seems like you and I have something in common."

"Oh?"

"We both care about Jesse."

She stopped upon reaching her horse and wagon. Clutching her bag as if her life depended upon it, she turned to face him. A straw bonnet framed her delicate face but failed to hide the strained expression of someone facing a hangman's rope.

"You came back because of Jesse?" she asked, clearly surprised.

He shrugged. "What can I say? The lad grows on you." That part was true, at least. He wasn't about to divulge that the real reason for his return involved her deceased husband. Not yet.

Her blue eyes darkened with emotion. "He *is* a good boy," she said. "I don't care what the sheriff says. He's doing the best he knows how." She heaved a sigh before adding, "His ma was a friend of mine."

Matt studied her. Her blue floral frock showed off her tiny waist and gentle curves to full advantage, but it was the gold-flecked sadness in her eyes that commanded his attention. Was the look there because she missed her husband? It had only been a little over a year...

"He is a good boy," he said. "And he should be in school. He has a bright mind. With the right guidance, he could make something of himself. But convincing him to continue his education will be a problem. He's determined to be a Ranger."

She looked at him through a fringe of dark lashes. "No doubt he thinks that what you do is more interesting than sitting in a classroom."

Recalling his own youthful beliefs on the subject, Matt shook his head. "He might think that, but he would be wrong. Sleeping in tents and spending long, tedious hours in the saddle is anything but glamorous."

She assessed him long and hard, as if seeing him for the first time. "Then why do it?" she asked. "What made you choose to be a Ranger?"

He narrowed his gaze. This was hardly the conversation he'd expected to have with her, or with anyone, for that matter. Most people knew better than to inquire about a man's past. Regardless, he surprised himself by answering her.

"When I was fifteen, my pa was shot during a holdup," he began, further surprising himself with his candor. He'd not talked of his pa's death in years—fifteen years, to be exact. It was no easier now to voice the words than it had been in those first early days. But for reasons he couldn't explain, the need to say them had never been greater. "He'd gone to the general store for kerosene and never came back."

As he spoke, her expressive blue eyes turned into two pools of sympathy. For the first time since meeting her, he sensed her lowering her guard.

"How awful for you," she said, her voice as soft and comforting as a summer breeze.

Awful didn't begin to describe the aftermath of what had happened. His mother had taken her husband's death so hard, she had been confined to a sickbed and never fully recovered.

"They never found the culprit," he said. "That's the reason I joined the Rangers. I figured if I could catch enough criminals, put enough outlaws in jail, it would make up for the one who might never be caught."

A thoughtful expression crossed her face before she asked, "How many?"

He raised a single eyebrow. "What?"

"How many criminals will it take to make up for what happened to your pa?"

He sighed and clamped down on his jaw. There weren't enough outlaws in the world to make up for losing his father. He hadn't known that in his late teens when he first joined the Rangers. But he knew it now.

"A lot," he said vaguely.

She pulled her gaze from his and lowered her lashes. "I hope you catch whatever number it takes," she said.

Though she'd sounded like she meant it, he sensed her putting up her guard again. Just like that, their newly established rapport had vanished, leaving him feeling oddly lost. Her sudden pulling away brought a depth of disappointment to him that had nothing to do with him being a lawman. It was more personal, more worrisome, more something...

"Thank you," he said, surprised to find himself wishing things could be different between them. Wishing they had met under very different circumstances. Wishing he wasn't driven to right a wrong that he now knew could never be made right.

Her lashes flew up as if she, too, had noticed the change between them.

A strange emotion that he couldn't decipher shadowed her face. Once again, her withdrawal felt like a door had been slammed shut between them. That was a good thing. A very good thing. For it reminded him that she was a suspect's widow and he had a job to do.

"I better go," she said.

He shortened the distance between them. "Before you go...I need to talk to you about something."

She raised her fine eyebrows. "Oh?"

"I talked to the Petersons," he said slowly, gauging her reaction. "They said your husband never showed up for the barn raising." Watching her closely, he paused for a moment. "Have you any idea why he didn't?"

She shook her head and drew in a ragged breath.

"No," she said in a hoarse voice. "I have no idea. It was a long time ago."

"Just thought I'd ask," he said.

She looked up at him with a glazed look of despair. "If there's nothing more…?"

"That's all," he said.

She turned to her wagon so abruptly, she dropped her purse and gasped in dismay.

They bent at the same time to pick up the purse, but he reached it first. He brushed the dust off the soft black leather before handing it to her. Their fingers touched for a mere second, but it was enough to bring a pretty flush to her cheeks.

"T-thank you," she stammered, refusing to meet his eyes. Grabbing hold of the wagon's handrail, she hoisted herself onto the driver's seat.

Looking up at her, he tipped his hat. "Always a pleasure," he said.

Not bothering to return the sentiment, she tugged on the reins and drove off. He wondered if it was only his imagination, but it sure did seem like even the sunlight was less brilliant now that she was gone.

Shaking away the disturbing thought, he turned and headed back to his horse. The lady had secrets. Of that he was certain. He just wasn't sure he wanted to know what they were.

Ellie-May raced her horse and wagon out of town. Fortunately, it was still early and the road relatively empty. Nevertheless, she garnered startled looks from shopkeepers sweeping doorsteps and a few pedestrians racing to get out of her way.

Matt Taggert had made her nervous—and it hadn't just been the incriminating evidence on her person, though that was a big part of it. She'd wanted to die when he'd picked up her purse. What if it had fallen open and he'd recognized the banknote inside?

She felt sick just thinking about it. It was bad enough that he now knew Neal had no alibi during the time of the robbery. Had he found her with stolen goods, there would have been no saving Neal.

But that wasn't the only thing that worried her. Whenever she was near him, her pulse raced, and her nerves threatened to snap. He had a way of looking at her that made her feel both womanly and girlish. Made her feel pretty, even. Made her feel special.

Not good. As long as he was in town, she needed to keep her wits about her at all times, especially in his presence.

She wasn't sure how or why he made her feel so fluttery. Certainly, it wasn't just his good looks or crooked smile. Maybe it was simply the power he had to destroy Neal's reputation—the power to bring her children's world tumbling down. Maybe that was what kept her nerves on edge.

She didn't want to think it was the way he looked at her at times. Like he could see into her very soul. Like he knew what was in her heart and could dredge up her darkest secrets.

With those troubling thoughts whirling in her head, she drove the horse and wagon back to the farm. Reaching the house, she tugged on the reins and gasped. Anvil was bent over the porch step and hammering away. Had he found the gunnysack?

Last night, she hadn't wanted to wake the children, so she'd simply retrieved a banknote and gently tapped the tread back in place. She had intended to do a more complete job of the step today while Lionel and Alicia were in school.

Setting the brake, she jumped to the ground.

Anvil straightened as she neared and tossed the hammer into his toolbox. "The dang thing came loose again," he said, and his eyes narrowed as he looked at her. "You okay?"

"Yes. Why do you ask?"

He brushed his damp forehead with the back of his hand. "All I knows is that you came barrelin' up the road like you were runnin' for your life."

"I was just…anxious to get home. I have a lot of things to do."

Anvil lifted his hat and ran his fingers through his graying hair. "Do you have a moment?"

He looked and sounded so serious, she was convinced he'd found the money.

She bit her lower lip and nodded. How in the world could she explain the loot without making Neal look bad?

She struggled to find her voice. "Yes, of course, Anvil. What is it?"

He replaced his hat. "It's that Roberts fella."

She stared at him. "Roberts? What about him?"

"Hope you don't mind, but I told him to go and not come back."

She frowned. "I don't understand." It wasn't like Anvil to make such decisions without consulting her. "Why?"

"He weren't here as no friend, I can tell you that. All he was doing was pokin' around. Like he was lookin' for something."

Though it was hot, cold shivers shot down her back. It wasn't what she had wanted to hear. If Roberts was looking for something, that could mean only one thing—he knew about the stolen money. If he knew, who else knew? Oh God, who else?

"Like...like what?" she asked cautiously. "What do you think he was looking for?"

"Don't know, and he sure in blazes wasn't talkin'." Anvil shook his head and hung his thumbs from the straps of his overalls. "Hopefully, we've seen the last of him."

Ellie-May gripped her purse tight. Was it possible that Roberts and Neal had been in cahoots? The thought made her stomach turn over in dismay, and she swallowed the bile rising in her throat.

"The Texas Ranger is back in town," she said. He'd told her he'd come back for Jesse's sake, but she wondered if that were true. It was hard to believe that a man as driven as Matt Taggert would take time away from his job to help a young boy.

Anvil raised an eyebrow. "Oh?"

Not sure of how much or little to say, she moistened her lips. "Anvil...you...you don't think that Neal had anything to do with that stage robbery, do you?"

Anvil's eyes grew round as brass buttons. "Glory be, Miss Ellie-May. What would make you think such a thing?"

She drew in her breath. "You said that Roberts was looking for something. If he thought that Neal—"

Anvil shook his head, and his gray eyes met hers. "Whatever Roberts has on his mind, it has nothing to do with Neal."

He said exactly what she needed to hear, and she afforded him a smile of gratitude. "You're right, of course."

"You're darn tootin' I'm right." He gathered up his toolbox. "I'll take care of your horse and wagon." He studied her a moment. "Don't you go worryin' none, you hear?"

Nodding, she clutched her purse in both hands and watched him drive her wagon to the barn, her troubled thoughts whirling in her head. Now that Matt Taggert was back in town, how could she not worry?

❧

Matt had no trouble finding the James place. Situated just outside town at the base of a bleak hill, the small house was built of logs and roofed with shingles.

Next to it, a large sycamore leaned to the side as if looking for a place to fall. The small yard was fenced by a crooked picket fence that was more hindrance than barrier.

Dismounting, he tied his horse to a wooden post and let himself through the rusty iron gate. The walkway to the house was covered in weeds. Somewhere in the distance, a dog barked, but otherwise, all was quiet.

Matt had to knock several times before the door finally creaked opened. It was hard to get a look at

Jesse's face through the curtain of long hair, but it sure did look like he'd been sleeping. Matt felt bad for waking him, but what he had to say couldn't wait.

"We need to talk," Matt said. Brushing past Jesse, he planted himself in the middle of the drab parlor. The room was dimly lit, and it took a moment for Matt's eyes to adjust.

A sagging sofa faced a stone fireplace and offered a startling contrast to the intricately carved oak tables that flanked each upholstered arm. A copy of the *Police Gazette*—or *Bachelor's Bible*, as it was called—yawned open upon the sofa. The air smelled stale and musty.

Turning to face the boy, Matt felt his irritation drain away. Instead, his anger was directed at the boy's neglectful pa. The boy had dreams, and anyone who could harbor a dream in such depressing surroundings deserved a break. That made him feel even more responsible for Jesse's safety and well-being.

"From now on, you're not to conduct any investigations on your own. And if you know what's good for you, you'll stay away from the sheriff. Do you hear me?"

Jesse crossed his arms, a defiant look on his face. "What gives you the right to tell me what I can do? You ain't my pa."

"Five dollars gives me the right," Matt said. "And until you pay me back the money you owe me for paying your fine, I have the right to tell you what you can and cannot do. Understood?"

Looking cornered as a trapped mouse, Jesse gave a reluctant nod, and his gaze dropped to the floor.

"You must have good, solid proof before you go

around accusing people of crimes." Matt hated being so stern with the boy, but it was for his own good.

Jesse looked up. "But I saw the mayor stuff the ballot boxes with my own two eyes."

"It's still your word against his." Since Jesse looked like he was on the verge of tears, Matt softened his stance along with his voice. "Things aren't always what they seem. That's why you need good, solid proof before you go around making accusations."

Jesse frowned. "How am I gonna get proof? Huh?"

"Far as the mayor's concerned, there probably isn't any tangible proof."

Looking more lost than defiant, Jesse's shoulders slumped forward. "You mean he gets away with cheating?"

"Looks that way," Matt said. His father's death taught him one bitter truth—not every crime is punished. "Now you know what makes a Ranger's job so tough."

Satisfied that he had the boy's cooperation—or at least less resistance—Matt tried to decide what to do with him. If the man Jesse overheard talking to Blackwell did indeed exist, Matt would need help finding him. Unfortunately, that meant having to depend on the boy's help, and that wasn't something he'd wanted to do.

"From now on, the only undercover work you do is for me," Matt said against his better judgment. "Understood?"

Jesse lifted his gaze. "Are you gonna pay me?"

"No, you're gonna work with me till your debt is paid. You owe me five dollars, remember?" That didn't even begin to cover the cost of feeding and clothing him. "Always pay your debts. Consider it a rule."

Looking more like himself, Jesse rolled his eyes. "You sure do have a lot of rules."

"Yeah, and if you want to do Ranger work, you best follow them." Matt held out his hand. "So what do you say? Deal?"

Jesse stared at Matt's offered hand for a moment before shaking it. "Deal."

"All right, then." Matt thought for a moment. "Meet me at the Feedbag Café at nine tomorrow morning."

No sooner were the words out of his mouth than the memory of breakfast with Ellie-May Blackwell popped into his head. Surprised at the warm though no less worrisome feelings that came to mind, he quickly turned on his heel and reached for the doorknob.

"Don't be late!"

12

AFTER WASHING AND RINSING THE LAST OF THE SUPPER dishes, Ellie-May reached for a clean towel and dried her hands. She'd been meaning to have a serious talk with her daughter for a week but had kept putting it off. Since Alicia's birthday was now only three days away, she could no longer postpone what she had to say.

"Alicia, about your birthday…" Ellie-May reached for the stack of clean plates and placed them in the overhead cabinet. Pausing for a moment to search for the right words, she then turned to face her daughter. "You know I love you very much."

Alicia twisted the damp towel in her hand. "I'm not gonna get the music box, am I?"

Ellie-May felt a sharp pain in her chest, like someone had punched a hole in her heart. A fortune was hidden beneath her porch steps, yet never had she felt so poor. It was at moments like this that she felt like such a failure as a mother.

"It costs a lot of money."

Alicia looked as if she was trying not to cry. "If Papa was here, he'd find a way to pay for it."

"Yes. Yes, he would," Ellie-May said and felt no pleasure in saying it.

Had she unknowingly driven her husband to a life of crime? Made too many demands on him? Appeared too needy? Had robbing that stage been his way of making up to her for what had happened in her past? Had he actually committed the crime out of concern for her and the children?

Grimacing, she heaved a sigh of disgust. She could not, would not make excuses for Neal. There was no defense for what he'd had done. None!

Aware, suddenly, that her daughter was staring at her, she moistened her lips. "Oh, Alicia. My dear daughter, don't you know how much it hurts to deny you something that means so much? I would give you the moon if I could. You know that, right?"

Alicia lifted her chin, and resignation fleeted across her face. "I know, Mama. It's okay."

Both surprised and gratified at Alicia's response, Ellie-May wrapped her arms around her daughter's thin shoulders and hugged her close. Ellie-May couldn't give her the moon or even a music box. All she could do was make sure that Alicia continued to be proud of her father and would never have to hang her head in shame. Never must her children know the truth.

In the end, all Ellie-May could do was hope and pray that protecting their pa's reputation would be enough.

Matt arrived at the Feedbag Café ten minutes early that morning to find Jesse already seated at a table. He nodded approval. Early was good.

What wasn't good was the boy's appetite. Never had Matt seen anyone gobble his way through a mile-high stack of flapjacks so quickly, and it didn't stop there. He'd also devoured all the bacon and half of everything else on Matt's plate.

Fortunately, the boy preferred orange juice to coffee, so Matt's brew was safe. All he could hope for was that they found their man before the kid ate a hole in his pocket.

Jesse was far less enthusiastic about the trip to the Haywire Bathing and Tonsorial Parlor, which followed breakfast. "I had a bath at the Ranger camp."

"What you had," Matt said, "was a splash of cold water that hardly penetrated the layers of dirt." He pointed Jesse toward the reception desk.

Matt paid extra so the boy could have clean hot water and towels, but even that failed to earn any gratitude.

When the attendant handed Jesse a towel and bar of lye soap, the boy balked. "I don't know why I have to take a bath. What's that gotta to do with being a Ranger?"

"Taking a bath will show me you know how to follow an order," Matt said, his voice stern. "It'll also keep you from warning off the bad guys with your smell. Cleanliness is—"

"I know, I know," Jesse said, rolling his eyes. "A rule." Jesse didn't look happy, but he begrudgingly entered the bathing room and slammed the door shut.

"And wash behind your ears!" Matt said, lifting his voice to be heard through the door.

Jesse emerged fifteen minutes later, his wet hair falling to his shoulders. "I don't have a comb."

"You don't need a comb," Matt said. "The barber will take care of it."

Jesse brushed the stringy ginger strands of hair away from his face. "You mean you even have a rule about haircuts?"

Matt shrugged. "If you want to be a Ranger, you have to look the part," he said and led the way down the street to the barbershop.

Less than thirty minutes later, Matt left the barbershop with Jesse in tow. The boy sure in blazes smelled better, and his haircut had improved his appearance, but his trousers still hung loose on him. The shirt Matt loaned him was clean, but it fell to his knees, and the sleeves had to be rolled up. Only the lack of straw kept him from looking like a scarecrow.

For now, however, he would have to do. There was work to be done.

For the remainder of the morning, they walked the entire length of Main Street, checking shops and businesses in town for the man Jesse claimed was in cahoots with Blackwell.

Jesse said he'd spotted the man in the Wandering Dog Saloon. If true, then chances were the man either lived in town or was staying there. They stopped to question the hotel clerk and checked with all the local boardinghouses. But trying to find a man with such a vague description was like looking for a needle in a haystack.

The sun was barely straight up in the sky when Jesse complained about being hungry again. Since the hotel was closest, they stopped at the hotel dining room. This time, Jesse wolfed down two plates of beef stew and half a loaf of bread.

By midafternoon, Jesse's eyes glazed over. "I thought we were gonna do Ranger work," he said.

"We are doing Ranger work," Matt said.

Jesse made a face. "This is boring."

"Son, you don't know boring. Wait till you're a Ranger for real." Matt didn't want to discourage the boy, but the sooner he faced reality, the better.

Jesse continued to complain. "I'm hot and hungry. And my feet hurt."

Matt glanced at the boy's worn shoes. No wonder his feet hurt. "A Ranger never advertises his problems. Consider it a rule. People are oversupplied with their own problems and don't want to hear about yours."

Jesse muttered something beneath his breath, but Matt decided not to ask him to repeat it.

Matt stopped in front of Gordon's General Store and reached for the brass doorknob. "Let's see what the owner has to say. Then we'll stop and get you some new foot leather."

The shop was empty except for the man behind the counter and a little girl listening to the tinkling sound of a music box.

Jesse waved to the girl.

"Know her?" Matt asked.

Jesse nodded. "Yeah. That's Alicia Blackwell."

"Black—" Matt took a closer look and could see a family resemblance. The girl had her mother's blond hair and delicate features. He couldn't tell from this distance, but he was willing to bet she also had her mother's pretty blue eyes as well.

"What can I do you fer?" the clerk called from behind the counter, saving Matt from dwelling too long on the memory of the girl's mother.

Matt checked the sign over the counter. "Are you Gordon?"

"That's me," Gordon said, pushing his spectacles up his nose.

Matt introduced himself. "We're looking for someone." Jesse had stopped to talk to the little girl, and Matt motioned him over with a wave of his hand. He waited for Jesse to join him. "Describe the man we're looking for."

"The man stands this tall," Jesse said, holding his hand slightly above his head. "He has a skinny mustache and a crooked nose."

Following Jesse's description, Gordon shook his head. "You just described half the men in town. Sorry." He regarded Jesse with narrowed eyes. "Don't tell me you're up to your old tricks again. Like I told you, you can only work here long as you stop making accusations."

Not wanting Jesse to lose his job, Matt quickly stepped in. "He's not making accusations. He's working for me now."

Gordon scratched the side of his neck. "That so?"

Nodding, Matt turned to Jesse and pointed to the men's ready-to-wear section. "Pick out a shirt and pair of trousers for yourself." He then turned back to Gordon.

"You'd better watch your step," Gordon said. "Jesse has a habit of accusing innocent people of crimes they ain't committed."

"Like I said, he's working for me now."

Jesse returned with a pair of canvas trousers and a plaid shirt. Matt took the clothes from him and laid them on the counter. Seeing Jesse hungrily eye the display of apples, Matt reached for a bag and placed it on the counter next to the new duds. He then dug in his vest pocket for his money clip and paid for the lot.

The music box started again, and Matt glanced over his shoulder at Ellie-May Blackwell's daughter.

Gordon handed Matt's change over the counter and tossed a nod at the little girl. "She comes in every day after school to play the music box. Says the song reminds her of her pa."

"She wants the music box for her birthday," Jesse said, reaching into the bag for an apple. "Said her ma can't afford it." He bit into the fruit with a loud crunch and started for the door.

Matt grabbed his purchases off the counter and fell in step behind Jesse. But before leaving the shop, he shot yet another glance at the little girl. Big mistake, for again a vision of her mother came to mind, followed by the memory of what it was like to lose a pa.

13

A SCREAM WOKE ELLIE-MAY FROM A SOUND SLEEP. Flinging off the covers, she sprang out of bed and ran from the room, her feet barely touching the hardwood floor.

Her sleep-clouded brain could barely make sense of the scene that greeted her in the parlor. Alicia was bouncing around the room like a rubber ball, her braids hammering her back like two drumsticks.

Thinking something awful had happened, Ellie-May clutched her hands to her chest. "What is it? What happened? Is your brother—?"

Alicia whirled about, a bright smile on her face. "Look, Mama. Look!" She held out something in her hands.

Ellie-May blinked, not sure she could believe her eyes. It sure did look like…

"It's the music box I wanted!" Alicia's voice trilled with excitement.

"I can see that," Ellie-May said, puzzled. "Where… where did you get it?"

"It was on the porch by the front door when I went

to feed the chickens." Alicia danced around the room, hugging the wooden box to her chest. "Oh, Mama! Thank you, thank you, thank you."

"Honey, I didn't—"

Lionel entered the room yawning. He was still dressed in his nightshirt, and his hair stood up like a picket fence. "You woke me up," he complained and knuckled the sleep from his eyes.

"Look, Lioney!" Alicia said, ignoring her brother's grumpy expression. Her voice rising another octave higher, she continued, "Today is my birthday, and I got the music box I wanted." Setting it on the table, she carefully turned the crank.

"Listen," she said and danced around the room to the tune. "Remember Papa singing that to us?" Eyes closed, she began to sing in a soft, sweet voice. "Hush-a-bye, don't you cry. Go to sleep, my dear sweet child. When you wake, you'll have cake, and all the pretty little horses." Lionel moved to his sister's side, and together they sang the second verse.

Hearing the words so often sung in Neal's baritone voice, Ellie-May blinked back tears. The song was actually a lullaby, but Neal had changed some of the lyrics as the children grew older, and the word *baby* had become *child*.

Ellie-May waited until the song ended. "Was there a card?" she asked, wiping away a tear.

Alicia carefully turned the wind-up key. "What?"

"A card. On the box."

Shaking her head no, Alicia broke into song again with her brother, their young voices blended in sweet harmony.

Puzzled, Ellie-May walked into the kitchen to make Anvil's coffee and a cup of tea for herself. Who could have given Alicia the music box? Anvil? She discounted the idea the moment it occurred to her. He could not afford such a thing. Not unless he found the money under the porch.

The thought almost made her drop the teakettle. Steadying herself, she tried picturing Anvil riding into town to purchase a music box and couldn't.

But if not Anvil, then who? The box didn't end up on the doorstep on its own. Who would do such a thing and, more importantly, why?

Matt had just finished shaving when a knock sounded at his door. Thinking it was Jesse, he reached for a towel and wiped the foamy soap off his chin.

"Give me a minute," he called. Dressed in trousers but no shirt, he moved away from the dry sink.

The knock came again, this time more urgently, and Matt shook his head.

If Jesse ever hoped to be a Ranger, he'd best learn the importance of patience. Fearing the boy would disturb the other hotel guests, Matt tore the door open, ready to scold him, but the words never left his mouth.

Much to his surprise, it wasn't Jesse at the door. Instead, Ellie-May Blackwell stood glaring at him, and she looked as steamed as a locomotive.

"Why are you giving my daughter presents?" she demanded.

He quirked an eyebrow. "How do you know I did?"

"Mr. Gordon told me."

He sighed in resignation. He should have known she would check. Not that he meant it to be a secret. He stepped aside. "Come in."

Her gaze lit on his bare chest. Cheeks turning red, she quickly lowered her eyes. "A lady does not enter a gentleman's hotel room."

He quirked an eyebrow. "I promise not to act like a gentleman if you'll promise not to act like a lady."

Her lashes flew up and her lips parted. "I'll do no such thing!"

He glanced up and down the hall. Three hotel guests peered from the doorways of nearby rooms and gazed at Matt with curious stares.

Thinking the lady might prefer airing her grievances in private, Matt grabbed her by the hand and pulled her into his room. Not that the paper-thin walls allowed for much privacy, but they were better than nothing. Releasing her hand, he slammed the door shut.

He reached for his shirt and quickly donned it. "You can look now."

She lifted her head and looked him square in the eye. The sweet, delicate scent of her perfume seemed at odds with her defiant stance. Despite her small stature, she looked as formidable as a bull seeing red.

"You haven't answered my question," she sputtered. "Why did you give my daughter that music box?"

He tucked his shirt into his trousers and reached

for his gun belt. "I thought you'd be pleased. It is her birthday."

Her eyes widened, allowing him to see the golden flecks in their depths. "How do you know that?"

"Jesse," he said and shrugged. "So what's the harm? Gordon said the box played music that reminded her of her father."

"The father that *you* accused of robbing stages!"

"I never accused him," Matt said, buckling his gun belt in place. At least not to her face. "I'd simply wanted to ask him for information."

Pursing her mouth, she studied him like a frog about to snap up a fly. "You still haven't answered my question. Why?"

"Why did I give your daughter the music box?" He hadn't given much thought as to the reason. All he knew is that he'd felt a strong compulsion to do it. "Maybe because I know how it feels to lose a pa at a young age."

The answer seemed to satisfy her. At least, she looked less inclined to do him bodily harm. "I don't want your charity."

"A music box hardly qualifies as charity."

"I'll pay you back," she said after a pause. "But it'll take time."

He shook his head. "I don't want your money."

Her forehead creased. "Then what do you want?"

"Nothing," he said.

"You bought my daughter an expensive gift and want nothing in return?" She looked and sounded incredulous.

"Is that so hard to believe?"

"You hardly know us."

"I know enough to want to make a little girl happy," he said.

A look of vulnerability crossed Ellie-May Blackwell's face, and much to his surprise, her eyes filled with tears.

He took a step forward but stopped short of touching her. "I didn't mean to make you cry," he said.

She swiped a tear away from her cheek. "It's just that…" she began and stopped. He sensed her hesitation. Saw a shadow of indecision cross her face. "I'm not used to such kindness."

His eyebrows shot up. "I'd say that's a real shame," he said. "A widow with two children deserves all the kindness and consideration she can get."

The tears magnified the pain in her eyes, and he felt an overwhelming need to comfort her. Protect her. He'd seen those same eyes flash with anger, harden in determination, and soften with tenderness for her child. But now, looking into her eyes, he felt as if her heart was opening to him like the petals of a flower, beckoning him to peer inside.

"There, now," he said soothingly. Cursing himself for the inadequacy of his words, he drew a clean handkerchief from his pocket and dabbed her cheeks dry. It seemed that all he could do was wipe away her tears, and he was grateful that she let him do it.

She studied him with grave intent, and a shadow of indecision fleeted across her forehead. "You'll probably find this out anyway," she began slowly as if each word had to be tested before spoken. "You might as well hear it from me."

He tilted his head. She looked and sounded as serious as a sinner in a confessional. The tension between them felt almost palpable. "Hear what?"

She drew in her breath as if bracing herself against even more pain. "Have you heard of a man named Arthur Grant?"

"I reckon everyone's heard of Grant," he said. The man's crime spree was way before his time, but it was still a topic of conversation among the senior Rangers. "Why do you ask?"

She took so long to answer that he'd almost given up on her and was about to repeat the question when at last she spoke. "He was my father."

It took a moment for the full impact of her admission to hit him. "Your fa—"

She nodded. "I was the same age as Alicia when I watched him hang." She shuddered as if the mere act of talking about it was too much to bear. "You have no idea what it's like growing up as an outlaw's daughter."

Feeling bad for her, Matt was momentarily at a loss for words. It was hard enough having to deal with an outlaw brother. How much harder it must be to live under the shadow of a notorious father!

"I have a little idea," he said at last. "My brother is a wanted bank robber." He gently dabbed at the watery pearls rolling down her cheeks with his handkerchief.

Her eyes widened. "You're a Texas Ranger and have an outlaw brother?" she asked, aghast.

Feeling the need to defend his brother, he said, "My pa was shot during a holdup, and my brother took his death hard. The whole family did." It was still hard to believe how one tragic event had led him and his brother in opposite directions.

"I'm so sorry," she whispered, and this time, she reached out to lay a hand on his arm.

He looked down at the small, pale hand seeming to burn a hole through his shirtsleeve and covered it with his own. "Nothing I went through compares to what you must have gone through," he said and lifted his gaze. "You were just a child. I can't imagine how hard it must have been to watch your father hang." At least he hadn't had to watch his father being gunned down.

Her expression softened, even as she looked at him with solemn eyes. "No one ever said that to me before," she whispered.

Not sure what she was saying, he tilted his head. "No one?"

She pulled her hand away from his arm. "People were certain that my father's bad blood ran through my veins." Moistening her lips, she continued, "I wasn't allowed to finish school or do any of the things that other kids could do. I didn't even feel welcomed in church."

As she described the ordeal, Matt thought of all the criminals he'd arrested or helped arrest in the past. He wondered how many of them had left children behind, children who were then shunned by society and forever scarred by their father's actions.

"What about your mother?" he asked.

Her intake of breath told him that talking about her mother was no easier than talking about her pa. "Mama told me to ignore what others said. But that's not easy for a child to do."

Fresh tears filled her eyes, and this time, he wrapped his arms around her. Resting his chin on her head, he held her close and inhaled her sweet womanly fragrance. For several moments, neither of them said a word. At last, he felt her trembling body still and her soft sobs fade away.

Stirring in his arms, she looked at him through rings of wet lashes, and it was all he could do not to cover her quivering lips with his own. Fortunately, she pulled away, saving him from doing something he would surely regret. Her late husband was still a suspect, and that made her off-limits. *Way* off-limits.

She straightened her shoulders as if pulling herself together. "I'm sorry," she murmured. "I don't know what's wrong with me. I'm not usually…like this."

"No need to apologize," he said. If anyone should apologize, it was him, for wanting to kiss away her pain. For wanting to hold her until her memories of the past had faded. For wanting to fix everything in her world even though he had no right to. No right at all.

"Why did you tell me about your father?" he asked. It wasn't the kind of thing one told a mere acquaintance.

She lowered her eyes before answering. "You've shown my daughter the kindness I never knew as a child." Face brimming with emotion, she looked up and continued. "For that reason, you deserve to know why I resent you trying to link my husband to a crime. Never must my children feel ashamed or inferior as I was made to feel. I want them to grow up able to hold their heads up high."

Her expression reminded him of a black bear he once saw defending its young. He felt for her, and a protective surge swelled in him once again.

"Their father died a hero," Matt said.

"Yes, he did." She lifted her chin. "And I aim to make sure he remains a hero."

Matt drew in his breath. He could hardly deny his interest in her husband. "It's not my intention to do anything that'll harm you or your children."

For the first time ever, he wished to God he wasn't a Ranger. Wished he didn't have a job to do. Wished he'd taken up carpentry instead, like his pa.

She opened her mouth to say something, but a knock at the door stopped her. This time, it was Jesse, and just like that, the tension in the room vanished.

Greeting the boy with a nod, Ellie-May complimented him on his haircut. "My, don't you look all grown-up?" she said.

Her praise made Jesse grin. "Do I look like a real Texas Ranger?" He turned a circle to show off his new clothes.

"Absolutely," Ellie-May said as she straightened his collar.

"I'm learning how to track bad guys," Jesse said with a note of pride.

"That…that's good," she said. She glanced at Matt and cleared her throat. "I best be going."

The look she gave him appeared to be filled with remorse, and Matt wondered if she regretted having been so open with him about her father. He tried thinking of something to say to relieve her mind but couldn't. There was no denying that Neal Blackwell's train ticket had been found at the crime scene. It also appeared that Blackwell had no known alibi for the time of the robbery. No matter how much Matt wished otherwise, Ellie-May's deceased husband was still a prime suspect.

After bidding Jesse goodbye, Ellie-May left the hotel room without further ado, and Matt immediately regretted her absence. It was as if she'd taken the very air with her.

He hoped and prayed that Neal Blackwell was innocent, but the only way to prove it was to find the man Jesse had overheard talking to him. But what if the man provided proof of Blackwell's guilt? What if the man was Blackwell's partner in crime? Feeling as if he was about to land on a double-edged sword, Matt sighed. What then?

14

ELLIE-MAY LEFT THE HOTEL IN A HURRY. MOMENTARILY blinded by the sun, she adjusted her bonnet before hiking up her skirt and racing to her horse and wagon.

She was shaken to the core. Her original intent in telling Matt about her father had been to warn him. She'd wanted him to know that she would do whatever necessary to protect her children, even if it meant fighting him tooth and nail.

Never had she expected Matt to react as he had, and her cheeks flared at the memory of being in his arms. Instead of treating her with scorn as so many others had done, he'd wiped away her tears and comforted her. The sheer power of him had been hard to resist, and like a child, she'd sobbed in his arms and rested her head against his strong chest. Her senses were still whirling from the kindness he'd shown.

The kinship they'd shared when he'd told her about his brother was unlike anything she'd ever experienced. Matt Taggert knew what it was like to have an outlaw in the family, and for the first time ever, Ellie-May felt like she wasn't alone.

No matter what happened in the future, no matter what unkindness was hers to bear, she could always fall back on the memory of being in the arms of the one person who truly understood.

Neal had tried his best to understand, he really had, and she would always be grateful for that. But they'd been married three years before he'd finally gotten around to telling her he'd shot his childhood friend. At first, she'd been angry that he'd taken so long to confide in her. His secret had created a block between them that had made her feel as though she was married to a stranger, and that feeling had never entirely gone away.

There had been so much she hadn't known about her husband. Still didn't know.

In contrast, she'd been acquainted with Matt Taggert for only a short time, but already she felt like she knew him better than she'd ever known Neal.

But that was only part of it. In the brief time she'd been exposed to Matt Taggert's bare chest, she'd somehow managed to memorize every plane and ridge, every well-defined muscle.

Her heart thudded at the memory, and heat rose up her neck. The pleasure she felt in recalling the Ranger's naked chest filled her with confusion and more than a little shame.

Since Neal died, she'd not given her own needs any thought. All she'd been able to think about were the children and the farm. Never once had she imagined herself being attracted to another man.

Had Jesse not arrived…

Dear God. What was she thinking? Nothing would

have happened. She wouldn't have let it happen. Hadn't wanted it to happen.

Okay, so that wasn't entirely true. There had been that one crazy moment, while locked in his arms, when she'd wondered what his lips would feel like on hers.

Appalled at the memory, she shook her head as if to banish the thought and climbed into the driver's seat. With a quick intake of breath, she reached for the reins.

If only Matt Taggert hadn't looked at her with such tenderness… If only he hadn't shown her daughter such unbelievable kindness. If only he hadn't shared his own family shame.

Refusing to linger yet again on the memory of being held by him, Ellie-May shook the reins and drove slowly out of town. She needed time to calm her still-racing heart before returning to the farm.

As for Neal, his secret was safe, his reputation secure. The money was safely hidden, and no one need ever know what was buried beneath her porch. Still, it near broke her heart.

Oh, Neal. Why? Why would you do such a thing?

How she hated living with secrets. Hated that Neal had pulled her into his. Everything about the life they'd shared now seemed like a lie. Had she done something, said something that had made Neal think she'd been dissatisfied with their marriage? With him?

Sure, they'd struggled to make ends meet, but what local family hadn't? Times had been tough. Still were.

Thoughts racing through her head like leaves in the wind, she left the town behind and turned up the road leading to her farm. Never had she felt more confused.

The lamplighter had already made his rounds by the time Matt and Jesse stopped for supper that night at the Feedbag Café. While Matt ate, Jesse continued eating. The boy had been scarfing down food all day.

After leaving the restaurant, they walked the distance to the Dead Line, which separated the moral part of town from the saloons and rowdy houses, and stopped beneath the sign that read THE WANDERING DOG SALOON. Saloons didn't generally start buzzing until after dark, which was why Matt had waited until now to check them out.

"This where your pa likes to hang out?" Matt asked.

Jesse nodded. "Yes, sir."

Matt pushed his way through the batwing doors. The place was packed, and the air hung heavy with the smell of tobacco, alcohol, and heated bodies.

After a quick scan of the noisy room, Matt asked, "So where is he?"

Jesse pointed to a corner table. "That's Pa over there."

Matt frowned. The same man had been slumped over the same table the last time Matt was at the saloon.

"Pa comes here every day," Jesse said.

Matt clamped down on his jaw. "Along with every other drunk in town," he muttered.

"What?"

"Nothing." Matt glanced around. A few glaring looks were cast his way. Some folks hadn't taken kindly to him asking questions about the town hero and had let him know it in no uncertain terms.

"Take a good look 'round and let me know if you see the man," he said. "I'll wait here by the door."

Moments later, Jesse joined him, shaking his head. "He's not here."

Matt rubbed his chin. It was no more than what he'd come to expect. Maybe the sheriff was right; maybe the boy had taken him on a wild-goose chase. Not that Matt could blame him. Knowing what he now knew about the boy's pa, he supposed the company of an unwilling Ranger was preferable to an empty house.

"Okay," he said, softening his tone. He couldn't help but feel sorry for the lad. "Go home and get some shut-eye."

"What time do you want to meet in the morning?"

Matt rubbed the back of his neck. "Meet me at nine for breakfast but…" He hesitated. "That's where it ends. I'm leaving town on the three o'clock train."

Jesse's mouth dropped, and his eyes darkened with emotion. "But we haven't found our man." The dismay on his face echoed in his voice.

Matt felt bad, but there was nothing more to be done there, and it wasn't in his nature to bide time. There were other outlaws to catch, his brother Charley among them.

"I've gotta get back to my company."

"Can I go with you?"

"No."

"I won't be any trouble."

"Jesse—"

"Pleeeeeeeeease."

Matt blew out his breath. He hated having to say no

to the lad, but what choice did he have? "We'll talk about this tomorrow over breakfast. Now go home and get some shut-eye."

Jesse looked about to argue but then turned and pushed his way outside through the swinging doors. Head low, back bent, he looked like he carried the weight of the world on his young shoulders.

Hours after leaving Jesse, Matt woke to the sound of loud banging.

"What the—?"

Battling his way out of bed, he staggered across the dark room. He felt for the brass knob and swung the door open. The flickering gaslight in the hall made him blink. "Not again," he groaned.

"I saw him!" Jesse said, his voice high with excitement.

Since Jesse spoke loud enough to raise the dead, Matt hushed him and motioned him into the room.

Turning, he felt for the oil lamp on the bedside table. Guided by the ribbon of light streaming from the open door, he removed the glass globe and picked up the box of safety matches. "Saw who?"

"Our man."

Striking a match, Matt lit the wick and replaced the globe. "Jesse—"

"Honest!" Jesse stepped into the room and closed the door. "He's at Pa's saloon."

Matt studied the boy. He sure did look and sound sincere. Blinking the sleep from his eyes, Matt picked his pocket watch off the bedside table and checked the time.

"It's after one. Why aren't you home in bed?"

Jesse lifted his chin. "I wanted to find him. Before you left town. So I kept checking all the saloons. I decided to check on Pa again, and there the man was. The bartender told me the man's name is Roberts."

"You got a name?" Now they were getting somewhere. Unless, of course, Jesse was trying to trick him into staying.

Jesse grinned. "Just doing what any good Ranger would do."

Matt studied the boy. "You better be telling the truth—"

"I am. You gotta believe me."

Stifling a yawn, Matt reached for his trousers. "All right, we'll check it out. But if I find that you're trying to pull the wool over my eyes…"

"I ain't. Honest!"

Satisfied that the kid spoke the truth, Matt quickly dressed. Less than twenty minutes later, he and Jesse arrived at the Wandering Dog Saloon.

"That's him," Jesse said, pointing to a man at the bar. "Are we gonna take him to jail?"

"Can't," Matt said.

"Why not?"

"*We*…don't have any proof that he's done anything wrong."

Jesse frowned. "So what *are* we gonna do?"

"I'm gonna talk to the man. And you're gonna take care of your pa. Soon's I'm finished here, I'll help you get him home."

"But—"

"That's an order, Ranger!"

Jesse clenched his jaw, but he straightened his shoulders and saluted. "Yes, sir!"

Shaking his head, Matt walked up to the bar and with a nod at Droopy, the bartender, took his place next to the man named Roberts. Of medium build and height, the man's unremarkable features made him hard to describe. Not even his crooked nose helped.

Acknowledging Matt with a brief nod, Roberts returned to his drink.

Matt was careful not to do anything threatening to make the suspect put up his guard. After casually chatting with the bartender, he ordered a shot of whiskey, which he left untouched.

He leaned sideways to make sure the man heard him over the noise. "Name's Taggert. Matt Taggert."

The man turned his head to stare at him, as if he couldn't decide whether to state his name. "Roberts," he said at last. "Dave Roberts."

"Pleased to meet you, Mr. Roberts," Matt said and offered his hand. The man had the shifty-eyed look of a dishonest horse trader.

The two of them shook hands, and Matt ordered Roberts another drink. He waited for the bartender to refill Roberts's glass before getting down to business.

"I understand you were a friend of Neal Blackwell."

Roberts visually stiffened. "What business is that of yours?"

Matt reached into his pocket for his badge and laid it on the bar. "Serious business," he said.

Roberts eyed the badge with hooded eyes. "I knew him. So what? No law against that."

Before Matt could answer, angry voices rang out behind him, followed by the sound of chairs and tables scraping across the straw-scattered floor. Hand on his gun, Matt spun around. Two men were going at it tooth and nail, pounding each other with flying fists. One man fell back against a table, sending coins and playing cards flying in every direction.

Soon others joined in the fray. Concerned for Jesse's safety, Matt craned his neck to look for him, but brawling bodies blocked his view.

Somebody fired a gun, and the mirror over the bar shattered, raining glass onto the shelf of whiskey bottles lined beneath.

Matt pulled out his Colt. "Stop!" he ordered. Some backed away, but the two men who had started the fight kept pummeling each other.

"I said stop!" Matt thundered, and this time, the battling duo drew apart, both with battered faces.

No sooner had Matt restored order than Sheriff Keeler came running through the swinging doors, suspenders flapping by his side. Wielding a pistol in one hand and handcuffs in the other, the sheriff carted the two troublemakers away.

Matt found Jesse hiding under a table. The boy looked scared to death, but his pa had slept through the whole ruckus. Grimacing in disgust, Matt was tempted to try to shake some sense into the man, but it would probably be a waste of time.

Matt scanned the room for Roberts, but he was nowhere to be seen. Evidently, he had taken advantage of the fight to make his escape.

Droopy caught Matt's eye to indicate that he still

owed for two shots of whiskey. Sighing, Matt reached for his money clip.

The night had been a bust.

15

ELLIE-MAY HAD JUST FINISHED ADDING CHOPPED carrots to the cast-iron pot on the stove when Lionel raced into the kitchen. "Ma, Ma!" Breathing hard, his face red from running, he could hardly get his words out. "Come quick!"

"Lionel, what is it? What's wrong?"

"Anvil was"—Lionel struggled to speak—"b-bit by a snake."

Ellie-May slammed her wooden spoon down with a gasp and raced to the pantry to grab the bottle of medicinal whiskey from the upper shelf. "Where is he?"

"In the barn."

Racing through the parlor, Ellie-May ran out of the house and down the porch steps with Lionel at her heel. Feet pounding the hard-packed ground, she sprinted across the yard and reached the barn out of breath.

She found Anvil slumped against a wooden post, the leg of his overalls pulled up. Next to him, Alicia held a bloody-tipped knife in her hand.

Ellie-May dropped to her knees by her daughter's side and set the whiskey bottle on the ground. After glancing at the rawhide tourniquet and cross-cut wound, she took the knife from her daughter's hand. "Did you?"

Anvil answered for Alicia. "I did the cuttin'. She tied the tourniquet." He grimaced as if in pain. "Dang, rattler snuck up on me."

Ellie-May uncapped the whiskey bottle and poured a dollop of the liquid on his wound. "Alicia, ride to the Buttonwood ranch and ask Mrs. Buttonwood to have one of her ranch hands fetch Doc Avery."

"Don't need no sawbones." Anvil looked like he was struggling to speak. "It was a dry bite."

"You don't know that," Ellie-May said, but already Anvil's eyes had drifted shut. She leaned over him, and his labored breathing worried her.

Lionel dropped to his knees by her side. "Is he gonna die?"

"Not if I can help it." Ellie-May pressed a hand on Anvil's forehead. "Hold on, dear friend. I'll be back."

Standing, she motioned her daughter to follow her with a wave of her hand. She let herself into the first stall and saddled her horse, Jingles, adjusting the stirrup for Alicia's height.

"Ride carefully," she said. She hated having to send her young daughter on such an errand, but she didn't want to leave Anvil alone in his condition.

"I can ride into town myself, Mama."

"No. It's too far." Alicia was a good rider, but she had never ridden as far as town. "Go to Mrs. Buttonwood. She'll know what to do."

Ellie-May helped her daughter fork the horse and readjusted the stirrups. "Be careful."

After Alicia had ridden away, Ellie-May turned to her pale-faced son. "Lionel, run to the house and fetch a bowl of water and a clean towel." She then hurried back to Anvil's side and took his hand in hers.

His skin had turned ash-gray, and his breathing was shallow. "I'm here," she whispered and said a quick prayer.

Moments later, the sound of hoofbeats outside made her shoot to her feet and hurry to the barn door. Alicia couldn't possible have made it to Mrs. Buttonwood's ranch and back in such a short time, but there she was.

"Alicia, what's wrong?" she called. "Why did you come back?"

Alicia slid out of the saddle. "I met a man on the road, and he said he would fetch the doctor for me."

"What man?" Ellie-May asked, taking the reins from her daughter and tethering the horse to a railing.

"I don't know his name, But he's a friend of Jesse's. He said he could travel faster."

"Jesse?" She thought a moment. "Did this man ride a black horse?"

Alicia nodded.

Ellie-May's heart skipped a beat. It sure did sound like Matt Taggert. Once again, she recalled how he'd held her and wiped away her tears. Now, as always, the memory of strong arms flooded her with warm feelings. Then her thoughts took a disturbing turn. She was now dependent upon the one man who could ruin her children's lives if she wanted to save Anvil.

Knotting her hands together, Ellie-May closed her

eyes and took a deep breath to calm herself. Feeling Alicia's hand on her arm, Ellie-May opened her eyes and gazed into her daughter's face.

"Did I do right, Mama?" Alicia asked with a worried look.

Ellie-May pressed her hand gently against her daughter's cheek. "You did fine, dear heart."

Lionel returned carrying a bowl of water and a towel over his arm. Though he was walking slowly and trying his best not to spill, water splashed over the side of the bowl. Snapping out of her troubled thoughts, Ellie-May took the half-empty bowl from him and rushed to Anvil's side.

∞

Matt spurred his horse to a full gallop and led the way along the dirt-packed road to the Blackwell farmhouse. The doctor's horse and buggy rattled behind him like a bag of old bones.

Ellie-May appeared at the door of the barn the moment Matt arrived at the farm and waved them over. Her young son and daughter stood by her side, looking every bit as grim as their mother.

Matt rode up to where they were standing and dismounted. For once, Ellie-May's guard didn't go up when she saw him. If anything, she looked glad to see him. Or at the very least, relieved.

He wrapped his horse's reins around a railing. "Your daughter said someone was bit by a belled snake."

Ellie-May nodded, her eyes dark beneath her

furrowed forehead. "Yes, my farmhand. His name is Anvil."

"How's he doing?"

She shook her head. "Not good."

The doctor drove up a moment later. He grabbed his black leather bag from the buggy floor and joined them. Dressed in black trousers and frock coat, a felt hat riding upon his wizened head, the doctor's presence seemed to have a calming effect on Ellie-May.

Greeting him with a look of relief, she motioned him to the barn. "Anvil's in there," she said.

Matt fell in line behind the doctor as Ellie-May led the way. The two children followed behind.

Matt took one look at the man named Anvil and shook his head. It sure did look as if Ellie-May's farmhand had been tossed by an angry bull. He was slumped over, his face gray and forehead damp with sweat. It didn't take much to see that Ellie-May had good reason to worry.

"Let's get him moved over there," Doc Avery said, indicating a straw-strewn pallet with a nod of his head.

Matt grabbed Anvil beneath the arms, and the doctor picked the man up by his feet. Together, they lifted him over to the pallet and laid him down flat. Matt reached for a saddle blanket. After rolling it up, he placed it under Anvil's head. He then moved away to give the doctor room to work.

Ellie-May stood motionless, her face pale and forehead creased with a worried frown. Matt sought her eyes and gave her what he hoped was a look of reassurance. Had her children not been clinging to her side, he might have been tempted to comfort her in his arms.

Instead, he reached for the piece of hay caught in her hair. A startled look crossed her face until he held the yellow stalk where she could see it.

"Thank you," she said, sounding breathless. Her hand flew to her hair where his hand had been.

"You okay?" he asked.

Dropping her hand, she moistened her lips and nodded.

Lionel stared up at Matt. "Is he a bad man, Mama?" he asked.

Arching an eyebrow, Matt locked Ellie-May in his gaze. He could hardly blame the boy for thinking such a thing. It wasn't that long ago that his mother had held him at gunpoint in this very barn.

"No, no. He's a Texas Ranger," Ellie-May said. Two spots of pink appeared on her cheeks, making Matt wonder if she'd recalled him holding her and wiping away her tears.

Kneeling by Anvil's side, the doctor pulled his monaural stethoscope out of his black bag and leaned over his patient. He checked Anvil's heart and lungs and examined the wound.

"Looks like a shallow bite," he announced.

"That's good," Matt said. A shallow bite meant less venom had been released. He'd hoped the news would relieve Ellie-May's mind, but the worried frown remained.

Doc Avery pulled back and slipped the stethoscope back into his bag. "Not much we can do right now 'cept make him comfortable."

"Will he be all right?" Ellie-May asked.

"We'll know better in a few hours." The doctor

glanced around. "Is there some place we can put him meanwhile?"

"He lives in the loft," Ellie-May said, pointing upward.

The doctor regarded the ladder with a dubious look before shaking his head. "I'm not about to carry him up there."

"He can use my bed," Lionel said. "I'll sleep with Alicia."

Alicia folded her arms across her middle. "You will not!"

"Hush, children," Ellie-May said. "We'll work it out later." She nodded. "Let's take him to the house."

With Matt doing most of the heavy lifting, he and the doctor managed to move Anvil from the barn, across the yard, and up the steps of the porch. Inside the house, Ellie-May led the way down a hall to a small but tidy room and turned down the covers on one of the two beds. She then stepped aside.

Matt and the doctor maneuvered Anvil's body onto the thin straw mattress.

After giving Ellie-May instructions for the man's care, the doctor prepared to leave. "I'll be back in the morning to check on him."

While Ellie-May showed the doctor to the door, Matt pulled off the man's boots. Lionel and Alicia stood a short distance away, watching quietly. The girl looked worried, but the boy assessed Matt through eyes that were as distrustful as they were curious.

Matt freed the man from his overalls. It was necessary to cut the canvas fabric with his knife so as not to disturb the wound. By the time Ellie-May returned with a basin of water, Matt had managed to strip Anvil down to his long johns.

He took the sponge from her. "Let me," he said.

Without knowing the full extent of Anvil's condition, he gave her an encouraging smile—anything to wipe the worried look off her face. His efforts paid off as the furrows melted from her forehead and the corners of her pretty pink mouth turned upward.

Pulling his gaze away from her, he dipped the sponge into the basin and squeezed out the excess water. He then set to work sponging Anvil's damp face and arms. The man felt hot, as if on fire. While he worked, Ellie-May sent the children out of the room and opened the window.

The sun was about to set, and the curtains billowed in the cool, light breeze. After dabbing Anvil's face and neck, Matt tossed the sponge into the basin.

Ellie-May moved to Anvil's side. She pressed her hand gently against her farmhand's rough cheek and brushed a strand of gray hair from his forehead. Watching her, Matt couldn't help but wonder what that same small hand would feel like on his own forehead, his own flesh.

"He feels a little cooler," she said. The eyes lifting to his begged for Matt to agree. He nodded, and her gaze softened. "Thank you," she whispered.

"I didn't do that much," Matt said.

"You did more than you know." She moved away from the bed with a sigh. "I don't know what I'd do if he…" She shuddered. "I couldn't have gotten through this past year without him. He's not just my farmhand; he's a very good friend."

"I'm sure he feels the same about you." Matt's gaze drifted to her lips, which looked just as tempting today as the other morning in his hotel room. Clamping down on his wayward thoughts, he tossed a nod at the door. "I reckon I'll let you attend to your family."

"Please." Hesitating, she reached for a strand of yellow hair that had escaped from her bun and wrapped it around her ear. "Won't...won't you stay for supper?"

The invitation surprised him. "Well, I...don't want to cause you any more trouble than you already have." He felt bad that she now had a patient to take care of, along with her other duties.

"No trouble," she said. "I can't offer you anything fancy. Just beef stew."

Now that she mentioned it, his stomach was growling. If the tantalizing smell that could only be coming from the kitchen was a clue, he'd be crazy to turn down her offer.

"If you're sure it's no bother," he said with a grin.

Ellie-May smiled back, and his heart did a funny little flutter. It was the first real smile he'd seen on her since arriving at the farm.

"It's no bother," she said. "Besides, I owe you for breakfast at the Feedbag Café." She called to her daughter. "Alicia, set another place at the table." After checking on Anvil once again, she led the way out of the room.

Following her to the kitchen, Matt ignored the niggling voice inside that cautioned him to leave before he got any more involved with Ellie-May and her family.

16

The house was small and sparsely furnished but had a warm, homey feeling that filled Matt with an unfamiliar longing. Gingham curtains fluttered from the open kitchen windows, and the table was set with a white linen cloth and vase of fresh flowers.

The savory smell rising from the cast-iron Dutch oven made his mouth water in anticipation. He tried to remember when he'd last had a home-cooked meal and couldn't. The hasty meals cooked over campfires by saddle-worn Rangers hardly qualified as edible, let alone home-cooked.

He'd not considered himself a family man, had never thought to settle down. But the domestic scene appealed to his senses, and he found himself relaxing for the first time in a long while. Of course, it helped that he didn't have Jesse to worry about. The boy was scheduled to work tonight, and that was a blessing. The truth was, caring for the boy and seeing that he got proper rest and plenty to eat had already taken up too much of Matt's time.

Ellie-May's voice cut into his thoughts. "Alicia, show Mr. Taggert where he can wash up."

Alicia led him out the back door to the rain barrel at the side of the house. The girl chatted the entire time, jumping from subject to subject with hardly a breath in between. In the span of only a few minutes, she had filled Matt in on all the details of her young life, which seemed to be made up primarily of school and chores.

Her brother remained silent. Instead, he watched Matt like a cat watched a mouse.

Matt tossed a nod at the homemade fishing pole leaning against the side of the house. "You like to fish?" he asked the boy.

The corners of Lionel's mouth tilted in a shadow of a smile, but before he had a chance to answer, Alicia spoke for him. "That's all he wants to do is fish," she said with a look of pained tolerance.

Encouraged by the boy's smile, however faint, Matt asked, "Catch any?"

Lionel shook his head with his usual seriousness. "Alicia makes too much noise and scares the fish away."

"I do not," Alicia said with an indignant toss of her head. "Anvil said fish can only hear sounds that are underwater."

"That's not true," Lionel said stubbornly.

Brother and sister were still debating the subject when the three of them returned to the house, which brought a frown to their mother's face.

"Are you two still arguing about fish?" she asked.

"I'm afraid I'm to blame," Matt said. "I didn't know I was bringing up a touchy subject."

"Lionel takes fishing seriously," Ellie-May said and set four bowls of steaming stew on the table, along with a basket of freshly baked bread.

"Fishing *is* serious," Matt said.

"Do you fish?" Ellie-May asked.

"Every chance I get." Matt sought the boy's eyes. "When you're on the trail, sometimes a fish is the only thing between you and starvation." For once, Lionel had dropped his suspicious look and now regarded Matt with keen interest. "Did your pa teach you to fish?"

"No," Lionel said, his face scrunched in a frown.

Ellie-May regarded her son with raised eyebrows. "How can you say that, Lionel? Your pa took you fishing all the time."

"Yeah, but he didn't teach me to fish." Lionel turned to Matt to explain. "Once I caught this really big fish, but it got away." He folded his arms across his chest and looked as indignant as it was possible for a six-year-old to look. "I asked Papa to help but he wouldn't. He said I had to reel it in by myself."

"Your pa helped you more than you know," Matt said, surprised to find himself defending his suspect. But he could hardly let a child think poorly of his father. Happy memories of the past might be all Lionel would have to fall back on, should his father be proven guilty of a crime.

"He did?" Lionel asked, looking unconvinced.

Matt nodded. "He helped you by teaching you the magic of fishing."

Lionel frowned. "The magic?"

"That's right. Had your pa helped you bring it in,

the fish would have been this big." Matt held his hands six inches apart. "But between the time a fish takes the bait and gets away, it magically grows this big." He spread his hands as far apart as he could. "That gives you bragging rights."

Lionel's eyes grew wide. "You mean I can brag about the fish that got away?"

"You're not a fisherman unless you do," Matt said. "It's a rule."

Ellie-May rolled her eyes, but she looked pleased. "I'm afraid you might have created a monster," she whispered for Matt's ears only and handed Alicia an empty pitcher.

"Not a monster," Matt whispered back and laughed. "I created a real fisherman."

Alicia filled the pitcher from the water pump and placed it in the center of the table. She then took the seat opposite her brother.

Ellie-May sat at the head of the table, and Matt took the chair across from her. Her gaze traveled the length of the table to meet his. "Would you care to say the blessing?"

He glanced at the children on both sides of him and cleared his throat. Before his father died, they had always said a blessing before meals. But since leaving home, he'd fallen out of the habit. Fortunately, he recalled the words to his father's simple grace.

"Our Heavenly Father, we thank thee for this food we're about to receive…"

No sooner had he said "amen" than Lionel dug into his bowl. He seemed oblivious to his sister's glaring looks.

"You're supposed to wait for the guest to start eating first," Alicia scolded.

"I'm here as a friend, not a guest," Matt said, catching Ellie-May's eye. It wasn't often that he got to enjoy such warm hospitality, and he meant to make the most of it. Tomorrow would be soon enough to get back to work and recall all the reasons why Ellie-May Blackwell was off-limits.

He couldn't tell for certain what she was thinking, but he hoped the slightly upturned mouth meant she regarded him as a friend and not an enemy, at least for tonight.

Savoring the appetizing smell, he dove into his meal. The stew tasted every bit as good as expected. Unfortunately, his pleasure didn't come without guilt. Jesse would probably miss out on a decent meal tonight.

"Delicious," he said, and his praise brought a pretty flush to Ellie-May's cheeks.

Lowering her eyes, she moistened her lips before turning to her daughter. "Why aren't you eating, Alicia?"

Alicia folded her arms across her chest. "I don't want Lioney sharing my bed," she said. "He kicks his feet and talks in his sleep."

Ellie-May gave her daughter a stern look. "We have a guest," she said and immediately corrected herself. "*Friend*. And I'm sure he doesn't want to hear our family squabbles."

"Don't mind me," Matt said, wiping his bowl clean with a piece of bread. "I had a brother who used to talk in his sleep, too." Thinking about Charley brought a stab to his heart. As if guessing his thoughts, Ellie-May regarded him with a look of sympathy before turning to her daughter.

"Alicia, why don't you sleep with me?" she said. "I promise not to kick or talk in my sleep."

The solution put an end to the discussion, and Ellie-May quickly changed the subject. "Mr. Taggert is the man who gave you the music box, Alicia."

Alicia turned her head to stare at him, her eyes rounded. "How did you know that's what I wanted for my birthday?" she asked.

"A little birdie told me," Matt replied.

"Was it a parrot?" Lionel asked.

Ellie-May gave her son a loving smile. "It's just an expression," she explained before addressing her daughter. "What do you say to Mr. Taggert?" she prompted.

"Thank you," Alicia said. "I really, really like it."

A look of exasperation fleeted across Lionel's face. "She plays it all the time," he complained.

Matt drew his napkin to his mouth and winked at the boy as if to commiserate.

"I'm sorry I can't offer you dessert," Ellie-May said. "I planned on making a pie but ran out of time."

Matt held up his hand. "Not to worry. I couldn't eat another bite."

Ellie-May glanced at her children in turn. "You are excused," she said.

Rising, Lionel and Alicia gathered up their dirty dishes and carried them to the sink.

"How big was the fish that got away?" Matt called to the boy.

Lionel's broad smile lit up the whole room. "This big," he said and spread his arms wide.

Ellie-May waited for the children to leave the room before speaking. "You're very good with them," she said.

Matt shrugged. "I've always had a fondness for young'uns."

She hesitated a moment before asking, "Your brother—?"

"Still on the lam," Matt said.

"I'm sorry."

He nodded. "Yeah, so am I."

She moistened her lips. "I apologize for my daughter's behavior," she said. "When Alicia is anxious, she tends to take it out on those around her."

"I hope she's not anxious because of me."

Ellie-May shook her head. "No. She's just worried about Anvil. Both children are very fond of him. He's been a blessing."

"Sounds like you're lucky to have him."

"I am," Ellie-May said, rising from her chair. "Would you care for some coffee?"

"Thank you, if it's not too much trouble."

"No trouble," she said and walked to the stove. Returning to the table with the coffeepot, she hesitated. "Alicia said she met you on the road." It was a question as much as a statement.

"Yes, I was on the way to the Rocking M Ranch."

"Oh?"

He waited until she filled his cup before explaining. "I'm looking for a man named Roberts. I heard that a man matching his description might work there. Do you know him?"

"Not really…" She set the coffeepot on a trivet and sat. She hesitated as if trying to decide how little or how much to say. "A Mr. Roberts arrived on my doorstep claiming to be a friend of my husband's," she said.

"Claiming?"

"Neal never mentioned his name. I had no knowledge of him until he showed up on my doorstep, offering his condolences and services."

"What kind of services?"

"He offered to repair the…roof and other things. He said it was his way of honoring his friend's memory. I told him I couldn't pay him, but he insisted upon doing the work for free."

"And did he?"

"No, Anvil didn't trust him and told him not to come back."

Matt sipped his coffee as he mulled over this new information. Recalling Roberts's shifty eyes, Matt didn't blame her farmhand for not trusting him.

Ellie-May had no way of knowing it, but she had just confirmed what Jesse had told him. Roberts and Neal Blackwell had a connection of some sort. Were they in cahoots? Even if they had been, that didn't explain why Roberts had come back and offered to work at the farm for free. Unless…

Matt sucked in his breath. Unless Roberts knew that the stolen money was hidden on the farm somewhere. If that were true, did Ellie-May know where it was? She sure in blazes was holding something back. He felt it in his gut. There had to be a reason why she was so guarded whenever he made mention of the stage robbery or her late husband.

"Can I get you anything else?" she asked. "More coffee?"

"No, thank you. I best get a move on." The longer he was in her company, the less objective he became. That was not good. A Texas Ranger couldn't afford to let his emotions get in the way of doing his job. Matt had allowed that to happen once with his brother, and he had no intention of making the same mistake twice.

He rose, surprised at how unwilling he was to leave the warm comfort of her home. "That was the best meal I've had in a month of Sundays, and I'm much obliged."

This time, Ellie-May smiled without reservation, and he couldn't recall seeing a prettier sight. It suddenly became necessary to make a quick exit.

Two disturbing thoughts accompanied him as he rode back to town. One concerned Roberts and his reason for volunteering to work on the Blackwell farm. The other thought was more personal, more worrisome, and involved haunting blue eyes and a dazzling warm smile.

17

THE FOLLOWING MORNING, MRS. BUTTONWOOD arrived on Ellie-May's doorstep minutes after Doc Avery had left. As usual, she was dressed in a pair of overalls, a man's shirt, and a floppy felt hat.

"Heard about Anvil," she said. It was obvious by the basket slung over her arm that she intended to take over his care. The basket held enough jars and vials to fill a druggist's shelves.

Sighing, Ellie-May stepped aside. She hoped Anvil would forgive her, but she welcomed the extra help. Taking care of Anvil along with all her other duties had already worn her to a frazzle.

So far, Anvil had survived the snakebite, but whether he would survive Mrs. Buttonwood's good intentions was another matter. The woman meant well, but she could be overbearing at times and wouldn't take no for an answer.

"I'll show you to his room," Ellie-May said.

Anvil was sitting up in bed when they walked in. That morning, the doctor had applied a poultice to the snake wound, and Anvil's lower leg was covered with white gauze.

His fever had broken but he was still weak. Judging by the horrified look on his face at the sight of Mrs. Buttonwood, he had recovered enough to know his troubles were far from over.

"I brought you some special salves," Mrs. Buttonwood said and set her basket on the floor next to his bed. "They're old family remedies and will extract the poisons from your body."

Ellie-May cast an apologetic look at Anvil and left the two alone before he could object. She returned to the kitchen where Lionel waited for her at the kitchen table. His schoolbook yawned open in front of him, and his beloved fishing pole was propped against an empty chair.

Unlike Alicia, who seemed to absorb knowledge like a sponge, Lionel struggled with schoolwork.

With her own limited education, Ellie-May had trouble helping him with history and grammar, but she was fairly good at arithmetic. Unfortunately, Lionel didn't take after her in that regard.

She sat at the table and watched him laboriously add the numbers of a problem and write down the answer.

"That's the way, Lionel. Now do the next one."

Anvil yelled out from the back bedroom, and Lionel looked up, his eyes rounded. "Is he okay?"

"I'm sure he is." Ellie-May sighed. "But I better go and check."

She hurried down the hall to the children's room and peered through the doorway. Anvil was yelling and kicking his feet, his bedcovers on the floor. Bent over him, Mrs. Buttonwood ignored his protests as she rubbed foul-smelling liniment on his bare chest.

Ellie-May had no idea what was in the ointment, but it sure did smell like ammonia and it stank up the room.

"That burns!" Anvil yelled, thrashing around.

"It's supposed to burn," Mrs. Buttonwood yelled back. "Now keep still!"

The yelling and screaming continued for a good half hour before silence prevailed. The sudden quiet was just as worrisome.

The next time Ellie-May checked on Anvil, it was to make certain he was still breathing.

"She's trying to kill me," he complained the moment Ellie-May entered the room.

Looking undaunted, Mrs. Buttonwood appeared about to attack him with another homemade concoction. "Trust me, it's for your own good."

The yelling and screaming that followed could probably be heard clear to the next state.

∽

Matt rode out to the McKnight Ranch that morning, hoping to track down Roberts. From what he'd heard, the Rocking M Ranch was the largest privately owned ranch in the county, and now that he saw it with his own eyes, he believed it.

The foreman went by the name of Boomer, probably because of his loud voice. Even when he was talking normally, he sounded like he was shouting through a speaking trumpet.

"Don't know a Roberts," he said in answer to Matt's question. "'Course that don't mean nothing.

No one 'round here goes by his real name. What does he look like?"

Matt described him the best he could.

Boomer rubbed his chin. "That sure does sound like the man we call Hobbs."

"Hobbs?"

"Yeah, we call him that on account of his leg," Boomer said.

Matt frowned. "What's wrong with his leg?"

"He hobbles."

Someone rang the triangle chow bell in front of the bunkhouse. Boomer tossed a nod at one of the men walking toward them. "Here comes Hobbs now," he said.

Even from the distance, Matt recognized Roberts, and it was easy to see that he favored his right leg.

"Hey, Hobbs," Boomer yelled. "Someone here to see you." Following his announcement, Boomer walked away.

Roberts didn't look happy to see Matt. He was dusty and sweaty, as if he'd been riding hard. "Oh, it's you again." He cupped his hands and dipped them into the trough on the side of the building.

"What's wrong with your leg?" Matt asked.

"Nothing that you need be concerned about," Roberts said. He splashed water all over his heated face, washing off the dust but not the scowl. "What do you want?"

"Our talk got rudely interrupted the other night," Matt said.

Roberts eyed him warily. "So?"

"So I don't like to leave things hanging."

Roberts yanked a dingy towel off a rusty hook. "Well then, say what you came to say and be done with it." He wiped his face dry. "I'm a busy man."

"The other night, you said you knew Blackwell."

Roberts frowned. "Yeah, so?" He slung the wet towel back on the hook. "What of it?"

"How well did you know him?"

"Well enough, I guess. Hadn't seen him for a while. I spent some time in Alaska. Didn't know he'd bit the dust till I came back."

"Alaska, huh?" Matt hung his thumbs from his vest pockets. "Heard that's beautiful country."

"Yeah, if you like dark, cold winters. I swear I went three months at a time without seein' the light of day."

"How long were you there?"

Roberts shrugged. "Dunno. Two, three years. Why?"

"What if I told you that someone claims to have seen you and Blackwell together just before he died? That would be a year ago."

Roberts eyes narrowed. "I'd say whoever told you that is lyin' through his teeth."

"Why would anyone lie about something like that?" Matt asked.

"How should I know?" Roberts scratched his bristly chin. "Maybe someone has it in for Blackwell. Maybe they don't like him being treated like a hero."

"Any reason he shouldn't be?" Matt asked. "Be treated like a hero, I mean?"

Roberts's eyes glittered with hostility. "You know what they say? Martyrs and outlaws are greatly improved by death."

Matt considered this a moment before asking, "So which was he? A martyr or outlaw?"

Roberts shrugged and tugged the brim of his hat. "Like I said, hadn't seen him in a couple of years. When I knew him, he was just a regular guy." He walked away without so much as a goodbye, his limp looking more pronounced from the back.

Until Matt saw Roberts walk, he hadn't given much credence to the guard's claim of having shot the stage robber. A well-placed bullet might cause such a limp. The problem was how to prove it. Roberts sure as heck wasn't talking.

Ellie-May worked the laundry plunger up and down until her arms ached. Though the back porch offered protection from the noontime sun, it was hot as Hades. It was a good day for drying clothes but not for the work involved in washing them.

Her wash load had nearly tripled in the last couple of days. Anvil had run a fever off and on, which made it necessary to change his bedding at least once a day and sometimes even twice.

Stopping to brush her damp brow with the back of her hand, she thought she heard laughter. Was that Lionel? It sure did sound like him. She couldn't remember the last time she'd heard him laugh so freely. Certainly not since his pa had died.

Curious, she set the plunger down. Stepping off the porch, she scanned the yard and heard more laughter. It appeared to be coming from behind the barn. Now what was Lionel doing that brought him such pleasure?

She crossed to the side of the barn.

Much to her surprise, they had a visitor, and it was none other than Matt Taggert. The mere sight of him made her heart do a funny flip-flop.

He was teaching Lionel how to cast a fishing pole. Even from a distance, she could see that Lionel was holding a real store-bought pole, not his homemade stick-and-string one.

She pushed the hair that had escaped her bun behind her ear and smoothed down her apron. Bracing herself with a quick breath, she joined them.

Lionel greeted her with an ear-to-ear smile that did her heart good. "Look, Ma! Look what Mr. Taggert gave me. It's a real fishing pole with a winder wheel and everything."

"Yes, so I see," she said and turned questioning eyes on Matt.

Matt met her gaze with a shrug. "I was in the area and thought I'd check on the patient. I also wanted to deliver that pole. Thought Lionel could put it to good use."

Once again, she was reminded what a handsome man he was. It wasn't just his finely chiseled features or arresting brown eyes that she found so appealing. His proud bearing made him seem even taller than his actual six-foot height. Then there was that devastating smile…

"Watch me," Lionel called.

Pulling her gaze away from Matt, she watched her son draw his rod back and release the button on the reel. The line shot out in a wide arc and fell to the ground a distance away.

Ellie-May clapped her hands, and Matt nodded approval.

"Good job," he said. "Just be sure to check behind you before you cast off. You don't want to snag anyone or get tangled up a tree."

"Oh yeah, I forgot." Lionel reeled in his line. "Mama, can I go to the pond and try it out? Maybe I'll catch something for supper."

"That would be mighty good." Ellie-May bent to gather Lionel's shoes. "Put these on," she said. "One snakebite is enough."

Matt waited for Lionel to put on his shoes before handing him a bucket. "Don't forget your bait."

Ellie-May gave her son a meaningful look. "What do you say to Mr. Taggert?"

Balancing fishing pole and pail in his hands, Lionel stared up at Matt. "Thank you."

"You're welcome," Matt said.

Lionel's gaze remained on Matt's face. "If you marry my ma, you can be my pa," he said.

Ellie-May practically choked. "Lionel! You mustn't say things like that!" She turned to Matt with flaming face. "I'm sorry," she stammered. "I don't know what Lionel is thinking."

Lionel frowned. "I'm thinking he would make a good pa."

"Well now," Matt said, looking somewhat befuddled. "That's the nicest thing anyone ever said to me." He reached out to straighten Lionel's hat. "What do you say that for now we just remain friends and fishing partners?"

Seemingly satisfied with Matt's response, Lionel nodded and took off in the direction of the pond.

Ellie-May drew in her breath and fanned her heated face with a wave of her hand. Matt's kindness to Lionel struck a chord deep in her heart, and she felt herself drawn to him in a new and worrisome way.

A moment of silence followed Lionel's departure before Ellie-May spoke. "You'd make 'a good pa' is the nicest thing anyone ever said to you?"

Matt flailed his hands with a sheepish smile. "What can I say? The people I arrest aren't generally inclined to hand out compliments." He chuckled. "Far as I know, none of them ever wanted me to be their pa."

Ellie-May laughed and then grew serious. "I… apologize for my son," she said and, by way of explanation, added, "Lionel misses his pa something fierce."

"No need to apologize. Lionel is a fine boy. You should be proud of both of your children."

"I am," she said. "But…" She cleared her throat. "We…we can't keep accepting gifts from you. First the music box. Now the fishing pole."

"Consider the fishing pole my way of thanking you for your hospitality the other night. That was the best meal I've had in a very long time."

Since he made it sound like his generous gift was his way of repaying a favor, she let the matter drop. "Could I offer you some refreshment?" she asked.

"Much obliged, but I can't stay," he said, and she wondered if she only imagined the note of disappointment in his voice. His gaze held hers for a moment before he tossed a nod in the direction of the house. "How's the patient doing?"

"I think he's better than he lets on."

Matt quirked an eyebrow. "Oh?"

"One of my neighbors has been helping out. Anvil pretends otherwise, but I do believe he likes all the attention."

"Can't say I blame him there." They stared at each other for a moment, and it was as if the world stood still. As if catching himself gaping, Matt cleared his throat. "I better get a move on. I told Jesse to meet me at the Feedbag Café."

Ellie-May tilted her head. "Sounds like you and Jesse spend a lot of time together."

"I guess in some ways, Jesse reminds me of myself when I was that age. Though I'm pretty sure I didn't eat as much as he does."

Laughing, she tried to visualize Matt as a skinny, awkward kid and couldn't.

Adjusting the brim of his hat against the sun, he let his gaze linger on her for a moment longer before he made a motion to leave. "Give your farmhand my best."

She nodded. "Will do." Turning, he walked to his tethered horse, and she called after him. "Thank you for the fishing pole. You made my son very happy."

He acknowledged her with a raised hand. "It was my pleasure."

She watched him ride away with conflicting emotions. The man was trouble, no question. He'd made it clear on several occasions that nothing would keep him from pursuing and catching his man.

Still, even knowing the damage he could do to her and her children, she was drawn to him in a way she couldn't explain. Perhaps it was his kindness to Jesse that appealed to her, or his concern for Anvil. Nor could she forget his generous gifts, first to Alicia and now Lionel. Then there was the empathy he'd shown when she'd told him about her father.

Whatever it was, it was hard not to like him. It was harder still to keep her wits about her whenever he was around, and that was a worry. A very big worry.

18

THE FIRST THING MATT DID THE FOLLOWING MORNING upon leaving the hotel was head for the sheriff's office. Last night, after sending Jesse home, he had been given a note by the hotel desk clerk stating that Sheriff Keeler had wanted to see him.

Stifling a yawn, Matt decided to walk rather than ride. He needed to clear his head. He'd not slept well. For some reason, Lionel's words kept him twisting and turning until the wee hours of the morning.

I'm thinking he would make a good pa.

A good pa.

Matt drew in his breath. He'd always liked children but wasn't ready to be a father. Not yet. Maybe one day. Right now, he had things to do. Criminals to catch. His brother to track down. So why Lionel's words had affected him so, he couldn't say. All he knew was the sooner he tied up his business in Haywire and left town, the better.

Matt found Sheriff Keeler seated in his office behind his weathered desk. "You wanted to see me?"

Keeler stuck his pen in the penholder and sat back

in his chair. "Thought you'd be interested in knowing that we had a break in the stagecoach robbery."

"Oh?"

The sheriff tossed a Wanted poster across his desk, and Matt picked it up. The name on the poster was James Stanford, but he recognized the likeness as someone else. "Roberts?" he said. "He's wanted for robbery in Kansas?"

"Was." The sheriff indicated the jail cells upstairs with a glance at the ceiling. "He's now behind bars."

"How do you know he's your man?"

"I had a visit two days ago from a Pinkerton detective," Keeler said. "He'd tracked Roberts all the way from Montana where he'd pulled the same stunt."

"You mean, he held up stages in Montana, too?"

"Yep. But guess what? When I arrested him, he thought I was arresting him for the stage robbery here. Said he didn't mean to do it and spilled the beans. How lucky is that?"

Matt frowned. "Did he say what he did with the stolen loot?"

"Nope. Soon as he realized what he'd done, he clammed up. Couldn't get 'nother word outta him."

"So you don't know if he worked alone or had a partner?"

The sheriff raised a questioning brow. "None of the witnesses saw a second man. If you can't trust a state senator as a witness to a crime, who can you trust? I think that pretty much answers your question."

Matt wished it were that simple, but there were still too many loose ends for his peace of mind. One of them being the conversation Jesse claimed to have overheard between Roberts and Blackwell.

"I need to talk to him."

"You'll be wasting your time. Far as I'm concerned, we got our man and the case is closed. The rest is up to the judge."

"It'll be hard to prove his guilt without the stolen money," Matt said. "Roberts could be the only way we'll find it."

The sheriff made a face. "Like I said, you're wasting your time. The money's probably long gone."

Matt had reason to believe otherwise. He doubted Roberts offered to help work on the Blackwell farm out of the goodness of his heart. He had to have been looking for something. If Matt was a betting man, he'd wager that something was the loot stolen from the stage.

"If it's all the same to you, I'll waste my time the way I see fit." With that, Matt turned and stumped up the stairs to the jail cells.

Reaching the second floor, he scanned all three cells, but today only the middle cell was occupied. "We meet again," he said.

Roberts sat on his cot with a blank stare and said nothing.

"Guess you got yourself in a heap o' trouble," Matt said. "Robbing stages is serious business."

Roberts's upper lip curled, but he remained silent.

"The penalty is pretty steep," Matt continued and made a motion across his neck to indicate just how steep, though Roberts's chances of being hung were slim. Most robbers nowadays got prison terms. All it took was a lenient judge or a halfway-decent defense lawyer. "If I were in your shoes, I'd do everything I could to gain leniency."

This time, he had Roberts's attention. "Like what?"

"You can start by telling us what you did with the loot you stole from the Haywire stage robbery."

"Don't know nothin' 'bout no Haywire robbery."

"Then why did you confess?"

"I got confused is all," Roberts said. "I admit to robbin' that stage in Montana, but that's before I got myself religion and became a changed man."

"I have a witness who said he overheard you talking to Blackwell about the stolen loot."

Roberts studied Matt with glittering eyes. "And like I told you, your witness is lying through his teeth!"

"Are you saying that you and Blackwell were never in cahoots?"

"I work alone," Roberts said, a note of pride in his voice. "Always have. Always will."

"Then I'm sure it won't pose any great hardship when you hang alone."

Roberts clamped down on his jaw and refused to say another word.

❧

Ellie-May dreaded having to attend the dedication of the new school, but if she failed to show, tongues were bound to wag.

She reached for her cloth bonnet and changed her mind. Today, only her Sunday-go-to-meeting hat would do.

She lifted the straw hat off the hat stand and carefully arranged it on her head. The feathers tipped sideways, and the ribbon was frayed. No question the hat had seen better days, but wearing it still made her feel like a lady and more self-assured. Today, she needed all the confidence she could muster.

She stepped back from the mirror for a full-body view. After examining herself with a critical eye, she sighed and reached in her glove box for the pair of white kid gloves saved for special occasions. At least her red callused hands would be hidden from public view.

"Come along, children," Ellie-May called. "We don't want to be late."

She waited for Lionel and Alicia to join her before marshaling them outside and helping them onto the narrow buckboard seat.

Alicia looked especially pretty in her blue dress. People often commented on how much Alicia looked like her, but Ellie-May couldn't see the likeness, except in the color of hair and eyes. It was much easier to see Neal in her son. They were alike in so many ways and not just in looks. They both had quiet, reserved personalities. Neal would hate all the fuss the town was making over him.

Seated in the driver's seat, Anvil greeted her with a toothy smile. "Morning, Miss Ellie-May," he said.

"Good morning," she said and took her seat next to her children.

Anvil had lost a lot of weight in recent days but had otherwise fully recovered from the snakebite. His skin was still red from Mrs. Buttonwood's treatments, and he looked like he'd been in the sun too long. It seemed that the so-called cure was worse than the poison.

Anvil gathered the reins in hand. "Ready?"

Ellie-May smoothed down her skirt and hoped no one noticed how faded it was. How frayed. "Ready."

Anvil clicked his tongue, and Jingles moved forward with a flick of her tail, churning up dust with each languid step.

Guiding the buckboard along the bumpy road, Anvil glanced over the heads of the two children. "You okay?" he asked when they were halfway to town.

Ellie-May straightened her daughter's bonnet and retied the ribbon beneath her chin. "Yes. Why do you ask?"

"You've not said a word since leaving the house."

"I'm just a little...nervous, I guess."

"You have no call to be nervous. This is a proud day for the family." Anvil tugged on his felt hat and addressed his next comments to the children. "Your pa was a fine man. Never met anyone quite like him."

Ellie-May took a deep breath, which made her regret wearing her whalebone corset. As much as she appreciated Anvil's kind words, the bag of money beneath the porch continued to haunt her. It was worse than a thorn at her side, and no matter how hard she tried, she couldn't put it out of her mind.

"Don't know if you've heard," Anvil said. "But it turns out I was right to be suspicious of that Roberts fellow."

"Oh?"

"Yep. Turns out he was a wanted man."

Ellie-May frowned. "Really? What was he wanted for?"

"Stage robbery."

Gasping, she stared at Anvil. "The Haywire stage robbery?"

"That's what I heard."

Ellie-May shook her head in disbelief. She'd always felt there was something strange about the man, but it had never occurred to her he was an outlaw. Chewing on a nail, she considered this new information with increasing alarm. Did that mean Neal had worked with someone else? That his partner was Roberts?

"W-why do you suppose he acted like he was Neal's friend?" she asked.

Anvil shrugged. "Who knows? Maybe he thought a friend of Neal's would not be considered a suspect."

Ellie-May knotted her gloved hands on her lap. It was a comforting thought but didn't feel right. The only way the sack of stolen money could have ended up under her porch was if Neal had put it there. Now that Roberts had been arrested, there was no telling what he would say or what lies he might tell to save his own skin.

Feeling herself begin to panic, she tried pushing her dark thoughts aside. Pushing away a boulder would have been easier, but it was either that or drive herself crazy with worry. For the children's sake, she needed to keep her wits about her. At least until after today's dedication.

It took longer than usual to reach the new school because of the traffic. The number of vehicles vying for a place to park made her mouth run dry. A large group of people never failed to remind her of the crowd that had gathered at her father's hanging.

Anvil drove past the new schoolhouse and pulled the horse and wagon onto an unfenced field where others had parked. He drew up behind a buggy and set the brake. "Here we are," he said.

Ellie-May's stomach churned from nerves. Determined to make this a day Alicia and Lionel would always remember, she lifted her chin and forced a smile. "Come along, children."

Moments later, the four of them joined the crowd gathered in front of the school. Ellie-May waved at Claudia Peterson, who juggled two small children in her arms and had two more tugging at her skirt.

Ellie-May could barely bring herself to look at the sign reading NEAL BLACKWELL GRAMMAR SCHOOL. Still, the building was impressive.

The original one-room schoolhouse had been replaced by a building with two classrooms. Children six to twelve years of age would occupy one room. The second room would be for older children. Two classrooms meant that the school would now require two teachers.

As usual, Mayor Wrightwood stood behind a podium ready to speak. Ellie-May hoped the mayor kept his remarks short, for the school grounds provided little shade and it was already hot. Next to him stood the teacher everyone called Miss Holly.

Ellie-May decided that the fashionably dressed woman standing next to her must be the new teacher. Her face was as round as a powder puff, and her stylish frock marked her as an Easterner. The stuffed bird occupying her three-story hat brought curious stares from children anxious to get a look at their new teacher.

Glancing down at her own plain homespun dress, Ellie-May pulled off a glove and fanned her heated face with it. How long before the new teacher learned the folly of such fashion and took to dressing more sensibly?

She'd failed to notice that Lionel had wandered off until a man's angry voice suddenly rose above the murmurs of the crowd. All eyes turned to a man holding Lionel by the shoulders and shaking him like a housewife shaking a dusty rug.

"You little brat. You're just like your outlaw mother!"

Ellie-May recognized the man as Hal Spencer, who'd once owned a farm not far from hers.

The man set Lionel down. Holding on to Lionel with one hand, Spencer raised his other hand as if to slap him. Jaw dropping, Ellie-May hiked up her skirt and charged toward him like an angry bull.

"Oh no, you don't!" she gasped.

With a swing of her arm, she clobbered Spencer over the head with her purse. He released Lionel, but she kept pounding on him. Yelling for her to stop, he held his hands to his head to ward off the blows. Someone in the crowd laughed at the unlikely sight of a pint-sized woman getting the best of a burly man like Spencer.

That only made matters worse. Spencer's face grew red with rage, and ugly blue veins stuck out from his neck. He grabbed her swinging purse and yanked her toward him with such force, Ellie-May almost lost her footing.

His vile breath in her face, he yelled, "Why you little—"

Matt Taggert suddenly appeared at her side and grabbed Spencer by the throat. "Let her go!"

Cursing beneath his breath, Spencer released his hold on Ellie-May and quickly turned on Matt. But Matt was ready for him. He grabbed Spencer's swinging arm with one hand and punched him square in the jaw with the other, knocking him clear off his feet.

The crowd backed away with a collective gasp as Spencer's unwieldly form hit the ground, but Matt wasn't done. He reached down, grabbed the man by the collar, and jerked him upright.

"You owe the lady and her son an apology," Matt said, his voice dead serious.

With her arm around Lionel, Ellie-May's mouth dropped open. No one had ever before demanded an apology on her behalf. She was so shocked, so touched, by Matt's actions and words that, for a moment, all she could do was stare at him, speechless.

When Spencer failed to apologize, Matt released him and pounded a fist into his palm as a warning.

Spencer rubbed his bloodied jaw with the back of his hand. Eyes glittering, he mumbled something beneath his breath.

Matt frowned. "I don't think they heard that."

This time, Spencer spoke louder. "I said, the bratty kid kicked me in the shin. He's the one who should apologize."

Lionel made a fist as if he was ready to fight Spencer himself. "He said a mean thing about my ma," he said.

Ellie-May held him back, but she couldn't help but feel a glimmer of pride. Her young son had defended her, just as Matt had, and she felt overwhelmed with emotion.

Spencer scoffed. "All I said was a man who married an outlaw's daughter don't deserve no hero treatment." He scanned the crowd as if looking for others who shared his opinion. "Did you all forget what her pa did to this town?"

Matt gave the man a good shaking, his fist posed in a threatening way. "Mrs. Blackwell and her son are still waiting for that apology."

Shooting Matt visual daggers, Spencer turned beady eyes on Ellie-May. "Sorry," he said.

"That's more like it." Matt let him go, though he looked reluctant to do so.

Spencer staggered to his feet, wiped his chin with the back of his hand, and shuffled away.

Her arm still wrapped around her son's shoulders, Ellie-May drew him close. Reaching for her daughter's hand, she shepherded both children past the staring crowd. Head held high, she looked neither left nor right and ignored the whispered voices that trailed behind them.

Anvil chased after her, looking visibly upset. "Are you okay?" he asked.

"I'm fine," she said. "Would you please just take us home?"

He frowned. "Are you sure that's what you want?"

"Yes." The day had been ruined, and there was no

way to salvage it. She quickly marshaled the children off the school property and across the street to where their rig was parked. She was shaking so much, she feared her knees would cave beneath her. Had Matt not come to her rescue, she wasn't sure what would have happened.

While Anvil took his seat, she helped the children aboard and then climbed up after them. Anvil grabbed the reins and snapped them, his face set in a grim expression.

The mare took off with a snort, and the wagon bumped up and down until they reached the main road. The children held on to each other to keep from being thrown from the seat.

Somehow, Ellie-May had lost a kid glove, and she sighed in annoyance. Not only was it her best pair, the gloves had been a gift from Neal. Now, she used the single glove to fan her heated face.

Alicia was the first to break the tense silence. "How come that man said you were an outlaw's daughter?"

Gripping the reins tight in his hands, Anvil shot Ellie-May a worried look. "The man is plain loco and don't know what he's talkin' about."

"It's all right, Anvil," Ellie-May said. She'd always known the day would come that she'd have to tell her children about their outlaw grandfather. Of course, she'd hoped—foolishly as it turned out—that the time and place would be of her own choosing.

"My pa…wasn't a very nice person," she began, searching for words.

"Was he a bad man?" Lionel asked in his usual blunt style.

Ellie-May exchanged a glance with Anvil. As a child, she'd heatedly defended her father. *He didn't do the things they said he did*, she'd argued. *It was all a terrible mistake.* Eventually, she'd had to face the truth, but it had been a long and painful journey to acceptance.

"Yes," she said simply, hoping that would be answer enough. She wasn't ready to tell them the rest. That her father was a thief and murderer.

"What did he do?" Alicia asked.

Ellie-May sighed. She should have known that Alicia's curious mind would demand more than the vague answers she was prepared to give. "He...hurt people."

"Does that mean we're bad, too?" Lionel asked.

"Heavens, no!" Ellie-May squeezed her son's hand. "We can't be responsible for another's actions. We can only control our own. That's why I don't want you hitting people." She never thought to say such a thing to her son, but today she had seen a side of him she'd not known existed.

"But, Ma...he called you an outlaw."

"I know, Son. I know."

"And *you* hit him."

"That's because I didn't want him hurting you."

Lionel gazed up at her with eyes that looked too old for his young face. "I didn't want him saying bad things about you."

Ellie-May's heart melted in her chest like ice in the sun, and she could no longer bring herself to scold him. "I know, Son. I know."

"And Ranger Taggert didn't want him saying bad things about you, either," Alicia said.

Lionel grinned. "I told you he'd make a good pa. That's cuz he won't let anyone hurt us."

Anvil met Ellie-May's gaze with raised eyebrows. "I won't let anyone hurt you, either," he said.

Ellie-May cleared her throat. "That's because you're a good friend," she said, emphasizing the word *friend* for Lionel's sake. "Just as Mr. Taggert is a friend."

She never thought to call Matt anything but a threat to her family. Still, for good or bad, their paths kept crossing. The man had come to her rescue twice in less than two weeks. Three times, if she counted his help with the broken step, and each time, she'd felt their bond grow stronger. They also had something in common—they both knew what it was like to have an outlaw in the family—and that connection had made her feel less alone.

If that didn't complicate matters enough, there was also the kindness he'd shown to her children. To Jesse. To her.

Matt Taggert had scared her from the first moment she'd set eyes on him in her barn. He'd seemed so formidable, so strong, so utterly sure of himself. At the time, he'd made the shotgun in her hands seem less potent than a broomstick.

He still scared her. Not only for what he could do to her and her family but for what he was doing to her heart.

19

MATT AND JESSE CAUGHT A LATE MIDDAY MEAL AT THE
Feedbag Café following the school dedication. Jesse was
wound up tighter than a toy soldier, and his constant
babble drew disapproving looks from the other diners.

Eyes shining, he made a fist and punched the air
with a triumphant look. "Pow!"

Watching him, Matt tapped the table with his fingers. He'd hoped to impress Jesse with his investigative
skills, not his fists, but he could hardly blame the boy
for seeing no merit in such a dull and unproductive
pursuit. Nothing worse than following a cold trail.

Neal Blackwell had taken his secrets to the grave,
and apparently that was where they would stay, for
Roberts sure in blazes wasn't talking.

But it wasn't Neal or Roberts on Matt's mind, or
even the fella who had ruined the school dedication.
It was Ellie-May Blackwell. He felt bad for her. Bad
for her children. Today should have been a special day
for them. Instead, Ellie-May had been forced to leave
under unpleasant circumstances and had missed the
dedication altogether.

He only wished he'd been able to catch up to her before she'd left. Maybe he could have persuaded her to stay. But he'd lost her in the crowd, and by the time he realized she had left the premises, the dedication ceremony was over.

Drawing a napkin to his mouth, Matt tossed a nod at Jesse's plate. The boy was so busy fighting off an imaginary foe that he'd hardly touched his food.

"Eat up. Your food is getting cold." Where Jesse was concerned, those were words Matt had never expected to say.

Jesse reached for his fork and stabbed at a piece of meat. "Would you teach me how to fight like that? I want to be a good Ranger, just like you."

"You don't have to be a Ranger to do what's right." Matt toyed with the food on his own plate. For some reason, he didn't feel like eating. "That man was about to hurt Mrs. Blackwell. I'd have gone after him even if I wasn't a Ranger."

Jesse gave him a knowing smile. "Is that cuz you like her?"

"I don't like…" Matt cleared his throat. "Not the way you mean."

Not only would involvement with a suspect's widow be unprofessional, he had no desire to settle down. Least not until he'd settled his business with his brother and found justice for his father's death.

Ellie-May had once asked him how many outlaws he would have to capture before he considered the score settled. He didn't know. What he did know was that he couldn't stop. Not yet. Maybe never.

Still, he couldn't shake the vision of clear blue eyes

and a wide, dazzling smile that had once again sprung to mind unbidden. The same vision came to mind a dozen times a day at the least expected times. It had even followed him in his sleep.

Aware, suddenly, that Jesse was watching him with a funny look on his face, Matt shook his thoughts away.

"Doesn't matter who you are—Ranger or not," he said. "You don't let anyone hurt a woman or child. Call it a rule."

Jesse's mouth was full of food, so all he could do was nod, but the knowing look remained.

Swallowing his irritation, Matt reached into his pocket for his money clip to pay for their meal. Instead, he found the lady's glove that he'd found on the ground. The delicate scent of violets did nothing for his peace of mind.

He stuffed the glove back into his pocket. Drat the kid. He knew too much or thought he did. But Jesse was wrong. Matt's interest in Ellie-May Blackwell was purely professional—nothing more!

"Eat up," he said, his brusque voice forbidding further discussion.

Ellie-May had just finished putting the last of the supper dishes away when a knock sounded at the door.

"Now who could that be?" she wondered aloud. It would soon be dark, and visitors rarely strayed out this far so late in the day.

Anvil looked up from the table where he was

teaching Lionel to play chess. "Want me to get that?" he asked.

Ellie-May wiped her hands on her apron. "I'll get it."

Leaving Anvil and Lionel to their game, she rushed from the kitchen to the parlor and opened the door. Surprised to see Matt Taggert on her doorstep, his tall form outlined by the fast-setting sun, she felt her heart take a leap.

He greeted her with a crooked smile. "Hope it's not a bad time."

"N–not at all," she stammered. Hoping, praying, that this was just a social call and had nothing to do with his investigation, she glanced over her shoulder at her daughter on the sofa playing her music box. Not wanting to chance the children hearing something they shouldn't, Ellie-May stepped outside and closed the door behind her.

The sun had stained the sky a vivid red, and a cooling breeze swept over the land, but it did nothing to calm her heated face.

"Just wanted to make sure you're okay," he said.

Pushing a strand of hair behind her ear, she regarded Matt with a wary look. "Yes, we're fine," she said. "Th–thank you for coming to my rescue today."

His mouth twitched. "The way you were beating up on your assailant," he drawled, "I believe he was the one in need of rescuing."

Embarrassed, she lowered her gaze. Never before had she raised a hand to another. But seeing Lionel in danger made her see red, and she'd hardly known what she was doing.

"He didn't hurt your son, did he?" Matt asked.

She looked up at him, and the concern written on his face near took her breath away. "No, Lionel's fine. Both children are, but they had a lot of questions." She bit her lower lip. "I had to talk to them about their grandfather."

His smoldering brown eyes held hers, telling her how deeply he sympathized. "That must have been hard."

"I should have told them before, but I kept waiting for the right time." She shrugged. "I guess there is no such thing, is there? As the right time, I mean."

"That's been my experience," he said. "How did your children handle it?"

"As well as they could, I suppose. All they know for now is that their grandfather did bad things. I'm sure they'll find out the rest soon enough."

"It would be better coming from you," he said.

"I know." She moistened her lips, drawing his gaze to her mouth for an instant before he lifted his eyes to hers.

"I'm sorry you missed the school dedication," he said. "I looked for you."

"Leaving seemed like the best thing to do at the time," she said. "People were staring, and…it brought back too many unpleasant memories."

"From your childhood?" he asked.

She nodded. "Yes, from my childhood." The intensity of his look made her heart flutter, and it was suddenly necessary to remind herself who he was and how he could hurt her family. "I didn't expect to see you still in town. Now that the stage robber has been caught."

"Just tying up loose ends," he said vaguely.

She wasn't sure what he meant by that and wasn't about to ask. All she could do was hope and pray that none of those loose ends had anything to do with Neal.

His forehead creased. "The man who attacked you… He's not gonna give you any more trouble, is he?"

She thought for a moment before shaking her head. "I don't think so. His name is Hal Spencer, and his problems were with Neal, not me." After a pause, she went on to explain. "He was always in competition with Neal. When Hal lost his farm, he took to drinking. Neal tried to help him, but it only seemed to make matters worse."

"I guess your husband's heroic death was too much for him."

"It didn't help," she said. Regarding Matt with a questioning look, she asked, "So what brings you out here? Not Ranger business, I hope?"

Matt shook his head and reached into his pocket. "I came to give you this," he said and held up her white kid glove.

Her hand flew to her chest. "Oh." Their fingers touched as she took the glove from him. She quickly pulled away, but not soon enough to prevent the flare of her cheeks. "You came all the way out here to give me this?" she asked.

"And to see that you were okay," he said.

The concern in his eyes and tenderness of his voice made it hard for her to breathe, let alone think. Overcome with emotion, all she could do was gaze up at him, her heart pounding against her ribs.

"Th-thank you," she managed at last, her voice shakier than she would have liked. His questioning eyes made her lower her gaze. "The gloves were a gift from Neal," she said softly. "I never thought to see this again." She tucked the glove into her apron pocket for safekeeping.

"Glad I could be of service," he said.

He was about to say more, but the sound of a galloping horse stopped him. "Looks like you're about to have company," he said.

The horseman came into view, but the long shadows prevented her from identifying the rider until a voice rang out.

"Ranger Taggert, Ranger Taggert!"

Matt spun around. "Jesse? What's wrong?"

Before the boy could answer, his horse whinnied and reared back on its hind legs. The gelding frantically pawed the air before its front legs crashed down, hard.

Jesse was thrown from the saddle and hit the ground with a sickening thud.

20

MATT LEAPED OFF THE PORCH AND RAN. WITH A CRY of alarm, Ellie-May chased after him. By the time she reached the unconscious boy, Matt had already lifted him off the ground and was holding him in his arms.

"Bring him to the house," she said.

Anvil and the children had apparently heard something, as the three of them came rushing outside.

"I'll round up his horse," Anvil said as Matt brushed past him.

Inside the house, Ellie-May moved the music box and books off the sofa to make room for the boy. She then arranged a pillow for Jesse's head.

Matt laid Jesse on the sofa ever so gently, and Ellie-May covered him with a quilt.

Bending over the boy, Matt tapped him gently on the cheek. "Jesse! Wake up."

While Matt tried to get Jesse to respond, Ellie-May rushed into the kitchen and pumped water into a basin. Grabbing a clean sponge and towel, she quickly returned to the parlor.

Jesse was awake now but barely. He looked dazed

and his eyes appeared unfocused. His face was a ghastly white, and a nasty red bump was centered on his forehead.

Ellie-May set the bowl on the low table and dipped a corner of the towel into the cool water. Squeezing it out, she then took her place next to Matt. "Jesse, I just want to wash the dirt off your face," she said soothingly. "I promise not to hurt you."

When Jesse made no response, Matt took the boy's hand in his and held it tight. "Hold on, Ranger. You're gonna be fine." He sounded more positive than he looked.

Wishing she could think of something to say to erase Matt's worried frown, Ellie-May gently dabbed at Jesse's forehead, taking special care not to apply any pressure to his injury.

Standing at the end of the sofa, Alicia and Lionel watched with rounded eyes. "Is he gonna die?" Lionel asked, his voice as serious as his expression.

"He'll be fine," Ellie-May said, her confident tone belying her fears. She glanced up at Matt, hoping he would agree, but the lines of worry remained on his face.

When she finished sponging the dirt off Jesse's forehead, she drew back so that Matt could take her place. "Jesse, what's my name?" he asked.

When Jesse failed to answer, Matt tried again. "How old are you?" Matt asked several more questions, but each time received the same blank stare. Finally, he gave up.

His frown deepened, and Ellie-May laid her hand on his arm. He glanced at her hand for a second before covering it with his own. For several moments, they stood side by side, gazing at the boy like two anxious parents.

The front door flew open, and Anvil entered voice first. "I caught Jesse's horse, and he's now in the barn. He's been watered and grained."

Ellie-May drew her hand away. "Thank you, Anvil."

Anvil's gaze fell on Jesse. "Anything else I can do? Do you want me to fetch the doctor?"

She glanced up at Matt. "What do you think?"

Matt met her gaze. "If it'll make you feel better. But there's not much a doctor can do for head injuries. The important thing is to keep Jesse awake as much as possible."

Ellie-May chewed on a fingernail. "We'll let you know, Anvil."

Anvil nodded, and after he'd left, Ellie-May drew in her breath and said a silent prayer. It promised to be a long night. "I'll wake him every half hour," she said.

Matt shook his head. "That's not your responsibility. It's mine. I'll watch over him." He drew his eyebrows together. "That is if you don't mind me staying."

"No, not at all," she said, alarmed by the way her heart pounded at the prospect.

Alicia piped up. "I'll play my music box to keep him awake."

"That'll be a big help," Matt said.

Ellie-May smiled but said nothing. She wondered if Matt would feel that way after hearing the same tune for hours on end.

"Shouldn't we let his pa know where he is?" she asked.

Matt's jaw hardened. "Trust me. He won't even know his son is gone."

Ellie-May's gaze lit on Jesse's pale face, and her heart ached. Jesse had always tried to look and act so grown-up, but now he looked only young and vulnerable. How could his pa be so uncaring?

∞

A sliver of sunlight slanted through the opening in the curtains early that morning, stirring Matt awake. His body stiff from sitting upright in a chair all night, he stood, yawning, and stretched.

Alicia had been as good as her word and had sung to her music box until her mother had finally made her go to bed around midnight. The box now sat silent as a brick, but the tinny tune and Alicia's voice still ran through Matt's head.

All the pretty little horses...

Shaking away the persistent tune, he wondered if he only imagined the smell of freshly brewed coffee. He pulled his watch from his vest pocket and flipped the lid open. It was nearly 6:00 a.m. The last time he'd checked on Jesse had been thirty minutes ago.

Returning the watch to his pocket, he ran his fingers through his hair and rubbed his chin, prickly with day-old whiskers. He'd been so focused on Jesse the night before, he'd paid scant attention to the surroundings. Accustomed to sleeping in a tent or hotel, he was surprised by how much he enjoyed waking in a real home.

Next to his chair, a well-read Bible with a worn leather cover took up residence on a polished side table along with an equally dog-eared Webster's Dictionary. A needlepoint plaque reading "God Bless Our Home" hung over the front door. A carefully stitched sampler was nailed to one wall next to a knickknack shelf filled with a collection of porcelain cats. Crocheted doilies protected the arms and backs of sofa and chairs. The only untidy thing in the room was an overflowing wicker sewing basket next to the hearth.

A shaft of light glanced off the mantel, drawing Matt's gaze to the daguerreotype draped in black ribbon. Moving to the fireplace for a closer look, he willed the picture to reveal something about its subject. Instead, Neal Blackwell stared back as if challenging him to a duel.

He'd seen the same look on Neal's son, but one striking thing separated the two—a deep-rooted sadness inherent in Neal's face.

Sighing, Matt returned to the sofa. If there were answers to be found in that room, they were safely hidden beneath a layer of domesticity.

He leaned over the sleeping boy. "Wake up, son," he said softly and gave Jesse a gentle shake.

This time, Jesse's eyes flickered open without much encouragement. Sighing with relief, Matt dabbed Jesse's parched lips with a wet sponge. Slipping his arm under the boy's head, he lifted a glass of water to Jesse's mouth.

"Take a drink."

Jesse took a sip.

Matt set the glass down and lowered Jesse's head

back onto the pillow. "Do you know where you are?" he asked.

Jesse glanced around the room and gave a slight shake of the head. He was still pale, but today his eyes looked more focused.

"You're at Mrs. Blackwell's farm." Matt spoke slowly, enunciating each word clearly. "Do you know how you got here?"

Again, Jesse shook his head.

"You were thrown from a horse." Matt waited for that information to sink in before asking, "Do you remember why you wanted to see me?"

Jesse frowned as if chasing after an elusive memory. "How do you know I wanted to see you?"

It wasn't the response Matt had hoped for, but it was a start. At least Jesse was more alert than he had been the night before. His memory loss wasn't too surprising, given the way he'd banged his head, but it was still worrisome. It wouldn't hurt to have the doctor take a look.

"You came barreling toward the farm like your tail was on fire, calling my name. That's how I know."

Jesse gazed up at him with a blank expression. "Can't remember," he said and struggled to sit up.

Matt arranged the pillows behind the boy's back. "Take it easy, son." He stepped back. "What do you remember? Do you know your name?" The reply took so long in coming, Matt had almost given up when at last the boy spoke.

"Name's Jesse."

Relief rushed through Matt only to be crushed a moment later when the boy added, "Jesse Taggert, Texas Ranger."

"Well, you got some of it right," Matt said.

Jesse studied him with narrowed eyes. "You told me to change my name."

Matt's gaze sharpened. It sure did look and sound like Jesse was back, or almost back, to his old self. "I didn't tell you to change your name to mine."

"It's the only one I could think of."

"Think harder."

"All right, I will!" Jesse said. The determined look Matt had come to dread returned full force. Today, however, it was a welcomed sight.

Not wanting to further upset the boy, Matt quickly changed the subject. "Where'd you get the horse?"

Jesse had a pinched look as if trying to remember. "From the stables."

"Figured as much."

"I…I told them it was Ranger business and you'd pay for it."

Matt stared at him. "What do you think I am? Your bank?"

"No, but you are my boss."

"I'm not your—" Matt blew out his breath. Arguing with the boy while he was still recuperating was not an option. "Sounds like some of your memory is back. Still can't remember why you wanted to see me?"

Jesse's forehead creased. "No. But it was important. I know it was."

Ellie-May entered the room, carrying a steaming mug. "Good morning," she said in a cheery voice. She looked as bright and fresh as morning dew, and Matt suddenly had a hard time catching his breath.

"Morning," he said.

"Was that Jesse's voice I heard?" she asked.

"It sure enough was," Matt said. "He has some of his memory back, but not all."

Aware, suddenly, that Jesse was staring at him with an annoying know-it-all smirk, Matt slanted a nod at the cup in her hand. "I sure do hope that's for me."

"It is," she said with a bright smile that ramped up his already fast-beating heart. She handed him the mug, handle first, and he took a sip.

"Just as I like it," he said with an appreciative grin. "Scalding hot and barefooted."

Laughing softly, she moved to the sofa and bent over Jesse. "How are you doing?" she asked.

"I'm okay," Jesse said. "'Cept my head hurts."

She straightened Jesse's blanket. "A cup of willow tea will fix that," she said.

Jesse brightened. "Can I have some flapjacks to go with it? And bacon and eggs and—"

Matt raised his free hand, palm out. "Whoa, there, Ranger. We don't want to eat Mrs. Blackwell out of house and home."

Ellie-May dimpled. "Don't worry. I'll be sure to keep a chicken or two in reserve," she said. "Flapjacks, bacon, and eggs coming up."

❧

After breakfast, Matt insisted upon helping to clean up, but Ellie-May declined his offer. "You're a guest," she said.

She might not have much in the way of book learning, but she knew how to treat company. Of course, that wasn't the only reason she didn't want his help. The kitchen was small, and she already felt overwhelmed by his nearness. Even when they were a distance apart, the space between them seemed to crackle as if on fire.

Strange as it seemed, she'd even sensed his presence in the parlor last night as she'd lain in bed.

"Jesse's a guest," he said. "I'm just riding shotgun. Besides, how else can I show off my impeccable kitchen skills?"

She laughed. Since he appeared determined to help her, she finally gave in and handed him a flour-sack towel. "Impeccable, eh? This I've got to see."

He grinned back, and her heart did a funny flip-flop. Normally, he was clean-shaven and neatly dressed. Today, he looked disheveled, and whiskers shadowed his strong jaw. Oddly enough, his rumpled appearance only enhanced his good looks.

She was surprised—shocked—to find herself longing to feel the rough stubble on his chin and run her fingers through his mussed hair. After her husband died, she'd never thought to be attracted to another man. Never wanted to be.

Shaken by the knowledge that some change had taken place within her, she turned to the sink and scrubbed a plate like her life depended on it. Such thoughts would never do. As long as Matt was in town poking around, he could still be a danger to her and her children—especially now that Roberts had been caught—and she'd best not forget it.

Seemingly oblivious to the battle she fought within, Matt stood mere inches away, ready to dry. Now, as always, he seemed to command the space around him.

His nearness put her nerves on edge, making it difficult to breathe. Though she tried not to look directly at him, she was aware of his every move, could feel the heat of his body, smell his masculine scent. She could even count each breath he took.

When his arm inadvertently brushed against hers, Ellie-May nearly dropped a dish. Heart racing, she tightened her hold on the plate and dipped it in the rinse water. Handing it to him, she was careful to avoid physical contact. But even when they weren't touching, she couldn't escape his embracing warmth.

Moistening her lips, she forced herself to breathe. "You really don't have to do this," she said.

Matt wiped the plate dry. "It's the least I can do for the hospitality you've shown me and the boy. Soon as we're done here, I'll take him home and we'll get out of your hair." He held up the plate. "See? Impeccable."

Laughing, she reached for the next dirty plate and turned serious. "Please...let Jesse stay." Meeting his gaze, she beseeched him. "At least till we know for sure he's okay and has fully recovered."

Matt tilted his head, and the golden light of approval in his eyes almost made her drop a second plate.

"That's mighty generous of you," he said, his voice warm. "But you've got your hands full as it is."

"Jesse's no trouble," she said. "And it will only be for a day or two. You know he won't get the care he needs at home." It was the truth, however much she hated saying it.

Matt hesitated. "If you're sure it's okay."

"I am. But you should talk to his pa. Let him know where Jesse is. It's...only right."

Matt scoffed. "I'll talk to him. It's high time someone did."

Ellie-May studied him. "If you think you're gonna change him, forget it," she said. "If you shot Patrick James full of lead, you'd see no blood. All you'd see is the devil's water."

"I owe it to Jesse to at least try," he said.

She reached for the last of the dirty plates and scrubbed it clean. "You really care for Jesse, don't you?"

"I guess you could say he grows on you." Matt set a dry plate atop the stack on the counter. "What's the story with his pa?"

Sighing, Ellie-May reached for a dish towel and wiped her hands dry. She wished she'd done more to help Jesse after his mother died, but after Neal's death, there had been so much to do. Taking care of the farm and her own children had been a full-time job.

"Jesse's father took his wife's death hard," she said. "That's when he started drinking." As much as she hated to admit it, she had been tempted to drown her own sorrows following Neal's death. Had it not been for Alicia and Lionel, she might have done just that, as distasteful as it now seemed.

"Losing someone is no excuse for neglecting a child," Matt said and, after a short pause, added, "You lost your husband, and I don't see you ignoring Lionel and Alicia."

Blushing at the faint praise, she moistened her lips. "I wasn't to blame for Neal's death."

His gaze sharpened. "Are you saying James was responsible for his wife's death?"

"He thinks he was," she said and quickly explained.

"Jesse's ma had stomach pains. Patrick thought it was something she ate and sent her to bed. It turned out to be her appendix. He blames himself for not fetching the doctor sooner."

Matt shook his head. "Even with a doctor's care, there's no guarantee that things would have turned out any differently."

Ellie-May inhaled sharply. Since finding that money under her porch, she better understood Patrick James's need to take the blame for his wife's death. She'd thought up a dozen ways to blame herself for what Neal had done. Accepting blame provided an answer when no other one could be found.

"We all told him that, even Doc Avery. But"— she shrugged—"nothing we said changed his mind." Taking the damp flour-sack towel from Matt, she hung it on a hook to dry. "I wish you could have known him before his wife died. You wouldn't think he was the same man. He was a cabinetmaker and made the most beautiful furniture."

"I think I may have seen some of his work at his house," Matt said.

"No doubt you did." She sighed. "I feel sorry for Jesse. I wish there was more I could do."

Matt held her gaze as he rubbed the back of his neck. "I wish I could, too. But I'm not gonna be around much longer to watch out for him. I have to get back to my company."

"Does…that mean you've completed your business here?" she asked. As much as she didn't want to admit it, she hated the thought of him leaving, even as she worried about him staying.

"More or less," he said. "Roberts is in jail. It's up to the judge to decide his fate."

His answer gave her small comfort. There was no telling what Roberts might say to save his own neck. He might even tell the judge the money was hidden on her farm—anything for leniency. Then it would be known that Neal wasn't the hero everyone thought he was.

Oh yes, she had plenty of reason to worry.

21

MATT FOUND JESSE'S PA EXACTLY WHERE HE'D EXPECTED to find him—at the Wandering Dog Saloon. Though it was still early afternoon, the place was already buzzing with activity. It was the first of June, and that meant payday for local cowhands.

The rattle of chips at a poker table competed with the drone of a faro dealer's voice at another. Someone played a harmonica, and a good-time girl dressed in a purple gown weaved in and out of tables, looking for a fast buck.

Ignoring the curious and, in Hal Spencer's case, hostile stares directed at him, Matt walked up to the slumped form at the corner table. He didn't want any trouble, but he was keeping his eyes and ears open in case it came a-calling.

Nose wrinkling in disgust, he shook Patrick James on the shoulder. "Wake up."

It took several good shakes before the man's bloodshot eyes fluttered open. "Don't know you," he slurred, his breath foul with whiskey.

"You will." Matt tried talking to him, but the

man was too far gone to understand. Finally, Matt grabbed James by the collar and yanked him to his feet. Apparently, Matt wasn't the only one who didn't want trouble. The saloon's patrons looked away, and he was able to drag James outside without interference.

When neither the heat nor glare of the late-afternoon sun revived James, Matt hauled him down to the horse trough and dunked his head in the water. A gelding tied to the railing whinnied in protest.

Matt apologized to the horse. "Sorry, but it's for a good cause."

Submerged to his shoulders, James flailed his arms wildly until Matt yanked his head up for air. Gasping, James cursed. "Let me go, you—"

"What's your son's name?" Matt all but yelled in the man's ear. Just thinking of the way James neglected Jesse made Matt want to wring the man's neck.

The question solicited more curses, and Matt plunged James's head into the water a second time. It took several more dunks before James had finally sobered up enough to give Matt the answer he sought.

"Jesse," James slurred. "Name's Jesse."

Only then did Matt let him go.

James backed away. Arms limp, he glared at Matt through a curtain of long, wet hair. Water dripped from his unkempt mustache and beard. He looked and smelled as if he'd just emerged from a watery grave.

Matt untied the red kerchief from around his neck and handed it to him. He waited for James to dry his face before breaking the news. "Jesse was thrown from a horse." Not sure how much James was able to comprehend, Matt paused. "Did you hear what I said?" He repeated himself several times, hoping for a response.

Comprehension dawned on James's face as slow as wet gunpowder, and he looked like he'd been stabbed. He moved his mouth long before he could get the words out. "He…he okay?" he managed at last.

Satisfied that James had the right amount of paternal concern, Matt softened his stance, along with his voice. Maybe there was hope for the man after all. "That's what we're hoping. He's staying at the Blackwell farm till we know for sure."

James stared at him, his face contorted with pain and what looked like self-loathing.

Matt was about to say more—wanted to say more—but he knew it would do no good. James looked like a wreck of a man. Matt didn't want to feel sorry for him, hated feeling sorry for him, but he couldn't seem to help himself.

With an irritated sigh, he grabbed James by the arm. Since leaving home at eighteen, Matt had avoided any entanglements or responsibilities that didn't involve his job. The decision had been made from necessity. Work required his full attention.

The last thing he wanted—indeed, needed—was to be tied down. But the longer he stayed in Haywire, the more involved he found himself becoming with Jesse and Ellie-May. Now with this man…

Not good. Not good at all.

"Let's get you home."

Matt glanced at the row of horses tethered in front of the saloon. Since there was no way of knowing which horse belonged to James, Matt led him over to where Justice was hitched and helped him onto the saddle.

Untying his horse, Matt mounted behind James. He touched his spurs gently to Justice's flanks and rode slowly through town. James flopped around in the saddle in front of him like a rag doll, and it was all Matt could do to keep him from falling.

Upon reaching his destination, Matt practically had to drag James's sorry figure into the house. Depositing him in a back room on an unmade bed, Matt yanked off the man's boots and opened a window to let in fresh air. James appeared to be out cold.

Since there was nothing more he could do for the man, he left the house and rode back to town. Feeling the effects of the long, sleepless night spent at Ellie-May's farm, he purchased a newspaper and stopped at the Feedbag Café for coffee.

The hot brew revived him somewhat, which might have been a good thing had thoughts of Ellie-May not kept popping into his head. Recalling in startling detail how she had looked that morning, he imagined he heard her laughter. Felt her touch. Smelled her sweet fragrance...

Clamping down on his thoughts, he mulled over the bill of fare. After the hearty breakfast Ellie-May had fed him, he wasn't hungry, but he decided to eat anyway. Without Jesse, he could eat his meal in peace and not have to share.

The distant sound of the train whistle reminded him that it was time to leave town. His job in Haywire had reached a dead end. There was nothing more to be done there. Roberts was in jail, waiting to see the judge, and Blackwell was dead. Much as Matt hated admitting failure, it looked like finding the stolen money was a lost cause. Even if it were buried on the Blackwell farm, as he suspected, it might never be found.

Shaking his thoughts away, he opened the newspaper and froze. his gaze glued onto the bold print of his brother's name. Charley had struck again and robbed a bank in Lockhart.

The sharp pain that shot through Matt's chest felt like an arrow to his heart. Charley had been such a bright, happy child with so much potential. The bullet that had killed their father had changed all that. It had created hate in Charley where love once resided and had turned his childlike innocence into festering guilt that could never be appeased. No matter how many times Matt had told Charley he wasn't to blame for Pa's death, Charley refused to listen.

Oh, Charley, Charley, Charley…

Matt wondered where he'd gone wrong. Why hadn't he known that Charley was heading down the road to destruction? What clues had he missed? What could he have done differently?

If he didn't know it before, Matt knew it now. His time and energy would best be spent tracking down his brother. Maybe Charley could be saved; maybe not. All Matt knew was that he had to try.

Matt pulled a hand-drawn paper map from his pocket and marked the town of Lockhart with a pencil. The holdup before then had been in Austin, twenty-some miles away from Lockhart. The proximity seemed to suggest that Charley was holed up somewhere between the two. It wasn't much to go on, but it was a start.

The proprietor, Mrs. Buffalo, arrived at his table to take his order. "I'll have the roast beef," he said, folding his map and returning it to his pocket.

"Where's the boy?" she asked as she wrote down his order.

"Jesse got thrown from a horse. He's staying at the Blackwell farm."

Mrs. Buffalo tutted. "The kid gonna be all right?"

Matt nodded. "Far as I know."

"Good to hear," she said. "Guess you got enough to worry about as it is."

He frowned. "You mean because of Jesse's accident?"

She shrugged. "That and the escape."

Matt sat back in his chair. "I'm not sure what you mean. What escape?"

She raised her thin eyebrows. "Guess you haven't heard. The stagecoach robber—Roberts was his name—escaped."

"Escaped?" Matt shot up from his chair. "When?"

"Dunno for sure. Yesterday…" She said more, but Matt didn't stay around long enough to hear the rest.

"Cancel my order," he called as he rushed out of the café and onto the boardwalk.

Moments later, he arrived at the sheriff's office just as Keeler rode up. Matt waited for him to dismount and followed him inside.

"Is it true?" he asked. "Did Roberts escape?"

Keeler hung his hat on a hook before answering. "Yeah," he said, his manner and voice reluctant. "It's true."

"Why am I only now just hearing about it? It wasn't even in the newspaper."

Keeler suddenly looked tired. "I was hopin' to capture him before soundin' the alarm."

Matt frowned. More likely the sheriff had kept Roberts's escape quiet to save his own skin.

As if guessing Matt's thoughts, the sheriff went on to explain. "He escaped without means or even a horse. Can't get far on shoe leather."

"How did he escape?" Matt asked.

Keeler rubbed his chin. "We were on the way to see the judge. Roberts started acting kind of funny. Like he was gonna faint or something. I tried to keep him from fallin', and he grabbed my gun." Shaking his head, the sheriff pulled out his chair and sat. He then reached for a cigar.

"Why wasn't he handcuffed?"

"Dang it!" The sheriff glared at Matt. "What gives you the right to question me?"

"Somebody needs to!" Matt fired back.

Keeler's eyes glittered. "For your information, he *was* cuffed but somehow had slipped out of 'em. I gathered up a posse, and we searched high and low. Found nothing. Not a trace."

"Do you think he had help?" Matt asked.

"How the heck would I know? All I can tell you is that the man's as slippery as a greased pig. He's probably halfway 'cross country by now."

Matt thought a moment. "Maybe. Maybe not."

The sheriff's gaze sharpened. "You know something I don't know?"

"There's still the matter of the missing money."

Keeler scoffed. "We don't know that the money is still around. Roberts could have gambled it away for all we know."

Matt shook his head. "None of the banknotes have turned up. In any case, something brought him back to Haywire." He doubted a man like Roberts would volunteer to work on the Blackwell farm out of the goodness of his heart. "If it wasn't the stolen loot, then what?"

22

ELLIE-MAY SET HER HAIRBRUSH ON HER DRESSING table and stifled a yawn. She was glad Matt had agreed to let Jesse stay. But worrying about him had taken its toll. She'd hardly been able to sleep and had checked on him several times during the night.

Instead of braiding or carelessly tying her hair back in a ponytail as usual, she smoothed it into a more fashionable bun at the nape of her neck.

She stared at her pale face and reached for the jar of rouge usually kept for special occasions and hid her pale skin beneath a rosy blush. She then dabbed tinted beeswax on her lips.

"Can I have some of that on my lips?" Alicia asked.

Unaware that Alicia had been watching from the doorway, Ellie-May screwed the top back on the jar and returned it to her dressing table. "No, you're too young."

Alicia moved into the room and caught her mother's gaze in the mirror. "But I want to look pretty, too."

Turning away from her dressing table, Ellie-May cupped her hands lovingly around Alicia's face.

"You're already pretty," she said. Her heart filled with pride as she gazed at her young daughter. "You're perfect just the way you are."

"How come you're getting all fancy?" Alicia asked. "Is it because of Jesse?"

Ellie-May dropped her hands to her side. Getting all fancy? Is that what she was doing? And with the thought came the memory of Matt's soft brown eyes and winning smile.

Startled, she straightened and stared in the mirror.

"Well, is it, Mama?"

Shaking away the disturbing thought, she forced herself to focus on her daughter. "Is what it?"

"Are you getting all fancy for Jesse?" Alicia made a face. "Jesse's a boy. He don't care what we look like."

"Maybe not, but I'm sure your teacher does." She reached for her hairbrush. "Let's fix your hair. I don't want you being late for school."

Alicia turned her back. "When is Jesse going home?"

Ellie-May carefully untied the ribbons on Alicia's night braids and drew the brush through the long, blond tresses. "Today," she said as she untangled a knot.

"Can I wear that shiny stuff on my lips?" Alicia asked again.

"It's called lip balm, and I already told you no."

"Why can't I wear lip bomb?"

"Balm," Ellie-May said. "It's lip *balm*, and you're too young to wear it."

"When won't I be too young?"

Ellie-May wanted to say never. Alicia and Lionel

were growing up too quickly. It seemed like only yesterday that she'd held them in her arms and nursed them at her breasts. If Neal were to see them today, he would hardly recognize them.

So far, she'd been able to shelter them both from the ugly realities she'd known as a child. Still, she lived in fear that something might happen to change all that.

Ellie-May laid the hairbrush on the dressing table and reached for a blue satin ribbon. "You can wear lip balm when you're a hundred years old."

"Ah, Mama. You always say that!"

"I know." Ellie-May tied a pretty bow on the top of Alicia's head and stepped back. "One day, the good Lord willing, you'll have children of your own, and you'll tell them exactly the same thing."

Alicia folded her arms across her chest, a defiant look on her face. "I won't make my children wait till they're a hundred," she said. "They'll only have to wait till they're ninety."

✷

After Anvil had left to take the children to school, Ellie-May made herself a cup of tea. She would have preferred coffee but wanted to save the few beans left for Anvil.

Matt was also a coffee drinker and might want a cup when he came to fetch Jesse.

The thought brought a feeling of anticipation, and she willed the butterflies in her stomach to go away.

She joined Jesse at the table and watched him wolf

down a mountain of flapjacks swimming in maple syrup.

The boy ate like a bear following a long hibernation. Matt was right—she was in danger of being eaten out of house and home and had already used up the rations for the week.

"I don't know where you put all that food," she said. The boy was skinny as a possum's tail. Pale as the animal's face, too.

Jesse finished the last morsel on his plate before looking up. "Thank you, Mrs. Blackwell. That was really good."

"Glad you liked it." She tossed a nod at his glass. "Drink your milk."

He picked up his glass and emptied it with one long gulp, then wiped the creamy mustache away from his mouth with his shirtsleeve.

"Where's Ranger Taggert?" he asked.

"It's early yet. I expect he's still at the hotel." She doubted Matt had gotten much sleep at her house and was probably trying to catch up. "Why?"

"I need to talk to him."

"He promised to stop by later to check up on you. I'd say you're well enough to go back with him."

"I need to talk to him now," Jesse said, looking and sounding serious. "Ranger business."

"Ranger business, eh?" She folded her arms on the table. "What's so urgent that it can't wait?"

He glanced around the room as if checking for eavesdroppers and lowered his voice to almost a whisper. "I remember why I came to the farm. I need to tell Ranger Taggert that the man escaped."

Ellie-May frowned. "Man?" she whispered back. "What man?"

"The man we were looking for. Mr. Roberts."

She stiffened. "Mr. R-Roberts has escaped?" Alarm racing through her, she sat back. How was such a thing possible?

Jesse nodded. "Yeah, and now he's gone." He brightened and gave her a lopsided grin. "See? My memory came back."

"That's good," Ellie-May said, her mind freezing on the one comforting thought—if Roberts had escaped before revealing Neal's name, then her secret was still safe.

Jesse leaned forward, looking as grave as a lawyer at a reading of a will. "That's why I came here. I wanted to tell Ranger Taggert that Roberts had escaped."

"I'm sure Matt…Mr. Taggert…already knows by now." News like that would travel through town with the speed of a bullet.

She balled her hands in her lap. There was no question in her mind that Roberts knew about the hidden money. He just didn't know what Neal had done with it. It all made sense now. The money was the reason Roberts had volunteered to work on the farm. It even explained why Anvil had caught him digging around the windmill.

A sudden, worrisome thought froze in her brain. What if Roberts came back to the farm to look for the stolen money? What then?

Matt knew the moment Ellie-May opened the door that something was wrong. Her eyes were as dark as storm clouds, and the smile on her face looked forced.

"Everything okay?" he asked. "Jesse?"

She stepped aside to let him in, and he caught a pleasant whiff of her perfume. "He's fine," she said, closing the door. "He's in the barn with Anvil." She glanced at the box in his hands. "What's all that?"

"Provisions," he said.

She blinked. "I'm sorry?"

"I don't know if this will replace what Jesse ate, but it's a start," he said and walked into the kitchen. He set the box on the counter and began pulling out packages of bacon, flour, tack bread, cheese, and jerky.

Ellie-May watched him unload with rounded eyes. "You...you really didn't have to do this," she gasped.

He held out a package of bacon. "It's just a small way to say thank you for taking care of Jesse."

"Jesse was no trouble." She took the bacon from him and put it into the ice chest. "Did you talk to his pa?"

"I talked to him." He pushed his hat back with the tip of his finger and nodded. "Not sure it did much good, but..." He studied her. "Everything else okay?"

She nodded. "It's just that Jesse remembered why he'd come to see you."

"Was it because of Roberts?" he asked, though he was sure he already knew the answer.

She lifted her gaze to meet his, and the pain in her eyes made his heart sink. He'd hoped that Neal Blackwell had nothing to do with the robberies, hoped Jesse had misinterpreted the conversation he'd overheard between Roberts and her husband. But her worried expression suggested otherwise, and that could mean only one thing. She knew something, knew something bad. Knew something she didn't want him to know.

"Yes," she said, slowly. Her voice—even her face—confirmed his suspicion.

He tried thinking of something to say to relieve her mind, but that would mean having to lie. "Had Jesse wanted to tell me that Roberts had escaped? Is that what had brought him to the farm?"

She nodded. "It's true, then?"

"'Fraid so."

Sucking in her breath, she lowered her lashes, blocking him from delving into her thoughts. "Like I said, you'll find Jesse in the barn."

He was about to leave the house when something made him stay. Maybe it was the way her lips trembled. Or the way she knotted her hands by her side. Perhaps it was the haunted look that shadowed her delicate face.

Whatever it was made him close the distance between them. "Ellie-May…" He heard her intake of breath. "I don't want to hurt you." Growing up as an outlaw's daughter, God knows she'd suffered enough without having to contend with an outlaw husband. Matt laid a hand on her shoulder. "You know that, right?"

She met his gaze briefly before looking away.

"I mean it, Ellie-May. If there's something you think I should know…"

"No," she said, her voice soft. Uncertain. "There's… there's nothing," she stammered.

He stared down at her tempting mouth, and every muscle in his body tensed. Since his hand was already on her shoulder, it took no effort to draw her slight body closer. She didn't fight him, didn't protest. If anything, she seemed to welcome the protective comfort of his arms. He was surprised at how natural it felt to hold her in his arms…how right it felt.

She stiffened as he tightened his hold, then relaxed, her hands against his chest.

Looking down at the woman in his arms, Matt drew in his breath. At that moment, it seemed that nothing else existed but the two of them. He yearned to press his mouth to hers and taste her sweet lips, but he forced himself to hold back. Right now, earning her trust was more important than satisfying his needs. Unless she was honest with him, he couldn't help her.

"I mean it," he said. "I would never purposely do anything to harm you or the children, but I have to know what I'm up against."

He sensed her lowering her guard. Her eyes softened, drawing him ever deeper into their smoky-blue depths. He felt a closeness, a connection, a spark, and it was an exhilarating moment.

Somehow his good intentions went by the wayside, and he brushed her lips with his own. Much to his delight, she offered no objection. Instead, she lifted her mouth to his, showing him that she welcomed his kiss as much as she had welcomed his arms. Only then did he claim her mouth fully with his own.

Her lips were every bit as sweet as he'd imagined, her mouth every bit as yielding as he'd hoped for.

She kissed him back with such sweet intensity,

he felt like he was in heaven. The fact that he was breaking his personal moral code didn't escape him. No doubt later he would have to deal with his guilt, but for now, he wanted to absorb her on all levels. He wanted to feel her, smell her, taste her.

Hands on her back, he pressed her closer to deepen the kiss and take in as much of her as possible. His pulse quickened when her arms found their way around his neck. Quickened even more when her fingers delved into his hair.

All too soon, she pulled away, a look of dismay on her face. "I can't do this..." she whispered.

Before she was able to explain, the kitchen door burst open, forcing them further apart.

It was Jesse, talking so fast he stumbled over his words.

Matt shook his head. "Whoa, boy," he said, raising his palms outward. "Slow down." It was good seeing Jesse looking more like his old self. Matt just wished the boy's timing had been better. A whole lot better.

Jesse started over, but he still talked a mile a minute. "I remember why I wanted to see you. I wanted to tell you that Roberts had escaped—"

"I heard," Matt said and immediately regretted it. Disappointment at not having been the one to break the news was written all over Jesse's face. "How did you know he'd escaped? The sheriff said he'd kept it quiet."

"I told you, I know things," Jesse said with a secretive smile.

"Yeah, you did," Matt said. "And you've made a believer out of me."

Jesse looked pleased. "Did you to talk to him before he escaped?"

"Yeah, I talked to him," Matt said. Acutely aware of Ellie-May's every move, he heard her intake of breath, sensed her stiffen. Roberts worried her, that much was clear. The question was, how much did she know about him?

"What did he say?" Jesse asked.

Matt frowned. "Privileged information."

Jesse's face dropped. "Ah, come on. I'm the one who told you what Mr. Blackwell said."

"That's enough," Matt said, glaring at the boy. Jesse opened his mouth to say something more, but Matt stopped him. "I said that's enough!"

Matt glanced at Ellie-May, and his heart ached. She looked as if she'd been punched in the stomach, and there wasn't a dang thing he could do about it. "What…did my husband say?" she asked, her voice trembling.

Matt silenced Jesse with a shake of his head, but the damage had been done.

Ellie-May's sapphire eyes bored into him. "I asked you a question." This time, her voice and manner made it clear that she had no intention of letting the matter drop.

Matt lifted his shoulders in resignation. "Jesse heard your husband talking about stolen loot from the stage holdup," he said, studying her face intently as he spoke. Whatever she knew, whatever dark secret she held, he hoped it had nothing to do with the crime.

She frowned. "Everyone talked about the robbery at the time. That doesn't make my husband a criminal."

"Maybe not, but Roberts is. I have reason to believe that he and your husband might have been in cahoots."

"That's not true!" she said, her voice strained in hot denial. "They were friends, nothing more. They were both from Hannibal, Missouri, and—"

"Roberts is from Ohio," Matt said. "Born and raised there. Far as I know, he's never been to Hannibal."

She drew back and looked at a loss for words. "Why?" she managed at last. "Why would he lie about a thing like that?"

Matt sucked in his breath. "Roberts might have thought it was the only way you would trust him enough to let him work on the farm."

Her forehead furrowed. "But…but why?"

"The money from the stage is still missing," he said slowly, watching her closely. "If Roberts thought it was buried on the farm, it would explain his interest in working here."

She stared at him with stricken eyes. "And you believe my husband stole it."

Not wanting to discuss the matter any further in front of Jesse, Matt told him to get his hat. "It's time to go."

After Jesse had left the room, Matt reached for her hand. "Ellie-May—"

She looked at him with a strange expression, as if seeing him for the first time, and snatched her hand away.

For a long moment, Ellie-May couldn't find her voice. The pain in her heart was so sharp, she could hardly breathe. She felt like her life was spinning out of control and she didn't know how to stop it.

She'd thought that by keeping the money hidden, her world would be safe, but that was no longer true. How foolish of her to think she could save Neal's reputation, save her children from scorn. But maybe most foolish of all was trusting Matt.

"So that's it," she managed at last, her voice a suffocated whisper. "That kiss… You used me." It seemed like almost everyone she had ever loved or cared about had betrayed her, but never before had she been betrayed by a kiss.

"Ellie-May—" He reached out to her, but she backed away.

"You used my children," she said, her voice rising. "All you wanted was for me to confirm your suspicions about my husband."

Matt shook his head. "You got it all wrong. It was nothing like that. I would never—"

She didn't let him finish. "That's why you've shown so much kindness to my children. Why you gave them presents. I should have known you'd do anything to get your man."

"No!"

Despite his denials, she persisted, her body shaking. "You worked your way into my family with gifts, hoping for information."

"That's not true." His voice broke. "Everything I did was because I've become fond of your family. Fond of you."

She shook her head in disbelief. His lips didn't just lie with their kisses, they lied with his words, and she didn't know which was worse.

"Get out!" she said.

"Ellie-May, please…"

Jesse returned, but even his presence failed to break the tension in the room.

"Go!" she sputtered and then in a lower but no less intense voice added, "And don't come back!"

23

ELLIE-MAY STOOD IN THE OPEN DOORWAY, WATCHING
Matt and Jesse ride away. Her heart was beating so fast,
she could hardly breathe.

Even after finding that money beneath her porch,
she hadn't wanted to believe that Neal had put it
there. She'd searched her head in vain for another
explanation. Someone else to blame. But now that she
knew Neal had been heard talking about it, the last of
her hopes were gone.

Only after Matt and Jesse had vanished from sight
did she slam the door shut and rest her head on
the cool, smooth wood. Since the pressure on her
forehead only reminded her of the feel of Matt's hard
chest, she quickly pulled away.

She closed her eyes and tried to sort through her
confused thoughts. She wished she hadn't felt Matt's
mouth on hers. Wished she hadn't tasted his lips,
tasted him. For it only filled her with a hunger that she
now knew could never be satisfied.

For a moment in time, Matt's kiss had made her
forget everything. In his embrace, no sack of stolen

money existed. In his arms, all the pain of the past had seemed to vanish. More than anything, he'd made her feel beautiful and feminine. He'd made her feel wanted. Made her feel whole.

Shaking her head, she pushed the memory away. How utterly foolish to think even for a moment—a second—that Matt's kiss had meant something. All he'd wanted was to ply her with affection in exchange for information. She should have known that he would do anything to get his man, including fake his kisses.

It hurt her deeply to think he would stoop so low. She didn't want it to, but it did.

Still, she had only herself to blame. He had no reason to protect her, protect her children. He owed her nothing. Trusting him was the last thing she should have done. The fault was hers. All hers.

Hands clenched, she paced the floor. If only she hadn't looked under the porch and found the sack of money! The bag beneath her porch weighed on her conscience to the point that it had given her nightmares. She was so tired of thinking about it. Worrying about it. Obsessing over it.

Now that Roberts had escaped, she had something else to worry about. He obviously knew the money was hidden somewhere on the farm. What if he came back looking for it?

Feeling as if the world was pressing down on her shoulders, she sank on a chair and held her head in her hands.

As she sat pondering, something suddenly occurred to her. The money was a problem—no question. But what if it were also a solution?

With this thought came another. What if the banknotes suddenly turned up? What if the money was returned to its rightful owner? That would certainly stop Roberts in his tracks, and he'd have no reason to stick around. Certainly, he'd have no reason to return to the farm.

Chewing on a nail, she weighed the problem of leaving the money in a safe place where it could be found. She didn't dare drop it off at the bank. The Haywire Bank was located in the center of town, and someone was bound to see her. Same was true of the hotel where Matt was staying. If she left it at the railroad station, it could easily be stolen by one of the vagabonds in the area.

After much thought, a solution finally occurred to her. She'd leave the loot on Mayor Wrightwood's porch. His house was located a way from town, and he was gone during the day. She could easily sneak to his house and back without being seen.

No doubt the mayor would welcome the attention he'd get for such a find and use the occasion to give one of his long-winded speeches.

The more she thought about it, the better her plan seemed. The sheriff wouldn't know who'd left it there, and Roberts would have no reason to return to the farm.

She paced the floor until every detail had been worked out to her satisfaction. There could be no room for error. Neither the sheriff nor the mayor must ever know where the money had come from.

With a new sense of resolve, she made her plans. She would retrieve the gunnysack from beneath the porch tonight after the children had gone to bed. Tomorrow, while they were in school, she would leave the bag on the mayor's doorstep and be done with it.

∞

Matt rode away from the farm with the memory of Ellie-May's stricken face very much on his mind and her accusations still ringing in his ears. He felt about as bad as it was possible to feel. Kissing her had been a mistake. It wasn't like him to act so forward where women were concerned. Especially when he had a job to do. He knew he would pay—and pay dearly—for kissing her and breaking his moral code, but never had he thought he would pay like this.

Ellie-May Blackwell had affected him in ways he didn't understand. Ways he couldn't control. Whenever he was around her, he felt like a schoolboy with his first crush.

It hurt that she thought he'd tried to trick her with a kiss. Nothing could be further from the truth. Never would he do such a thing. Using a woman in such a way went against everything he believed in. It cut him to the quick to think that Ellie-May thought otherwise.

He waited until he'd ridden a mile away from the Blackwell farm before reining in his horse. Turning in his saddle, he waited for Jesse to catch up.

He'd picked a shady spot next to a sprawling syca-more tree and reached for his canteen. He wasn't the only one taking advantage of the shade. On the other side of the barbed-wire fence, a mama cow rested next to her two calves. The peaceful scene did little to quell his tumultuous thoughts.

Watching Jesse with furrowed brow, he bit back his anger. The boy drove him crazy at times, but then he'd turn around and do something impressive. Like today. After causing a scene with Ellie-May, Jesse had gotten on a horse without a moment's hesitation. Being tossed from a saddle caused most people to lose their riding nerve. But not Jesse. The boy had grit, that was for sure. He also had the uncanny ability to pick up on things that most people would miss.

"What's the problem?" Jesse asked, nudging his horse closer to Matt's.

Matt uncapped the canteen and took a quick swig before answering. "The problem is you. If you ever hope to be a Ranger, you've got to learn to keep your trap shut."

Jesse stared at him from beneath his floppy hat. "What did I say?"

Matt raised an eyebrow. "What did you say? You mentioned overhearing something Blackwell said. That's what!"

The panicked look on Ellie-May's face had to have meant she knew more about the robbery than she'd let on. Matt had long suspected that, but he didn't want to believe it. Now he had no choice.

"I didn't know it was a secret," Jesse said defensively.

"We don't discuss Ranger business in public," Matt said. "Call it a rule."

Jesse wrinkled his nose as always whenever Matt mentioned rules. "All I did was state the truth."

"We don't know that. Things aren't always what they seem."

Jesse slanted Matt a sidewise glance. "Is it cuz you like her? Is that why you don't want me talking about her husband?"

"I don't…" Matt cleared his throat. "It's part of an ongoing investigation. That means you don't talk about anything you know or think you know. From now on, you're not to say a word about Roberts or Blackwell. Understood?"

"Yeah," Jesse murmured, looking properly chastised. "So what are we gonna do now?"

"*We* do nothing." Matt handed the canteen to Jesse. "You're going to the stables to return the horse. I'm heading for the sheriff's office. See if there's any news."

Jesse took a quick gulp of water and handed the canteen back. "If they haven't caught Roberts, are you gonna look for him?" he asked, wiping his mouth with the back of his hand.

Matt capped the canteen and hung it over the saddle horn. "No sense in that. No doubt he's miles away by now."

Jesse thought for a moment before asking, "Can I come to the sheriff's office with you?"

"No."

"Why not?"

"I want you to get some rest." In the glare of the sun, the boy looked pale, and the bump on his head had turned almost purple. "You took a bad fall." The corners of Jesse's mouth turned down, and Matt found himself relenting. "Get some rest and meet me at the Feedbag Café at six for supper."

"Can't. I gotta go to work at six."

"Okay, then meet me at five."

Jesse nodded. "Will you tell me if there's any news then?"

"What? So you can blab it all over town?" Matt pressed his knees against his horse's sides and urged the horse forward.

Jesse rode to his side. "I won't blab," he said. "Honest!" When Matt didn't respond, Jesse tried another tactic. "I won't even tell anyone that you like Mrs. Blackwell. Or that she likes you, too."

"I told you…" Steering his horse with one hand, Matt eyed the boy with curiosity. "What makes you think she likes me?"

"She looked like she was going to punch you. That's how girls show they like someone. A girl named Becky keeps hitting me on the arm. That's cuz she likes me."

Matt laughed without mirth. Oh, to be that young and naive again.

Jesse frowned. "What's so funny?"

"Trust me," Matt said, alarmed to find himself wishing that what Jesse said was true. "Mrs. Blackwell might have wanted to punch me, but it sure in blazes wasn't because she likes me."

"Oh, she likes you all right." A know-it-all smile curved Jesse's mouth. "Sometimes things really *are* what they seem."

With a whoop and a holler, Jesse waved his hat over his head and spurred his horse into a gallop. Against his better judgment, Matt gave chase.

Ellie-May waited until the children were asleep that night before donning her shawl and stepping onto the porch. Earlier, she'd fetched a crowbar from the toolshed and now held it tightly gripped in both hands.

The air was still, and the countless stars splattered across the moonless sky appeared to be eyes gazing down on her. Some blinked, some stared, but she imagined all were critical.

The memory of accusatory eyes that had followed her all through childhood made her more determined than ever to go through with her plan. Never would she let her children suffer the way she had suffered. Never must they hang their heads in shame or be made to feel inferior or in some way lacking.

She craned her neck to make sure the upstairs barn window was dark before dropping to her knees. It wouldn't do for Anvil to catch her pulling the step apart.

Light fanned across the porch from the open doorway, barely illuminating the middle step. Hesitating, she assured herself she was doing the right thing. At last, the money would be returned to its rightful owner, and her children would never know what their father had done. No one would ever be the wiser.

With a new sense of determination, she set to work. Wedging the V end of the crowbar under the lip of the step, she exerted power with her shoulders and arms.

Anvil had been the last to hammer the tread in place, but it was the memory of Matt that came to mind. Matt measuring the tread. Matt hammering the nails in place, the muscles rippling beneath his shirt. Matt holding her in his arms.

Matt's kiss…

Startled by the intensity of the last memory, she pushed her thoughts away and applied all the force she could to the end of the crowbar. The man had used her. Worse, used her children, and she'd best not forget it.

In the quiet of night, the sound of ripping wood seemed uncommonly loud. Pausing, she swiped a wayward strand of hair out of her eyes and glanced toward the barn to make sure there was no movement. No light shone from the loft window, and all was quiet. Sighing in relief, she set to work again.

It took longer than she'd thought it would to pry the tread off the riser, but at last the wood came free.

She set the crowbar down and rubbed her sore hands together. Telling herself that this whole nightmare would soon be over and she would never again have to think about the stolen money or worry about protecting Neal's reputation, she reached into the gaping, dark hole. Patting the ground with her hand, she felt for the rawhide tie and couldn't find it.

She drew her hand out of the hole and wiped the dirt off on her apron. Standing, she carefully stepped over the missing tread and went inside to fetch a lantern.

Moments later, she held the lantern in such a way as to illuminate the entire area beneath the porch.

As she drew back in disbelief, her jaw dropped. It couldn't be. *Oh, no, please, God, no.* The gunnysack couldn't be gone!

24

Doc Avery opened the door to Matt's knock, and his gray eyes lit up beneath his bushy white eyebrows. "Come in, come in."

"Sorry to bother you so early," Matt said.

"No bother," the doctor said, leading the way into a small, crowded room. Shelves crammed with books lined two of the four walls. A Penn Medical University degree was displayed in a gold frame and hung next to the open window.

Doc Avery motioned Matt over to a leather chair and took his own place behind a weathered oak desk piled high with unopened mail and periodicals. "Hope all is well and this isn't a medical call."

"Not exactly," Matt said.

The doctor raised an eyebrow, and his white mustache twitched. "Anvil recovered from the snakebite?"

"Far as I know." After a pause, Matt added, "I'm here because of Jesse James."

"Ah, Jesse. How is the lad?" the doctor asked. "Nothing wrong, I hope."

"He was thrown from a horse," Matt said. "He has

a nasty bump on the head but seems to have recovered with no problems."

"I'll be glad to look at him if you like."

"Much obliged, but that's not the only reason I'm here. Since I've been in town, Jesse's been more or less under my"—he'd almost said *foot*—"wing."

The doctor nodded in approval. "It's good to hear that someone is looking out for him."

"It wasn't as if I had a choice," Matt said. "The thing is, I'm not gonna be in town much longer, and I'm worried about him. I thought about asking Ellie-May...Mrs. Blackwell to keep an eye on him, but she already has her hands full." He didn't mention that as far as Ellie-May was concerned, his name was Mudd and she never wanted to see him again. It was a depressing thought.

The doctor leaned back in his chair and folded his arms across his chest. "If it'll make you feel better, I'll look in on him from time to time. See that he eats proper. That sort of thing."

"That'll be a big help," Matt said. "Just so you know, he's got the appetite of a bear."

The doctor chuckled. "They used to say the same about me, and I was skinny as a toothpick. Now I eat like a bird and look at me." He patted his rounded belly. "Speaking of Mrs. Blackwell, I'm glad to hear Anvil's recovered. You never know how those snake-bites will turn out. He's been a real blessing to her since her husband died."

"So I gathered." Matt balanced his hat on his knee. "How long did you know him?"

"Anvil?"

"Blackwell."

The doctor pursed his lips. "Long enough to know he was the finest man I ever had the privilege of knowing. How does that old saying go? Never judge a man till you've seen him with a woman, a child, and a stubborn mule? I saw him with all three, and he passed each test, hands down."

"I heard he did a lot of good for this town," Matt said.

"That he did. A pity the way it turned out. Did everything I could, but his lungs just couldn't take all that smoke." He paused for a moment before adding, "I sure do give his missus credit, though. She's kept the farm going and is determined to do right by her young'uns."

"I agree," Matt said. The mere mention of Ellie-May brought back another round of painful memories, and he hungered for the feel of her, the scent of her, the taste of her. Suddenly aware that he'd missed something the doctor had said, he leaned forward. "I'm sorry?"

"I was just asking when I can see Jesse. I have some free time this afternoon."

"I'll make sure he gets here," Matt said.

The doctor nodded. "Is there anything more I can do for you? Besides checking in on Jesse when you're gone, I mean?"

Matt rubbed his chin. *Make me stop thinking of things I best not think about. Make me forget.* "Your offer to keep an eye on the boy is enough," he said. The doctor's interest in Jesse's welfare seemed genuine, and that was a relief. "He's got a bright mind and should be in school. Unfortunately, he's got his heart set on being a Ranger, even though he's too young."

"Maybe I can persuade him to go back to school," the doctor said. "Now that there are two classrooms, he can be with children his own age."

"Good luck," Matt said. He hated adding to the doctor's burdens, but he really didn't know who else to turn to. "His pa… Is there nothing that can be done for him?"

Dr. Avery folded his hands on his desk. "You mean…?"

"He seems bound and determined to drink himself to death."

The doctor let out a long sigh. "He blames himself for his wife's death. I've told him it wasn't his fault, but it's like talking to a lamppost."

"Why do people do that?" Matt asked, thinking about his brother. "Take on blame for things that aren't necessarily their fault?"

"Well, I'm not an alienist," Avery said, referring to the specialists who dealt with mental illnesses. "If you ask me, all this recent talk about so-called mental alienations is a bunch of hogwash. But from what I've observed in my practice, some people do have the need to punish themselves."

Matt rubbed his chin. Was that why Charley had alienated himself from family and friends and turned to a life of crime? To punish himself for Pa's death? Did he not think he deserved a better life? A better future?

"As for the drinking…" The doctor paused for a moment. "There is a method that has shown promise."

Matt sat back in his chair. "Oh?"

The doctor stabbed a medical journal on his desk with his finger and explained. "There're some in the medical community who think dipsomania should be considered a disease and not a vice."

Matt frowned. "How can imbibing be a disease?"

"It sounds crazy, I know. But it's not the actual drinking that's the problem: it's the craving for it. That's what makes some people think it should be treated medically."

"But how?" Matt asked. "Don't tell me you know of some magical potion that can cure the problem?"

"Cure? No. But some people have been able to control their drinking by staying at an inebriate home."

Matt shook his head. "Never heard of such a thing."

"They've been around for a while. At least fifty years or so, but they're only now becoming more widespread." The doctor tossed a nod at the journal on his desk. "According to the article I read, it's all done with mutual aid. These homes bring a bunch of drunks together, and they help each other stay sober."

Matt frowned as he tried to imagine such a thing. "Does it work?"

The doctor shrugged. "Some say it does. Only one way to find out. I've been toying with the idea of opening up a place like that here in Haywire."

"Oh?"

Doc Avery nodded. "Been thinking about it for a while. The drought has caused financial burdens that have driven some men to drink. You may have inspired me to actually put the idea of an inebriate home into practice." He paused for a moment. "Do you think we can convince James to move into it?"

Matt turned the idea over in his mind before answering. "Don't know. But it's worth a try for the boy's sake." He didn't have a lot of confidence in the doctor's proposal, but who knew? Maybe something good would come of it. "How long would it take to put something like that together?"

The doctor thought for a moment. "Not long. I've got a spare room in back, but I can't take more than three or four at a time."

Matt stood, donned his hat, and reached across the desk to shake the doctor's hand. "Is there anything I can do to help?"

"You figure out a way to get James here, and I'll handle the rest."

"Sounds like a task for the Texas Rangers," Matt said with a grin.

Doc Avery made a face. "Knowing James, you might also want to call in the cavalry."

Ellie-May had hardly slept that night and had gotten up feeling tired and out of sorts. All she'd been able to think about was the missing gunnysack. She was so deep in thought, she'd burned the first batch of flapjacks and had to start over.

"Alicia, where's your brother?" she asked. "His breakfast is getting cold."

Alicia looked up from the table, fork in hand. "He went to feed the animals. It's his turn this week."

Ellie-May frowned. "He's been gone for a good long while."

Anvil entered the kitchen to help himself to another cup of coffee. He waved his hand through the blue haze in the air. "What happened in here?"

Alicia wrinkled her nose. "Mama burned the flapjacks."

"My mind was on Lionel," Ellie-May said by way of explanation. "Have you seen him? It's his turn to feed the animals."

Anvil shook his head. "Sorry, no. Maybe he snuck out to go fishing." He reached for the metal coffeepot on the stove and filled his cup. "You know how that boy likes to fish since he got that new fishing pole."

Ellie-May did know. Lionel loved his fishing pole and had already caught several good-sized bass. Thinking about it only reminded her that Matt had used her son—had used both her children—to worm his way into her heart, hoping she would reveal the truth about Neal.

Pushing through the hurtful memories that thoughts of Matt now triggered, she studied Anvil with questioning eyes. She was dying to talk to him about the missing money, but it would have to wait until they were alone. He was the only one who could have moved it—no one else.

"Lionel knows better than to take off on a school day," she said.

Anvil shrugged. "Do you want me to go and look for him?"

Ellie-May thought for a moment before shaking her head. "I'd rather that you took Alicia to school. No sense them both being late, and Lionel hasn't eaten yet." It would serve him right if she sent him to school hungry.

Anvil drained his coffee cup and set it in the sink. "Ready, Alicia?"

"Ready." Jumping up from the table, Alicia grabbed the leather strap holding her schoolbooks together and dashed out of the room.

Anvil turned to follow but stopped at the doorway and looked over his shoulder. "You okay? You don't seem like your usual bright self."

Ellie-May moistened her lips. "When you get back, we need to talk."

He raised a questioning brow. "Sounds serious." He waited for her to explain. When she failed to do so, he shrugged his shoulders and left.

The moment she was alone, she cleared the few dirty dishes from the table. Usually, concentrating on mundane chores relaxed her, but not today. Thoughts of Matt, Neal, and the missing money popped in her head like kernels of heated corn.

The table cleared, she glanced out the kitchen window. Lionel had still not returned. She had fully expected him to come running into the house when he'd heard the horse and wagon take off. Why hadn't he?

Leaving the dishes in the sink, she yanked off her apron and tossed it on a chair. He better not have gone fishing. She stepped outside. Shading her eyes with her hand against the bright morning sun, she scanned the yard. "Lionel!" she called.

She checked the chicken coop first, and the hens

had not been fed. She then walked to the barn, and the cow's trough was empty. That was odd.

She walked outside again and checked behind the barn. Lionel's fishing pole was on the ground. Frowning, she stooped to pick it up and stood it against the side of the barn.

Lionel was not one to be careless with his belongings. Nor was he one to neglect his chores. So why had the animals not been fed? And what had made him drop his beloved fishing pole?

More worried now than irritated, Ellie-May circled the barn again, calling Lionel's name. Something was seriously wrong. She felt it all the way to her bones.

25

MATT LEFT THE DOCTOR'S OFFICE DEEP IN THOUGHT.
He had no idea how to persuade James to stay at the
doc's inebriate house, but he had to give it a try. For
Jesse's sake.

Though it was still early morning, he had intended
to head straight for the Wandering Dog Saloon to
confront James. But upon noticing several horsemen
gathered in front of the sheriff's office, he changed
his mind. It sure did look like the sheriff was putting
together a posse.

Dodging around a horse-drawn wagon, Matt jogged
across the street and reached the office just as the sheriff walked outside. "What's going on?" he asked.

The sheriff strode past him to his horse before
answering. "We have reason to believe Roberts is still
in the area."

"Oh?"

The sheriff mounted his saddle before explaining.
"Roberts broke into the Peterson farm and helped
himself to their pantry."

Matt's stomach clenched. If he remembered

correctly, the Peterson farm was only about a mile from Ellie-May's. "What makes you think it was Roberts?"

"Oh, it was him, all right," Keeler said. "Peterson spotted him trying to steal a horse and scared him off."

"Think he's still around?"

The sheriff shrugged. "No horse thefts have been reported. Far as we know, he's still on foot. Care to join us?"

Surprised by the invitation, Matt nodded. "I'll catch up."

The sheriff took off without another word and led his posse out of town in a cloud of dust and the sound of thunderous hooves.

Watching the group ride away, Matt's mind whirled. If Roberts was still in the area, it could mean only one thing. He had no intention of leaving until he had the stolen money in hand. If the money was at the Blackwell farm as Matt suspected, Ellie-May and her children could be in danger.

He spun about and ran for his horse. Moments later, he raced out of town, heart pounding.

❧

"Lionel!"

Ellie-May scanned the property for as far as she could see, panic rising inside her. She checked the tree he liked to climb and looked inside the shed. She found no sign of him, not even his shoes, which he loved to cast aside. *Oh, Lionel, where are you?*

Standing next to the side of the barn, Ellie-May

shaded her eyes against the sun and looked toward the pond. Without his fishing pole, she doubted Lionel had gone there, but it wouldn't hurt to check.

Just as she'd started in the pond's direction, a movement caught her eye. Turning, she gasped in horror. Roberts stood a short distance away, his arm around Lionel's neck. In his free hand, he held a gun pointed at her.

"Let him go," she said when she could find her voice. Her poor son looked scared to death. His face was white and his eyes round as saucers.

"Do as I say," Roberts hissed, "and the boy won't git hurt."

Icy fear twisting inside, she swallowed hard and knotted her hands by her sides. "What…what do you want?"

"I want what's mine. I want the loot. Where is it?"

Ellie-May forced herself to breathe and not panic. If she and her son had any chance of coming out of this alive, she had to remain calm and think clearly. If she told Roberts the truth—that she didn't know where the money had gone—he probably wouldn't believe her.

"It's…it's under the front porch," she said. Last night, after finding the money gone, she'd hammered the tread back in place and was grateful now that she had. Prying off the step would likely keep Roberts occupied until Anvil returned.

"Show me where," he snapped, keeping his hold on Lionel. "And you better not be pulling any tricks."

She struggled to find her voice. "First you have to let my son go."

Eyes as hard as stone lit into hers. "Not till you show me the money."

The dark expression told her he meant business and she'd best do as he said. "Th-this way," she stammered.

Casting Lionel what she hoped was a look of reassurance, she started across the yard toward the house. She prayed her knees wouldn't buckle and her heart wouldn't stop. She searched the distant road for signs of Anvil. Where was he? What was taking so long? He should have been back from taking Alicia to school by now.

After what seemed like the longest walk of her life, she finally reached the porch and pointed to the steps. "It's hidden under there."

Roberts gave the porch a visual inspection. "Where do you keep your tools?"

"In the toolshed behind the barn."

A look of impatience fleeted across his face. "Get 'em. And don't try any funny business."

She gazed at Lionel, not wanting to leave him alone with Roberts.

"I said get 'em!" Roberts thundered.

"Don't go, Mama," Lionel cried. "Don't go!"

Roberts shook him. "Shut up, kid!" he said, waving the gun at her. "If you know what's good for you and the boy, you'll do as I say."

"D-don't be scared, Lionel," she stammered, backing away. "I'll be back as quick as I can."

It almost broke her heart to leave him, but what else could she do? She held on to Lionel's gaze for as long as she could before turning. Hiking up her skirt, she ran to the toolshed as fast as she could and fumbled with the rusty latch.

"Come on, come on," she muttered beneath her breath.

At last, the door creaked open. Her hands were shaking so hard, she could hardly grab the crowbar from the workbench. Holding her raw emotions in check, she forced herself to breathe. Where was Anvil? If only Matt were there. He would know what to do.

Appalled that her thoughts had turned to Matt in her hour of need, she rushed back to the house on shaky legs, her feet pounding the hard clay soil. Roberts hadn't moved in her absence, and his arm was still wrapped around Lionel's neck.

Noting the crowbar in her hands, Roberts tossed a nod at the step. "Pry it off."

"First let him go," she pleaded.

"I said pry it off!"

Since there didn't seem to be anything else to do but follow his orders, Ellie-May dropped to her knees. Fumbling with the tool, she worked the claw beneath the tread lip. Biding for time, she pretended to exert pressure. Though her back was turned, she could hear Roberts's seething breath hiss between his clenched teeth.

"Stop!" he yelled at last. He moved his arm from around Lionel's neck and grabbed hold of her wrist, his fingers digging into her flesh.

"You!" he said, addressing her son. "Go into the house and stay there. You hear me?"

Lionel's gaze found hers, his eyes glittering with stark fear.

"Do it!" Roberts yelled.

Still Lionel refused to move. "Do what he says." Ellie-May smiled and hoped it didn't look as forced as it felt. "I'll be okay."

Lionel hesitated a moment before turning. He ran up the steps and into the house, slamming the door shut behind him.

Seemingly satisfied that the boy would give him no trouble, Roberts turned his full attention on Ellie-May. "Give me that!" He snatched the crowbar out of her hands. "Stay there where I can keep my eye on you," he said, pointing a short distance away. "And don't move."

Holding the gun in his left hand, he aimed it at her and worked to pry the tread loose with his right hand. As the wood began to splinter, Ellie-May held her breath, and her mouth ran dry. There was no telling what Roberts would do when he found the area beneath the porch empty.

Ellie-May eyed the road leading to the farm. *Where are you, Anvil? Where are you?*

The sudden blast of a shotgun startled her. Crying out, she jumped. Eyes rounded, her mouth fell open, and Roberts looked equally shocked. His hat had blown clear off his head, and he'd dropped both the crowbar and gun.

Acting purely out of instinct, Ellie-May reached down to grab the gun that had fallen mere inches from her feet. Pointing the weapon straight at Roberts with shaky hands, she glanced at the doorway where her young son stood, the smoking shotgun still posed in his hand.

Swallowing hard, she searched for her voice. "If you know what's good for you, you'll leave now and not come back."

Roberts glared at her but said nothing. Instead, he reached for his hat and examined the bullet hole in the crown.

"This isn't the end," he muttered at last and lumbered away on foot.

Ellie-May kept the gun aimed at him until he was out of sight. Shoulders sagging in relief, she rushed up the steps to her young son's side.

"He was a bad man, Mama," Lionel said, sounding remarkably calm given the situation.

"Yes. Yes, he was." She grabbed the shotgun out of his hands. "Quick! In the house."

The moment they were both safely inside, she slammed the door shut with her foot. After standing the shotgun in a corner, she locked the door with her free hand.

She wasn't ready to give up Roberts's gun, so she kept it with her as she ran around the house closing windows and checking the back door. Assured that all the windows and entrances were secure, she returned to the parlor. Only then did she place the gun within easy reach on the mantel.

Hand on her chest, she tried catching her breath before turning to face her son. He hadn't moved since entering the house and now stood watching her with rounded eyes.

Drawing him into her arms, she hugged him tight. He was safe—they both were—and her heart nearly burst with gratitude. *Thank you, God.*

"When…when did you learn to fire a shotgun?" she asked when she could finally think clearly.

The question seemed to perplex him. "Don't you remember?" he asked. Stirring in her arms, he gazed up at her. "Papa taught me."

She released him. "Oh, that's right."

How could she have forgotten? At the time, she remembered thinking a five-year-old too young to use a gun and had argued with Neal about it. But he'd been adamant about teaching his son the proper handling of a weapon. It wasn't hard to understood why he had been so insistent. Neal had wanted to make sure his son never shot anyone by accident as he himself once had.

"That bad man said Papa stole his money." An indignant look crossed Lionel's face, and she could almost see the man he would one day become. "That's not true, Mama. It's bad to steal, and Papa wouldn't do nothing bad."

Praying that her children would never find out the truth about their father, she hugged him tight. "You did good, Son," she whispered, her voice wavering. "Your pa would have been proud."

Lionel looked up at her, and once again she was reminded how much he looked like Neal. How much he was like his pa in so many other ways as well. "I'm hungry, Mama. Can I eat now?"

Ellie-May drew back. "Hungry? Oh, that's right. You haven't had breakfast."

Marveling at her son's resilience, she took him by the hand, and together they walked into the kitchen. Releasing him, she set to work cooking up a plate of flapjacks and bacon, taking special care this time not to burn them.

Roberts was gone for now, but there was no telling when he would return. The only way to prevent him from doing so was to go through with her plan of leaving the sack of money at the mayor's house. But what if Anvil refused to tell her where he'd hidden it? Since he still hadn't returned from taking Alicia to school, he might have already absconded with the money. As much as she hated thinking such a thing, it was a possibility.

After setting Lionel's breakfast on the table, she glanced out the window and chewed on a nail. *Oh, Anvil, not you, too.*

26

MATT CAUGHT UP TO THE POSSE JUST AS THE SHERIFF ordered his men to spread out. In all, there were twelve men.

"I'll check the Blackwell farm," Matt called. Without waiting for the sheriff to approve or disapprove, he took off at a gallop.

The farm looked peaceful enough as he rode up the narrow dirt road leading to the house. He dismounted and cautiously looked around. Nothing seemed amiss, except for the crowbar on the step.

Wrapping the reins of his horse around the railing, he leaped up to the porch and banged on the door. Recalling how Ellie-May had ordered him to leave the house, he wasn't sure what kind of reception awaited him.

"Ellie-May," he called. "It's Matt."

He knew as soon as she opened the door that something was terribly wrong. Her face was strained, and she held on to her son as if to never let him go.

He fully expected her to tell him to leave, but instead she said, "Roberts was here."

"When?" he asked, senses alert.

"About twenty minutes ago."

Lionel pulled away from his mother's arms. "I shot him," he said proudly.

Matt stared at the boy. "You...shot him?"

Lionel nodded. "He was a bad man."

"He caused Roberts no harm," Ellie-May added quickly and shuddered.

Worried that she was about to collapse, Matt stepped into the house and took her by the arm. "You okay?" he asked, leading her to a chair.

Sitting, she gazed up at him and relayed all that had happened.

"What did Roberts want?" Matt asked.

Her lips parted but she didn't answer. She didn't have to. He knew. He didn't want to know, but he knew.

"That's his gun," she said, pointing to the weapon on the mantel. "He's not armed. Least as far as I know."

"Did he have a horse?"

She shook her head. "None that I saw."

"I'll check around," Matt said. "He couldn't have gotten far on foot." Noting the quiver of her lips, he dropped to a knee by her side and took her hand in his.

This time, she yanked her hand away. The gesture, along with her dark look, told him that nothing had changed. She still thought the worst of him.

"About the other day," he began slowly, watching her face. "I had no right..." It hardly seemed like the time to talk about a moment they'd both be better off forgetting. But he hated her thinking the worst of him, hated her thinking he would use amorous tactics to trick her.

"I know it looks bad," he said, "but it was never my intention to deceive you." The instant their lips met, the stagecoach robbery and Neal Blackwell had been the farthest thing from his mind. "It was unprofessional of me, and I apologize. It won't happen again."

She searched his face as if to validate his sincerity, but the suspicion remained in her eyes. "Why else would you give my children gifts?" she asked. "Why else would you—" Biting her lip, she looked away.

"Did it ever occur to you that maybe I…" Surprised that the word *love* was on the tip of his tongue, he clamped down on his jaw and stood. Mustn't go there. Wouldn't go there. He had a job to do and should be thinking of only that. Nothing else.

"Lock the door after I'm gone," he said, crossing to the door with long, quick steps. "And stay inside."

❧

Ellie-May watched Matt walk out of the house with confused feelings. How strange that a man who could do her and her family so much harm could, at the same time, make her feel so utterly and completely safe.

He said he was sorry for kissing her. She wanted to believe him when he said he hadn't meant to trick her. But that was a hard thing to do. For that would mean that his kiss had meant something, and as much as she wanted to believe such a thing was true, she couldn't.

What would a worldly man like Matt Taggert see

in a woman like her? Not only was she the daughter of an outlaw, but it appeared she had also married one. Even without knowing her background, a man would have to be crazy to involve himself with a poor widow who had two children and a dilapidated farm.

The rattle of wagon wheels drew her away from her thoughts, and she raced to the window. It was Anvil. Finally! Relief rushing through her, she ran to the door just as he pulled up in front of the house.

He quickly joined her on the porch. "I ran into the sheriff. He said that Roberts was in the area."

"It's true," she said and motioned him inside.

Anvil listened to her ramble on about what had happened in his absence, and a look of horror shadowed his face. "You shouldn't have had to face him alone," he said when at last she fell silent. "I should have been here for you."

"I wasn't alone," she said. "Lionel saved me."

Lionel walked out of the kitchen upon hearing his name. "He was a bad man," he managed around a mouthful of food.

Anvil turned questioning eyes on Ellie-May. "I'll explain later," she whispered. In a louder voice, she asked, "Where were you?" It didn't take that long to drive to the school and back.

He cleared his throat and ran a finger along the inside of his collar, his neck all red. "Well...I...um..."

"Why, Anvil. You're blushing." She regarded him with a sideways glance. "You didn't by chance stop by to see Mrs. Buttonwood, did you?"

"You c-caught me there," he stammered. "I...

thought I should stop by and thank her for taking such good care of me during my recovery."

"Such good care?" Ellie-May tilted her head sideways. "That's not what you said before."

"I might have said a few things I shouldn't have. But that was the fever talking. Not me."

Ellie-May gave him a playful punch on the arm. "Don't tell me you've taken a fancy to Mrs. Buttonwood."

Anvil reared back. "Now don't go jumpin' to conclusions. You're not the only one who had a bad mornin'. All I done is made a friendly call. How could I know she was gonna go all crazy-like on me?"

Ellie-May frowned. "What do you mean? Crazy-like?"

Lifting his chin, Anvil pulled himself up to his full height. "Do you know what the fool woman did? I'll tell you what she did. She proposed marriage. That's what!"

Ellie-May drew back. "She did what?"

"She asked me to marry her," he repeated. He somehow managed to make it sound as if the marriage proposal had been every bit as horrifying as her ordeal with Roberts. "Don't that beat all?"

"What did you tell her?"

"What do you think I told her? I said no, I wouldn't marry her. It's a man's job to propose. Not a woman's."

Ellie-May studied him with serious regard. "Is that the only reason you turned her down? Because she proposed and not you?"

Anvil dismissed the idea with a shake of his head.

"No, it ain't the only reason. Give a woman like that an inch, and she'll start thinking she's the whole ruler. Gosh-a-livin', a man would have to be a dang fool to give up his freedom for a woman like that."

"If you say so," Ellie-May said. Not wanting to give him a bad time, she let the matter drop. Anxious to question Anvil about the missing money, she glanced at her son, who'd been listening to the conversation with rapt attention. "There're still some macaroons left in the cookie jar." Macaroons were his favorite.

Lionel brightened. "For me?" he asked.

"For you," she said and smiled. She waited for her son to leave the room before turning to Anvil. "We need to talk." She lowered her voice. "I know you took the gunnysack from beneath the porch." Without giving him a chance to confirm or deny it, she added, "No one else could have done it."

Anvil frowned. "So you know about the money?"

She drew in her breath. "I found it when I went to repair the step."

"Same here," he said. "Couldn't believe my eyes. All that dough just sittin' there."

Detecting awe in his voice and maybe even surprise, she knitted her brows. "Where…where do you think the money came from?"

He gave a casual shrug of his shoulders, but she noticed he avoided her eyes. "Beats me."

She hesitated before asking the next question. "You don't suppose…Neal robbed that stage, do you?" Even as she said it aloud, everything inside protested the thought, and the words felt like acid in her mouth.

Anvil's gray eyes met hers. "We don't know that."

"How…how else could the money have gotten there?"

He shook his grizzled head. "I don't know the answer to that. All's I knows is that the Neal Blackwell I knew was no thief."

Ellie-May knotted her hands by her side. She wished with all her heart that she had Anvil's faith in her late husband and could believe in his innocence. But when all the signs pointed to the contrary, what else could she think?

"Why…why did you move it?" she asked.

"The way those steps keep rotting away, I didn't want to leave it there. I was sure someone would find it and…"

She flinched as she finished the sentence for him. "Know what Neal had done?"

Anvil gave his head an emphatic shake. "Like I said, we don't know that."

Ellie-May clasped her hands to her chest. "If this comes out, I won't be able to protect the children."

"Now, don't you go worryin' none, Miss Ellie-May. I plan to burn the money." He made a motion with his hands as if striking a match. "That way, no one will ever know what we found."

The thought of all that money going up in flames made her feel sick. "That would be wrong, Anvil. The money doesn't belong to us. It should be returned to the bank."

Anvil wrinkled his nose. "I don't disagree," he said slowly. "But if we walk into the bank and drop off a sack of money, they might start askin' questions."

"I have a different idea," she said and told him her plan for leaving it on the mayor's doorstep.

He frowned, and his eyebrows twitched. "I don't know, Miss Ellie-May. Riding around with all that money could be dangerous. What if you get caught? I still think burning it is the better option, much as it pains me to say so."

She shook her head. "The only way to get rid of Roberts for good is to convince him that the money isn't here at the farm. That...it's in the sheriff's hands."

Anvil ran his hand over his whiskered chin. "I still think my plan is best."

"My son was in danger today and almost killed a man." Shuddering at the memory, she suddenly felt cold and rubbed her hands up and down her arms. "That's something he would have had to live with for the rest of his born days. Do you know what a thing like that can do to a person?"

Anvil frowned. "No one would have blamed him."

"Maybe not," she said, her voice edged with doubt and frustration. Would a town that had blamed her for her father's deeds be less judgmental of her son? Somehow, she doubted it. "You know he's a sensitive child." Sensitive like his pa.

Anvil thumbed his suspenders and blew out his breath. "Okay, if your heart is set on returning the money to the bank, let me do it."

She shook her head. "This is something I have to take care of," she said. She would never know what madness had caused Neal to rob that stage, but she wanted to believe that he would approve of the money's return.

The next morning, Anvil stood in front of the barn, waiting for her when she returned from taking the children to school.

The moment she pulled up in front of him, he heaved the burlap sack into the back of the wagon. Earlier, she had stuffed the single banknote she'd taken into the sack and it was a relief to be rid of it.

"Do you want me to go with you?" he asked.

Grasping the reins of her horse in her hand, she shook her head. "I'll be all right." If something should go wrong, she didn't want to involve Anvil.

His frown told her he didn't approve, but he backed away. "Okay, then."

Tossing him a nod, she shook the reins and circled the wagon around. It was already hot and the air as thick as a wet blanket, but that was the least of her concerns.

If she got caught with the sack of stolen money, that would be the end. She would land in prison and would probably never again see the light of day. What would become of her children then? She had no family, and who in their right mind would want to adopt an outlaw's young'uns?

Cold sweat dripped off her forehead as she drove her horse and wagon to the mayor's house. Her heart pounded whenever she passed another on the road. She smiled and waved as she normally would, but her heart wasn't in it.

The mayor lived a couple of miles out of town, his house hugged by a small grove of trees. All was quiet when she pulled up in front. It was as if the very earth held its breath. Her heart thumping madly, she took a moment to calm down before climbing from her seat.

She wiped her damp hands on the side of her skirt and walked on wooden legs to the back of the wagon. All she had to do was place the sack on the mayor's porch, and the nightmare would be over. No one would know who put it there and her secret would be safe.

Just as she was about to reach into the back of the wagon, the door flew open, startling her. She whirled about just as the mayor stepped onto the porch.

"Mrs. Blackwell!" he called out in a cheery voice. "What a surprise. What brings you here?"

She stared at him, unable to move. "I...I..." Swallowing hard, she forced herself to think. "I was on the way to town and thought something...eh...was wrong with my wagon wheel."

"Well, we can't have that now, can we?" Much to her horror, he joined her and checked the back wheel.

The gunnysack was in plain sight, and there was nothing she could do about it except pray he didn't see it.

"Looks okay to me," he said.

"Th-thank you," she stammered, hoping he would leave. Instead, he proceeded to check the other three wheels.

"I don't see any problems, but you might want to stop at the wagon works in town and have Bobby Joe check."

"Thank you, I will," she said. Anxious to leave, she

climbed into the driver's seat and grabbed hold of the reins. "I won't take up any more of your time."

He looked up at her. "I wonder if you'd mind doing me a favor?"

"A favor?"

"My horse threw a shoe, and I don't have any way of getting to town. Since you're heading that way, I hope you don't mind giving me a lift."

She sucked in her breath. "Oh."

He gave her a questioning look. "You are headed for town, right?"

"Yes, of course," she said, and since there didn't seem to be any way out of it, she added, "I'd be happy to give you a lift."

"Much obliged. I have a meeting in town and don't want to be late." He indicated the house with a nod. "Let me just get my hat."

While the mayor returned to the house, Ellie-May glanced over her shoulder. The sack was in plain sight. Worse, so was the bank's name stamped on the side. She frantically scanned the wagon bed in search of something that could be thrown over the bag. Finding nothing, she visually searched the side of the road for a hiding place, but before she could act, the mayor returned and heaved his bulky form onto the passenger seat.

"You can drop me off at the stables," he said. "I need to make arrangements for the farrier to shoe my horse."

Nodding woodenly, she drove the wagon forward, her heart in her throat.

27

AFTER DROPPING THE MAYOR OFF AT THE STABLES, Ellie-May raced back home.

Anvil rushed out of the barn to greet her. Spotting the sack of money still in the back of the wagon, he frowned. "What happened?"

She jumped down from the wagon and quickly explained, her words tumbling out like rushing waters. Even now, long after the danger of being caught had passed, she was still shaking.

"So what do we do now?" Anvil asked.

"I don't know, but there's got to be a way of returning the money without being caught." It was the only way to end this nightmare.

Anvil scratched the side of his head. "I don't know, Miss Ellie-May. Times are tough. Much as I hate sayin' this, most people findin' that much loot ain't likely to turn it in."

She pressed her hands to her chest. Anvil was right, but the only way she could think to keep Roberts away was to get rid of the money. "There's got to be someone we can trust," she said.

Anvil looked dubious. "Until we figure out who that someone is, we best hide it." He reached into the wagon and groaned, hand on his back.

"Let me help you," she said, rushing to his side. The bag was bulky but not that heavy, weighing little more than forty pounds.

As they lifted the sack from the wagon, a thought suddenly occurred to her. "What about the church?" she asked. Pastor Wayne was a man of integrity. He would see that the money was returned to its rightful owner.

"What about the church?"

At the sound of Matt's voice, both she and Anvil froze, the sack of money slung between them like a dead body.

Matt stared at the bulging gunnysack Ellie-May and her farmhand were holding. The sack was tied with rawhide and filled his nose with a musky smell.

Her face ashen and eyes bright with fear, Ellie-May released her end of the bag, and it dropped to the ground. "What...what are you doing here?" she stammered.

"I hired a couple of men to watch your property should Roberts return," he said. "I was showing them around."

Her mouth dropped open. "You...you did that?" she said, clearly shocked.

"Yeah, I did. Like I told you, I don't want to see you or your children harmed."

She covered her trembling lips with her hand, and her shoulders slumped forward in defeat.

Matt tossed a nod at the gunnysack. Curiosity mingling with dread, he stared at Ellie-May with raised eyebrows. "Is this—?"

A look of despair crossed her face. "You got what you wanted," she said, her voice but a whisper.

Matt clenched his jaw. There was no denying he had wanted to find the stolen money, but he'd hoped to do it without implicating her or her family.

Anvil let go of the bag like it had suddenly burned his hands and stepped away.

Matt moved closer to the sack and squatted. Untying the rawhide string, he pulled out a stack of banknotes held together with a paper band. He rifled through the crisp bills and tried to ignore the sick feeling in his stomach. It was the loot he'd been looking for, all right. No question. He couldn't be certain, but it looked like it was all there.

He returned the banknotes to the sack and straightened. "What are you doing with it?"

Ellie-May seemed at a loss for words, so Anvil spoke in her place. "We were gonna return it to its rightful owner, and that's the God-honest truth."

Matt glanced at Ellie-May with a raised eyebrow. "After all this time, you finally decided to return it?"

"I only recently found it," she said, dropping her hand to her side. "I had no idea it was beneath the porch till the day I tried to fix the step."

His eyebrows drew together. "Was that when—?"

She nodded. "I was so sure you'd see the sack hidden there."

He remembered the day all too well. Even now, he could recall how fetching she'd looked. How they'd worked together. How, after he'd fixed the step, she'd given him her first real smile and the warm glow had followed him all the way back to town.

Funny how he could recall everything about her that day in startling detail but could hardly remember repairing the broken step. He remembered the captivating way she'd blushed when their fingers touched, her eyes shifting from sky blue to almost sapphire in color. At the time, he'd thought she was reacting to the spark that had flown between them. Now he knew the reason she had been so tense had nothing to do with him as he'd hoped and everything to do with protecting her deceased husband.

Silently cursing himself for having been so easily distracted, he shook his head. The money had been practically at his fingertips, and he'd missed it.

"Why didn't you just leave it hidden? Why return it now?"

She closed her eyes, her hands clutched to her chest, and he heard her intake of breath. After a long moment, she opened her eyes with a sigh. "I was afraid Roberts would come back. I couldn't take the chance of putting my children in further danger." She shuddered. "I can't forget that Lionel almost killed a man."

She fell silent and studied him with troubled eyes as if trying to decide how far she could trust him. When at last she spoke again, her voice was so soft, Matt had to lean forward to catch every word.

"Please don't think poorly of Neal," she pleaded.

"When he was Lionel's age, he accidentally killed his childhood friend. He was cleaning his rifle when it went off." Ellie-May paused for a moment, her face more serious than Matt had ever seen it. "Don't you see? Neal spent his life trying to make up for what he'd done. Even so, it haunted him till the day he died. That's why he was always doing for others." She wrung her hands together. "Why he ran into that burning school."

Anvil nodded. "He was a good man, that one."

Matt rubbed a finger along his upper lip. A childhood tragedy had defined Neal Blackwell's life, just as the death of his father had defined his.

Had his father not been shot, he doubted he'd be a Texas Ranger. His plan had always been to buy land and raise horses. Being a lawman had been the last thing on his mind.

As for his brother Charley... Had he not blamed himself for his father's death, would he still have turned to a life of crime? Matt doubted it.

Forcing such dark thoughts away, he stared at the bag of money. Even with the proof staring him in the face, he was reluctant to believe Blackwell guilty of robbing that stage. Matt didn't want to think that his desire to protect Ellie-May—protect her two adorable children—had blinded him to the truth, but there didn't seem to be any other explanation.

"The man you described doesn't sound like someone who would suddenly turn to stage robbery," he said.

His words softened her features. "I know," she said. "It makes no sense." Her eyes filled with tears.

"I never thought the man I married would do such a thing. Neal was good and kind and loving and…" She shook her head. "I don't know how to explain"—she tossed a nod at the gunnysack—"I don't know how to explain that."

Matt reached in his pocket for a clean handkerchief and handed it to her. He'd once worried that she had been involved in the holdup, but he now knew that wasn't true and he felt greatly relieved.

Murmuring thanks, she balled the handkerchief in her hand and dabbed at her eyes.

"You have what you came to town for," she said and implored him with tearful eyes. "Must you reveal where you got it? Can't you just return it to its rightful owners and be done with it?"

He backed away from her but only so he could think more clearly. Reminding himself that he was a Texas Ranger with a job to do, he shook his head. "I'll have to write a full report. It's my job."

"Please," she whispered. "Can't you leave Neal's name out of it?"

He sucked in his breath. "You're asking me to lie."

"I'm asking you to protect my children. If it's known that their father—" A sob stifled her words.

"Ellie-May…"

She looked away, and he felt about as bad as it was possible to feel. He wanted to protect her, protect her family. Heck, he even wanted to protect her deceased husband. He just didn't know how. Or even if he could.

Her gaze collided with his. "I don't want them growing up in the shadow of an outlaw father like

I did," she said, her voice barely above a whisper. "Surely, you can understand that."

He understood all right, but that only made his job harder. Grimacing, he stared at the sack of money. Usually, when he reached the end of an investigation, the pieces fell into place. But not this time. He'd come across other men who'd led double lives but not at the extremes Neal Blackwell had. It didn't seem possible that a man could be both a town hero and stage robber.

Things just didn't add up. Why would a man intent upon righting a terrible wrong done as a child suddenly turn thief? It made no sense. And why hide the money under the porch where it could do neither him nor his family any good?

"If it's known that the money has been turned in," Matt said, "Roberts will likely leave town."

"Good riddance!"

He frowned. "Ellie-May, I need time to figure out how to handle this."

She glared at him. "All you're interested in is catching your man! You don't care who gets hurt in the process."

"That's not true. I care, more than you know. But"—he paused, searching for words—"there's more to this story than we know. If we let Roberts get away, we might never know the truth."

"What truth?" she asked, her voice shaking. "The money was under my porch, and there's only one person who could have put it there." She twisted the handkerchief in her hands. "I just hope and pray that when the truth comes out, the town is kinder to my children than it ever was to me."

28

AFTER A SLEEPLESS NIGHT, ELLIE-MAY PREPARED HER-self to talk to Lionel and Alicia about their pa. She wasn't sure what would happen next, but once it was known what Neal had done, things were bound to get ugly.

She planned to keep the children home from school, and Anvil had taken over their chores. Until she knew for certain that Roberts had either been captured or had left the area, she didn't want to let the children out of her sight.

It was obvious by the way Lionel and Alicia kept looking at her during breakfast that they knew something was afoot.

She sat at the head of the table and waited for them to finish eating. Clasping her hands on her lap, she cleared her throat. "I need to talk to you about something,"

"Is it about the bad man?" Lionel asked.

"No, no, it's about your pa," Ellie-May said. After a moment's hesitation, she added, "We love him very much even though he can't be with us. And he loved us."

"He was a hero," Alicia said proudly.

Ellie-May smiled at her daughter. "Yes, yes, he was." She'd hoped and prayed that Alicia would always think of her father as a hero, but that now seemed unlikely.

Lionel's face was as serious as an old clock. "That bad man said Papa stole his money."

Alicia folded her arms across her middle, a defiant look on her face. "Papa didn't take anything that wasn't his. He wouldn't!"

"Why did he say those things about Papa?" Lionel looked to Ellie-May for an explanation.

The words she'd rehearsed now seemed all wrong. There was simply no way of explaining the stage robbery without destroying the memory of the father they adored, and that she couldn't do.

"I don't know," she said. It was the cowardly way out, but it was the best she could do for now.

"What did you want to talk to us about?" Alicia asked.

"I...just wanted to tell you that you're not going to school today."

Lionel frowned. "Is it cuz that bad man wants to get us?"

Alicia gasped and looked close to tears. "I don't want him to get us, Mama."

Ellie-May reached over to squeeze her daughter's hand. "No one's gonna get you, dear heart. We just have to stay in the house until Matt...Ranger Taggert says it's safe to leave."

Lionel gave his sister a sympathetic pat on the arm. "Don't worry. If that bad man comes back, I'll save you."

Lionel's promise seemed to satisfy his sister, but an uneasy tension filled the air for the rest of the morning. Ellie-May tried to carry on as usual. After washing the breakfast dishes, she had the children help her roll out dough for pies. But every sound, either real or imagined, sent her flying to the window, heart in her throat.

The rest of the day fared no better. The hours trickled by slowly, and still nothing happened. The wait was pure torture.

Ellie-May had no idea what to expect once news of the stolen money became known. Would angry citizens flock to her door? Would they tear down Neal's statue? Storm the new school? What?

Following yet another sleepless night, Ellie-May sent Anvil into town to see if there was any news.

"Nobody knows nothin'," he said upon his return. "Don't know what your Ranger friend did with the money, but he sure hasn't told anyone about it."

Ellie-May chewed on a fingernail. "That means Roberts is probably still in the area."

Anvil looked about as serious as she'd ever seen him look. "Could be, but don't you go worryin' none. Taggert's got two men watchin' the place just as he promised."

That relieved her mind a little but not completely. "I need to talk to Matt. Would you mind watching the children while I go to town? Promise me you won't let them out of your sight."

"Don't worry," Anvil said with a determined nod. "I'll watch them like a hawk. There ain't nobody gonna get to them as long as I'm around."

"Thank you, Anvil. You're a good friend." She then hurried to her room to change.

Less than an hour later, Ellie-May arrived in town and headed straight for the hotel. Matt wasn't in his room, and the desk clerk had no knowledge of his whereabouts.

"Where are you?" she muttered to herself as she stormed out of the hotel. "Where are you?"

So deep were her thoughts that she almost bumped headlong into Jesse. He looked almost as startled as she was. "Oh, sorry," she said and frowned. The boy looked close to tears. "Are you okay?" she asked in alarm. "What's wrong?"

"Nothing," he said with a quick swipe of his eyes.

She laid a hand on his shoulder. "Jesse, you can tell me. I'm your friend. Please. I can see that you're upset."

He hesitated for a moment before answering. "It's Pa."

She drew her hand away. "What about him?"

"Ranger Taggert arranged for him to stay with Doc Avery, but he refuses to go."

"Why Doc Avery?" she asked. "Is your pa sick?"

"He's not sick. It's cuz he drinks too much." Jesse gave her a hopeful look. "Doc Avery thinks he can help people like him." He sniffled as if to hold back tears. "Do you think he can?"

"I don't know, but if anyone can, it's Doc Avery," she said. "Maybe…maybe your pa just needs time to think about it."

"He said he won't go, and nothing will make him change his mind." Tears glimmered in the depth of Jesse's eyes.

Feeling bad for him, Ellie-May tried to think what to say to make him feel better. "Has Matt…Mr. Taggert talked to him?"

Jesse shook his head. "He thought it would be better if I talked to Pa first."

She squeezed his arm. "Don't give up, Jesse. Give your pa time. He may change his mind yet."

Jesse blinked and rubbed his nose with the back of his hand. "I don't think so, Mrs. Blackwell. Pa's not like that. If he says he won't do something, he means it."

"Where is your pa now?" she asked.

"He's at the Wandering Dog Saloon."

Ellie-May drew in her breath. "What do you say we stop at the Feedbag for ice cream." She was anxious to return home to her children but didn't want to leave Jesse in his present condition. "We can talk there. Maybe we can think of a way to make your pa change his mind."

Jesse shook his head. "Sorry, but I have to go to work. Mr. Gordon got a new shipment in and wants me to stock it. I gotta go or I'll be late."

Ellie-May watched him zigzag his way through traffic to the other side of the street, and it looked like he carried the world on his young shoulders. It nearly broke her heart to see him looking so dejected. As she stood watching him scamper up the steps to the opposite boardwalk, her pity turned to anger, and something snapped inside.

She whirled about and, after a moment of hesitation, stormed along the wooden sidewalk, her feet pounding the boards like two angry woodpeckers.

Looking neither left or right and pushing her own problems aside, she crossed the Dead Line separating moral businesses from the rest. No decent woman would be caught dead entering this section of town, but she was too incensed to care about propriety. Between concern for her children and now Jesse, she felt as if something was about to explode inside her. If she didn't do something, she would scream.

She stopped outside the swinging doors of the Wandering Dog Saloon for a moment before barreling inside.

The saloon was dimly lit, and it took a moment for her eyes to adjust. The bartender looked up from behind the long bar, the corners of his mustache drooping all the way to his chin. He arched an eyebrow as if to question her presence, then went back to drying glasses.

Since the place was almost empty, she had no trouble locating Jesse's pa slumped over a corner table.

Just as she reached his side, his arm shot out for the half-filled whiskey bottle. She grabbed the bottle first and moved it out of his reach. That got his attention.

James looked at her with bloodshot eyes. "Whatcha do that fer?"

"We need to talk."

"I ain't talking."

"Then I'll talk and you listen." She pulled out a chair and plopped herself down. "Jesse said you refuse to accept Doc Avery's invitation."

"You don't understand," he slurred.

"What don't I understand?" She lowered her voice. "What it's like to lose someone I cared about? How it feels to raise children alone?" *How it feels to know that your world is about to come to an end?* "What?"

James held his head in both hands and said nothing.

Arms on the table, Ellie-May leaned forward. "Penelope was my best friend. She would hate seeing you like this. Hate what you're doing to Jesse."

"The boy's fine. He can take care of hisself."

Ellie-May pounded her fist on the table, rattling his empty glass. "The boy is not fine. Do you know how he spends his time? How many jobs he works just to support your drinking habit? He's out all hours of the day and night. Shall I go on?"

James hid his face in his hands. "Leave me alone," he muttered.

She lowered her voice but spoke with no less urgency. "All Jesse's asking is that you give Doc Avery a chance."

"It won't work," James said, running his words together. "I can tell you that right now."

"Maybe it'll work. Maybe it won't." She had no idea what the doctor had proposed, but she trusted him. She'd known him almost all her life, and he was one of the few people who hadn't judged her for her father's deeds. "Doc Avery will do whatever he can to help you if you let him."

James dropped his hands. "Can he take away the hurt?"

The raw agony on his face made her heart ache. "No. No, he can't," she said quietly. "Only time can do that." She covered his hand with her own. "But you alone can ease Jesse's pain." She paused a moment before adding, "He hates seeing you like this. He lost his ma, but he's also lost his pa, and that's no less painful."

James failed to respond, and she couldn't tell by his closed expression if anything she'd said had penetrated his foggy brain. Not knowing what else she could say or do to make him change his mind, she fell silent. For several moments, they sat quietly, each in their own thoughts.

She finally withdrew her hand and stood. "I have to go." There didn't appear to be any more she could do there, and she was anxious to go home. She'd been away from her children longer than intended.

Without looking up, James asked, "How long would I have to stay?"

Feeling a flicker of hope, she sat down again. "That's up to you and the doctor."

He raised his eyes to hers. "What if it don't work?"

She patted him on the arm. "At least Jesse will know that you tried."

They sat side by side, neither saying a word. For some odd reason, she suddenly sensed a change in the room, a change in the air, and when she looked up, she saw him. Saw Matt—and he was looking straight at her.

She couldn't tell by his face what he was thinking. All she knew for sure was that the mere sight of him made her heart pound and her pulse race.

She leaned closer to James. "You don't have to do it alone. There's someone here who will help you get settled."

"Jesse…"

"Jesse will help you, too," she said. "All he wants is to get his pa back. That's all any of us want for him."

James didn't agree verbally to go to Doc Avery's, but his shoulders slumped forward as if in surrender, and a look of submission—maybe even hope—crossed his face.

Ellie-May sought Matt's eyes and nodded.

Matt joined them. "You did good," he mouthed, his eyes warm with approval. He then reached for Patrick James's arm and gently helped him to his feet.

29

ELLIE-MAY PACED THE FLOOR OF THE DOCTOR'S parlor, waiting for Matt and the doctor to get Jesse's pa settled. *What was taking so long?* She was anxious to go home but needed to talk to Matt.

When at last Matt appeared, he looked surprised to see her still there.

"Is he okay?" she asked.

"We'll know better in a day or two." His gaze softened. "You should go home and get some rest."

The look in his eyes and gentle tone of his voice brought her an unexpected jolt of pleasure. She didn't want it to. She still didn't trust him—not fully—and it wasn't just because of the kiss. Matt now knew the full truth about Neal and had within his power the ability to bring her world tumbling down.

She lowered her lashes. "I will," she said. After taking a moment to regain her composure, she looked up. Reminding herself of all the reasons she had to be wary of him, she said, "But first, we need to talk. Roberts…?"

He shook his head. "Still on the lam."

Weary with worry, she felt her temper flare. "As long as he thinks the money is at the farm, I can't let my children out of the house. I'm afraid to even let them out of my sight."

Hushing her, he motioned her to the door. "We can't talk here."

He led her outside, and she whirled around to face him. "If Roberts harms either one of my children—"

Matt pushed his hat back with the tip of his fingers. "I have a plan," he said, his voice low. "Do you want to hear it?"

She sucked in her breath. "What kind of plan?"

"I will make a call for volunteers to search the farm on Saturday."

She drew back. "Search the farm? For what?"

"Stolen loot."

"I don't understand," she said and frowned. "You have the money."

"Yes, but Roberts doesn't know that. I'm willing to bet he'll want to beat the crowd and get to the money before they do. When he shows up at your place, I'll be waiting."

"That's it?" Her temper snapped. "That's your plan? Bring him to the farm and endanger my children?"

"My plan is to catch him," Matt said, making it sound easy. "So he doesn't do you or your children any harm."

She bit her lower lip. "What makes you think he's still around? He might have left town by now."

"Possibly. But as far as he knows, the loot is still hidden beneath your porch. Saturday gives Roberts two days to retrieve it. Like I said. When he does, I'll be waiting for him."

"My children—"

He took both her hands in his, and the tender look in his eyes took her breath away. "Ellie-May, I won't let anything happen to them. You know that, right?"

She snatched her hands away, but only so she could think. "Don't make promises you can't keep. Once the truth is known, there'll be no saving them!"

"We don't know that. Your husband did a lot of good for this town. People aren't likely to forget that." He tilted his head. "Work with me."

She started to protest, but something in his eyes, his face, his voice stopped her.

"Please," he pressed, and this time, he held out his hand.

No longer able to deny his touch, she placed her hand in his.

He curled his fingers around hers, jolting her senses and adding to her torment. "Are you sure?"

Against her better judgment, she nodded, but only because she didn't know what else to do.

A look of approval crossed his face. "You won't be sorry. I promise, this whole thing will soon be over."

She hoped he was right, but in her heart, she knew otherwise. Once the truth was known about Neal, it would never be over. Not ever. Alicia and Lionel would always be known as the outlaw's children, and there wasn't a darn thing she could do about it.

No sooner had Matt watched Ellie-May leave in her horse and wagon than he heard his name. Turning, he saw Jesse waving his hat and calling to him from across the street.

"Ranger Taggert!" Ignoring the oncoming traffic, Jesse darted into the street and was almost hit by the hotel omnibus.

"Watch out!" Matt yelled.

The omnibus driver raised his fist and shouted obscenities, but Jesse didn't seem to notice. Instead, he leaped up to the sidewalk where Matt was standing and surprised him by throwing his arms around him.

As he hugged the boy back, Matt's memory shifted to another time, another place. It had happened the day his father had been shot and the sheriff had come to the house to break the news.

Charley had flung himself into Matt's arms, and the two of them had clung to each other as if to never let go. Matt hadn't known it at the time, but not only had he lost his pa that day but also his brother. For Charley was never the same after that.

Somehow, he'd failed Charley, but he hoped and prayed he didn't fail Jesse.

With that thought in mind, Matt gazed down at the boy wrapped in his arms. Jesse reminded him of Charley in so many ways. For that reason, Matt feared for him, feared for his future. He now knew how quickly things could go wrong. The best-laid plans could be wiped out in a single day, a single moment. A single heartbeat.

Surprised by the sudden blurring of his vision, Matt swallowed the lump in his throat and blinked the moisture from his eyes. "To what do I owe this?" he asked, his voice thick with emotion.

Jesse lifted his gaze to his. "You got Pa to go to Doc Avery's house."

"How do you know your pa's there?"

"Mrs. Avery saw me working at Gordon's and told me."

"Actually, it was Ellie... Mrs. Blackwell is the one you should be thanking."

Jesse pulled away, though he seemed as reluctant to do so as Matt was to let him go. "Do you think the doctor can cure Pa?"

Matt considered his answer with care. He didn't want to give Jesse false hope. But neither did he want to discourage him. "I don't know if a cure is possible, but I think Doc Avery can help him."

Jesse pursed his lips. "How long will he have to stay there?"

Matt laid his hand on Jesse's shoulder. "I reckon that's up to your pa, son. All we can do is hope and pray."

"Is that a rule?" Jesse asked, a glint of humor in his eyes.

Matt laughed. "I guess you could say that." He tossed a nod up the street. "Here's another rule for you: never miss a chance to celebrate a good thing. I believe this calls for a big bowl of ice cream."

The smile spreading across Jesse's face told Matt that was one rule the boy wouldn't fight him on.

All was quiet when Ellie-May reached home. Anvil and Lionel were playing chess, and Alicia was perfecting her sewing skills on a linen sampler.

"Everything okay?" Anvil asked. He and Lionel were seated opposite each other at the kitchen table.

"Yes," she said. Now that Jesse's pa was under Doc Avery's care, everything was more than okay. "Any… problems?"

"Other than the fact that Lionel just called checkmate, no," Anvil said, feigning disgust.

Lionel grinned. "Want to play another game?"

Anvil stood. "And get whupped again? No thank you. 'Sides, I have chores to do."

Ellie-May walked Anvil out to the porch where she could talk to him in private.

"Did you talk to the Ranger?" he asked.

She nodded. "We talked," she said and described Matt's plan to capture Roberts.

"Sounds good to me," Anvil said. "So why so glum?"

"I don't know. I just have a bad feeling about it," she said.

"I don't blame you for worryin'. But you can trust the Ranger."

She studied Anvil's well-lined face. The only person she'd ever really trusted was Neal, and look where that had gotten her. Her stomach twisted into a knot just thinking about how he'd betrayed her trust.

"How can you be so sure?" she asked.

"I just am," Anvil said with a mysterious smile. "Just as I'm sure Mr. Neal didn't steal no money."

30

Jesse walked into Matt's hotel room late that afternoon, looking glum as dry mud.

Watching him through the mirror, Matt reached for his gun belt and buckled it around his waist. "Why the long face?"

"Saw Pa this morning. He didn't look happy."

Matt felt bad for the boy. Jesse had been so worried about his pa, he'd insisted upon sleeping on the floor of Matt's hotel room so he could be close to him.

Matt turned away from the mirror. "Like I said, it'll take time."

Jesse sat on the edge of the bed and watched Matt don his vest. "How come you're going to the Blackwell farm?"

Matt's eyebrows shot up. "Who said I was?"

"You usually only shave in the morning."

Matt rubbed his smooth chin. The boy had a point. Blast it all. Nothing escaped Jesse's notice, that was for sure.

Stalling for time, Matt reached for his vest. No sense lying. Jesse wouldn't believe him if he did. On the other hand, he didn't want Jesse knowing the real reason he was heading to the farm was Roberts.

"Can't a man make a social call if he's got a mind to?"

Jesse's mouth curved in a slow smile. "I knew it. You *do* like her."

Matt grimaced. His feelings for Ellie-May Blackwell were too complicated to explain even to himself. She was a suspect's widow, for crying out loud. She claimed she'd found the money under the porch, and he wanted to believe her. But for all he knew, she could have been her husband's accomplice. As much as he didn't want to believe her guilty of any crime, no lawman worth his salt would overlook that possibility.

"I thought you liked her, too," Matt said, pretending to misunderstand.

"Yeah, but I don't want to kiss her." Showing his youthfulness, Jesse wrinkled his nose in disgust.

Matt stared at him. He was pretty sure Jesse hadn't seen them kiss, but apparently he'd seen enough. Great thunder, had his desire to kiss Ellie-May Blackwell been so obvious that even a thirteen-year-old had noticed?

Swallowing his irritation with the boy for making him recall the feel of Ellie-May's sweet lips on his, Matt pulled out his pocket watch. "Shouldn't you be getting ready for work or something?"

Jesse slid off the bed. "Oh yeah." He stopped at the door and looked over his shoulder. "What time will you be back?"

"When I get here," Matt muttered, turning to the mirror. "When I get here."

Matt waited until just before sunset before riding out to the Blackwell farm. After sending the two guardsmen he'd hired home, he hid his horse in an empty barn stall. He then settled down on Ellie-May's front porch where he could view the yard without being seen.

He'd done his share of surveillance through the years, but it never got easier. It wasn't in his nature to wait for things to happen. He only hoped that Roberts would take the bait and prevent the necessity of him having to spend a second night there.

Around nine o'clock, Ellie-May stepped out of the house and handed him a warm quilt and cup of coffee. Though she had agreed to work with him, he knew she didn't approve of his plan. For that reason, her thoughtful gesture came as a surprise.

Their fingers touched as he took the steaming mug from her, and he felt a physical jolt that was as pleasant as it was worrisome. "Much obliged."

She spread the quilt over his lap. "It gets cool at night," she said.

He took a deep breath and caught a whiff of lavender perfume. In the pale moonlight, her luminous eyes looked like stars and her hair shone like spun gold. But the moon also revealed a tightness of expression that he longed to smooth out.

He wished he could think of something to say to put her mind at ease. But now that the stolen money had been recovered, there was no way of protecting her or her children. If things were indeed as they seemed, soon everyone would know that the town hero was a thief.

He sensed her hesitation as she studied him. "You okay?" he asked.

She nodded and after a pause said, "I saw your brother's name in the paper. I know how hard it must be for you."

He heaved a sigh. *Hard* didn't even begin to describe it. Suddenly, the frustration that had been building inside him since reading about his brother's latest heist needed release.

"I'm sorry," she said, apparently misunderstanding his silence. "I didn't mean to..."

"It's all right," he said, not wanting her to feel bad. "I'm glad you did. You understand what it's like to have someone you love—" He didn't finish his sentence. Couldn't.

She commiserated with a nod of her head. "What are you going to do?" she asked.

"Do?"

She hesitated as if not wanting to put her thoughts into words. "If you catch him?" she said at last.

He sucked in his breath. "Funny, my captain asked me that very same question. I told him I would treat my brother like any other outlaw. At the time, I meant it."

"At the time?"

His thoughts traveled back for a moment before he explained. "When I finally did catch up to Charley, he pulled a gun on me and got away." Even now, it pained him just thinking about it. "That wouldn't have happened had it been anyone else. Because he was my brother, I'd let down my guard."

"That's understandable," she said, and even in the soft light, he could see the sympathy in her eyes.

He shook his head. "Not for a Texas Ranger."

"You were a brother long before you were a Ranger," she said.

"It didn't matter to Charley that we were brothers." Matt rubbed his chin, but nothing could be done about the ache in his heart. "I'd hoped to stop him before someone got hurt." Before Charley got hurt. "His Wanted posters read 'Dead or alive.' Some bounty hunters aren't fussy how they haul someone in. Long as they get the reward."

"Maybe you can still get to him first," she said. "Now that your job here is almost done."

He didn't have a lot of hope of saving Charley, but still he nodded. "You better go in," he said, even as he wanted her to stay. There wasn't enough shadow on the porch to hide them both.

She hesitated. "Do you really think Roberts will show?" she asked.

"Don't know. But if he does, I'm ready."

"Good night," she said, her voice as troubled as her expression. "Be careful."

Her concern for his safety touched him, and he swallowed hard. "I will."

Silently, she turned to the house. She stopped in the doorway and glanced at him over her shoulder. Their gazes locked for a moment before she stepped inside and closed the door, leaving him to his disturbing thoughts and the long, lonely night ahead.

And the night was long, and it was lonely.

As dawn began tiptoeing across the distant hills, he

wondered if he had Roberts pegged all wrong. Maybe the man had decided to forget about the money and run. Maybe he'd sensed a trap. A dozen other possibilities sifted through Matt's head like sand in an hourglass.

Yawning, he stood and stretched. Every muscle in his body ached. Rubbing his neck, he surveyed the land. It looked to be another hot day. The sky was clear, and already the air felt warm.

Peace and serenity greeted the early morning light, but so did the effects of the drought. What grass had survived was brown and the soil barren. Nevertheless, it was a good piece of land with a lot of possibilities and reminded him of his long-forgotten dreams.

Dreams about owning a horse ranch. Dreams that included a wife and family. Dreams that had been wiped out by a single bullet to his pa's chest.

He was saved from his thoughts by the sound of children's voices, along with the music box playing "All the Pretty Little Horses." A rooster greeted the rising sun with a lusty crow.

The door creaked opened, and Lionel peered at him, his eyes round with curiosity. "Breakfast is ready," he announced.

"Thanks, son." Matt hadn't counted on breakfast, but he wasn't about to turn down the offer. He entered the house and followed the welcome smell of coffee and bacon to the kitchen.

Ellie-May looked like she hadn't gotten any more sleep than he had. Her face was pale, and blue shadows skirted her dark, solemn eyes.

He answered her silent query with a shake of his head. No sign of Roberts.

She tucked a strand of hair behind her ear and reached for the coffeepot.

"Smells good," he said.

"Scalding hot and barefooted. Just how you like it," she said. After filling his cup, she set the coffeepot on the stove and shoved her hands into her apron pockets. "Now what?"

He leaned back against the kitchen counter and took a sip of the hot brew before answering. "We do it again tonight."

"And if Roberts doesn't show?" she asked. The look on her face told him she still didn't approve of his plan.

"I'll cancel Saturday's search and turn the money over to the sheriff," he said.

She drew in her breath as if bracing herself for the worst. It suddenly became necessary for him to move as far away as the small kitchen allowed. It was the only way to keep from taking her in his arms and telling her that everything would be all right.

❧

The following night, Ellie-May stepped outside again with coffee and quilt. She couldn't see Matt in the dark shadows of the porch, but she could feel his strong, masculine presence. Just knowing he was there was both comforting and alarming.

Alarming, because she hated what he was doing. Though she'd agreed to work with him, she still hated how her family's welfare hung in his hands. Hated more than anything how he'd used her. Even though he'd denied it, she had a hard time thinking his interest in her family was real. But even as she doubted his sincerity and worried about the wisdom of his plan, she still felt compelled to see to his comfort. It made no sense.

"Brought you coffee," she said, keeping her voice low.

She heard him shift in his chair. "And not a moment too soon," he murmured back. He sounded tired.

Irritated at how his nearness made her feel all fluttery and nervous inside, she handed him the steaming cup. Their fingers touched for a mere second, but it was enough to make her heart beat faster. Ignoring the temptation to lean in closer, she stepped back. Careful to avoid the stream of moonlight that flooded half the porch, she was grateful for the shadows that hid her blazing face.

"Ellie-May, we need to talk about tomorrow," Matt said, his voice as low as it was serious.

The tone of his voice made her pull her shawl tight around her shoulders and stare at his dark form. Tomorrow, the truth would be known, and she'd no longer be able to protect Lionel and Alicia from the scorn that would surely come their way.

"If nothing happens tonight," he said slowly, "I'm gonna have to turn the money over to the sheriff."

"I know," she managed to squeak out.

"No one's gonna blame you or your children."

Something snapped inside her. "You don't know that."

"I won't let anyone hurt you," he said, his voice thick with meaning.

She wanted to believe he meant what he said, but he was a relative stranger in town and didn't know it the way she did.

"And who's gonna to protect us after you're gone?" she asked. Giving him no chance to answer, she continued. "They've treated Neal like a hero. How do you think people will feel once they know that he—"

"Things aren't always what they seem," he said, and something in his voice told her he was no longer talking about tomorrow; he was talking about something more intimate. He was talking about the kiss they'd shared. The kiss that continued to haunt her, even as she'd tried denying it had ever happened.

Not wanting to go there—unable to go there—she forced herself to concentrate on the immediate problem. "No one else could have hidden that money beneath our porch," she said. "Only Neal."

Fighting back tears, she turned to the door. But just as she reached for the doorknob, something made her stop.

The sound of a galloping horse.

Matt heard it, too, as he was on his feet in a flash, a speck of moonlight glinting off the gun in his hand.

"Quick! In the house," he ordered, not bothering to lower his voice. No sooner had he spoken than the night was shattered by the blast of gunfire.

31

MATT DUCKED LOW. AFTER MAKING SURE THAT ELLIE-May was safely inside the house, he peered between the porch railings.

Ears ringing from the sound of gunfire, he quickly assessed the situation. The shots had been fired from behind the toolshed. He knew where Roberts was. What he didn't know was the identity of the horseman.

The galloping horse came to a quick halt in front of the house, and another shot rent the air. The horse reared back on its hind legs with a loud whinny and tossed its rider to the ground.

Matt caught only a quick glimpse at the rider as he fell, but it was enough to send a cold chill shooting through him. *What in blazes is Jesse doing here?*

Fearing the worst and mindless of his own safety, Matt leaped off the porch, gun in hand, and ran to the still-dark form on the ground. More shots were fired, and the bullets hit the ground by his feet as he ran.

"Jesse!" He dropped to his knees by the boy's side and shook him. "Are you hurt?"

Jesse raised his head. "Pa's gone," he said, seemingly oblivious at having been shot at or even the danger that he was still in.

Matt reared back. "What?"

"Pa left Doc's house, and I can't find him."

Cursing, Matt quickly checked Jesse over for injuries. He felt no blood, but the boy winced when Matt moved his right arm. "I want you to go to the side of the house. Can you do that for me?"

"Yes, sir."

"Stay there and don't move. Understood?"

"Yes, sir."

For once, Jesse didn't argue, which was proof enough that the boy was hurting or scared or both.

Matt shielded Jesse with his body and waited for him to reach safety before springing into action. Crouching low, he leaped forward and darted behind a tree.

"Roberts! Come out with your hands up!"

Roberts fired again, a flash of light showing he was still behind the woodshed. Matt held his gun steady but didn't fire back.

The big, orange moon was straight up, and there was no way of reaching the toolshed without being an open target.

His best chance was to get Roberts to fire until he had to reload again. It took what? Fifteen, twenty seconds to load a gun. With his long legs, Matt could cover a lot of ground in that amount of time.

With this new plan in mind, Matt pulled the trigger, careful not to aim at the man. He wanted Roberts alive.

As predicted, Roberts fired back. *One, two, three*...

Roberts kept firing, which could only mean he had two guns. Cursing beneath his breath, Matt ducked low and considered his other options. He then heard a yell, a grunt, and a groan. What the...?

Bolting forward, he found Anvil and Roberts rolling on the ground behind the toolshed, both clutching a single gun between them.

Timing his move, Matt jammed his weapon against Roberts's back. "Hold it right there!"

Roberts froze in place, allowing Anvil to roll away and stagger to his feet.

"Drop the gun," Matt said. When Roberts didn't immediately obey, he repeated the command, this time sharper. "I said, drop it."

The gun fell from Roberts's hand, and Matt kicked it away. He glanced at Anvil.

The older man stood panting like an old hound, blood trickling down the side of his face.

"You okay?"

Anvil nodded. "There's rope in the shed," he said. "I'll get it."

Moments later, Roberts's hands were cuffed and his feet secured with rope at the ankles. Matt wasn't about to take chances on Roberts escaping a second time. He was about to ask Anvil to check on Jesse when the boy's voice rang out behind him.

"We got him!"

"What do you mean *we*?" Matt muttered.

"I mean you and me," Jesse said.

Matt frowned. Jesse had almost gotten himself killed, but now didn't seem like the time or place to scold him. Even in the dim light, he could see the boy was hurting. His arm hung at a strange angle, like it was broken, and his face was as white as new-fallen snow.

"Anvil, you better take him to town and have the doctor look at that arm. Might not be a bad idea for you to be checked out by the doc as well."

Anvil nodded. "Come on, boy."

Jesse grabbed his arm and groaned. "Rangers don't leave their partners during a takedown," he said, his voice weak. "It's a rule."

"Yeah, well, here's another rule," Matt said. "If you want to be a Ranger, you're gonna have to make staying alive a priority. Consider it rule number one."

Ellie-May hunkered down in the dark, the shotgun in her hands pointed at the closed door. Outside, the shooting had stopped, but the stretch of silence was even more frightening than the gunshots had been, and her brain conjured up all sorts of scary images.

Was Matt all right? What if he was wounded? What if he was lying on the ground, bleeding? What if he were…? Even knowing how he'd used her, she didn't want to see him hurt.

A dozen unsettling thoughts raced through her head. Clamping down on the worst of them, she tried to think what to do. It was still hours until daylight, and by then, it could be too late to save him. On the other hand, Roberts could be waiting to pounce the moment she opened the door, and she couldn't take the chance with her children's safety at stake.

She strained her ears, hoping to hear something—anything—that would tell her Matt was uninjured, but the harrowing silence continued. The gunfire hadn't awakened Alicia or Lionel, and for that, she was grateful. It seemed that no matter how much she'd tried protecting them, danger kept landing on her doorstep.

Seconds turned into minutes, and minutes turned into what seemed like hours.

At long last, she heard something. Footsteps on her porch. Clutching the shotgun, she felt her mouth run dry and her knees threaten to buckle. Nerves taut, she held her finger on the trigger, ready to fire.

The knock made her jump, and she almost dropped her weapon. "Ellie-May. It's me, Matt!"

With a cry of relief, she lowered the shotgun. Jumping to her feet, she ran to the door and released the lock. The moon was now behind the house, and the porch was in total darkness. Still, she could see that Matt wasn't alone.

"Can we come in?" he asked.

"Yes, of course." Stepping aside, she stood her shotgun against the wall and turned to reach for the box of matches on the table. She lit the gas lamp with shaking hands and blew out the match.

Turning, she gasped upon seeing Roberts. His hands cuffed, he was bleeding at the mouth.

"He and Anvil got into a tussle," Matt explained.

"Is Anvil…?"

"He's okay. So is Jesse."

She blinked. "Jesse's here, too?"

A resigned expression flitted across Matt's face. "Oh

yeah, he's here, and he's lucky to be alive. He hurt his arm and Anvil's taking him to see the doc." Matt turned to his prisoner and pushed him into a chair. "Our friend here has an interesting story to tell." Matt leaned over him. "Mrs. Blackwell is gonna want to hear it. Suppose you start at the beginning."

Roberts looked up at Matt with hate-filled eyes and clamped his lips tight.

Matt leaned closer. "You heard me. Start talking!"

"I ain't sayin' no more."

Matt drew back, "Wrong answer." He pulled out his gun and held it to the man's temple. "If you know what's good for you, you'll start by telling the lady how you and her husband met."

Roberts glared at Ellie-May, and his face brought back terrible memories. Recalling how he'd frightened Lionel, something snapped inside her, and she flew at Roberts with pommeling fists.

Roberts yelped when her fists landed on his already wounded jaw. "All right, all right," he yelled. Eyes rounded, he looked more scared of her than Matt's gun. "We met on the road outside town."

Ellie-May backed away, hands clutched to her chest. Not sure whether she wanted to hear more, she held her breath and froze.

Matt pressed Roberts to continued. "How did you meet?"

"I'd been shot, and Blackwell found me."

Matt locked Ellie-May in his gaze a moment before asking the next question. "Was that before or after you'd robbed the stage?"

"After."

The air left Ellie-May's lungs. "After?" she whispered.

Matt nodded. "Your husband had nothing to do with the robbery." He nudged Roberts again. "Go on. Tell her the rest."

Roberts continued in a low, rambling voice. "I took a bullet in my leg and was bleeding bad. My horse had bolted, and I had no way of getting back to town. Your husband found me on the side of the road. I told him I was on the stage when it was robbed and was shot by the highwayman. Blackwell bandaged me up and was gonna take me to the doctor, but I begged him not to. I said I couldn't afford to pay no doctor. So he drove me here to his farm to doctor me up himself."

"He brought you here?" Ellie-May asked, shocked.

Roberts nodded. "Yeah, but when your husband pulled up to the farm, he spotted the bag of money I'd snuck into the back of his wagon, and that's when the truth dawned on him."

Ellie-May gasped. "That means that Neal never—"

Oh God. How could she have ever thought otherwise? Tears of relief stung her eyes. Guilt filled her chest. She should have trusted in Neal. Believed in him. Why hadn't she?

"Then what happened?" Matt asked.

"When he threatened to turn me in, I lied about having a sick wife at home, and we made a deal."

Matt backed away and holstered his gun. "What kind of deal?"

"I begged Blackwell to give me time to do the right thing and go to the sheriff myself."

"And he agreed?"

"He didn't want to, but I told him I needed to talk to my wife and square things with her first. He insisted that the money stay with him. Said I had twenty-four hours to do the right thing before he turned the money over to the sheriff hisself."

"So you left the money with Blackwell," Matt said.

Roberts's face darkened. "What else could I do? My leg hurt like the dickens. I'd lost a lot of blood. I knew if I tried anything, he could overtake me. I had no choice but to agree to his terms. He then drove me to town to the doctor's office and told the doc that I had accidentally shot myself while cleaning my gun. He then paid the doctor outta his own pocket."

"Neal did that?" Ellie-May whispered and then thought of something "But…but I don't understand. The day you came to the door, you knew so much about Neal. About what had happened to his child-hood friend. How did you know all that?"

After a moment of silence, Matt pressed the tip of the gun against Roberts's head. "The lady asked you a question."

"Okay, okay." Roberts glared at her. "I asked around and found out he was from Hannibal. Turns out I have a cousin there. A couple of wires later, I had all the information I needed. It was the only way I could make you believe your husband and me were friends."

Ellie-May let out her breath. She couldn't believe she'd been so easily duped.

Matt reached in his vest pocket. "This is Blackwell's train ticket," he said, waving it. "How did it end up at the crime scene?"

Roberts stared at the ticket and shrugged. "Beats

me. 'Less he dropped it when he checked out the location of the robbery. He insisted upon checking it before we drove to town."

Matt frowned. "Why would Blackwell do that?"

"He was worried that the driver or one of the other passengers had been injured. By the time we got there, the stage was gone."

Matt returned the ticket to his pocket. "What made you come back to Haywire?"

Roberts rubbed his sore chin before answering. "I read about the statue dedication in the paper. That's when I found out that Blackwell died before my twenty-four hours were up. I figured that meant the money was still here on the farm somewhere." He glared at Ellie-May as if she were to blame for all his troubles. "If it weren't for her brat of a son—"

Not giving him a chance to finish, Ellie-May darted toward him a second time, but Matt stopped her with a hand to her wrist.

She gazed up at him with tear-filled eyes. "Neal. Didn't—"

"I know, Ellie-May." Matt said in a soothing voice. "It's over."

"Thanks to you," she whispered, her heart filled with gratitude. Had he not set a trap for Roberts, she might have spent her whole life thinking Neal had robbed that stage. "Thanks to you."

32

MRS. BUTTONWOOD WAS THE FIRST TO ARRIVE AT THE farm the following day. "Heard you had some trouble out here last night," she said, brandishing a basketful of medicinal concoctions. Without waiting for a reply, she added, "Heard Anvil got himself injured again."

Ellie-May motioned her into the house. News traveled quickly in Haywire, but never as fast as it seemed to reach Mrs. Buttonwood's ears. "Yes, but not seriously. He just has a few cuts and bruises."

A look of horror crossed Mrs. Buttonwood's face. "Mercy me. I swear he needs a full-time nurse. Thank goodness he was around to save you."

"Yes…uh… He was a big help." Ellie-May led her to the kitchen where Anvil was eating breakfast. "Look who's here," she announced.

Setting his fork down, Anvil stood politely and studied the widow with wary regard.

Mrs. Buttonwood quickly inspected his bruised face. "Oh, you poor thing," she cooed.

Anvil gave her a sheepish grin. "It looks worse than it is," he said.

"We'll see about that." Mrs. Buttonwood waited for him to finish his breakfast, then set to work giving his wounds more attention than they deserved. Since no snake poison was involved, she treated his wounds more gently this time, and Anvil relished her attention like a puppy lapped up milk.

After Mrs. Buttonwood had left, Ellie-May couldn't help but tease him. "Why, Anvil. I do believe you've set your cap for her."

Anvil's eyebrows practically reached his hairline. "Set my cap, nothing," he grumbled. "I was just being polite."

"Hmm." Ellie-May leaned her back against the kitchen counter and folded her arms. "Have you ever thought about getting married again?"

"No! Like I told you, I have no intention of marryin' Mrs. Buttonwood."

"I don't mean to her. But to anyone?"

Anvil refilled his coffee cup before replying. "Tried that once and it didn't work out. My wife thought she'd married a banker, and I thought I'd married a homemaker."

Anvil hadn't talked much about his early days except to say his wife had run away with a traveling salesman. That was when his life had fallen apart, and he ended up living by the railroad tracks.

"I don't see Mrs. Buttonwood running off with a salesman," Ellie-May said.

"Maybe not," he said, cradling his cup in both hands. "But what can a man like me offer a woman like her? She owns her own ranch. All I own are the clothes on my back. And I'm not exactly celebrated for my beauty, you know."

"You have a lot to offer," Ellie-May said. "Your kindness and protection."

Anvil scoffed. "Trust me. That woman don't need no protection. Anyone messin' with her would rue the day." He took a long sip of coffee and put the empty cup in the sink. "'Sides, I belong here. You and the children are the closest thing I have to family."

"We'd still be your family, no matter what," Ellie-May said. "Nothing would change that."

"Yeah, but it wouldn't be the same if I was livin' somewhere else."

She laid a hand on his arm. "I don't want you giving up a chance of future happiness out of an obligation to me."

His eyebrows shot up. "Is that what you think I'm doin'?"

She removed her hand. "You tell me. Is it?"

"You and Mr. Neal saved my life," he said with meaning. "I ain't 'bout to forget that."

"You've more than paid us back for anything we did," Ellie-May said. "I don't know what I would have done this past year without you."

"Yeah, well, enough 'bout me," he said. "What about you?"

"What about me?"

"Ever think 'bout gettin' hitched again?"

Ellie-May laughed. "Who's gonna marry a poor farmer like me with two children?" And an outlaw's daughter, no less.

He shrugged. "A man with a good head on his shoulders, that's who."

She sighed. "Aren't many of those around, I'm afraid."

"You might be surprised," Anvil said.

Irritated that the mere mention of marriage conjured up memories of Matt Taggert, Ellie-May cleared the dirty dishes off the table to signal the subject closed. Much to her annoyance, Anvil refused to take the hint.

"I kinda thought that you and that Texas Ranger might, you know…"

"You thought wrong," she said a bit too hastily and immediately regretted being so abrupt. Knowing that Anvil meant well, she apologized. "I'm sorry. It's just that so much has happened."

"It's me who should do the apologizin'. I know when I've overstepped the line."

"If anyone is allowed to do that, it's you," she said. "You're family. And…" She bit her lower lip. "You believed in Neal when I didn't."

"Now don't you go blamin' yourself for that," Anvil said. "I have to admit that when I first found that money, I had my doubts, too."

"Thank you," she said, feeling somewhat better. "You're a good friend."

He gave his head an emphatic nod. "Remember that the next time I go stickin' my nose where it don't belong," he said and started for the kitchen door. "I best get back to work."

"Would you mind rigging the wagon?" she called after him. "I need to go to town."

"Will do."

Matt found James at the Wandering Dog Saloon, sitting at his usual table. Swallowing his anger, Matt pulled out a chair and sat. "Why'd you leave the doc's house?"

"Got my reasons," James said without looking up.

Matt pounded the table with his fist. "Your son's lucky to be alive, no thanks to you!"

James pulled his gaze away from the still-untouched bottle of whiskey. "Yeah, so he said."

Matt regarded James with more than a little surprise. The whites of James's eyes looked more pink today than red, and his speech wasn't slurred. "You talked to him?"

"Yeah. He told me what happened."

"Did he tell you that you leaving the doc's place almost got him shot?"

James let out a long sigh. "I had to leave. I'm cured. See?" He pointed to the full bottle. "Haven't touched it."

Matt scoffed. "You were only at the doc's place for three days. That's not long enough to cure a blister."

James folded his elbows on the table and clenched his hands together. "You try staying in a room with a bunch of drunks and see how fast you get cured." His face grew dark. "After I sobered up, I got a good look at the others. Never saw a more sorrowful bunch of losers in my life. I realized that's how I must have looked to Jesse."

Matt scoffed. "You just realized that?"

"Things are a bit clearer when you're sober." The corners of James's mouth turned down. "Ellie-May was right. Penelope might forgive me for causing her death, but she would never forgive me for neglecting our son."

"So now what are you going to do?" Matt asked.

"The doc called in Pastor Wayne, and after a lot of prayin', the two talked me into reopenin' my woodworkin' business. The doc said he'd needed a chest of drawers, and the coffin-maker had made him one." James made a face. "I swear, the thing looks like a pine box."

Matt laughed. "So are you going to take their suggestion?"

"Thinking about it. That pine box in the doc's office might give his patients the wrong idea. I gotta fix that."

"You up to it?" Matt indicated the whiskey bottle with a toss of his head. "Could be a hard road ahead."

James hesitated a moment before answering. "I know. But Pastor Wayne made me realize that the bottle ain't gonna fix my grief." He fell silent for a moment before adding in a lighter tone, "It won't be easy living on just food and water, but I did it once. With the pastor and Doc's help, I reckon I can do it again."

Matt studied James with narrowed eyes. He sounded sober. Heck, he even sounded sincere, but that didn't mean his troubles were over.

"So what are you doing here?"

James leaned back in his chair. "Needed to make sure I was strong enough to resist it before I went home."

Matt glanced at the brown bottle that stood like a sentinel in the middle of the table. "And if you're not?"

"Then may I rot in Hades."

33

ELLIE-MAY STOOD IN FRONT OF NEAL'S STATUE AND stared up at her husband's face with mixed emotions.

Neal had had nothing to do with the stage robbery, and her children's future was safe from scorn. For that, she was greatly relieved and, more than anything, grateful. She might have even felt happy had it not been for the guilt pressing down on her like a heavy weight.

Such was her remorse that she imagined that the blue jay sitting on Neal's shoulder was squawking at her in disgust.

"Shoo!" she yelled, waving her arms. The bird took to the sky, leaving her alone with her thoughts.

Even the act of breathing seemed to hurt. *Oh, Neal. Will you ever forgive me?*

She must have been out of her mind to think that her dear, sweet husband would do something so awful as rob a stage. One sack—one lousy sack of money— and she had jumped to all the wrong conclusions and believed the worst about him.

She should have known better. She'd done to Neal

what the town had done to her: judged him unfairly. To some, she would always be an outlaw's daughter. Nothing she could do about that.

She'd heard it said that people see in others what they see in themselves. If true, then what did assuming the worst about Neal say about her? That it wasn't just the town that saw her as an outlaw's daughter but that was how she saw herself?

Such were her thoughts that she failed to notice that she was no longer alone until a voice broke through the early morning quiet.

"Thought I recognized your horse and wagon."

Startled by how the mere sound of Matt's voice made her pulse pound, she turned, and her heart took another leap.

Matt touched the brim of his hat in greeting. "Just wanted you to know, Roberts made a full confession to the sheriff. Your husband is officially in the clear."

"Thank you," she said, and though the words came from the deepest part of her heart, they seemed lacking in some way. Inadequate.

"Just doing my job."

"It was more than that," she said. "You believed in Neal even when I didn't. For that, I'll always be grateful."

His gaze softened as he studied her. Today, his dark eyes reflected glimmers of light that were more gold than brown. "I don't think you stopped believing in him. I think you stopped believing in yourself. Believing in your own judgment."

The kindness of his reply—maybe even the truth of it—caught her off guard. His effect on her only added to her remorse. To have such confused and unresolved feelings for a man not her husband added yet another layer of guilt to her already burdened shoulders, and tears sprang to her eyes.

Concern shadowed Matt's face as he reached into his pocket for a handkerchief. "I didn't mean to make you cry." Stepping forward, he dabbed at her moist cheeks, and his gentle touch sent warm ripples trickling down her spine. He must have felt her tremble as he pulled his hand away. "You okay?"

She nodded. "I just feel terrible. I knew the kind of man Neal was, and yet I believed the worst about him."

"The evidence was pretty compelling."

"But not to you," she said.

He shrugged. "I have to admit, I had my doubts. But something didn't sit right. Comes with years of experience. I've been around long enough to know things aren't always what they seem. So don't be so rough on yourself. Anyone in your shoes would have jumped to the same conclusion. And I think if your husband were here, he'd tell you the same thing."

"That's…very kind of you to say." His words didn't completely absolve her guilt, but they did make her feel better. Especially the part about Neal.

"I'm not just saying it. I mean it." He tilted his head, and his brow furrowed. "I hope you don't still believe I tried to trap you. I would never use you or your children in such a way."

She studied him. If what he said was true, then his kiss had meant something, and his interest in her family had been real. The thought brought a jolt of pleasure followed by another surge of guilt. *Forgive me, Neal…*

"It looks like I was wrong on two accounts," she said. "I was wrong about you and wrong about Neal."

"Kissing you was a mistake and should never have happened. I don't blame you for not trusting me."

Biting her lower lip, she wondered how he could so easily discount something that had affected her so deeply. Not wanting him to know how much his words cut her to the core, she lowered her lashes and moistened her lips. "I guess now that your work is done here, you'll be on your way."

"That's the plan," he said, dashing any hope she had of him staying. "I asked Doc Avery to keep an eye on Jesse."

She met his gaze. "Jesse will miss you," she said. *I'll miss you…*

Matt smiled fondly and rubbed the back of his neck. "Much as I hate to admit it, I'll miss him, too."

They gazed at each other for a moment without speaking. Unable to tell from his expression what he was thinking, she waited for him to say something. To reach out and touch her. To tell her he didn't want to go. To say that he'd miss her, too, and that kissing her had not been a mistake. But the words she longed to hear didn't come, and the silence hung between them like a thick veil.

"I guess this is so long," he said, snuffing out the last of her hopes.

"Guess so," she said, her voice hoarse.

"Take care of yourself."

She lifted her chin and squared her shoulders. "You, too," she said, sounding brighter than she felt.

He looked about to say something more but instead turned and walked back to his horse. Not wanting to see him leave, she swung around to face her husband's statue.

Caught between the two men who were lost to her, she felt her heart break into a thousand little pieces.

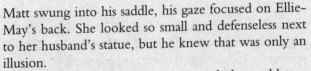

Matt swung into his saddle, his gaze focused on Ellie-May's back. She looked so small and defenseless next to her husband's statue, but he knew that was only an illusion.

Where her children were concerned, she could turn into a lioness in a blink of an eye. That was one of the things he most admired about her. If his own mother had been more like Ellie-May, perhaps Charley wouldn't be in the bind he was today. Instead, their mother had folded like a wilted flower after his father's death and had never recovered.

Not wanting to dwell on the past, Matt pushed his thoughts aside, but the future wasn't looking that great, either. He knew saying goodbye would be tough but never had he imagined how tough. The call to duty was great, but the call of his heart was even greater.

He was tempted to go back to her—to say the things that had been left unsaid—but she'd turned to face her husband's towering image, and that told him where her heart was.

Neal Blackwell was the town hero and deservedly

so. What mortal could compete with such a man? Matt sure couldn't. Wasn't sure he wanted to.

He had a job to do. There were outlaws to catch and still that business with his father's death and the need to seek justice. But the uppermost thing in his mind was the burning hope he could still save his brother.

Oh yes, there were reasons aplenty for not giving in to the dictates of his heart.

Once he hit the road and returned to his unit, he would put Ellie-May Blackwell out of his mind for good. Had to.

His thoughts as tangled as straw in a mattress, Matt tugged on the reins and headed back to his hotel. After paying his bill, he raced upstairs to his room to grab his bedroll and other belongings and left.

Moments later, as he stood tying his bedroll to the back of his saddle, Jesse ran up to him, his arm in a sling. Today, he was all smiles.

"What's up, Ranger?" Matt asked. "Your pa okay?"

"Yeah. He spends a lot of time with Doc Avery, but he stays away from his saloon."

"Not his saloon anymore, son," Matt said. The good Lord willing, it would never be again.

Jesse's grin almost reached his ears. "Came to tell you that Pa's gonna reopen his furniture company, and he's hiring me as his partner. He's getting a new sign that reads 'James and Son, Fine Furniture.'"

Matt arched an eyebrow. Never had he imagined James had it in him to turn his life around. "That's good news."

"I told Pa what you said about changing my name,

but he said that would be a mistake. Said it was high time that people started thinking fine furniture when they heard the James name. Not outlaws."

Matt nodded approval. "I agree with your pa," he said. "Guess that means you'll have to quit your other jobs."

"Already have." Jesse flashed a quick smile before turning serious. "Pa said that if I ever see him touch a bottle, I'm to fetch the doc right away."

Matt nodded approval. It sounded like James was doing everything right. "Glad things worked out," he said. His bedroll secure, Matt tightened the saddle's tie strap. "What about your plan to join the Rangers?"

Jesse hesitated. "I guess it'll have to wait. Pa needs me."

Matt squeezed the boy's shoulder. "I'd say you need each other."

Jesse scraped the ground with the toe of his boot. "I'm gonna miss you," he said, narrowing his eyes. "You have to promise to write to me."

"Will do," Matt said, pulling his hand away. "Any chance I can talk you into returning to school?"

Jesse made a face. "Pa said if I wanted to be his partner, I had to go to school in the mornings and work for him the rest of the day."

Matt grinned. Good for his pa! Since Jesse looked about to tear up, Matt reached into his pocket for a coin. "James and Son calls for a celebration. I'd say ice cream is in order."

Jesse's face broke into a wide grin. "Oh yeah. I forgot. Celebrating is one of your rules."

"Here's another rule—take care of yourself. And take care of your pa."

"I will," Jesse said.

Surprised once again by his reluctance to leave, Matt sucked in his breath. "I gotta go. Got a train to catch."

The corners of Jesse's mouth drooped. "Wish you didn't have to go."

"It's time. My job is done here." Matt slipped his foot into the stirrup of his horse and mounted. "Will you do me a favor? Will you check on Mrs. Blackwell from time to time?"

Jesse's forehead creased. "I was right. You do like her."

Matt sucked in his breath, and a wave of emotions washed over him. *Like* didn't begin to describe his feelings. Still, if he admitted even to himself any more than that, he'd never be able to leave town.

"Yeah, I like her," he said.

"Then why are you leaving?"

"Got work to do," he said, and before Jesse could ask any more questions, Matt snapped the reins and rode off with a wave of his hand.

His heart seemed to grow heavier by the minute as he arranged for his horse to be transported on the animal car and boarded the train himself. He didn't even chance a glance out the window for a last glimpse at the town. Didn't dare.

34

FOR THE NEXT THREE MONTHS, MATT TRIED FORGET-
ting Haywire and all that had happened there. Tried
forgetting a certain pretty lady and her two adorable
children. Tried focusing solely on work and tracking
down his brother.

Other than the fact that Charley was still on the
lam, it had been a productive three months. The
Rangers had helped settle a labor dispute and tracked
down a group of fence cutters. They'd also caught a
gang of cattle rustlers that had been plaguing the area
for months.

Catching the rustlers had required Matt's company
to spend long hours in the saddle. Matt spent even
longer nights tossing and turning on the hard ground
beneath the starry skies while the others slept. This
gave him plenty of time to think about things he
didn't want to think about. Remember things he'd
best forget. Like pretty blue eyes and a winning sweet
smile.

Though he was tempted to chuck it all and return
to Haywire, he wouldn't. Couldn't. He had things to

do. Outlaws to catch. Responsibilities. Promises to keep.

Charley was now one of Texas's most wanted men and always seemed to be one step ahead of the law. No bank was safe. He had even managed what many had thought impossible; he had single-handedly held up a train.

It was this latest holdup that convinced the captain to relent and let Matt work solely on the case.

Matt immediately set to work questioning witnesses, hoping for that one vital clue that had so far eluded him. Eluded everyone.

Finally, he got his wish. It happened shortly after Charley robbed a stage outside Austin.

One of the passengers was a telegraph operator by the name of Abigail Meadows. Miss Meadows was a small, meek, birdlike spinster who hardly seemed like the kind of person to give anyone trouble, let alone an outlaw like Charley. But she had noticed something that no one else had—the man who'd robbed her stage wore an unusual deer head signet ring.

During the excitement that followed the holdup, she'd forgotten about the ring. It wasn't until she'd spotted the same exact band on a man in town that she thought about it.

She then did something unexpected and most likely out of character for her—she bravely followed the man to his cabin.

It was the very same cabin that Matt scoped out late that afternoon from behind a grove of trees. Rangers Parker and Madison were supposed to have met him there, but so far neither of them had shown up.

Matt grimaced. Should he wait for them to arrive or move in? The fact that the captain had arranged for the other two Rangers to meet him was proof that he still didn't trust Matt to treat his brother like any other outlaw.

Rankled by the thought, Matt studied the house with narrowed eyes. Built from white-washed adobe with a flat roof, it was just as Miss Meadows had described it. The ends of wooden support poles jutted out from beneath the roofline, and green shutters hung haphazardly from a single window.

It had been roughly built as a square box with a stone porch leading up to a weathered wooden door. The house probably once belonged to a miner. Years ago, gold and silver were discovered in the area, and people had flocked there in droves. Cabins sprang up like mushrooms after the rain. Unfortunately, the hoped-for boom failed to materialize, and the makeshift cabins were deserted as quickly as they'd been built.

Matt had imagined this moment many times over—the moment he came face-to-face again with his brother. He thought about what he would say to him. If he could get Charley to surrender, a judge was more likely to be lenient. The outlaw Jesse James's brother Frank had turned himself in. He then stood trial and was acquitted. Word was that the man had gone straight. Matt hoped the same for Charley.

Wishing he had a spyglass, Matt narrowed his eyes against the glare of the late-afternoon sun. The only sign of life was a single brown gelding tethered in front. The horse was saddled, which suggested that Charley planned to go out.

His impatience growing by the minute, Matt forced himself to wait for the other two Rangers. Did they get lost? What?

The sun sank lower into the sky, sending long shadows creeping across the earth like giant fingers. It was the fading light that made Matt decide to act.

Eyes alert for the least bit of movement at the house, he crept to the edge of the trees. The gelding twisted its head to one side, cocked its ears, and stared at Matt.

Matt covered the twenty or thirty feet between the trees and house without making a sound. The soil was soft, muting his steps. The horse maintained its intense stare but didn't move.

Speaking softly to the horse, Matt untied it and kept hold of the reins. He'd hoped that releasing the horse would bring Charley outside on the run. The cabin was miles from town, and the loss of his horse would present a hardship. The problem was the soil was soft and the sound of horse's hooves might not be heard from the house.

In the end, the gelding solved the problem by tossing his head back with a loud neigh. Matt barely had time to slap the horse's rump to get him running before the door to the cabin sprung open. He ducked out of sight by the side of the porch just in the nick of time.

Seemingly oblivious to everything else, Charley ran down the porch steps, waving his hands over his head and yelling for his horse to come back.

Matt stepped up behind him, gun drawn. "Hi, Charley."

Charley whirled around, hand on his holster. Quickly recovering from his initial surprise, his lips thinned into a smirking smile. "Well, if it's not my dear brother. How'd you find me?"

"I have my ways," Matt said. Charley was younger than Matt by five years. Maybe it was the mustache, or even the cynical expression, but today, he looked considerably older. "You'll make it a lot easier on us both if you throw down your gun and put your hands up."

Charley scoffed. "When have I ever taken the easy way out?"

"I don't want to see you get hurt."

"Oh no? Then what are you doing here?"

"Hoping to take you in nice and peaceful-like," Matt said. "You have a price on your head. Better to come with me than to chance facing a bounty hunter."

Charley gave a short, hollow laugh. "Go with you? What? And get my neck in a loop? No necktie party I ever saw was nice and peaceful."

"Far as I know, you're only wanted for robbery," Matt said. "Frank James turned himself in and was acquitted."

Charley scoffed. "You think that'll happen to me?"

Matt shrugged. "Maybe. Maybe not. The most you'll get is time in the state pen."

"You have it all figured out, don't you? Like always. After Pa was shot, the family fell apart, but not you. You were the big man. You didn't even blame me for his death."

"Wasn't your fault."

"There you go again." Charley sniffed. "Always

taking the high road. 'Course it was my fault. Pa wouldn't have been at that shop had I not forgotten to pick up kerosene on the way home from school."

Matt studied his brother and remembered something Ellie-May had said. "So how much longer do you plan on punishing yourself?" Matt knew arguing with his brother would do no good. Still, he had to try.

"Is that what you think I'm doing?" Charley asked. "Punishing myself?"

"If living on the lam isn't punishment, I don't know what is."

"So what's your excuse?"

Matt arched an eyebrow. "My excuse?"

"Granted, what you do is more respectable than what I do. But the results are the same. We're both running from the past. So what do you have to feel guilty about?"

Matt stared at him. True, he'd wondered if he'd let his brother down in some way. But it had nothing to do with guilt. Nothing to do with choosing to live life on a saddle rather than settling down. Nothing to do with leaving the woman he loved.

Startled by the last thought, he drew in his breath. "I'm not running," he said.

Charley shrugged. "Whatever you say."

"Right now, I say to drop your gun," Matt said. "Let's not make this any more difficult than it already is."

"You're the one making it difficult," Charley said.

Matt's patience snapped. "Do you think I like this? Like having to arrest you? You have no idea how many nights I've spent wondering what I could have done differently. How I could have saved you."

"I'm not a child anymore," Charley said. "You don't have to save me."

"You're still my brother," Matt said. "Nothing's ever gonna change that."

Some undefined emotion crossed Charley's face just before he turned and walked away.

"Stop. Where do you think you're going?"

Charley paused midstep. "What are you gonna do? Shoot me in the back?" He peered over his shoulder. "My money says you won't." He started walking away again.

"I said stop, dang it!"

Charley kept walking, and Matt fired a warning shot. The bullet hit the ground no more than two feet away from Charley's feet, but he kept walking.

When a second warning shot failed to stop him, Matt took off after him. Just as he reached out his hand, Charley swung around. With lightning speed, he grabbed Matt's arm at the wrist and wrenched the gun upward. Before Matt could gain control of the gun, Charley kneed him between the legs.

The gun dropped out of Matt's hand. "Arrgh." Bent over in pain, he looked up to find Charley's gun pointed at him.

"Don't move," Charley said.

"Or what? You'll shoot me?"

"Don't make me do something we'll both regret." Releasing the safety catch of his gun, Charley kicked Matt's Colt away. He tossed a nod at the handcuffs hanging from Matt's belt and inclined his head toward the porch. "You know what to do."

Hands held outward, Matt searched Charley's face

for some sign of the brother he'd once known, the brother who would have sooner jumped off a cliff than hurt someone. But the eyes looking back at him belonged to a stranger.

Charley's expression darkened. "You heard me. Move it!"

"Don't do this, Charley. Let me take you in. We'll find you the best lawyers. It's what Pa would have wanted—"

"Shut your mouth," Charley said, scowling. "I don't want to hear it." With a nod of his head, he indicated the porch. "Move!"

Matt started toward the porch without another word. Charley had been so sure that Matt couldn't shoot him, and dang it, he'd been right. All that business about treating his brother like any other outlaw had been a lie. Not only had Matt failed the Texas Rangers, he'd failed himself.

As if guessing his thoughts, Charley said, "If you're wondering whether I could pull this trigger, let me assure you I can and will. If you know what's good for you, you'll do as I say."

Looking into Charley's hard, cold eyes sent a chill crawling down Matt's spine. At that moment, he had no doubt that Charley meant every word.

Matt unclipped his cuffs. "This isn't how it was meant to be. You and me. We were meant to be a team."

Charley indicated the cuffs in Matt's hands with a nod of his head. "Shut up and do it!"

Even as Matt snapped one cuff on his own wrist and the other cuff to the porch railing, he kept talking.

What he couldn't do with his gun, he hoped he could do with his words. To that end, he spoke of their childhood and the battles they had fought together and won.

Charley stared at Matt long and hard, a suspicious gleam in his dark, sad eyes. Matt felt his hopes rise, only to be dashed a moment later. ,

"Sorry, Brother," Charley said, his voice breaking. "Maybe you'll have better luck the next time we meet." He then holstered his gun and lumbered away.

35

ELLIE-MAY LOWERED HER MENDING TO HER LAP. "That's a very nice picture," she said to her son, who had spent most of the afternoon drawing.

"This is Anvil," Lionel explained, pointing to a stick figure. "And he's catching a big fish."

"So I see," Ellie-May said.

"I drew a picture for you, too, Ma." He held up a second drawing. "It's you trying to cook Anvil's fish."

Ellie-May laughed at the large fish flopping over the length of a stove.

Lionel looked pleased. "I knew I could make you laugh," he said, his eyes solemn. "I don't like it when you look sad." He brightened. "Maybe my drawing will make Anvil laugh, too."

Ellie-May studied her son and felt the frozen lake of her heart begin to melt. Since Matt had left, she hadn't felt much like laughing. Hadn't felt much like doing anything. She'd been so wrapped up in her own feelings, she'd failed to notice how her dark mood affected her children. Now that she thought about it, Anvil hadn't been himself lately, either.

Knowing the reason behind her own melancholy, she had a pretty good idea what was going on with Anvil. The question was what to do about it.

It took Ellie-May most of the night to think up a plan. She wasn't sure it would work, but it was worth a try. She found Anvil the following morning in the barn, changing a wagon wheel. He looked up as she approached.

"Something wrong?" he asked.

She drew in her breath. "Yes...you're fired." It wasn't the speech she'd practiced, but judging by the look of disbelief on his face, it had shocked him out of his lethargic mood.

"Wh-what did you say?" he stammered.

She folded her arms across her chest. "You heard me."

Anvil tossed his wrench into his toolbox and stood. "You can't fire me," he said.

"I just did."

He frowned. "How are you and the children gonna get along without me? Eh? Tell me that."

"I'm sure we'll manage," she said. She hated letting him go, but it was for his own good. She doubted he could survive another winter in the drafty loft.

His forehead ridged like a washboard, he studied her. "What's this really about?"

"Ever since you stopped seeing Mrs. Buttonwood, you've been moping around like a lost puppy. Even the children have noticed."

"I wouldn't talk if I was you. You ain't exactly been a barrel of laughs yourself, you know." When she made no comment, Anvil narrowed his eyes. "So you think that firin' me will make me what? Accept her proposal?"

"Actually, I was hoping me firing you would make you propose to Mrs. Buttonwood yourself."

He stepped back, an incredulous look on his face. "You want me to propose to her? B-b-but if I do that, we might end up gettin' hitched," he stammered.

She laughed. "That's usually how it works."

His eyebrows drew together. "I don't know, Miss Ellie-May," he said, shaking his head. "I don't even know if she's the right woman for me."

"Maybe it's time you found out," Ellie-May said.

"Maybe." He thumbed the straps of his overalls. "But then there's the promise I made to myself after your husband died. I promised to take care of his family like he took care of me."

"You've done that," Ellie-May said, her voice breaking with emotion. "And I'll always be grateful. But Neal would have wanted what's best for you. He would have wanted you to be happy."

"I *am* happy," Anvil said. "Or at least I was till you fired me."

Ellie-May sighed. "All right, you're not fired. For now."

He tossed a nod at the wagon wheel. "Does that mean I can go back to work?"

She nodded. "But only if you promise to think about what I said."

"I'll think about it. But don't go 'spectin' me to change my mind."

Ellie-May sighed. "All right. You win for now. But I'm not giving up."

Anvil lifted his eyes to the ceiling. "Unfortunately, neither is Mrs. Buttonwood."

∞

By the time Parker and Madison arrived at the cabin and released Matt from the handcuffs, it had already turned dark, and Charley was long gone.

Most of the others, including the captain, had turned in by the time the three of them rode into camp, and only a few glowing embers of the campfire remained.

Without bothering to undress, Matt threw himself on his cot and spent the rest of the night staring at the dark and going over everything that had happened.

He felt about as bad as it was possible to feel, and his throbbing head had nothing to do with it. His brother had escaped, yet again, and it was all his fault.

He should have planned better. Should have waited for Parker and Madison. Should have done a dozen things differently. Once again, his impatience had gotten the best of him.

Or maybe it was his arrogance. He'd been so certain he alone could save his brother. Well, Charley had relieved him of that notion.

Never would Matt forget Charley's expression while holding him at gunpoint. Would his brother have pulled the trigger? It was a question Matt didn't want to answer.

After a long and sleepless night, Matt greeted the bright morning sun with a groan. He kicked off his thin blanket and rose. Running his fingers through his hair, he left the tent without bothering with his morning ablutions and immediately regretted it. He'd hoped to grab a cup of coffee before having to face the captain.

But Captain McDonald was already up and immaculately groomed, with not a hair out of place. He greeted Matt with a frown and thrust a cup of coffee in his hand. "You look like you need that more than I do."

Wishing he'd taken the time to at least shave, Matt took a sip of the hot brew and waited for the captain to pour himself another cup. "I let Charley get away again," he said.

The captain arched an eyebrow. "Let him?"

Matt drew in his breath. "I told you I would treat him like any other criminal. I didn't. For that reason, I have no choice but to turn in my resignation."

The captain took a sip of his coffee before speaking. "You're one of my best men," he said, surprising Matt with his praise. "Men as dedicated as you are hard to come by. It would be a shame for you to quit."

For a long while, Matt didn't say anything. He kept thinking of something Ellie-May had said. *You were a brother before you were a Ranger.*

The echo of her words ringing in his head, he gripped his cup. "You once told me that your men had to be Rangers first. Everything else had to come in second."

The captain nodded. "I still stand by those words."

"I put Charley before my job. I put family first. For that reason, it's best if I go."

The captain stared at him long and hard. "Anything I can say to make you change your mind?"

Matt shook his head. "No, nothing."

"So what are your plans?"

Matt drew in his breath. Good question. "Haven't got that far yet." He hadn't thought much past that moment.

The captain took another sip of coffee and said. "Sorry to see you go."

"Yeah, me, too." Matt drained his cup and walked back to his tent. Glancing at the stained canvas walls, he wondered what would be next. He didn't know anything but how to be a Ranger. That had been his life for more than ten years.

He shaved and packed up his few belongings. He was just about to leave the tent when he heard a shout outside.

"We got him."

Frowning, Matt stuck his head through the tent opening. "Got who?" he called.

"We got Charley," Madison called from atop his horse.

His heart in his throat, Matt stepped outside the tent. That was when he saw him—his brother astride a pony, his hands cuffed behind his back. As much as he'd wanted to be the one bringing him in, it was a relief to see Charley unhurt.

"Where'd you find him?" Matt asked.

Madison dismounted before answering. "It was the strangest thing," he said, shaking his head. "We found him by the side of the road. Just sitting there as if he was waiting for us." According to Madison's account, Charley had seemed like he wanted to be caught.

Matt turned a questioning gaze in Charley's

direction. For a split second, Matt caught a glimpse of the brother he'd once known. The brother who used to follow him around and climb into his bed at night. The brother who had clung to him the day of their father's death.

All too soon, the sneering face and mocking eyes returned. But Matt had seen, and he knew. What Madison said was true; Charley had wanted to be caught.

Maybe he was just tired of running. Or perhaps his conscience had gotten the better of him. Maybe he'd finally punished himself enough for Pa's death. Maybe something Matt said had finally penetrated Charley's thick skull. Whatever the reason for his brother's change of heart, one thing was clear—Charley had wanted to be stopped. Needed to be stopped. He just didn't want Matt to be the one stopping him.

For one fleeting moment in time, Matt had caught a glimpse into his brother's soul…and maybe even his heart. It was enough to know that Charley had protected him as he had so often protected Charley. He'd done that by making sure that Matt would never have to go through the agony of arresting him.

The two of them were still a team.

∞

Ellie-May set her basket of clean laundry next to the clothesline. The sky was crystal clear and the sun blazing hot, but she'd hardly noticed.

Matt was very much on her mind and for good reason. News of his brother's capture had graced the front page of the *Haywire Dispatch* that morning.

She'd searched the newspaper in vain for Matt's name. The Texas Rangers were given full credit for the man's capture, but no individual names were mentioned.

Sighing, she reached for a wet towel. Matt had been gone for more than three months, but the memory of him was just as strong now as it had been the day he'd left. The misery of missing him just as intense.

Such were her thoughts, so when she noticed the black horse by the barn, she thought at first she was imagining things. But it sure did look like Matt's horse, Justice.

Abandoning her wash, she hiked up her skirt and rushed to the barn.

Inside, Matt greeted her with a smile. "Hello, Ellie-May."

Her breath caught in her chest. He looked every bit as tall as she remembered. Every bit as handsome. "I...I didn't expect you to come back," she said. It irritated her that after all this time, the mere sight of him could still make her heart beat faster.

"I didn't expect to come back," he said.

She gave him a questioning look. "What are you doing here?"

He glanced around the barn. "Right now, I'm thinking about the first time we met," he said. "You with a shotgun."

The memory brought a flush to her face, and she moistened her lips. "I...I read about your brother's capture in the paper," she said. "I looked for your name."

"He's serving time in the state pen."

"I'm sorry," she said. "It must be hard for you."

"Not as hard as it was when he was on the loose. At least now I know he's safe. With good behavior, he'll be out in a few years."

"That's...that's good to hear."

"The thing is..." He looked away for a moment as if to gather his thoughts. "I didn't capture him. Someone else did." He paused for a moment as if to let that sink in. "Made me realize there are dozens of men who could do the job I'd set for myself. Dozens of capable men who can bring outlaws to their knees." His voice grew hoarse. "But there's only one man who can love you the way I love you. Love your children the way I do, and that man is me."

She stared at him, not sure she could trust her own ears, let alone her eyes. Was she dreaming? Was he really standing there? Had he really said what she thought he'd said? Or was she simply imagining him there as she had so many times before.

"Why...why are you saying these things?" she stammered.

"Because they're true. Every last word." Closing the distance between them, he took both her hands in his. Only then, upon feeling his touch, did she dare believe this wasn't a dream. He was real. The moment was real. She tried to speak but couldn't find her voice.

He gazed into her eyes with such tenderness, he took her breath away. When he spoke again, his voice was thick with emotion. "For three long months, I've been telling myself that I'm not the kind to settle down, but it turns out that I was only lying to myself. You're all I could think about. The only one I want to be with. Lionel said I'd made a good pa, and I'd like the chance to prove him right."

Tears sprang to her eyes. Never did she think to hear such sweet words. "Oh, Matt," she managed at last. "Are you sure? Your pa...?"

He nodded and squeezed her hands. "You once asked me how many criminals it would take to make up for my pa's death. I don't know if there is an answer to that. But I do know this: it would only take loving one woman—loving you—to make me the happiest man in the world. I love you, Ellie-May Blackwell. And I think Pa would approve. But"—he searched her face—"I need to know if there's any chance that you and I—"

Locking his words in her heart, she pulled her hands from his and threw her arms around his neck. Staring up at him with tear-filled eyes, she whispered, "Oh, Matt!"

Hands around her waist, he held her tight and grinned down at her. "Does this mean what I think it means?"

Joy bubbling inside, she didn't know whether to laugh or cry. "It means I love you, too, and being with you would make me the happiest woman in the world."

His grin widened. "I think I loved you the moment I first set eyes on you," he said, his voice catching with emotion.

She drew in her breath and tried to think when she had first fallen in love with him. "I think I fell in love with you the day I came to your hotel room."

He looked at her with a mischievous glint in his eyes. "It was my bare chest, right?"

She blushed at the memory. "Not exactly. It was your kindness when I told you I was an outlaw's daughter. That meant a lot to me." Still did.

He gently knuckled away a tear on her cheek and caressed her face with his hands. "I don't want you thinking of yourself as an outlaw's daughter. Once we're married, I want you to think of yourself only as my beautiful wife."

"I think I can manage that," she whispered. "Long as you think of yourself as my handsome husband."

"Handsome, eh?" He laughed and then kissed her tenderly but oh so thoroughly on the lips.

Epilogue

FOR HER WEDDING DAY, ELLIE-MAY HAD LOANED Anvil Neal's frock coat and dark pants. Surprisingly, the suit fit him without much in the way of alterations. "Don't you look handsome?" she said, straightening his bow tie.

Anvil looked pleased. "And you look mighty purty yourself," he said, bringing a blush to her face.

"Thanks to Mrs. Buttonwood," she said. The woman had insisted upon making Ellie-May's wedding gown. The ivory dress with its lace bodice, satin paniers, and short train was far more elegant than anything Ellie-May had ever owned.

She had decided against a veil. Instead, she chose to wear the blue and yellow wildflowers in her hair that had been picked by Alicia and Lionel.

Anvil crooked his elbow. "Ready?"

Smiling up at him, Ellie-May slipped her arm through his. "Ready," she said. "More than ready."

Matt had insisted the wedding take place inside the barn where he'd first set eyes on her. Thanks to Mrs. Buttonwood and the ladies of her quilting bee, the barn had been transformed with candles, streamers, and satin bows.

"I'm ready, too," Lionel said, looking sharp in his knee pants and little bow tie.

Alicia adjusted the basket of rose petals on her arm. "Me, too."

Her children's affection for Matt filled Ellie-May's heart with unbelievable joy and thanksgiving.

Anvil nodded. "What do you say we get this over with so we can get to the good stuff."

Ellie-May arched an eyebrow. "The good stuff?"

Anvil grinned. "Me and Mrs. Buttonwood are gettin' hitched, too."

"Anvil, that's wonderful!" Ellie-May arched an eyebrow. "Who proposed this time?"

"Who do you think?" Anvil said, avoiding her gaze.

Ellie-May laughed. "I can't believe you said yes."

"Why wouldn't I?" he said, sounding defensive. "I saw how happy you and Taggert are together. Made me want some of that good stuff for myself."

"Oh, Anvil." She gave him an affectionate hug. "I'm so happy for you, and I wish you all the happiness in the world."

The sound of a fiddle playing "Here Comes the Bride" drifted from inside the barn. "I think that's our cue," Anvil said, signaling Alicia to move with a nod of his head.

The thrill of anticipation rushed through Ellie-May as she and Anvil followed Alicia and Lionel into the barn and down the center aisle. Matt stood in between the minister and his best man, Jesse. Mrs. Buttonwood had insisted upon being Ellie-May's bridesmaid and had even relinquished her usual manly attire for a dress. Anvil's eyes lit up when he saw his future bride, and Ellie-May gave his arm an affectionate squeeze.

When the two of them reached the front of the barn, Anvil took her hand and placed it in Matt's. "I love you," Matt said, his eyes filled with tenderness.

Locking the moment in her heart, she whispered back, "I love you, too."

Jesse flashed a know-it-all grin. "See? I told you," he said in all seriousness. "It's a rule. Sometimes things *are* exactly as they seem."

Matt laughed. "Yes, they are," he said, gazing deeply into her eyes. "Yes, they most certainly are."

Author's Note

Dear Readers,

I hope you enjoyed Matt and Ellie-May's story. This is the third and last book in the Haywire Brides series. If you missed *Cowboy Charm School* and *The Cowboy Meets His Match*, both books are still available.

I don't know if this happens to other writers, but I've had some strange things happen during the writing of a book. I once turned a manuscript in to my editor at the same time as another writer turned in hers. Oddly enough, our protagonists shared the same first names and professions. There were also many other similarities throughout our manuscripts, and all had to be changed.

Another time, I was hiking a trail in Mammoth when I met a geologist who was the spitting image of the geologist hero in the book I was working on. Even weirder, his first name was Damian, and I'd named my hero Damon. Close enough, right?

But the strangest thing that happened occurred recently. I'd been toying with the idea of taking an Ancestry DNA test for quite some time, so my daughter decided to gift me with one for Christmas. The results were pretty much what I expected, with one surprise. It turns out that the outlaw Jesse James and I share a common ancestor.

The timing was especially weird since Jesse James was a character in *The Outlaw's Daughter*, which I had just completed. Come to think of it, it's not the first time Jesse James has popped up in one of my books, and I can't count how many blogs I've written about the outlaw.

That's because Jesse is an interesting person to write about. Not only was he controversial, but he had both a light and a dark side. The son of a Baptist minister, he was known to pass out press releases to witnesses at his holdups and had no qualms about exaggerating his height. He might also be the only person on record to take a gang on his honeymoon. I don't know what his bride did while he and his partners in crime robbed a stage. Maybe she went shopping.

Jesse James lived for only thirty-four years, but there was never a dull moment. He was a Confederate guerrilla, was shot in the chest on two separate occasions, and once overdosed on morphine. He also claimed to have murdered seventeen people, although some historians suspect that number was exaggerated.

Jesse went by many aliases, but his nickname was Dingus because he shot off the tip of his finger while cleaning his pistol. After forming a friendship with the editor and publisher of the *Kansas City Times*, he wrote many letters for the newspaper about his gang and political beliefs. He also claimed that they robbed the rich and gave to the poor, though all indications are that the gang kept the spoils to themselves.

Far as I know, he was also the first person to prove that housework can kill. While cleaning a dusty picture, he was fatally shot in the back of the head by his new hire Bob Ford, who hoped to collect a reward and promised amnesty for his own crimes.

I can't tell you what it was about Jesse James that first caught my interest. I can't even tell you why this writer, who's allergic to horses, writes Westerns. All I can say is that it must be in my DNA.

Until next time,

Margaret

Acknowledgments

I always feel a little sad whenever I finish writing the last book in a series, and this time is no different. *The Outlaw's Daughter* is book number forty-eight for me. When I sat down all those years ago to write my first book, I never imagined such a thing.

If I were to thank everyone who made this amazing journey possible, it would require another whole book. For brevity's sake, I'll mention just a few, starting with my publisher, the amazing Sourcebooks, whose motto is "Books change lives."

I'm especially grateful to my editor, Mary Altman, whose editorial help, keen insight, and thoughtful suggestions help turn my flaws into strengths and make my books better than I thought they could ever be.

As always, I can't say enough about my super-agent, Natasha Kern, who gallantly leads the way through the crazy maze of publishing. I'll always be grateful for having her as a mentor, friend, and cheerleader!

Also, a big thank-you to my family and friends who patiently put up with me spacing out and talking about people who don't exist.

Finally, I want to thank my readers. So many of you have written to say my words mean a lot. Well, your words mean a lot to me, too, especially when you take the time to post a review on one of the many media outlets. Nothing sells books better than word of mouth, and I thank you one and all!

margaret-brownley.com

Read on for an excerpt from

LEFT
at the
ALTAR

The first book in the A Match Made in
Texas series by Margaret Brownley

1

Two-Time, Texas
1880

"Fifty-four minutes."

Her father's booming voice made Meg Lockwood want to scream. But airing her lungs in church wasn't an option, and thanks to the whalebone corset beneath her wedding gown, neither was breathing.

"Mama, make him stop."

Her mother straightened the garland of daisies in Meg's hair for perhaps the hundredth time so far that day before turning to her husband. "Henry, must you?"

Papa kept his gaze glued to his gold pocket watch rather than answer, his wagging finger ready to drop the instant the minute hand moved. Not by any means a formal man, he'd battled with Mama over his wedding attire until, like a defeated general, he'd thrown up his arms in surrender. Unfortunately, the knee-length coat Mama had chosen emphasized Papa's ungainly shape, which bore a striking resemblance to a pickle barrel.

The finger came down. "He is now fifty-five minutes late."

Meg's hands curled around the satin fabric of her skirt. Where *was* her bridegroom? She hated to keep the wedding guests waiting, but she didn't know what to do. Time meant nothing to her erstwhile fiancé, but he'd promised not to be late for their wedding. She'd trusted him to keep his word.

Just you wait, Tommy Farrell!

When he finally did show up, she wouldn't be responsible for her actions.

Tommy wasn't the only reason for her ill temper. As if her too-tight corset wasn't bad enough, the ruffled lace at her neck made her skin itch, and the butterfly bustle hung like a brick at the small of her back. Worse, the torture chambers disguised as dainty white slippers were killing her feet.

The church organ in the nearby sanctuary moaned louder, as if even the organist's patience was spent. The somber chords now rattled the walls of the tiny anteroom, threatening the framed picture and forcing the glass beads on the kerosene lamp to jiggle in protest.

She met her mother's worried gaze in the beveled-glass mirror. At forty-five, Elizabeth Lockwood still moved with the ease and grace of a woman half her age. The green velvet gown showed off her still-tiny waist and slim hips.

A wistful look smoothed the lines of worry on her mother's face. "You look beautiful."

Meg forced a smile. "So do you, Mama."

Meg had inherited her mother's honey-blond hair,

turquoise eyes, and dainty features, but her restless countenance was clearly thanks to her father's side.

"Fifty-*six* minutes late," her father exclaimed, and Meg's already taut nerves threatened to snap.

Clenching her hands tightly, she spun around to face him. "You never change!"

"Change? Change!" Papa looked indignant as a self-righteous preacher. "Why would I? Someone has to maintain a healthy respect for time."

The door swung open. *Thank goodness.* Meg whirled about again, ready to give her errant fiancé a piece of her mind, but it was only her older sister. The worried frown on Josie's face told Meg everything she needed to know, but still she had to ask.

"Anything?"

Josie shook her head. At twenty-three, she was two years older than Meg, and at five foot ten, stood a good six inches taller. Today she wore a dusky-rose gown that complemented her dark hair and gave her complexion a pretty pink glow. She took after Papa's side in looks, but of the three Lockwood girls, she was most like Mama in calm disposition.

"Ralph looked all over town." Ralph Johnson was Josie's husband, and he owned the saddle shop at the end of Two-Time's main street. "You don't suppose something might have happened to Tommy, do you? An accident?"

"It better have," Meg muttered.

Gasping, Mama looked up from straightening Meg's gown. "Of all the things to say!"

"Sorry, Mama." Hands balled at her sides, Meg

gritted her teeth. Her mother was right, of course; such uncharitable thoughts didn't belong in church.

Neither did thoughts of murder.

"Fifty-eight minutes," her father announced.

"I'm sure he'll be here soon, Papa." Josie always tried to see the bright side of things, but even she couldn't hide the doubt in her voice.

Papa's gaze remained on his watch. "Soon's already come and gone. Now he'll have to answer to me for keeping my daughter waiting!"

Her father didn't fool Meg one whit—he'd been against the marriage from the start. If she didn't know better, she would suspect him of causing her fiancé's absence just to prove he was right.

"Fifty-nine minutes!"

"Henry, please," her mother cajoled. "You're upsetting her."

"She *should* be upset. The boy's irresponsible and will never amount to a hill of beans. He's like a blister; he never shows up till the work's all done. Doesn't even know whether to wind his watch or bark at the moon. I should never have agreed to this marriage."

"You didn't agree to anything, Henry."

"And for good reason! Furthermore—"

A knock sounded, but before anyone could answer it, the door cracked open and Reverend Wellmaker popped his head into the room. "Is everything all right?" he asked, eyes round behind his spectacles. "We're almost twenty minutes late."

"*Fifty-nine* minutes late!" her father roared.

The difference in times raised no eyebrows, since no standard time existed in Two-Time. It was common practice for communities to set watches by the local jeweler, but unfortunately, their town had two—Meg's father and Tommy's pa. Both stubbornly insisted they alone had the right time.

The feud dividing the town for more than fifteen years was expected to end the minute the two families were joined by marriage. Both fathers had agreed—albeit reluctantly—to standardize time once the deed was done.

"Shh, Henry, not here." Her mother gave the minister an apologetic smile. "Soon."

Josie left with the pastor, and Papa continued his sonorous count until interrupted by another knock on the door.

"Meg, it's me, Tommy."

"It's about time!" She hiked her skirt above her ankles and started across the room.

Her mother grabbed her by the arm. "It's bad luck for the groom to see you in your wedding gown," she whispered.

"It's worse luck for the groom to be an hour late for his own wedding." Meg pulled free from her mother's grasp and ripped open the door. "Where have you been? You agreed to get married on Lockwood time and—" Suddenly aware that something was terribly wrong, she bit back the rest of her sentence.

Tommy looked as sober as an owl in a barn. Even more worrisome was his attire—old canvas trousers held up by blue suspenders. He appeared haggard, as if he hadn't slept, and his unruly red hair stood on end like a rooster's comb.

"We have to talk." He grabbed her by the hand and pulled her out of the room and down the hall.

She held back. "Thomas James Farrell, stop right now. You hear me? I said *stop!*"

But he didn't stop, not until they reached the cemetery behind the church. It took a moment for Meg's eyes to adjust to the bright autumn sun.

Tall, granite grave markers stood at attention like pieces on a chessboard waiting for someone to make the first move.

She snatched her hand from his. "What do you think you're doing? What's going on?"

Tommy grimaced. "Meg, I'm sorry, but I can't do this. I can't marry you."

She stared at him, dumbfounded. *This can't be happening.* "What are you saying?"

"I'm sayin' I can't be the husband you want. I can't spend the rest of my life workin' on watches in my father's shop. All those hairsprings and gears and stems and—"

"*This* is how you give me the news?" She gave him an angry shove. "Tommy Farrell, I've known you nearly all my life, and you've caused me plenty of grief along the way, but this takes the cake!"

"I'm sorry." He slapped his hand to his forehead. "I'm goin' about this all wrong. It's not that I don't want to marry you. I just can't."

"And you waited for our wedding day to tell me this?"

"I feel bad, I do."

"*You* feel bad? How do you suppose our guests feel after being kept waiting all this time? And what about the town? Our fathers promised to end their feud—"

"I know, I know." He grimaced. "Right now, I'm only thinkin' of you."

"By humiliating me in front of the entire world?" She stared at him as if seeing him for the first time. For years, she'd made excuses for his lackadaisical ways and had even defended him to his own father. She'd forgiven him for forgetting her birthday—not once but twice! But this...this was by far the worst thing he'd ever done.

"I'd make you miserable," he continued, his Texas twang even more pronounced than usual. "I'm not ready to settle down. I want to see the world. To travel to Europe and Asia and...and the Pacific Islands. I read somewhere that they're real nice."

"You've said some mighty dumb things in your life, but this has got to be the dumbest."

"I knew you wouldn't understand."

"No, I don't understand," she cried. "I don't understand how you could wait till today to throw me over for a bunch of islands!" She backed away from him, fists at her side. "I should have listened to Pa."

"Meg, don't look at me like that. It really is for the best. Maybe in a year, or two or three, I'll be ready to marry and settle down. Maybe then we can—"

"Don't you dare say it, Tommy Farrell. Don't you even think it! I'd sooner die a spinster than marry the likes of you."

"You don't mean that..."

"I mean every word. I don't ever want to see you again. Not ever!"

"Meg, please."

"Just...just go!"

He stared at her as if making certain she wouldn't

change her mind. Then he swung around and rushed along the narrow dirt path leading out of the cemetery as if he couldn't escape fast enough.

Watching him flee, Meg felt numb. Today was supposed to be the happiest day of her life, but instead, it had turned into a nightmare. How would she break the news to her family? To the guests? To the folks counting on this marriage to bring peace to the town? She pulled the garland from her hair, threw it on the ground, and stomped on it.

A movement caught her eye, and a tall figure stepped from behind an equally tall grave marker. Her gaze froze on the man's long, lean form. A look of sympathy—or maybe even pity—had settled on his square-jawed face, crushing any hope that the humiliating scene had somehow escaped his notice. Her cheeks flared with heat. Could this day possibly get any worse?

He pulled off his derby and nodded at her as if apologizing for his presence.

"Sorry, ma'am. Forgive me. I couldn't help but overhear." If his dark trousers, coat, and vest hadn't already marked him as an easterner, the way he pronounced his words surely did.

In no mood to forgive a man—any man, even one as tall and good-looking as this one—she grabbed a handful of satin, turned, and rushed to the church's open door, snagging her wedding gown on the door-frame. She glanced over her shoulder to find him still watching her. In her haste to escape, she yanked at her skirt, and it ripped. The tearing sound might as well have been her heart.

Inside, the thundering organ music rang like a death knell. Hands over her ears, she kicked off her murderous slippers and ran down the hall in stocking feet.

2

GRANT GARRISON LEFT HIS BOARDINGHOUSE AND RODE his mount down Peaceful Lane. Two-story brick residences lined the street, the boardinghouse where he lodged among them. Either the street name was a misnomer or someone had once had a strange sense of humor, because the street was anything but peaceful.

Even now, angry voices filled the morning air, the loudest coming from Mr. Crawford, who took regular issue with his next-door neighbor's bagpipes. But he wasn't the only one airing his lungs.

Mr. Sloan was yelling at the Johnson boy for stealing his pecans; Mrs. Conrad could be heard expressing her disapproval at the goat eating her flowers. Next door to her, Mr. Quincy was arguing with the paperboy, who had thrown the morning newspaper on the roof for the second time that week.

Grant tipped his hat to the two women gossiping over a fence and steered his horse around the wagon belonging to the dogcatcher. A terrible commotion drew Grant's attention to an alleyway, and the dogcatcher emerged running, chased by a big yellow hound.

A half block away, the widow Rockwell walked out of her tiny house carrying a lamp. Compared to the other buildings on the street, the two tiny residences she owned looked like dollhouses. She waved at Grant, and he tipped his hat in greeting.

"Need any help?" he called. He'd already helped her move twice that week.

"No, not today."

The widow's two houses were located directly across from each other. Almost identical in size and style, they were called Sunday houses and had originally been built so that immigrant farmers could stay in town during weekends to run errands and attend church.

The problem was, the widow could never make up her mind which one to live in. No sooner would she haul her belongings to one side of the street than she decided to live on the other. So back and forth she traipsed from house to house, moving, always moving.

It had rained the night before, and puddles of mud dotted the dirt-packed road, causing the widow to pick her way across the street with care.

Except for a few lingering clouds, the sky was clear, and the air smelled fresh with just a hint of fall.

It was a normal day on Peaceful Lane—except for one thing. In the middle of the roadway, a woman was fighting with a pushcart.

Grant reined in his horse and narrowed his eyes against the bright morning sun. Did he know her? He didn't think so. Still, something about her small, trim frame struck a familiar chord.

The lady pushed the cart one way and jerked it

the other. A trunk or chest of some kind was perched precariously on top of the hand wagon, and it teetered back and forth like a child's seesaw.

Apparently seeing the futility of her efforts, she leaned over to examine one of the wheels stuck in the mud. This afforded him an intriguing glimpse of a white lace petticoat beneath an otherwise somber blue dress. She surprised him by giving the pushcart a good kick with a well-aimed boot.

Hands folded on the pommel of his saddle, he leaned forward. "So what do you think, Chester? Should we offer to help before the lady does injury to her foot?"

For answer, his horse lowered his head and whickered.

"I quite agree."

Urging his horse forward in a short gallop, Grant called, "May I be of service, ma'am?" He tugged on the reins. "Whoa, boy."

She whirled around, eyes wide as she met his gaze. Two red spots stained her cheeks, but whether from exertion or embarrassment at being caught in a less-than-ladylike predicament, he couldn't tell.

"Thank you kindly," she said with a soft southern lilt.

"My pleasure."

Her face looked vaguely familiar, but he still couldn't place her, which struck him as odd. Her big turquoise eyes should not be easily forgotten. Hatless, she wore her honey-blond hair piled on top of her head, but a couple of soft ends had fallen loose. The carefree curls didn't seem to belong to the stern, young face.

He dismounted and tethered his horse to a wooden fence. He guessed the woman lived nearby, but that still didn't tell him where they might have met.

He tipped his hat. "Name's Grant Garrison."

She studied him with a sharp-eyed gaze. "You!"

Since she looked fit to be tied, he stepped back. At that point, the flashing blue-green eyes jarred his memory.

"You're the"—he almost said *jilted*—"bride." He hardly recognized her out of her wedding gown. According to local tongue-waggers, her name was Meg Lockwood. Best not to let on how last week's disastrous nonwedding was still the talk of the town.

She glared at him, eyes filled with accusations. "That day at the church…you had no right to eavesdrop on a private conversation."

He extended his arms, palms out. "Please accept my apologies. I can assure you the intrusion was purely unintentional. I was visiting my sister's grave."

Uncertainty crept into her expression, but her combative stance remained. "You…you could have announced yourself."

He also could have stayed hidden, which might have been the better choice. "I considered doing just that. I'm afraid that had I done so, I might have flattened your bridegroom's nose."

This failed to bring the smile he hoped for, but at least she looked less likely to do him harm. She glanced up and down the street as if trying to decide whether to accept his help.

"I would be most obliged if you didn't mention… what you heard."

Her request confused him. Everyone in town knew the wedding had been called off.

"About the Pacific Islands," she added.

Never would he profess to understand the way a woman's mind worked, but her concern was indeed a puzzle. Would she *rather* her fiancé had left her for another woman, as some people in town suspected?

"I promise." He pretended to turn a lock on his mouth. "Not a word."

She let his promise hang between them for a moment before asking, "What brings you to Two-Time, Mr. Garrison?"

He hesitated. "I'm a lawyer. Since the East Coast is overrun with them, I decided to try my luck here. I just opened an office off Main." He replaced his hat and tossed a nod at the cart. "Where are you taking that?"

"To my sister's house." Her gaze shifted to the end of the street. "She lives in the corner house with the green shutters."

"Well, then." He grabbed hold of the handle and yanked the cart back and forth before giving it a firm push. The wheels gave a reluctant turn and finally pulled free of the gooey sludge with a *slurp*. But just as it cleared the mudhole, the cart tipped to one side and the chest shot to the ground, splashing mud everywhere.

Miss Lockwood jumped back, but not soon enough to prevent mud from splattering on her skirt. "Oh no!"

Muttering an apology, Grant quickly turned the chest upright, leaving an intriguing assortment of corsets, petticoats, and camisoles scattered on the ground.

He never expected to see such a fancy display in a rough-and-tumble town like Two-Time.

While she examined the chest for damage, he quickly swooped up the satin and lace dainties and shook off as much mud as possible. Did women actually need this many corsets?

"I have to say, ma'am," he began in an effort to make light of the situation, "there are enough underpinnings here to fill an entire Montgomery Ward catalogue." He couldn't help but look at her curiously before dumping the garments back into the chest.

Checks blazing, she slammed the lid shut and double-checked the lock.

He offered her his clean handkerchief, which she turned down with a shake of her head. Silence as brittle as glass stretched between them, and Grant couldn't help but feel sorry for her. They seemed doomed to meet under trying, if not altogether embarrassing circumstances.

Since the lady seemed more concerned about the wooden chest than the corsets...uh...contents, he studied it more closely. It was obviously old but had been well cared for. Intricate engravings of birds, flowers, and a ship graced the top and sides, along with several carefully carved initials.

"No damage done," she said, her voice thick with relief. The red on her cheeks had faded to a most becoming pink. "My family would kill me if something happened to it."

"A family heirloom?" he asked.

She nodded. "All the way from Ireland. It's called a hope chest."

Grant knew about such things, of course, from his sisters. But never before had he been privy to a hope chest's contents. It was hard to know what disconcerted him more—manhandling Miss Lockwood's intimate garments, or the possibility that something of a similar nature filled his sisters' hope chests. Whatever happened to filling a hope chest with household goods?

Tucking the handkerchief into his trouser pocket, he struggled to lift the chest off the ground. He set it atop the cart and wiggled it back and forth to make sure it was balanced just right. "I'm afraid the contents may be ruined."

"Th-they'll wash," Miss Lockwood stammered, refusing to meet his gaze.

He brushed off his hands and grabbed hold of the cart's handles. This time, the wheels turned with ease, and he pushed it slowly down the road. She fell in step by his side, and a pleasant whiff of lavender soap wafted toward him. With heightened awareness, he noticed her every move, heard her every intake of breath.

"You said you were visiting your sister's grave," she said in a hesitant voice, as if she wasn't certain whether to broach the subject.

He nodded, and the familiar heaviness of grief rose in his chest. "Mary died in childbirth a month ago. Her husband owns a cattle ranch outside of town."

They had reached the gate leading to the two-story brick house with the green shutters. The rail fence enclosed a small but well-cared-for garden. A hen pecked at the ground next to a row of sprouting squash plants.

Miss Lockwood afforded him a look of sympathy. "I'm sorry for your loss," she said.

"And I'm sorry for yours." In danger of drowning in the blue-green depths of her eyes, he averted his gaze. "Where would you like me to put it?"

"Put it?"

He shot her a sideways glance. "The corset…uh"—he grimaced—"hope chest."

She lowered her lashes. "The porch would be just fine," she murmured.

Since the cart wouldn't fit through the gate, he had no choice but to haul the chest by hand. Fortunately, only two steps led up to the wraparound porch. Even so, he was out of breath by the time he set the heavy chest next to a wicker rocking chair.

She'd followed him up the porch steps. "I'm much obliged." Her prettily curving lips made the sadness in the depth of her eyes all the more touching.

"My pleasure." He studied her. "I hope you don't mind my saying this, but…if I had someone like you waiting at the altar, I would never walk away. Not in a million years." The expression on her face softened, and he was tempted to say more but decided against it. Better stop while he was ahead.

With a tip of his hat, he jogged down the steps and headed back to his horse. The memory of all that silk and lace remained, as did the shadow of her pretty smile.

Meg stood on her sister's porch, surprised to find herself shaking. *If I had someone like you…*

Never had anyone said anything like that to her, not even Tommy. Just thinking of Mr. Garrison's soft-spoken words sent a shiver racing though her, one that ended in a sigh.

Pushing such thoughts away, she knocked and the door sprang open almost instantly.

Josie greeted her with a questioning look. "Who's that man I saw you with?"

"Just…someone passing by. He stopped to help me." Meg seldom kept anything from her older sister, but she didn't want to discuss Mr. Garrison. Not in her confused state.

Josie looked her up and down. "Oh dear. You're covered in mud. What happened?"

Meg glanced down at her skirt. "I had a little accident."

"I told you to wait for Ralph," Josie scolded. "That hope chest is far too heavy for a woman to manage alone."

Meg hadn't wanted to ask her brother-in-law for help. Not with the way he'd been coughing lately.

"It's a good thing I have you to help me, then." Meg cleaned the sludge off the soles of her high-button shoes on the iron boot scraper, then shook as much of the mud off her skirt as possible. Satisfied that her sister's pristine carpets would not be soiled, she circled the hope chest. "Grab hold of the other side."

Carved by her great-grandfather, the wooden piece had been handed down to family members for generations. Each bride carved her initials into the old wood before passing it on to the next woman in line.

Mama had passed it down to Josie who, after her own wedding, had handed it over to Meg during a ritual that had made all three Lockwood sisters roll on the floor with laughter.

Today, however, no such happy ritual was in play as she and Josie struggled to carry the massive chest inside the house and into the small but tidy parlor. They set it on the brick hearth so as not to get mud on the carpet.

"Whew! I forgot how heavy it was," Josie said.

Meg brushed a hand over her forehead. Good riddance. The hope chest that once held her girlish dreams was now a dismal reminder of a day she'd sooner forget.

"I don't know why Amanda refuses to take it. It's only fair. You and I both had our turn."

Josie frowned, as she was inclined to do whenever their younger sister's name came up. "Amanda's too independent to get married. She's only interested in stirring up trouble."

By trouble, Josie referred to Amanda's many causes. One—her campaign to close saloons during Sunday worship—had almost created a riot. Their youngest sister was the black sheep of the family and was always on the warpath about one thing or another.

"Poor Mama," Meg said. "All she ever wanted was to see the three of us married and bouncing rosy-cheeked babies on our laps." She gasped and quickly covered her mouth. "Oh, Josie, I'm so sorry."

"It's all right." Josie patted her on the arm. "I haven't given up hope that one day I'll have a child of my own. Some things just take time."

Meg flung her arms around her sister's shoulders and squeezed tight. "I wish I had your patience."

Josie hugged her back. "I love you just the way you are."

Meg pulled away and smiled. Spending time with Josie always made her feel better. "Thank you for taking the hope chest off my hands. If I have to look at it one more day, I'll scream." She and Josie had spent hours working on her trousseau—and for what?

"I'm afraid the clothes inside are a mess. The chest tipped over, and everything is covered in mud." Just thinking about that handsome new lawyer's hands all over them made her cheeks blaze.

Josie opened the hope chest to check the contents. She lifted the carefully sewn garments one by one and examined them.

While her sister inventoried the damage, Meg glanced out the parlor window and froze. There rode Mr. Garrison on his fine black horse. Her breath caught, and she quickly stepped behind the draperies so as not to be seen gaping. Did she only imagine him staring at the house? *If I had someone like you...*

Josie's insistent voice brought her out of her reverie. "I'm sorry?"

"I said I'll wash and press the garments, and they'll be as good as new." Josie studied her a moment, and her expression softened. "Are you okay?"

Meg moistened her dry lips. "I'm fine."

Josie lowered the hope chest's lid and stood. "It's been nearly a month. You can't keep hiding. Papa misses you at the shop. You know what a terrible bookkeeper he is, and with Christmas just around the corner..."

Guilt surged through Meg like molten steel. How selfish of her. Staying hidden like a common criminal had done nothing but place an extra burden on Papa's shoulders. It was her job to keep the shop records, order supplies, and serve the customers, thus freeing her father to spend his time repairing watches and clocks. And yet...

"I don't know that I'll ever be able to show my face in public again."

"Meg, that's ridiculous. No one blames you."

Taking the blame wasn't what bothered Meg; it was the feeling that she had let everyone down. Papa had promised to make peace with Mr. Farrell as a wedding present. Now that the wedding had been called off, the feud between the two men had resumed. If anything, their animosity toward each other had grown worse, each blaming the other for the disastrous affair.

"Go and clean up while I fix us something to eat."

Meg nodded and started down the hall, but not before taking another quick glance out the window. The deserted road looked as forlorn and lonely as she felt.

∞

Moments later, Meg joined her sister in the sun-filled kitchen, her skirt still damp where she'd washed off the mud.

Josie's kitchen table had become the sisters' sounding board. Everything that happened—good, bad, or otherwise; every crisis, every problem—was hashed out, analyzed, resolved, or left to die upon that maple table.

Meg pulled out a chair, plopped down, and rested her elbows on the smooth-polished surface. "I don't understand why Papa and Mr. Farrell continue to fight." For as long as she could remember, bad blood had existed between the two men. Mama blamed it on professional differences, but Meg was almost certain their warfare had more personal roots.

Josie filled the kettle and placed it on the cookstove. "Sometimes I wonder if even they remember what started it. It happened so many years ago." She wiped her hands on her spotless white apron and pulled a bread knife out of a drawer.

Through the open window over the sink came the sound of bells pealing out the noon hour for the residents living and working north of Main. The rest of the town, including her father, had stopped for the noontime meal a good forty minutes earlier.

"Josie…how did you know you were in love with Ralph?"

Josie gave her an odd look. "What a strange question."

"I'm serious. How did you know?"

Josie thought a moment, cheeks tinged a pretty pink. "It was the way he made me feel. The way my heart leaped whenever he came into sight."

Meg chewed on a fingernail. She had known Tommy nearly all her life. Next to her two sisters, he was the best friend she'd ever had.

In school, he'd dipped her braids in ink and helped her with geography and science. In turn, she'd teased him about his red hair, drilled him on his numbers, and made him read aloud until he became proficient.

Knowing how their fathers disapproved of their friendship only strengthened the bond between them and forced them to meet in secret. It had been Romeo and Juliet all over again. Still, during all those years she'd spent in Tommy's company, never once had her heart leaped at the sight of him.

Josie dumped a loaf of bread out of a baking tin and proceeded to slice it. "I know you're still hurting, Meg, but I never did think you and Tommy belonged together."

A month ago, Meg would have argued with her sister, but now she only nodded. "I guess there're worse things than being jilted for the Pacific Islands."

Josie laughed. "I hope we never find out what those things are."

Meg laughed too, and for the first time in weeks, her spirits lifted.

3

THE BELLS ON THE DOOR OF GRANT GARRISON'S OFFICE danced merrily. Grant slid the last of his legal books onto the newly arrived bookshelves and stood to greet his visitor.

The welcoming smile died on his face the moment he turned. He knew the man at once—the gangly fellow with the pasty skin was Miss Lockwood's wayward bridegroom. He'd recognize those flyaway ears and that carrot-colored hair anywhere. Although today, the former groom's hair was neatly combed and parted down the middle.

"Mr. Garrison, is it? I'm Thomas Farrell." He offered his hand.

Swallowing his dislike, Grant shook the man's hand before walking around his desk. He sat, and the new leather chair squeaked beneath his weight.

"What can I do for you, Mr. Farrell?" Grant asked, his manner as cool and abrupt as his voice. A man so heartless as to leave a woman at the altar didn't deserve the time of day, let alone civility.

If Farrell noticed anything odd about Grant's

demeanor, he didn't show it. Instead, he lowered himself onto the ladder-back chair in front of the desk. He mopped his forehead with a handkerchief and crossed and uncrossed his legs. He looked like a man about to be hanged.

Grant waited. One minute passed, then two. The *clip-clop* of horses' hooves and the rumble of a wagon floated through the open window. The clock on top of the bookshelf clucked like a hen on a nest. It was exactly two—or two forty, depending on which time zone one favored. According to railroad time it was probably closer to three, but few people paid attention to train schedules unless they were leaving town.

"Mr. Farrell?" Grant prodded at length, if only to save what remained of the hat clutched in the young man's hands.

The man gulped, and his Adam's apple bobbed up and down like a rubber ball. "I'm bein' sued," he said.

Grant's eyebrows shot up. For the love of Pete, what other dastardly deed was Mr. Farrell guilty of? "Do you owe someone money?" he asked.

"No, no, nothin' like that."

"Did you cause injury?"

The question seemed to perplex the man, or at least render him momentarily silent.

"No…not really."

"Then why are you being sued?"

Setting his misshapen felt hat on the desk, Farrell reached into his trouser pocket and drew out what looked like an official document. He carefully unfolded the sheet of paper and smoothed out the wrinkles before sliding it across the desk.

It *was* a legal document. Grant scanned it quickly until he came to Meg Lockwood's name. A vision of a pretty, round face seemed to float up from the page. He remembered everything about her: her pretty pink cheeks, small dainty frame, and large, expressive eyes. He also remembered how she had struggled to smile the day they met on the street, even though her heart had been so recently broken by this very man.

Grant sucked in his breath and forced his gaze down the rest of the document. "It says here you're being sued for breach of promise." Miss Lockwood was asking for damages amounting to ten grand. That was a lot of money, even by Boston standards.

Farrell rubbed his chin. "Can she do that?"

"'Fraid so. It says you broke a promise to marry her and left her at the altar." The memory of Miss Lockwood standing alone in the cemetery in her wedding gown tugged at Grant's insides, and his hands clenched. It took every bit of professionalism he possessed not to toss Farrell out on his ear.

Farrell grimaced. "I don't deny any of that, but there were extinguishin' circumstances."

Garrison tossed the document on the desk. "I believe you mean *extenuating* circumstances."

"Yeah, that too." Farrell leaned forward. "I need a lawyer, and no other lawyer in town will touch my case."

Elbows on the desk, Grant tented his fingers. "What makes you think I will?"

"You're new in town. You can take sides, and no one will think the worse of you."

Grant opened his mouth to say something, but Farrell quickly stopped him.

"Before you go sayin' no, let me explain what happened."

Rubbing his neck, Grant considered Farrell's request. Personally, he disliked the law that allowed a woman to sue a man for promises that were so often only implied, or even imagined. The Boston courts were filled with such cases. Recently, one unfortunate man had been forced to pay twenty thousand dollars to a woman he hadn't set eyes on in eighteen years. His one mistake had been peering into her baby carriage and declaring her a beauty. Based on that one innocent gesture, he was accused of backing out of a promise of marriage when she came of age, and he was financially ruined.

Of course, in Miss Lockwood's case, no question existed about the nature of the promise. As much as he found such lawsuits distasteful, Grant didn't blame the lady for taking revenge.

He tapped his fingers together. "I don't handle these kinds of cases."

A lawyer could hang a reputation on a single sensational case. In that regard, a heart-balm tort was made to order—alienation of affection, seduction, breach of promise; they were all sensational. But fame didn't pay the bills and was often more of a hindrance than an asset. A lawyer's real bread and butter came from land disputes and routine legal chores, and that's what Grant had intended to concentrate on when he'd moved here.

"Please, there's no one else. At least listen to my side."

"I don't have much time." He had all the time in the world.

Farrell's gaze traveled over Grant's desk, empty save for the blotter and inkwell. "It'll only take a few minutes."

Grant blew out his breath. "Very well."

Farrell sat back. "I guess you could say it started at last year's winter dance." His skinny red mustache twitched. "Everyone kept askin' when Meg and I would set the date. Meg said she wouldn't marry me unless her pa and mine stopped bickerin' and agreed to a single time zone."

Farrell pulled out his handkerchief and dabbed his forehead. "Then my pa surprised us all by sayin' he would agree to such a thing if Mr. Lockwood did the same." His twang grew more distinct as he continued. "Everyone badgered Meg's pa until he finally agreed to end the feud and"—he snapped his fingers—"just like that, Meg and I were betrothed."

Grant narrowed his eyes. He didn't want to sympathize with the man, but he could see how small-town peer pressure might have put Mr. Farrell in a difficult position.

"How could you have gone along with this if you didn't love her?" A promise to marry was considered a legally binding contract. A man would be foolish to pledge such a thing unless he was serious.

"Oh, I love her all right. I've loved her ever since I was five and she was three, and I saw her runnin' down the street stark naked."

Grant blinked and cleared his throat. Erasing the memory of her intimate garments from his memory took considerable effort. "Did…did Miss Lockwood feel the same about you?"

"I-I think so."

"You think so?" Grant frowned. "Did…Miss Lockwood have no other suitors?" he asked.

"Oh, plenty," Farrell said with a nod. "But old man Lockwood chased them all off. He tried to get rid of me too, but I refused to go away." Farrell rubbed his chin. "Meg was the best friend I ever had, and I miss her somethin' awful, but we're as different as night and day. She's perfectly content to stay in Two-Time, and I want to see the world. Her idea of a good time is to curl up with a book." He wrinkled his nose. "I want to sail an ocean, and she wants to read about it."

Farrell looked so distraught and sounded so sincere that Grant felt sorry for him despite all his efforts to the contrary. At least Farrell had been man enough to own up to his feelings before ruining Miss Lockwood's life. His instincts were sound, even if his methods left much to be desired.

"Please, I need a lawyer. You're the only one in town who didn't turn me down before hearin' my side."

Grant hesitated. His office had been open for a month, and to date, Farrell was the only one soliciting his services. He'd had no idea it would be so difficult for a big-city lawyer to earn a small town's trust.

He mentally ran through his options. If he could talk the two feuding families into accepting a compromise, perhaps people would view him more favorably. Eighty percent of the breach-of-promise cases in

Boston were settled out of court. Still, he didn't want to take sides against the lady.

"By way of disclosure, you should know that I happen to be acquainted with Miss Lockwood and my sympathies lie with her."

Farrell nodded. "She has my sympathies too, but not ten thousand dollars' worth."

Grant folded his hands on the desk. "Hell has no fury like a woman scorned."

Farrell leaned forward. "It's not Meg's fury that worries me. It's her pa's. He's using this as an excuse to ruin my pa and run him out of business. Please say you'll help me."

About the Author

New York Times bestselling author Margaret Brownley has penned more than forty-eight novels and novellas. She's a two-time Romance Writers of America RITA finalist and has written for a TV soap. She is also a recipient of the *Romantic Times* Pioneer Award. Not bad for someone who flunked eighth-grade English. Just don't ask her to diagram a sentence.